A Romantic Entanglement Series

CHARISSE C. CARR

Copyright © 2024 by Charisse C. Carr

All rights reserved.

Any unauthorized reprint or use of the material is prohibited. No part of this book may be reproduced or transmitted in any form or by any means, electronic or mechanical, including photocopying, recording, or by any information storage without express permission by the publisher.

This is an original work of fiction. Names, characters, places, and incidents are either products of the author's imagination or are used fictitiously, and any resemblance to actual persons, living or dead, is entirely coincidental.

To The Readers:

This is a rerelease of my very first book and spin-off series that I wrote two and half years ago. The standalone was called "Kane and Candy: A Romantic Entanglement". The spin-off series, which consisted of two novellas, was called "A Romantic Entanglement: Autumn and Knowledge Story". They have been combined into one book. If you have already read this series, please enjoy it again. I added a family update at the end of it. If this is your first time, welcome and enjoy the ride!

Chapter One

CANDY

"Shut the fuck up, bitch!" I mumbled under my breath as I stormed to my room and slammed the door. My mom got on my goddamn nerves. She was always riding my ass but allowed my brother to get away with murder. Sometimes I thought she wished I was a boy too because I didn't think she wanted a girl.

Junior was always in trouble and barely went to school. He was my sixteen-year-old little brother. My mom worked the night shift at our local hospital from seven p.m. to seven a.m, so she was oblivious to what went on here. He took full advantage of the situation too because as soon as she headed to work, he ran to the streets. I heard he was hanging with the wrong crowd, and they were out there robbing folks. When I confronted his ass, he denied it.

Sitting on the edge of my full size bed, I could feel tears rolling down my cheeks. I needed to stop being so sensitive, but I was sick of her yelling at me. Even though I cooked, cleaned and did all the laundry, it still wasn't good enough for her. She always found something to complain about. So what if there were a few dishes left in the sink? Junior was the one who dirtied them up anyway.

He needed a positive male figure in his life because his daddy wasn't shit. The muthafucka stopped coming around when he was six. My uncle Pete could have been a role model, but he was in jail for the rest of his natural born life for murder. My mom hated him anyway. She never said why, though. And my daddy... Well, he was dead. At least that was what my mom told me. I never questioned it, but I wished I could have met him.

I knew I would have been a daddy's girl because I damn sure wasn't a momma's girl. He probably would have left just like the others. My mom couldn't keep a man to save her life. I've seen so many come and go. I was surprised she only had two kids. Junior was the only consistent man in her life, which was probably why she favored him.

I laid across my bed listening to music, trying to change my mood. I suddenly realized it was Friday, and my mom didn't have to work tonight. I'd be damned if I stayed home with these negroes. I decided to call my cousin Autumn and see what was popping for the night. She was my auntie Rose's daughter.

Auntie Rose and my mom were like oil and water. You

could cut the tension between them with a knife. I remembered one particular argument between them as a young girl.

I was coming in from outside to use the bathroom and heard them yelling at each other, so I stood at the door and listened.

"You have always been jealous of me and wanted everything I had!" shouted Auntie Rose.

"In your dreams. You have nothing to be jealous of, absolutely nothing," my mom taunted.

"You're not a sister, you're a whore! A heartless bitch who takes comfort in my pain."

You could hear the hurt and sadness in my auntie's voice.

"How many times do I have to say sorry to you? It was a drunken mistake that I am reminded of every single day of my life. I can't take back what happened, and I'm not gonna keep apologizing for it anymore. Get over it."

"You ruined all of our lives, and all you can say is get over it? I should spit in your face!"

"If you do, I will be the last person you spit on because sister or not, I'm gonna beat your ass," my mom threatened.

At this point I wanted to storm in and stop them both, but if I did they would know I was listening. They would tear my behind up for being in grown folk's business and tell me to stay in a kid's place. I never went in. Instead, I went to Auntie Rose's house to use the bathroom.

I never told anyone about the conversation I heard, not even Autumn. No matter what our parents went through, we never allowed it to affect our relationship. Autumn and I grew up thick as thieves and were more like sisters than cousins. We were both twenty-one, but I was a few months older.

I loved my cousin, and at times wished I could live with them. Don't get me wrong, they used to live in the same public housing development as us, but my Auntie Rose's name came up on the Section 8 list, so they got a house a few blocks over down by the beach.

My bitter ass mother was hating hard on them, but I was happy they were able to move out these projects. She wouldn't even help when it came time to pack up their old apartment, and never said congratulations or nothing. They didn't get along, so I wasn't surprised.

"Hey, cuz, what's good?"

"I was just about to call you," Autumn replied. "There's a party tonight in Red Bank, and Peanut said we can ride with her," she continued.

Peanut was our friend from the neighborhood we grew up in. She was always the driver because neither Autumn nor I had a car. We were some bus hopping, cab catching, always needing a ride, chicks. I was a CNA at a nursing home, but only part time, and was saving my money to get my own place, so I couldn't afford car payments and insurance right now.

"I'm down! What time are y'all coming to pick me up so I'm ready? Matter of fact, I'm just gonna walk to your house after I get dressed. This way she doesn't have to make two stops."

"Okay, just call me when you're outside, so I can let you in. I need you to fix my hair when you get here too, bye!"

Every time we go out she thinks I'm her personal hair stylist, I thought, laughing.

On my way to the bathroom, my mom yelled out for me to bring her a cup of ice water. Junior's funny looking ass was sitting right across from her on the loveseat. She purposely waited for me to come out of my room to ask me to do it. Prince Charming does nothing around here while my Cinderella ass constantly gets ordered around by the Wicked Witch of the East.

"Here you go!" She just took the glass from me and turned her head. I didn't even get a thank you. "Next time I'll put a little Shug Avery pee in it," I blurted, jokingly.

She definitely didn't find that funny by the look on her face, so I hurried on and took my shower. As I stepped out of the tub and wrapped up in a towel, my phone rang.

"Hey, babe!" I answered, smiling from ear to ear.

On the other end was, Rah, short for Raheem, my fiancé. He was locked up, but I made sure I kept money in my AdvancePay account so he could call me every day.

Rah proposed to me the day before he got caught up. I never told anyone and put the ring in the safe with the money I was holding for him. It was all he had left. We have been rocking ever since I was sixteen years old. He was my first, and my last at this point. I had never been with anyone else.

Right now he was doing a bid on a gun charge. They had him for possession too, but he used most of his money to hire one of the best criminal attorneys around, and those charges were dropped on a technicality. Someone in the DA office fucked up. Thank goodness because he had a lot of weight on him and was facing big numbers.

"Yo, I miss you so much, C!" he exclaimed. You could hear the love in his voice.

"I miss you too, and I can't wait for you to hold me in your arms."

"Well, hopefully you won't have to wait too much longer. My lawyer is supposed to come see me tomorrow. She said she got some good news for me."

"That would be awesome, and it's about time. You been in there for over fourteen months already. They act like you shot somebody."

"That's New Jersey for you. Anyway, whatcha up to?"

"Nothing much, just got out of the shower. About to get dressed and meet up with Autumn. We—" Before I could finish my sentence, he cut me off.

"Wow, so you about to hit the streets and be hot in the ass? You giving my pussy away?" He only said that because he doesn't like my cousin and thinks she's trying to set me up with different dudes.

"What the fuck are you talking about, Rah? Don't be disrespecting me because I've always been faithful. Too bad I can't say the same for your trifling ass!" Now I was pissed.

"We left that in the past. You forgave me, and we moved on from it. But now, you wanna throw it in my face."

"I'm only matching your energy. You know they're listening in on our calls, and you're making me sound like some trick ass bitch. You on some bs, I don't have time for this shit."

I banged on his ass. Now he could talk to his bunk buddy, the CO, or whoever else, but it wasn't going to be me.

Forgiveness doesn't mean I forgot what happened, and how could I? It was on my eighteenth birthday and with my best friend Tanya.

My favorite auntie, Bird, my mom's baby sister, let me have a party at her house. Everyone was chilling, having a great time. I needed to use the bathroom, but the one downstairs was occupied, so I went to use the one in my auntie's master bedroom. When I opened the door I couldn't believe my eyes.

Rah was sitting on the toilet with the lid down while Tanya was on her knees sucking his dick. I knew she was a whore, but didn't think she would cross me. Probably wasn't the first time either because they were too bold to do it with a house full of people.

Before I knew it, I had her hair balled up in one hand, punching her all up in her face. I tossed her to the side, then started hooking off on his ass. By this time, other people heard the commotion and rushed upstairs, breaking it up.

Needless to say we were no longer friends, and I did break up with Rah for a few months. He begged me every day to take him back, and I did. Everyone kept saying I was dumb as hell, and if he did it once, he'd do it again. Their words fell on deaf ears because I was in love.

Just thinking about it had me in my feelings, so I rolled up a blunt once I got back to my room, so I could relax and ease my mind. I cracked the window open and put a towel at the bottom of my door to keep the smell from traveling throughout the house once I lit it. Junior would definitely rat me out.

Once I put the blunt out, I searched my closet for something to wear and found a brand new pair of black skinny jeans I forgot I had. I was a solid size twelve, and they hugged me tight in all the right places. I put on a white tank top, white Air Force Ones, and my Gucci crossbody bag. I wanted to be cute but comfortable, and now that I accomplished that goal, my hair was next.

The great thing about having locs was the fact that I could rub some coconut oil in them and go. Peaches, my neighbor across the way, washed, deep conditioned, and retwisted them the other day, so they were still fresh. I needed to leave before Autumn called looking for me.

It took me longer than usual to walk to her house. The weather was perfect, so I decided to take my time and enjoy it.

"Hey, I'm outside." I called Autumn as soon as I got on her block.

"It's about time, damn! Whatcha do, take the scenic route?" she questioned sarcastically.

"Listen, don't start your shit. I just got here. I stopped and got you something on my way."

I stuck my hand in my bag, and then pulled it back out, displaying my middle finger as I pushed the door closed with my foot.

Chapter Two

AUTUMN

"You probably were on the phone with your prison bae. That's why you took so long to get over here," I implied.

"Umm, no, but I was on the phone with my boo earlier. Our call didn't last long at all. Once I mentioned I was meeting up with you to go out, things went all the way left."

It was no secret that Rah and I didn't get along, so I wasn't shocked to hear he got his panties in a bunch when my name came up. He thought I was a bad influence on Candy and doesn't want her around me. I would do anything to protect her from being hurt by anyone, and that included his funny looking ass.

She probably wouldn't speak to me again if she knew I was the reason he was sitting behind bars right now. I figured if he was out the way, Candy would be able to find someone else who would treat her better. I would never forget the agony in her voice that night. Just thinking about it made me weak in the stomach.

One night I happened to be at the right place at the right time and saw Rah with some chick I never seen before. He didn't see me because it was dark, and I was sitting in a car about to go inside the same bar they just came out of. They were holding hands, all comfortable and shit. He probably figured since he was out of town, no one would recognize him or see them. I was livid and had enough of him playing my cousin out.

Taking matters into my own hands, I googled the number to the police station and called them. When they answered, I explained to them that this guy leaving the bar appeared to be drunk and just drove off. I described the car he was driving and provided the license plate number. Rah loved to drink and always rode dirty. I wanted him gone. Usually, I didn't play with the police, but for my family I crossed all boundaries.

Candy called me later on that night, hysterically crying, and said the police had locked Rah up during a traffic stop. She was so upset she could barely get her words out. I felt horrible and wished I could take it back.

"Enough talk about your wanna be Nino Brown boyfriend. Let's start my head. Give me a top knot ponytail with some baby hairs," I requested.

We caught up on everything that happened since we last saw each other.

"Alright, you're done, now let's head outside before Peanut gets here. She's already driving us, so I don't want her to have to wait," Candy ordered.

Peanut finally pulled up in her royal blue Honda Civic, looking like a dude. She was one of those studs that really could pass for a man. Her voice didn't even sound feminine.

I saw her staring at me when I was getting in the car. The black V-neck bodysuit I wore had my titties pushed all the way up. My ass cheeks were hanging out of my booty shorts, and the Louis Vuitton slides I had on my feet displayed my freshly manicured toes.

"You look beautiful, Autumn," Peanut complimented as I sat back in the front passenger seat.

"Thank you, Nut." I smiled.

I knew she was sweet on me. We spent one night together, exploring each other's bodies because I was curious, but it wasn't for me. She scratched my itch, and that was it. We agreed to keep it our little secret and didn't let it affect our friendship.

"Whose party is this anyway?" Candy inquired as we pulled up to this beautiful home along the Navesink River.

"Does it matter? We're here, shit," I replied, shrugging my shoulders.

We followed the lighted pathway that led to the backyard once we exited the car. This house was amazing, so now I was interested in who threw this here shindig. The house was a mansion, like the one you saw in magazines.

"Can y'all smell the money in the air? I have to locate the

owner of this here estate." I snickered while taking in a deep breath, scanning the scene.

"Don't worry, your money meter reader will go off once you see him," Peanut joked.

"She's going to start beeping like a damn dump truck backing up," Candy chimed in, making the sound.

"Fuck both y'all hoes." I rolled my eyes and made my way over to the bar.

I did have a rep in the streets for only fucking with dudes that had money. Some would call it prostitution. I called it payment for services rendered. I had daddy issues, and only dealt with men I knew could provide for me.

I blamed my mother because I didn't know who my dad was. She said they had a one-night stand, and claimed to know nothing at all about him but his name, David. I knew she wasn't being totally honest because I found her diary one day, and inside of it was a picture of her and a man who looked just like me.

We had the exact same eyes, which I thought I got from my mother's side of the family because Candy had the same eyes as me. Once I saw this picture, I was convinced otherwise. We even smiled the same. I took a pic of the photo with my cell phone. One day I would build up the courage to ask her about it. Hopefully by then, she would be ready to come clean with the truth. She owed me that for having me suffer all these years.

It was hard watching my friends with their dads, especially on Father's Day. Most of them didn't live in the homes with their kids but came around and took them places. I wasn't able to go to my dad when I had questions about boys. There was no one to protect me from the heartache they caused as I got older.

"I know you're looking for trouble with that outfit on." A man interrupting my thoughts sneered.

"Yes, and I think I found it," I replied, turning around, looking him up and down as I bit on my bottom lip.

He was fine as hell with skin the color of cocoa that appeared to be rubbed down with oil. His thick lips were surrounded by a goatee that was perfectly trimmed.

This man had warm, dreamy, brown eyes, a broad nose, and a Caesar haircut. You could see the muscles through his shirt as he towered over me. To say I was attracted to him was an understatement.

"Would you like a drink?" I was next in line to get mine, so I could be nice for a moment.

"I'll have a double shot of Jack and a Corona with a lime," answered the mystery man with a raspy voice.

"Great party, Knowledge." Some random walking by complimented him as they smacked hands and did a hood embrace.

"So, this is your dwelling?" I inquired as I handed him his drinks.

"Absolutely," he assured me as he stared directly into my eyes. I wanted to pounce on him at that very moment. It was something about him that drew me in like a moth to a flame.

"You throw parties all the time, or is there a special occasion for today?" I questioned, not really caring about the answer, just making small talk to keep him near me.

"My brother moved to Baltimore with some chick two years ago. They didn't work out, but he stayed out there because the business he started flourished. Now, he decided it was time to come back home. This party is for him, but he's running late, stuck in traffic."

"Is he as fine as you because my cousin needs a new man," I flirted.

I got rid of Rah's ass physically, but now I needed him mentally gone from Candy's mind.

"You're straight to the point. You don't mince your words," he admired.

"I like to seize every opportunity placed in front of me," I boasted as I licked my lips, grabbed my drink, and walked away.

I looked back to see if he was following along, and he was. I had Knowledge on the line. All I needed to do now was reel him in. So, I purposely let my napkin fall on the ground in front of me. I bent over to pick it up, giving him a bird's eye view of my pussy print. This nigga was hot on my trail after that.

"Knowledge, meet my cousin Candy and our friend Peanut. This is his home, and the party is for his *single* brother that is on his way."

Candy knew I threw the single part in there for her and cut her eyes at me.

"Nice to meet you ladies, hope you are enjoying yourselves? By the smell of that good purple haze in the air, I can tell that y'all are," Knowledge acknowledged.

"Do you care to join us for a smoke?" Candy asked, waving the blunt in the air.

"Absolutely, I just need to steal this one away from y'all for a minute."

Knowledge placed his hand on the small of my back, ushering me toward the door on the side of his home. He grabbed my hand, leading me through the kitchen to a staircase that was center stage of a huge foyer. As we climbed the stairs, you could tell it was like an East and West wing to this mansion.

There was a bedroom located all the way in the back corner. No one would ever know we were up here. Once he closed the door, he wasted no time getting me out of my clothes. He pushed me onto the bed and had his face buried in between my legs, licking and sucking on me like he knew me for years.

He was experienced, and I was about to reach my peak. Before I could, Knowledge rolled over onto his back while holding my hips, sitting me on his face, not missing a beat. He was making me wetter than ever. I could feel my pelvic muscles contract, then relax.

"I'm about to cum. I'm about to cum!" I exclaimed.

I fell backwards off of his face and was sprawled out on the bed. As he placed the condom on, I laid there in awe of his manhood. Knowledge positioned himself in between my legs and slid inside me. It felt like he was splitting me wide open, in a good way. I was moaning and groaning with each thrust. They were long and deep.

When I wrapped my legs around him, his strokes became shorter but harder. I could feel his body tense up as he sped up. He was about to release for sure.

Knowledge relaxed on top of me once he erupted. We laid

there, trying to catch our breath. I could stay here all night, but I knew Candy and Peanut had to be looking for me by now. I freshened up in the bathroom that was attached to the room then headed back out.

"Where your nasty ass been?" Candy questioned once I made my way back to the table they were sitting at.

"Knowledge and I decided to get to know each other a lil better. " I smiled as I basked in the afterglow of my romp with Knowledge.

"I hope y'all—" Sounds of celebrations interrupted Peanut.

Everyone was crowding around a dude that resembled Knowledge, just darker. I guess the man of the hour had finally arrived.

Chapter Three

KANE

"Peace! Thank you for coming. It's great to see you." I greeted everyone while making my way over to my brother Knowledge.

"Miss you, bruh. Glad you're here to stay!" he exclaimed as we hugged each other.

Even though I wasn't that far away, it was far enough that we didn't see each other on a regular basis.

"I think you went a little overboard with the festivities."

Knowledge had an open bar, DJ, buffet stations, and an ice sculpture.

"Nothing's too much when it comes to you and me. We all we got."

Our parents died tragically ten years ago, Thanksgiving day, in a car accident. They went out to pick up breakfast and never returned. A drunk driver ran a red light at a high-speed and crashed into them, causing their car to flip over three times. I could still remember the look on the policemen's faces when they knocked on the door to deliver the horrible news. It was as if it was their own parents that had died.

I was sixteen and Knowledge was fifteen when they removed us from our home that day. We bounced around the foster system until I turned eighteen, because no one in my mom's family wanted two teenagers. Our dad was an only child. His parents were too old to take us and lived in a senior building.

Our parents left us life insurance policies, and I was able to cash them in. There was a clause written that if they passed away in an accident, the payout tripled. My dad dabbled in the stock market and taught us from the time we could read all about it, so I invested the money and we were still living off of it today. We never touched the stocks our dad had. Knowledge and I agreed to leave those for our kids.

"How's my nephew?" I questioned Knowledge.

"Man, listen, Keelie be on that bullshit. If I'm not fucking her, I can't see my son."

"Yo, what the fuck is wrong with her?"

"Everything! I haven't seen him in two months. I don't want the system involved, telling me when I can see my son. That's the only reason why I haven't dragged her ass into court."

"Too bad we don't have any sisters to get her ass straight. Well, let me make my rounds, and I'll get back with you."

As I was chopping it up with the guests, trying to hit each table, I bumped into two beautiful ladies, literally. I turned around, and they were standing right behind me.

"Hey, I'm Autumn, and this is my cousin, Candy," she greeted as she pushed her cousin toward me.

"It's a pleasure to meet you, and please forgive her, she had a few too many and was raised by wolves," Candy joked.

"It's all good. I'm Kane, and the pleasure is all mine," I replied while raising up her right hand, kissing it.

I could see by her timid reaction I caught her off guard, but I was the one taken back by her very presence.

Candy's beauty had me mesmerized. Locs that smelled like an island breeze framed her face. Her skin was the color of a cinnamon stick and appeared soft and smooth. Her dark brown, almond shaped eyes put you in a trance, but there was an innocence about them.

She had a button nose that added to her delicate features. When she smiled, it was so bright that even the sun would be jealous. Hopefully, they weren't on their way out of here because I needed her to stay.

"Where were you ladies heading to?" I questioned.

I'd probably follow her out if they were leaving. The attraction I had for her was very strong.

"Ummm, t-t-t-o the bar. The drinks are really good," Autumn stuttered.

I could tell she made that up, but I escorted them to the bar anyway. They grabbed their drinks, and I walked them back to their table. My brother was talking to one of our childhood friends, but I would have to interrupt because I needed more info about Candy.

"Where are they from?" I inquired of Knowledge, pointing toward the trio.

"I don't know. Tonight was the first time I've ever met them, but I already bust down shorty with the bun on her head right before you got here," he responded, smiling, like it was nothing.

"Bruh, you still out here acting up? That's why you're in a messy situation with your baby moms now."

"I wrapped up. I can't take another Keelie. That's why Kyle is my only kid, and he's five."

Knowledge lived life in the moment. If he was hiking on a trail and saw a woman who he vibed with, Knowledge would fuck her in the woods next to a deer. My brother didn't care. I wasn't on that type of wave. Eventually, I wanted to settle down and have a family.

"Her cousin said she needed a new man. You better go lock that down for the night before they bounce," Knowledge encouraged.

"I'm definitely not letting her leave before I get her info, but she doesn't seem like the type to just give it up. I'm not looking for that anyway." I needed to get Candy alone.

"Hey, boo!" I was cut off mid step.

"Hey, Shonda, how are you?" The cloud I was just floating on disappeared.

I used to mess around with Shonda before I moved away. It wasn't anything serious, but it was consistent. Once I decided to commit to the shorty I moved away with, I cut her off.

"I'm good, and I see you still handsome as ever. You know I had to come through and welcome you back."

Shonda pushed up on me. I could tell she wanted to pick up where we left off, but I wasn't interested.

"Glad to see you, and I appreciate you coming through. I'm going to holla at you later, though." Brushing her off, I kept it moving.

"Fuck you, nigga," she mumbled as I walked off.

"Can I talk to you alone for a minute?" I asked Candy, gesturing for her to take my hand.

"I don't want any problems with your lady friend. Y'all looked a little cozy over there just now." She nodded her head toward the direction I just came from.

"Naw, you good. She's someone from my past, and that's where her ass is staying."

"That's where she better stay because I don't play about my family." Autumn chimed in as she downed another drink.

"She's in great hands with me. I won't let nothing happen to her," I assured Autumn.

We headed away from the crowd, down to the gazebo that faced the river. The stars shone like little diamonds up in the sky while the moon casted a dim light on the water, adding to the ambiance.

"So, Miss Candy, tell me about yourself."

I really didn't know what to say. The fact that she was

willing to let me have a moment alone with her was good enough for me.

"What is it you would like to know?" The curves of her lips were perfect.

"How old are you? What do you like to do for fun?"

I needed to find out as much info about this alluring creature as I could. The universe was too kind by placing her in my path. I knew it was fate.

"I'm twenty-one. My birthday is on Halloween, so I'm looking forward to that. I like to read, dance, skate, watch movies, you know simple stuff."

Her vibe was everything, and I hung onto her every word.

"You live around here?" I was curious to see if she stayed within my reach.

"Twenty minutes away, if that."

She was so soft spoken. I had to lean in a little closer, just to make sure my ears caught every word that left her velvety lips.

"Does your man know you out here looking as good as you do?" I could see her nipples pressing through her shirt, and it was making my temperature rise.

"I mentioned having a man? My mind must be slipping," Candy replied while cracking a smile and raising her eyebrows.

"Your cousin said you needed a new man, so obviously someone is hitting that."

She rolled her eyes up in her head while frowning her face.

"Autumn crazy ass is always talking shit, so pay her no mind. As for who's hitting this." She pointed between her legs.

"The water coming out my shower head is the only one getting any action right now."

"In that case, I think you are the most beautiful woman I've ever seen and would like to get to know you better."

Candy crossed her legs and exhaled.

"I'm really not looking to get involved with anyone right now, so I don't know if that is a good idea."

She didn't exactly say no, so she must be feeling me as well.

"I'm not asking for your hand in marriage. Well, not yet," I smirked. "Just let me take you out to dinner or Barnes and Noble."

We both laughed and started heading back.

"You seem like a really sweet guy. I'm glad we had the chance to meet," she complimented then gazed up at me with those spellbinding eyes of hers.

"Well, hopefully this won't be the last we see of each other. My offer to take you out still stands."

"Put your info in my phone, and if I'm bored one night, I might give you a call," she teased as she unlocked her phone, handing it to me.

"It's about damn time y'all resurfaced!" yelled Autumn. "I kept looking, making sure he didn't toss your ass in that water," she slurred.

"We about to leave because you are done, done."

"Candy, you're not the driver soooo you don't say when we leave."

"You're right. I'm the driver, and I say we're leaving," Peanut confirmed, and with that, they were gone.

* * *

I'd been home for a few weeks now and still no call from Candy. I was staying with Knowledge until I figured out exactly where I wanted to settle down at. Plus, he had plenty of room.

As I'm sitting at the island on my laptop, looking at some properties I was interested in buying, Autumn entered the kitchen. Her and Knowledge had been fucking like rabbits ever since my party. She was here so much, I thought she moved in.

It surprised me as well because usually Knowledge didn't hang on to them this long. He really must be feeling her.

"Morning, you making breakfast?" I only asked to hear her response.

Autumn was funny and quick-witted. She definitely brightened up the place.

"No, I'm making coffee, but Burger King is. And you can have it your way."

"What's up with Candy? She went ghost on me."

I guess she wasn't bored enough to give me a call, or she really does have a man.

"She stuck on that useless ass nigga, Rah, and I can't stand it."

"Who's Rah?" I questioned while sitting up straight.

"Her man who thinks he's Stringer Bell from *The Wire*, but he's more like Bodie. That's why his ass is locked up now. They have been messing around since high school, so she's sweet on him."

"You think you can give me her number? I just want to holla at her and see what's good."

"If you can take her away from that no-good bastard, I'll give you her social security number."

She was laughing, but something in me knew she was very serious. After Autumn gave me Candy's number, I wasted no time hitting her up.

"How did you get my number?" Candy giggled as she answered my call.

She had an infectious laugh that instantly made you smile and laugh too.

"You already know how, but that's irrelevant at this moment. Why haven't I heard from you?"

"I've been busy, working and doing stuff around the house. I just didn't have the time to be social."

It sounded like Candy was giving me a bunch of lame excuses. Being the man that I was, I went after everything I wanted and got. This situation wouldn't be any different.

"Well, tonight you will make time. I'm going to pick you up at six p.m, and I'm not taking no for an answer. Wear something comfortable and be ready to enjoy yourself," I demanded.

"You don't even know where I live," she sassed back.

"I'm sure the same person that gave me your number has your address. See you soon."

I ended the call and checked the time, realizing I better hurry up and get ready myself.

Before long, I was exiting the house and putting the address Autumn provided me with into the GPS. When I pulled up to

Candy's complex at six p.m. sharp, she was already standing outside. She started heading toward my truck to get in as I was getting out. Candy seemed confused as to why I walked over to the passenger side of the truck. I opened the door for her. Candy gave me a puzzled look and got in.

"You never had anyone open the door for you?" I quizzed once I got back inside the truck.

"To be honest, no I have not. And it was nice, thank you."

"Well, I don't know what type of dudes you've been surrounding yourself with, but where I come from, that's what we do."

"Okay, Mr. Kane. So, where are we going?" She smiled and so did my heart.

"You will see soon enough. Just sit back, relax, and enjoy the ride."

Candy smelled just as sweet as her name. There was nothing in the world that smelled better than a woman who just stepped out of the shower and put on her body butter with a spritz of her favorite perfume behind her ears and on her wrist.

I pulled off and headed to our destination before my mind filled up with indecent thoughts of what I wanted to do to Candy.

When we arrived at the skating rink, a huge smile took over her face. We went inside, Candy stopped and turned to face me with a confused look.

"Where is everyone else?" she inquired while looking around.

"I rented it out. For the next two hours it's just us. Let's go get our skates, so you can show me what you're workin' with."

"Why would you do such a thing? This is just too much. I can't believe it."

Candy covered her mouth with her hands as her eyes glistened with delight.

"Well, believe it because it's real. This is just the beginning."

I put my hand at the small of her back, steering her over to the counter. We traded in our shoes for some skates. The music was great, and the colorful bright lights were flashing.

Candy was an excellent skater and showed off her skills by skating backwards. We skated until we were out of breath and needed a break.

They had old school video games lined up against the wall. Ms. Pac Man was both our favorite. We must have gone through three rolls of quarters, determined to break the high score. She beat me every time and would do a victory dance each time.

I challenged her to a game of pool, determined to beat her at something. She was horrible, losing every single game we played. Candy could rack them but couldn't break them. The pool stick slipped right out her hand.

"You ready to go get something to eat? I'm starving."

I knew she had to be hungry and our two hours were up.

"Since you chose this, I get to choose dinner. Deal?"

She extended her hand out to me, so we could shake on it.

"Deal. Where would you like to go?"

"Popeyes. I know it's not caviar and lobster, but I like it."

"Listen, I eat fast food too, and I've never had caviar. So, I don't even know where you came up with that." I laughed.

"You picked me up in a Bentley Bentayga. What am I supposed to think? Like for real?"

Candy thought she had me figured out and judged me based on what she saw, not what she knew.

"I work hard and deserve everything I have, and so do you. That truck doesn't define who I am as a man, and it damn sure doesn't tell you my appetite. You will be surprised at the things I eat." I licked my lips, and she blushed.

We left the skating rink, went to get some food, drove over to the beach, and parked. I rolled down the windows, so we could feel the night air. It was always a lot cooler down by the ocean than in town, especially once the sun rested for the night. I grabbed a hoodie I had in the back and gave it to Candy to put on since she had on short sleeves.

"This is very nice and different, thank you."

Candy smiled then opened up her box and started eating.

"You're welcome. I'm enjoying your company. So, what did your man do to become state property?"

She immediately stopped eating and closed up her bag.

"I hate Autumn. She's always running her mouth. Her ass is over there booed up with your brother and needs to worry about that situation and stay the fuck outta mine. She had no right to tell you that."

"She wasn't being malicious. I inquired about you, and Autumn just responded," I explained.

"You don't know her like I do. She was definitely being

messy because of how she personally felt about him." Candy sighed.

"I just wanted you to admit you had a man. Now, I know why he let you out of his sight and ain't taking care of you like he should."

"I'm really starting to think this was a mistake, and I should have never agreed to going out with you."

Candy was pissed and a little embarrassed, so I drove her home.

As we pulled up to her house, I could see from the look on her face that she was really upset with me. There was no way I'd let her get out without telling her how I felt.

"I just want you to know I really had a great time with you tonight, and that it wasn't a mistake. You agreed to come with me because obviously you were feeling a certain way about your situation. Hopefully, this isn't the last time that I get to show you how a woman should be treated by her man."

"You don't know how he treats me, so miss me with all of that, and I can let myself out."

She hopped out, slammed my door, and stormed away. I struck a nerve, so I must have been right. Even in her rage, Candy was sexy as hell, making me want her even more. I drove off smiling because I knew she was the one.

Chapter Four

CANDY

It had been a week since I last saw or talked to Kane, and I couldn't get him out of my mind. Yes, he pissed me off, but there wasn't one lie spoken. Everything he said was true. It was like he held up a mirror to my face and forced me to look at my relationship through it.

After just a few hours with Kane, I realized I settled when it came to Rah. I wasn't happy at all in our relationship, just comfortable. Rah had been the only man I've ever been with, so I had nothing to compare him to, until now. I understood at this very moment that I was never a priority in his life. The streets were, and where did that get him? Behind bars and away from me.

I'd become a slave to my phone, waiting for him to call. Putting money I didn't have on his books because my dumb ass didn't want to touch the money I was holding for him because it was all he had. I put him before myself; something he would never do if the roles were reversed. If I was in jail for even half the time, Rah would have already moved on.

I never even thought about entertaining another man because I was committed to Rah. Every night I'd come home and please myself. I have not felt the touch of a man in over a year, and I was okay with that, until Kane entered my atmosphere like a shooting star. He interrupted my happy place, my safe place, and I liked it.

Kane was such a gentleman. I still couldn't believe he opened my door and rented out the skating rink. You see shit like that on TV and in movies, but never thought it would happen to you in real life. He took time out of his day to make me feel special, and it wasn't my birthday or a special occasion, just because he wanted to see me smile.

Rah would only take me out if I planned it, and it was never nothing really fancy. He had no problem buying me stuff but it had to be a holiday or something like that, not just because he was thinking of me. I really was content with everything because it was our norm.

Now, one little date had me questioning everything. One date I wished never had to come to an end, but I didn't know how to handle being triggered by Kane's questions and accusations about Rah. It made me uncomfortable, and I could no longer look him in the face, even though it was a handsome face.

The way he stared at me when he was talking did something

to me. His eyes were dark, deep, and intense. It was like he could see down into my soul. Kane's skin was the color of midnight, and his smile was like a blanket right out the dryer, warm and comforting. I had a thing for tall men as well, which was funny because Rah was only a few inches taller than me.

When we were skating, I almost fell. Kane caught me, and I didn't want him to let me go. He was so strong and fit, with broad shoulders and huge hands. I could tell he worked out every day. The only exercise Rah ever did was running the streets.

"Uggghhh!!!" I bellowed into a pillow that I planted my face in.

I was so mad at myself because now I was torn. Rah was all I knew, and I loved him. I just wasn't sure that I was in love. Kane was this stranger that came out of nowhere, stirring up so many emotions that had me ready to end my relationship with Rah and take a chance with him, knowing it could go nowhere. We just met. I knew nothing about him but wanted him in the worst way.

How did I get here and what do I do?

Autumn was my go to when I needed to talk and think life through. I didn't want to call her, though. She'd throw the fact that she was right in my face, but I had no one else to confide in. My mother and I didn't have the type of relationship where I could talk to her about it, or anything for that matter.

She didn't like Rah either, and probably would say I was being fast in the ass because I went on a date with someone else. My mom never even had the sex talk with me. I learned about it from my friends, Autumn, and TV. I knew my mom was aware that I was sexually active, but she never cared to ask or made sure I was being safe.

I put myself on birth control pills when I was sixteen by going to Plan Parenthood. They also gave you free contraceptives, so I would take handfuls of condoms each visit to share with my friends and Autumn's crazy ass.

"Hey, cuz, you laid up under Knowledge or are you home?"

Autumn was rarely around now since she had someone. I missed her.

"Naw, I'm home. He dropped me off last night. His baby momma finally let him see his son, so I wanted to let them have some alone time."

"Cuz, I'm over here stressing so bad. I'm about to smoke twenty blunts."

We both started cackling like hyenas with laughter.

"Oh wow, that's saying a lot. What's wrong, boo?"

"I'm feeling Kane, and now, I'm questioning everything about my relationship with Rah."

She started hooting and hollering in my ear so loud, I wanted to hang up on her ass.

"Yes, bitch! I'm so glad you are finally coming around and seeing Rah's punk ass for what he really is. A pile of horse shit!" Autumn just kept going and wouldn't let me get a word in. "He never treated you like the young queen that you are. Rah disrespects you every chance he gets. When that muthafucka did that shit with Tanya, I wanted to skin his ass!"

Well, damn, she's acting he did the shit to her.

"I wanted to slice his ass open with razors and pour salt in his wounds. He deserved to be rolled in honey and thrown in the woods, so the insects and bugs could feast on his ass—" I had to cut her off and bring her back down to earth.

"Alright already, Autumn, damn! I get it. You don't like his ass."

"I despise the very sight of him and wish his father would have busted in a condom instead of his momma and flushed his ass."

Autumn's feelings were valid. She didn't play about me, and I didn't play about her, period! That night when Rah and Tanya played me out, Autumn went crazy after they stopped me from beating on both of them.

She cracked Rah in his head with a lamp. He still wore the scar from that today. Autumn caught Tanya's ass at the top of the steps and dragged her down all of them. She put a hurting on Tanya her ass would never forget.

Growing up in the projects you had to learn how to fight, and we fought a lot. Autumn was known for kicking ass and asking questions later. With that being said, I needed to get her focus off of Rah and onto Kane.

"Cuz, enough about my man because we are still together, for now. My dilemma is that Kane has my nose wide open."

"Yo, did you let him smack it, flip it and rub it down?"

The excitement in her voice made me chuckle.

"Absolutely not. Actually, he pissed me off. I ended the night early but can't stop thinking of him. Would it be misleading if I called him? He knows about Rah, so I guess not."

"Listen, there is nothing wrong with seeing what's out there. Rah is in jail and not coming home anytime soon."

"That's not true. He might be getting out early. Rah mentioned something about his lawyer having good news."

I've been avoiding his calls, so I don't know what his lawyer said or if they even talked, and I didn't care at this point.

"Are you fucking kidding me?"

Autumn's whole mood changed. She got quiet as hell. You could hear a pin drop.

Knock! Knock!

Who the hell would be knocking on my door this time of night?

Junior had a key, so it wouldn't be him unless he lost it. It was never good news when someone came by this late.

"Cuz, I'm going to have to call you back. Someone is knocking on the door."

"I'm staying on the line to make sure you okay, just in case I have to run over there and fuck something up," Autumn spewed.

"Who the fuck is it?" I questioned in a very unpleasant tone.

"It's me, babe, open up." My heart dropped.

I opened the door and stood there speechless, not believing my eyes.

"Rah!" I managed to screech out.

Autumn immediately hung up after hearing me say his

name. I wrapped my arms around his neck and held on for dear life. He hugged me tight as well. Neither one of us wanted to let go. A million thoughts and questions rushed through my brain.

"When did you get out?" I inquired while letting him in and sitting the phone down.

My mom was at work, and Junior was out in the streets as usual. He knew my mom didn't want Rah here.

"Today, I came straight here from off the bus. I had to see you. Babe, I missed you so much."

He held my hands and stared at me with his bright eyes and creamy brown skin. Rah grew out his hair but kept his face clean-shaven.

"I missed you too, and I'm sorry about hanging—" He cut me off with a kiss.

It felt so good to feel his lips against mine and his tongue in my mouth. My whole body started to heat up. I could feel his erection through his pants. We stumbled back to my room and locked the door.

I was wearing an oversized T-shirt that he snatched off. He started aggressively sucking on my titties while pressing me up against the wall. He pulled down my boy shorts, and I stepped out of them. Rah rubbed on my bottom lips while kissing on my neck then slid his fingers up in me, feeling all of my wetness.

"Yeah, it's still nice and tight," he whispered in my ear.

I grabbed a condom to put on him. It was old as hell but better than nothing. He turned me around and bent me over. Rah entered me from behind and started his attack. I placed my hands on the wall, so I could brace myself. His hands were on my hips as he rammed his dick into me, over and over again. As I enjoyed the feeling I longed for, my mind began to wander. I couldn't help but think of Kane, wishing it was him instead.

"Uhhhhhh!" Rah exclaimed as he climaxed and relaxed on my back.

Damn, that was quick as hell.

We climbed in the bed and laid there, not saying a word. It felt good to rest my head on his chest, to feel a warm body next to mine, but once again my mind wandered off. Kane's face just kept popping up. Rah rubbed my back and kissed the top of my head.

"I thought of you every day, dreaming of this moment right here," Rah expressed.

"So, are you going to tell me how you got out so soon?" I inquired while shifting my body, so I could look him in the face.

"I kept calling, trying to let you know, but you weren't taking my calls," he replied sarcastically.

He knew exactly why I wasn't answering the phone for him. I wasn't going to bring it back up because it was in the past. Rah was out now and hopefully for good.

"My lawyer said it was an illegal search and seizure. She got a hold of a recording of a call that came into the police department. The caller made false accusations against me. The D.A. should have never filed charges. He was aware that the tape existed."

What he said made no sense to me, but I let him continue.

"The police lied and said I failed to signal when I turned the corner. Come to find out, they were only on me because of that caller."

"Do you know who it was?"

"No, it was anonymous, but the caller was a female. I want to listen to it. If it was a setup, then I probably know the person and can recognize her voice. I'm going to visit my family up north tomorrow for the weekend. I'm meeting up with my lawyer since her office is up that way."

Rah grew up in the same projects as us, but his immediate family moved up north while he was locked up. His mom came into some money from a lawsuit and was out. He had a few cousins still around here, but that was it. This nigga just got out but was leaving me already and didn't ask me to go with him.

I rolled my eyes and got up to go to the bathroom. It probably was some hoe ass trick he was dealing with because why would a complete stranger do such a thing. More than likely, he was out there doing me dirty again! I was glad his ass got locked up and wished he was still there. Being loyal to him all this time got me nowhere. Kane's face popped into my head once again, causing me to smile. I was calling him tomorrow.

Chapter Five

KANE

Thought I wasn't going to see Candy again after she almost broke my door the last time we were together. Now, I was waiting for her to arrive. Our first date didn't end so great, so this weekend I planned on making up for it. I rented an Airbnb in Atlantic Highlands, at the top of the hills. I figured a more intimate setting would allow us to get to know each other better.

"How was your ride?" I greeted Candy as she stepped out of the car and walked toward me.

"It was very nice. An unexpected surprise, thank you."

She was wearing a black, form fitting dress that accented every one of her curves. Candy had her locs pulled back and smelled like a bed of fresh flowers that had just bloomed. I could feel my manhood instantly rise.

Down boy, not yet.

By now the sun had set and the moon hung in the sky shining over us like a scene in a movie. I ushered her inside and closed the door.

It took everything in me not to devour her right there. I wanted to lift Candy up and press her up against the wall while her ass rested in my hands, and I licked and sucked on her plump lips. Instead, I asked her to join me in the living room, so she could relax.

"Something smells delicious. Did you cook for us too?" Candy questioned as she took off her shoes and got comfortable on the oversized couch.

She had the prettiest feet with a fresh manicure.

"No, I actually had a chef come in earlier and whip us up something. She's staying in the guest house in the back and will be taking care of us while we are here."

I sat down next to her, opening up a bottle of Pinot Grigio that I had chilling on ice, pouring us each a glass.

"You just pulled out all the stops. This house is amazing and so are you," she complimented, taking a sip of wine.

"A small gesture to apologize for my actions the last time we were together. I made you feel a certain way, causing us to end the night way too soon. It wasn't my place to question your relationship or make assumptions about it."

"Yes, I admit it had me in my feelings, but if this is how you apologize, I might let you piss me off again."

Candy gazed into my eyes when she spoke. I didn't care about the food anymore. The only appetite I had now was for her. I leaned in and our lips touched. Candy's lips were even softer than I imagined. My tongue parted them and entered her mouth.

Our kisses were slow but constant. We had a rhythm going, and I could tell she was enjoying it just as much as I was. I placed my hand on her back, bringing her in closer, slowly kissing her cheek, then her chin, working my way down to her neck while showering her with kisses on both sides. As my tongue traced her collarbone, Candy's breathing started to pick up and her body relaxed even more.

I unzipped the back of her dress, just enough to cause her spaghetti straps to fall down. Applying soft kisses to each shoulder. Candy lifted her head slightly. She leaned back with her eyes closed and lips parted. Freeing the dress the rest of the way, I revealed her titties. Her nipples were small and firm.

"Lay back and let me take control. All you need to do is enjoy the ride."

I slid off her dress and tossed it to the side. Once I was positioned in between Candy's legs, I traced her areola with my tongue. I could see her body react while flicking my tongue back and forth over her left nipple, giving it a slight tug with each suckle. I gave the same care to the other nipple.

"Mmmmmm. Ooooooo."

She let out soft moans that excited me even more. They were low and long, making me harder than a brick as the tips of her nails softly raked my scalp. I continued downward toward Candy's belly button, leaving a trail of wet kisses. I pushed her legs wide open, so I could get to the sweet spot that was bare as the day she was born.

Now face to face with her pussy, I gently placed kisses on both lips, then ran my tongue down her center, grazing her clit. Candy's legs trembled. I took the first two fingers on my right hand and entered her gushy center while spreading her lips open with my other one, fully exposing her. Candy's moans were getting louder and deeper as my fingers slid in and out, feeling her wetness.

She rubbed on her own titties and played with her nipples. I removed my fingers and flipped her over onto her stomach. Candy was now face down, ass up. I licked and sucked her from behind as if she was a ripe mango.

"Aaaaaahhh."

She tried to crawl away, and I snatched her ass back while continuing to please her, placing my hand on the center of her back, so she stayed put. I could feel the sweat on her body.

My beard caught her juices as they dripped down my face. I kept this up until I felt her petite but voluptuous body spasm.

"Ssssssss, oh, oh, oh. Shit." Candy came hard.

I undressed and laid down beside her, fully erect and protected. She climbed on top, slowly sliding onto my dick. Candy rocked back and forth with the rhythm of a belly dancer as I gripped her hips. I put my hands on her titties. Candy placed her hands over mine and started to bounce up and down.

Any other time I had the stamina of a bull, but between the

death grip her pussy had on my dick, and Candy's determination to show me she was no amateur, I was about to bust at any moment. She leaned in toward my chest and increased her speed. We both climaxed at the same time.

"Candy, Candy, Candy," was all I could say.

"Whew, that was great. My body thanks you." she exclaimed, trying to gather her breath.

"Well, I hope it thanks me again later," I replied, kissing her forehead.

I got up to retrieve the surprise I had for her. In the text message I sent her, she was told to just bring herself, and I would take care of the rest. I hired a personal shopper to pick up a few things for her to wear over the weekend. With the pic I snuck of her at my party, and my description from recollection, the young lady did a great job.

"What's this?" Candy inquired, looking puzzled but smiling as I handed her the bag.

"Just a lil something I had put together for you. Hopefully, everything fits and is to your liking."

She pulled out the silk rope and put it on.

"This feels so soft and smooth. I love it."

Candy placed a kiss on my cheek as she stood on her tiptoes.

"Good, now I don't know about you, but I worked up an appetite."

I headed toward the kitchen and she followed. The chef had prepared an array of different dishes and placed them in the buffet warmers. Candy compiled mostly seafood onto her plate.

I was more of a meat and potatoes type man, but I did put some king crab legs on my plate as well.

We grabbed a couple beers and headed to the dining area. This house was modern with a cozy feel to it. Smokey gray, cushioned chairs surrounded a glass, rectangular shaped table. There was a beautiful chandelier hanging above that you were able to dim.

Candy and I sat down next to each other, and I lit some candles. They smelled of exotic fruits, adding a fresh fragrance to the room. I opened our drinks and took a swig from my bottle but poured hers into a glass.

"So, what else do you have planned for us this weekend? I'm already in awe of everything so far. The chef really outdid herself. I can't get enough of this seafood paella. It's delicious."

She sipped her beer and gave me a smile that could melt an iceberg.

"Well, I'm glad you are pleased with everything and enjoying your food. As for what else I have planned, you just have to wait and see. I like the element of surprise. Seeing your reaction excites me."

Her eyes lit up with anticipation of what was to come.

We finished up with dinner, and I took her by the hand, leading her to the master bedroom. It was decorated in an Arabian nights theme. So many beautiful colors adorned the room. There was a king size canopy style bed with steps leading up to it. It was covered with plush pillows and throw blankets draped the edges of the bed.

I went into the master bathroom that was off to the left. There was a double sink, and all the handles were embellished with jewels of many colors. The toilet was kept private in a separate area. A walk-in shower that was made for two people to shower at once took up most of the space. I grabbed fresh washcloths from the linen area built into the wall. There were two gold terry cloth robes hanging up next to it.

I started one of the showers and yelled for Candy to come join me. She came to the opening of the door and just stood there like a deer caught in headlights. I chuckled and summoned her with my hand. Candy entered, and I pulled her in under the water.

"Are you nervous or just acting shy?" I questioned, sensing her hesitation.

"A little of both, I guess. I never showered with anyone else before. So, umm, yeah."

I kissed the side of her neck while standing behind her. Pumping some of the soap that was sitting in the caddy onto one of the washcloths, I lathered it up and proceeded to wash her entire body. She returned the favor. As we were rinsing off, Candy rubbed on my dick, making it stand at attention.

Next thing I knew she was on her knees, taking most of me into her mouth. She sucked the head and gave me a hand job at the same time. Candy pleased me until she could feel I was about to bust and aimed it at her breast. I wasn't expecting that but was pleasantly surprised.

"You tryna make a nigga fall in love." She smiled.

We rinsed off, put on the robes, and headed back to the room.

"Join me outside." I spoke to Candy.

Our room had a balcony that overlooked the lower New York Bay. You could see Manhattan in the distance. I knew she liked to smoke too, so I had a tray prepared of different strains of weed. It had an assortment of wrappers, an herb grinder and a lighter.

I also had a cooler of different beverages on ice and a pork free charcuterie board that the chef put together for us.

We sat on the couch of the outdoor wicker furniture set. Everything was on the table in front of us. It was a beautiful summer night, but you could tell Fall was on the horizon. There was no other place I would rather be but here in this moment with her.

"I'm in awe of you. At such a young age, how do you know so much about how to care for a woman? You put so much thought into every detail," Candy questioned.

"I watched my dad love and care for my mom. That gave me the blueprint on how to treat that special lady in my life."

From a young boy I could remember my dad kissing on my mom, making her smile. He would always place his hand at the small of her back, whenever he escorted her somewhere. They would dance to old school music in the kitchen while she was cooking. My dad would bring her flowers or chocolate just because. I admired him and how he took care of our family.

"I can't believe you are single. Like, how are you available?

Is this a front, or is this truly who you are? Are you wooing me so I fall for you, then you turn into someone else?"

Candy bombarded me with all these questions as she rolled up a blunt.

"This is me, not a facade. Some women don't know how to appreciate a good man. They are broken and scarred from their previous relationships. All the baggage they are still carrying gets unloaded on the next man."

That was what happened in my last relationship. She couldn't get past what other men had done to her and constantly accused me of things I never did. I eventually got tired of defending myself and being verbally attacked, so I ended it.

"So, you're Mr. Perfect? You come with no flaws or scars?"

Candy passed the blunt to me as she blew smoke out her mouth. Even that was sexy. Her lips made the perfect pucker.

"Absolutely not. We all have imperfections and things we need to work on. I work too much and lose myself when I take on a new project. It causes me to be neglectful at times, but I'm working on that. And I like to be in control. That can be a double-edge sword, depending on the situation," I admitted.

"I'm too trusting and naïve. People show me who they are, and instead of believing them, I'm like no, show me again."

Candy laughed, causing me to do the same. It was infectious and joy to my ears.

"There's nothing wrong with trust. It's the foundation of any relationship. Who you trust is the problem."

I took another pull of the blunt, and she raised her eyebrows at me.

"Puff, puff, pass, bruh!"

Candy reached for it, and I stole a kiss. I put the blunt out, scooped her up, and carried her inside. I tossed her onto the middle of the bed, on her back. She smiled then bit down on her bottom lip and untied her robe. It was going to be a long night.

Chapter Six

CANDY

It was morning, and I awakened to the smell of goodness. I looked over, and Kane wasn't in the bed next to me. Scanning the room, I noticed a pair of pajamas on the nightstand next to the bed with a note. It was from Kane.

"*Candy... I went for a quick run. Everything you need is already laid out for you in the bathroom. Once you are done freshening up, go out on the balcony. See you soon.*"

I jumped in the shower then brushed my teeth and washed my face. After slipping on the pajamas, I headed outside to the breathtaking view. Looking down, I located the source of the wonderful aromas filling the air. Kane must have had the chef prepare this tray of deliciousness.

The homemade pastries and fresh coffee, which was on a warmer, were calling my name. I sat down and fixed myself a cup while taking a huge bite of a croissant. All this felt like a fairytale that I didn't want to come to an end. My Cinderella ass finally made it to the ball. I couldn't have dreamt this up if I tried.

As I took it all in, Rah came to mind. I was just as bad by doing exactly what he did to me to him. Two wrongs didn't make a right, but why did doing wrong feel so good? My feelings tried to take over, but they were interrupted before it could happen.

"Hey, beautiful, how was your sleep?" Kane inquired as he placed a kiss on my forehead.

"It was great. Just missing you when I woke up."

"I have an adventurous day planned for us, so when you are done here, get ready. The car will be here in an hour."

He was definitely a take control type of man. Kane didn't ask, he demanded. It actually turned me on.

* * *

The car arrived, and Kane opened my door, so I could climb in. It was the same driver that drove me here at the wheel. I guess he was our personal driver for the weekend.

There were fresh flowers and a card on my seat. They smelled amazing. The card simply said *"thank you"* and was signed by Kane.

"Thank you for what? I should be the one thanking you." I looked over at him.

"For being you and coming here. I know we are just getting

to know each other, but I feel a connection to you already. You give off an aura that is very beautiful and pure. It's not too many genuine people out there, but I can tell you're one of them."

"You're too sweet, and I appreciate you."

I placed my hand on the side of his face. He was so damn fine. Kane removed my hand, kissed it, and held it in his hands until we reached our destination.

The ride was short, like ten minutes. We pulled up to the waterway, and I almost died inside. Even though I grew up by the beach, I didn't play with the ocean. Getting my feet wet was fine, but I never sailed on the deep, blue sea.

"Have you ever been on a ferry?" Kane inquired with a smirk on his face.

"Never, and I'm nervous as hell. I hope I don't get seasick."

Just the thought of it made my stomach queasy. I didn't want this bitch to sink like the Titanic.

"Hopefully, you won't get sick, and we can sit inside if you like. It should take us about forty minutes to arrive in Manhattan. Just rest your head on my shoulders if you start to feel ill, okay?" I nodded my head.

The ferry ride was good. The views were spectacular, but I was glad to have my feet on solid ground once we made it into the city.

We walked around, taking in the fresh air and stopping at street vendors to buy souvenirs. I wanted to eat something from every food truck we saw. Where I lived in New Jersey, they didn't offer such amenities, so I wanted to enjoy all of it while I could.

As we made our way down the long blocks, we came upon an empty building. Kane stopped walking.

"Why are we stopping? There's nothing here but this unoccupied space."

"You mean *my* unoccupied space." Kane answered, opening the front door with a key.

"Ok, I'm intrigued and also a lil confused."

"I needed an office space in New York because I'm expanding my business here," he explained.

"What exactly do you do for a living, if you don't mind me asking?"

I wondered how he could afford his lifestyle. His brother too because his home was straight out of MTV Cribs.

"Simply put, I buy and sell property, for the most part. Whenever I see land or houses for sale, I do my research to make sure it's a good investment. The homes, which are mostly foreclosures, are fixed up and sold as is. I hold on to the land, waiting for the right developer to take it off my hands."

"Hmmm, I'm impressed, and it puts my mind at ease as to where all this money was coming from." I crossed my arms across my chest.

"All of us aren't drug dealers, Candy. It's a stereotype not only placed on us by society, but our own people too. You probably thought that about me and my brother. Our parents died when we were teenagers and left us money. I invested and started a family business to build generational wealth. I'm also employing other young black men and women." Kane seemed a little offended.

He was right, though. I did think they were doing something illegal. Everyone wasn't Rah or the other dudes in my hood that lived that street life. I just wasn't used to seeing young, black men thriving in such a way. It also showcased my ignorance, and proved how much I needed to explore life outside of my environment.

When we left his office, Kane took me on a horse and carriage ride through Central Park. It was so romantic. We talked and laughed, sharing kisses along the way. Before long, we were back where we started.

"Well, it's time to head back to the ferry. I wanted to get you out of the house, so it could be prepared for the evening festivities." Kane had a devilish grin on his face as he held down a cab.

"You don't stop do you?" I had a huge smile on mine, showing all my teeth.

"It's our last night away, so I wanted it to be special." He entered my personal space.

"Yes, this is our last night together. Then my carriage turns back into a pumpkin, and my weekend fairytale is over."

"It doesn't have to be. How this story ends is totally up to you."

Kane leaned in, placing a kiss on my forehead. I melted like butter in a hot skillet every time he did that.

He ushered me into the cab that took us to the ferry. The ride back to Jersey seemed faster, or maybe I was more relaxed. On the way to the house, all I could think about was how I would break things off with Rah. He probably was out there cheating on me again, but I didn't care because I was basically doing the same thing. In his mind we were still a couple.

"Here, put this on," Kane instructed, interrupting my thoughts.

We had arrived at our weekend home, and he handed me a blindfold to cover my eyes with.

"What do you have up your sleeve that I can't see?"

"Something I hope will make your night. I wanted it to be a surprise."

He took me by the hand and led the way. As we were walking, I wondered what it could be. Kane was so thoughtful and strategic with his planning.

I could tell we didn't go in the house, and this area was surrounded by a bunch of trees and bushes. One winding hill after another. I loved the seclusion of it, but I needed some Skin-So-Soft to sit out in these woods. These damn mosquitoes would bite my ass up.

"You can stop walking and take your blindfold off."

Kane had the backyard turned into a movie theater. There was a huge projector screen set up in the middle of the yard. Tiki torches, emitting the smell of citronella, surrounded our sitting area, creating a circle. My eyes teared up a little because no one ever made me feel this special.

I sat down in one of the enormous reclining chairs that was so comfortable. You literally became immersed into the cushions. I let my head fall back, so the tears couldn't escape my eyes. I took a deep breath and got myself together.

A small table was placed in between us, complete with an assortment of boxed candies, popcorn, and nachos. Beverages in an ice bucket sat in front of the table. I unfolded the blanket that was resting on the arm of the chair and covered my legs.

"You took me skating on our first date. Now, this." I smiled.

"I pay attention when you talk. What movie would you like to watch?"

His handsome face filled with warmth stared at me.

"Something to make us laugh. I love comedies. How about *Girls Trip*? I know it's a girly movie, but I like it."

"Hey, I'm cool with that. This weekend is all about you."

When the movie started, I grabbed my popcorn and got comfortable. What a wonderful end to a magical weekend.

Now that I was back home, my phone kept blowing up. I turned it off for the entire weekend because I didn't want anyone trying to reach me, especially Rah. I texted Autumn that I was going with Kane, so someone knew where I was.

"Where the fuck you been at? I tried to reach you all weekend, and your phone kept going straight to voicemail!"

Rah was pissed, and I didn't care. He got a taste of his own medicine and didn't like it.

"First of all, pipe down talking to me crazy! I turned my phone off because I was working. There was a private duty case I signed up for to get extra money. I went away with my client and her family. I couldn't make personal calls."

"Whatever, yo, I don't believe that shit, but we have bigger fish to fry."

I didn't give a shit what he believed. He has lied to me so many times, I lost count.

"Why, what happened now? Your ass going back to jail?"

"Fuck no, but your hoe ass cousin was the reason I was in there in the first place!" he spewed. I heard the words that came out of his mouth, but just sat there with the phone to my ear. "C, are you listening to me?"

"I know you don't like Autumn, but don't call her out her name again. And why would you lie on her? This is a whole new low, even for you!"

Rah must be getting high because he was talking out of his ass.

"She was the one on the goddamn recording. I know her voice. She didn't even try to disguise it. Probably thinking I would never listen to the tape."

"I'm going to call her because she needs to tell you that it wasn't her—"

"Don't call her! I want to see Autumn face to face, so she can't lie. I'm on my way, so we can go to her house," explained.

"Oh, hell no. We are not bringing this drama to my auntie's house. I will tell Autumn to meet us at the basketball court."

Rah was fucking tripping. My auntie doesn't like his ass either.

"You can't let her know I'm coming because she won't show up. You don't believe me C, but I'm telling you the truth. I'll text you when I'm close."

"Just come straight to the courts. I will have her meet me there now, so she won't get suspicious. You know how I feel about my cousin. If you're lying, I'll never speak to you again."

Rah had to be mistaken. Autumn wouldn't betray me like this. I knew she despised his ass and had wished death upon him on many occasions, but playing with the police. Nah, not her.

I called Autumn, hoping she wouldn't answer the phone.

"Bitch, I know you fucked him. Tell me all about it because if he's holding like his brother, I know you had an amazing weekend and walking like you need a wheelchair." Autumn laughed.

"Well, damn, hello to you too."

This was the first time we went all weekend without a call or text from each other. I knew she missed talking to me and wanted all the tea.

"Girl, bye! Nobody has time for formalities. I want the scoop on big daddy Kane."

"You did not just call him that. Yo ass really need help. Anyway, meet me at the courts, so I can tell you all about it. I want to see your reaction in person."

"Okay, I'm about to leave now. Just give me a few minutes to throw something on."

I felt horrible lying to Autumn, but I had to get to the bottom of this. If she had been keeping this secret from me all this time, I would be heartbroken. I trusted her with my life, and she knew everything about me. Just like I knew everything about her.

When I got to the courts it was pretty empty, which was

good. I'm dealing with two hot heads here, and neither one of them mind causing a scene.

I found refuge in the shady area all the way in the back by the tables with benches that were bolted into the ground. The trees leaning over from the outside provided a covering from the sun.

"Whew, we should have met inside the church. It's too damn hot out here."

Autumn walked up complaining as usual. My hands started to sweat a little, and it wasn't from the heat. I was nervous about confronting her. This shit could go all the way left.

"Hey, cuz. It's cooler over here, especially when you're sitting still."

I gave her an ice-cold water bottle that I grabbed for each of us before leaving the house as soon as she sat down..

"Spill the tea while it's popping hot, and don't leave anything out. I want all the details. I still can't believe you got up the nerve to cheat on Rah. It does my heart good to see you finally doing you."

She had a huge ass, cheesy smile on her face. I don't know how happy she was going to be when Rah pulled up.

"It was the best time of my life. I felt like royalty. The sex was amazing. Kane actually made love to me, instead of just screwing me in order to fulfill his needs. I've never fucked that many times in one night. He was like a drug that I couldn't get enough of."

"I think it's in their DNA because Knowledge had me the same damn way. I needed a break from him, though. That nigga got too much baby momma drama but continue. This is about you, not me."

"He had a whole damn staff, just waiting on us hand and foot. I took a ferry ride for the first time. You know me and the ocean ain't cool like that, but Kane made me feel safe..."

My phone interrupted me. It was Rah texting that he was about to pull up.

"Who is it? Why do you look nervous?" Autumn questioned.

"Listen, Autumn. Rah will be here any moment. He has this crazy notion that it was you who called the police on him the night he was arrested. I told him he was crazy as hell, but he wanted to hear it from you. So, when he gets here, just tell him that. We both know he's not going to let it go until you do."

She just sat there motionless, then a tear escaped from her eye.

"Bitch, you did do it!" I yelled, jumping up.

My heart was beating so fast I thought I would pass out.

"Candy, please, let me explain."

She reached for my hand, and I snatched it back. I could see Rah swiftly approaching us.

"I can tell by y'all lil interaction just now her trick ass admitted she did it."

Rah wasted no time insulting my cousin, once again.

"The only trick is your momma, you dirty dick bastard."

Now Autumn was up on her feet, looking Rah dead in his face with nothing but pure hate in her eyes.

"Suck my dick, bitch!" Rah countered.

"From what I hear, it ain't much to suck!"

Rah looked over at me like I betrayed him. I did tell her that but in confidence.

"Enough you two! What I want to know is why, Autumn? I cried to you that night, and you said nothing. What did he do to you that would make you send him to jail?"

My eyes swelled up with tears. This was the biggest betrayal ever. The fact that it came from her made it hurt even more.

"It's not about what he did to me. It's about what he does to you, over and over again. This lil dick muthafucka is a womanizer and a low life and—"

"You don't get to decide who's right for me!" I slammed my fist down on the table.

"He was cheating on you once again, Candy. That's why I called the police. He didn't even see me, but I saw him and some chick holding hands, all cozy and shit. Meanwhile, yo ass is at home, alone, being a good girlfriend. You deserve better!" Her lips were quivering with rage.

"And you deserve your ass kicked and need to mind your fucking business. Go get you a man. You got too much time on your hands, out here playing detective and shit." Rah barked at Autumn, pointing his finger at her face.

I noticed he didn't deny what she accused him of, though.

"I had to go *Law and Order* on your ass because my cousin just sits by while you shit on her. You don't deserve her then, and you don't deserve her now, muthafucka!"

"You could have just come to me, cuz. You know how hurt and sad I was with him being locked up. How many times did we discuss it? You just played dumb and faked like you were so concerned for me. We're family. I can't believe you, of all people, would do this to me."

"I'm sorry, Candy, and I hope you can forgive me. We are family, and I thought I was protecting you. I didn't mean to cause you more pain. He's a lying cheater, and you know it."

"She also knows you're the town whore, bitch."

Autumn opened her bottle of water and squeezed it, making the water splash all over Rah. Then she snatched my bottle and hit him in the face with it. I jumped in front of her, just in case he tried to retaliate.

"Rah, I told you before to stop calling my cousin out her fucking name."

At this point my head was hurting, and the tears wouldn't stop flowing from my eyes. I felt so betrayed by both of them. I knew Autumn wasn't lying, but she went too far. Rah was unfaithful, but he didn't deserve what she did.

"You defend her when she's the reason we've been apart for almost one and a half years! Man, fuck this shit. You betta watch your fucking back."

Rah wiped the water off his face with his shirt and walked off.

"You threatening me, Tiny Tim?" Autumn yelled, making sure he heard her.

All of this was crazy and had my head spinning. I just wished I could fucking disappear. Once again, Rah played me like a fool. It was sad, but it wasn't his first time, so I was used to it. Now, the betrayal from Autumn cut me to my core.

"Fuck that punk muthafucka. Let's go back to my house, roll a blunt, and hash this out." Autumn acted like what she did wasn't a big deal.

"I'm about to smoke, but it won't be with you. I love you like a sister. That's the only reason I didn't run up in your mouth, but we're going to need some time apart. What you did was fucked up and it hurts!"

I turned on my heels and left.

Chapter Seven

AUTUMN

All I could do was watch Candy walk away. I hurted her in the worst way, and that was the only part I regretted. Rah could burn in hell and go back to jail for all I cared. Candy asked for space, and I had to respect that. The shit stung, though.

We had never had any conflict with each other like this before. Yeah, we made each other upset here and there, but we always made up before the day was over. The grief I caused was visible in her eyes. Candy wasn't going to forgive me anytime soon.

I didn't want to go home, but I needed to go somewhere to process everything that just happened. So, I called the only other person I trusted with my feelings.

"Hey, Nut, if you're not busy, can you come grab me real quick from the courts by my house?"

Peanut didn't live that far from us, like ten minutes away in the next town over.

"You good? You sound like you've been crying."

"I'll explain everything to you. I just need to get the fuck away from here."

I was trying my best to hold my emotions in. Showing weakness, especially in public, was something I didn't do.

"Say less. I'm on my way."

Thank goodness Peanut didn't take that long to come get me. Once I got in the car everything hit me like a ton of bricks. I started hysterically crying. That ugly, snot cry where bubbles came out your nose.

"Wow, Autumn, did someone die? What the hell is going on?" Peanut questioned as she handed me a couple of those brown, rough ass napkins from fast food restaurants. It was like wiping your nose with sandpaper.

"I fucked up really bad this time, Nut. Like really, really bad. Candy will probably never speak to me again. I thought I was helping her, but I should have just stayed out of it."

On the ride back to Peanut's house I explained everything that went down, from seeing Rah with the chick up until now. We stopped at the liquor store along the way. A drink would help calm my nerves. A blunt would be even better. Peanut had weed. That was her side hustle and where I get all of mine from. She just gave it to me, refusing to take my money.

"Oh, no, Nut, I hope I wasn't interrupting anything." I apologized as I entered her home.

She had candles lit. The aroma of food coming from the kitchen filled the air while classic R&B played in the background. The stuff our mommas listened to on Saturdays while cleaning the house.

"No, this is all for you." I spun my head around, looking at her, confused.

"You sounded so distraught over the phone. So, I just threw something together real quick before I left, figuring you needed to relax. Don't get excited about the food. It's just Hungry Man frozen dinners I'm heating up in the oven," she explained.

"Awe, you're so sweet and such a great friend. I'm lucky to have you in my life."

I hugged Peanut and gave her a kiss on the cheek. She hasn't just been a great friend to me, but Candy too. It was always us three together wherever we went.

After I washed my hands and made myself comfortable, I cracked open the bottle of Hennessy and started sipping.

"Candy loves you. Just give her time to process everything. You fucked up. I understand why you did it, but it wasn't your place. You always let your emotions make bad decisions," Peanut explained as she rolled up.

"You're right. I should have just got out of the car and punched him in the face, instead of calling the police. This way I wouldn't be in this situation right now."

"No, mind your business! She doesn't need you to save her.

Candy is a grown ass woman and is in love with that nigga, whether you want to believe it or not."

"She might love him, but she's not in love. Her ass just spent the weekend with Kane, getting dicked down. So, ummm, yeah, that part!" That wasn't my business to tell, but oh well.

"Wow. I'm so surprised because Candy is usually the good one," Peanut uttered with no regard for my feelings.

"So, what are you saying? I'm the bad one? Why, because I like to fuck?"

I was tipsy at this point and needed to eat one of these instant meals to soak up some of this liquor.

"It's not the fact you like to fuck. You just let any rooster walking by enter your hen house." She shrugged her shoulders.

"Fuck you, Nut! You had no problem when you were all up in my hen house, pecking around and shit. Pass me the blunt, with yo ugly ass."

Peanut had a lot of nerve judging me. That low key hurt my damn feelings. She wasn't really ugly either, but she damn sure wasn't anything to write home about. Every time we were out together people thought she was mine or Candy's man.

She dressed just like a dude and kept her hair cut low with a fresh shape up at all times. Peanut was short, like me, with a strong jaw structure and a wide nose. She had beady eyes and skin the color of a dark chocolate candy bar. Her lips are thick with a slight discoloration on the bottom one. We called it a liquor lip. It was pinkish in color.

"And I'll gladly peck around it again."

We both busted out laughing. I needed to laugh because I was so tired of crying. Peanut got up and got our food. She cut off the music and put on Netflix.

Before long, hours passed by. I was high as hell and couldn't take another sip. Peanut was in no condition to drive me home, and I wasn't taking an Uber in this inebriated state.

I texted my mom, letting her know I'd be staying at Peanut's house for the night; not that she cared anyway.

"Don't touch my butt either. Stay on your side before I elbow you in the titty," I warned Peanut as I climbed into her bed.

Her couch wasn't comfortable enough to sleep on, and her floor was hard as hell.

"You know you want me to make that kitty cat purr," she teased.

When I was this wasted, my ass got very horny and definitely liked to be done dirty. Peanut and I already went there before, and it wasn't for me. But at this point, a mouth was a mouth, and I needed to feel good.

"You can do me, but I'm definitely not doing you again. We both were uncomfortable with that part."

Eating pussy was way more difficult than sucking on a dick to me. I figured since I had one and knew what I liked done, my ass would know what to do. Wrong! It was a horrible experience I didn't want to relive.

"Agreed."

Peanut wasted no time lifting my shirt up. She teased my nipples with her tongue then stopped, went to her dresser drawer, and pulled out a strap-on dildo. My eyes got big as hell. I'd never been fucked with a fake dick before. This muthafucka was feeling extra adventurous tonight.

"Hold up. I'm not that fucked up, bitch." I waved my hand at her.

"You gone love it. If you don't, I'll stop," Peanut promised.

"Put a condom on that thing. I know this ain't the first time you used it."

After Peanut made me drip like a leaky faucet when she ate my pussy from behind, she slid up inside me. It wasn't bad and got the job done, but I still preferred the real thing.

When she pulled out and turned me over on my back, I could tell we were in for a long night from the sparkle in her eye.

In the morning I jumped in the shower and put on the same shit I wore yesterday. Peanut was cooking breakfast, but I wasn't staying for it. Last night was amazing, nothing like the first time we tried it. I guess because she was home with all her equipment and shit, it put her in a different zone.

"Where you going? I'm making your favorite, shrimp and grits," Peanut questioned, looking bewildered.

"Knowledge is on his way to pick me up. I don't feel like going home, so I'm gonna go hang out at his house."

"Damn, Autumn, you foul as hell."

Peanut slammed the bowl she was holding down on the counter hard as hell, but it didn't break. Those Dollar Tree bowls and plates are hard to crack. I think they were made with gorilla glue.

"What got your boxers all up in a bunch?"

Peanut looked at me like she was ready to fight. I knew I would regret sleeping with her ass again. Being all up in my feelings over Candy then drinking and smoking had me doing dumb shit, once again. Now, this muthafucka was in here acting out a scene from a *Lifetime* movie.

"You could have told me you were leaving. I'm up here making breakfast, tryna feed you. Meanwhile, yo ass already called a ride."

If she was a cartoon character, steam would be coming from out her nostrils and ears.

"Since when do I have to tell you my every move? Just because you fucked me with a silicone dick last night, doesn't make you my man, so miss me with that bullshit," I informed her.

"You can wait for him outside. Grab yo shit and get the fuck out!" Peanut ordered as she pointed at the door.

Did this muthafucka really just dismiss me because she wanted to play house with my ass?

"Whatever, I didn't do shit to yo ass. Be mad at yourself for catching feelings. Obviously you have mistaken last night for something more than what it was, just sex between friends. If you couldn't handle it, you shouldn't have done it. Tuh!"

"You know exactly how I feel about us, and you took advantage of that. I'm not a fucking toy that you can play around with. You used me."

This bitch must have bumped her head. Peanut was almost foaming at the mouth as she yelled at me. I couldn't believe she was acting like this.

"Can I have my food to go because I see you need some time to be alone?" She gave me the dirtiest look ever and clenched her fists. "I guess that's a no. Call me when you get outta your feelings."

Before she could even respond, I was already out the door. Nobody had time for the craziness. If I would have stayed a minute longer, we might have come to blows.

As I waited for Knowledge to pull up, I sent Candy a text, apologizing again, but it wouldn't go through. She had me blocked. That really fucked me up because now I was out here alone for real. Both my day ones had me on their shit list.

"Took yo ass long enough, punk." I joked with Knowledge, getting into his truck.

"Get yo smart ass in here and stop talking shit all the damn time."

Knowledge's mouth was just like mine, reckless, and I loved it.

"Did you miss me?"

I haven't seen him in weeks because his baby momma, Keelie, was a real bitch. She would just pop up and start shit. The hoe had the nerve to try to swing on me one day, and I was about to push her wig back, but Knowledge stopped me. I figured he didn't want his son to watch his mommy get beat the fuck up, so I just stayed away. The last thing I wanted to do was come between him and his son.

"I missed that tight ass pussy of yours. Let me touch it."

He reached over, and I slapped his hand. Knowledge was so nasty, and I was turned on, but tried to play hard to get.

"I need to stop by my house and get something to wear. I'm out here looking like yesterday."

My ass was clean, but I wasn't going to be seen in the same shit, especially if we went out somewhere.

"You had clothes in my wash from when you stayed over. You better put that shit on because I'm going straight home to tear that ass up, and this ain't no fucking Uber."

"Well, I'm hungry, so can we stop at Starbucks? It's on the way, so don't say anything smart to me."

I knew he was sick of me already, and it had only been five minutes. He blew his breath but made sure I got what I needed before heading home.

When we pulled up to the house, Keelie's ass was waiting on the front steps. I rolled down my window but stayed in the car. Knowledge got out and she started going in on his ass. I didn't see her son at all and from what I could hear, she wanted to know why I was in the car. He must have been fucking with her when I wasn't around, not that I cared.

What he did when I wasn't around wasn't my business because he wasn't my man. Knowledge knew not to play in my face, though.

"You're not my girl, so I'm confused on why you worried about my dick. I do what I want. I'm a grown ass muthafuckin' man!" Knowledge scolded her.

I sat back and sipped on my chai latte, watching the drama unfold.

"What is it about her dusty ass that you keep bringing her over here where my son be?"

Now see, she crossed the line and invited me into the conversation when she called me dusty. I was over here minding my business but gladly accepted the invitation.

"It's because my pussy is tighter, and my head game is stronger than yours, bitch!" I screamed.

My voice was loud enough for her to hear me clearly. When I started laughing, it really pissed Keelie.

She gave me the finger, and I stuck my tongue at her, wiggling it. Her dumb ass charged at the car, and when she got close enough, I threw my drink right in her face. Keeling started yelling. That shit was hot as hell. I got out of the car to beat her ass, and once again, Knowledge stepped in my way.

"Your son ain't here to save you this time, bitch! Like I told you before, you don't want this smoke. I will beat a layer of skin off ya ass! Take yo ugly ass home and be a mother to your child."

She tried to get past him, but Knowledge's ass was too big and strong. He held her back.

"Go home, Keelie! This shit is getting old, damn!" Knowledge pushed her toward her car.

"You let this hoe throw a hot drink in my face, then tell me to go home? Fuck you, and the next time you see ya son, he will be graduating college."

Keelie climbed into her car and looked at her face in the

rearview mirror. It wasn't third-degree burns, but the shit was blistering up.

"Oh my fucking god, my face! Bitch, you better watch yo fucking back! I'm coming for yo ass!"

"Ooohh, I'm so scared. That's what the fuck you get for trying to run up on me. Get your herpes face ass on outta here and go home like he told you to. Bye, bitch!"

I waved as Keelie sped off like she was auditioning for *The Fast and the Furious*.

"You foul as hell Autumn for throwing that drink in her face like that. Now my son is about to be scared of her ass."

"I was at a disadvantage sitting in the car, so I had to think fast, shit. She's lucky you didn't let me get to her. I was going to put hands and feet on her trifling ass. Keelie would have been looking like the elephant man when I was done."

"Get your crazy, hood ass in the house and take your clothes off." Knowledge smacked me on the ass.

Chapter Eight

CANDY

It had been two weeks since the shit hit the fan with Rah and Autumn. All I've been doing was going to work and coming home. I missed Autumn like crazy. We've never been apart this long before, but I refused to give in. She needed to know just how hurtful her actions were.

Rah was on his way over to get the money I was holding for him. I told him to come get it last week, but now all of a sudden, he wanted it today. My mom already left for work, but Junior was here, surprisingly.

"Candy, Rah is at the door."

Junior was so damn lazy he wouldn't even open the door for him.

"You're sitting right here but rather yell at me. Just fucking useless." I mush his forehead.

"Shut up and keep your hands off me before I tell mommy he was here," he threatened.

"Go ahead, so I can tell her you're the neighborhood thief, you asshole."

I haven't seen Rah since that day at the courts, but we had been texting. I just didn't want to see or talk to anyone. When Kane reached out, I told him I was dealing with family drama and needed some time to myself.

Rah stood there with a stupid grin on his face when I opened the door to let him in. I was still agitated by the fact that he proposed to me, and the next day was with another chick. He definitely had some explaining to do.

"Here, it's all there. You can count it."

I put the money and the ring on my dresser once we made it back to my room.

"I don't need to count it. I trust you with my life and know you would never do me dirty."

Rah looked over at the ring then back at me. It was as if someone took all the air out of his lungs.

"C, what are you doing? I got that ring for you. I want to marry you one day."

He sounded so sincere and actually teared up.

"Are you freaking kidding me?" I laughed right in his face.

"What's so funny? I'm being serious as hell right now," he expressed.

"Give it to whoever you were with the night Autumn saw you. And before you even open your mouth, we all know my cousin is a lot of things, but a liar she is not."

Autumn was too damn blunt to make shit up. She always spoke her mind.

"I fucked up. I ain't even gone hold you. Autumn did see me with someone else, and maybe it was my karma that landed me in jail. You have always been faithful to me during our entire relationship, even now."

If he only knew how I allowed Kane to slut me out when we were together. That man made me have multiple orgasms during sex without even stimulating my clit. He awakened parts of my body that have been dormant, elevating me sexually. My body never responded to Rah in such a way. Kane did things to me I would have never imagined.

"Sitting there all that time, away from you, made me realize just how much I took you for granted. I didn't deserve your love, and you continued to give it to me anyway."

Here he goes, saying all the things I wanted to hear, pulling on my heart strings.

"Rah, don't say things to me you don't mean. You're just trying to get me to forgive you, so you can hurt me again." He stepped in close and grabbed my face.

"C, I love you. I mean every word, and I will never hurt you like that again."

He started kissing me while removing my clothes. My mind was saying stop, but my body said keep going. I could feel the wetness between my legs. Rah laid on the floor, pulling me on top of him. He had me right where he wanted me. I fell for it every single time.

Once I allowed him to enter me, I rocked back and forth

slowly, squeezing his dick with my pussy muscles on each forward motion. I grinded my hips, closed my eyes, and leaned my head back.

Rah grabbed my ass and slammed me up and down. Next thing I knew he climaxed. I covered his mouth, so Junior couldn't hear him.

"You know you were supposed to tell me beforehand, so I could have jumped off," I whispered through clenched teeth.

Rah knew he wasn't wearing a condom and probably did the shit on purpose.

"It happened so fast, and you seem to be somewhere else."

"What the hell do you mean by that?" I questioned, trying to play it off.

"I don't know, something just felt different, and usually you can tell when I'm about to bust. But like I said, you seem to be off in fucking LaLa land some damn where."

Pissed off, I got up and sat on the edge of my bed. I did see Kane's face as I was riding him. And the fact that Rah came faster than a freight change, it wasn't even worth my time.

"Whatever, Rah, what do you plan on doing with that money? I hope you're not going back to the streets. That shit is getting old," I questioned, changing the subject as I cleaned myself up with some baby wipes I kept in my underwear drawer.

"I can't live off $30,000. I have to re-up and do what I have to do. We can't live, I mean."

Everything was I, I, I with his ass. He never said "us"

because I wasn't part of his plan. He only cleaned it up because I gave him a funny look.

"No, you said it right the first time, with your selfish ass. You need to take the money and invest it. Start a business. Do something constructive with it. I'm done waiting for jail calls, sending money, visiting, and stressing! I ain't doing any more bids with you. I don't care who put you there. It's time for you to grow the fuck up."

I put my clothes back on, so I could walk Rah's raggedy ass outside. Before we could walk out. Junior came banging on my door. He was screaming my name, over and over again, like a crazy person.

"What the fuck is wrong with you banging on my door like that and—"

I stopped talking because I could see he was visibly shaken. Tears were flowing down his face, and he had his phone in his hand. Instantly, I felt ill because nothing made him cry. Something awful had to happen.

"Junior! What's wrong? Tell me." I had my hands on his shoulders.

"Mommy said she's been trying to call you. The ambulance and police just brought Autumn to the emergency room. She's been shot, and it's bad."

I fell to the ground and started wailing uncontrollably. My head felt like it had its own heartbeat as my body went numb. Rah picked me up and held me tight.

"She can't die. She can't die. I will never forgive myself."

I sobbed all over his shirt. The tears wouldn't stop falling.

"Don't talk like that. She will be fine. Autumn isn't my favorite person, but I don't want nothing to happen to her. I know what she means to you. Come on, I'll drop y'all off at the hospital."

"You okay, Candy?" Junior questioned, trying to hold back his own tears.

He got on my last nerve, but the love we had for each other was real. Autumn was like his sister too.

"No, I'm not, and I won't be until I know she is okay. Let's go check on her."

On the way over to the hospital, everyone was calling me, but I couldn't talk right now. They were probably wondering where I was, and why I wasn't with her. We were always together. My heart had never been in so much agony as it was now.

I told Rah to let us out on the side of the hospital because I didn't want anyone to see me with him. The last time we both saw Autumn, he threatened her. I knew he didn't shoot her because he was with me, but now wasn't the time to bring him back around.

Junior and I walked into the ER, and the first people I saw were my aunties, Rose and Bird, and my mom. They look drained and exhausted. Junior went over to console my mom. I let them have their moment while I checked on my auntie Rose. She was trembling as she hugged me so tight.

We didn't have the best relationship. My aunt loved me but never really got to know me. I stayed at her house more than mine, visiting Autumn, but it was like she tried to avoid me. It was weird.

"Auntie Rose, do you know what happened?" I looked around for tissues.

"No, I rushed over here when your mom called. I'm so scared and nervous."

My mom worked in the ER, so she must have seen Autumn come in.

"You girls are always together. I thought you might have been hurt too," she continued.

"Sit down, auntie. Let me get you some water."

I headed over to the water cooler.

"Hey, my love, I miss you. So sorry we have to see each other under these circumstances."

My auntie Bird whispered in my ear as she hugged me from behind. I could feel her tears on my cheek.

She didn't mess with her older sisters, so she rarely came around. As kids, Autumn and I were always at her house. Auntie Bird picked us up every other weekend. She would let us stay up late, watch movies with us, and take us to parks and carnivals. Auntie Bird was a travel blogger, so she stayed on the go, exploring the world.

"I miss you too auntie. This is crazy. Someone has to tell us what's going on." I sighed.

"Check with your mom. I saw her talking to a nurse or doctor when I arrived."

I walked over to my mom, after giving my auntie Rose her

water. She was sitting with her hands over her face while Junior was at the vending machine.

"Hey, mommy, how are you holding up?" I questioned while giving her a hug and kiss on the cheek.

"I was working when all this commotion started. The EMTs came in yelling about a female gunshot victim who lost a lot of blood. I get up from my desk, and it's Autumn covered in blood. I almost fainted."

"Oh, man, mommy. I'm sorry that you had to experience that."

"They rushed her into surgery, so now we just have to wait and see. Why would someone want to hurt her? We need to know what happened!" She slammed her fist on the small table next to her. I've never seen my mom so angry and upset. It was a lot to process. We all had a lot of questions and no answers.

I started pacing back and forth, trying to make sense of this all. Who was she with? Where was she at? She was at our local hospital, so maybe she was in the hood, but someone would have hit me by now, letting me know what went down if that was the case.

This hospital was also a trauma center, so maybe that was why they brought her here instead. My mind just kept racing.

"Candy, come on, the doctor is here to talk to us," Junior informed me.

"Autumn suffered a gunshot wound to the left shoulder and chest area, causing her to lose a lot of blood. The bullet to her shoulder was a through and through. We were able to remove the bullet lodged in her chest. It missed her major arteries, but it did collapse her left lung. She's on a ventilator because of the injuries she suffered. She has a long road ahead of her but should make a full recovery. Autumn will be heading to the ICU unit soon. Once she is admitted there, you guys can visit two at a time, but only for five minutes each. She won't be able to communicate with you, but she can hear you."

"Lord, thank you! Thank you, father God. You spared my child's life. I praise you in the name of your son Christ Jesus, Hallelujah!"

My auntie Rose raised her hands up in prayer, tears streaming down her face. She was usually a couch Christian on Sunday mornings. I'd never heard her pray out loud.

We all cried and hugged each other, joyful that Autumn made it through. Now, we just needed to know who did this, and why.

Chapter Nine

KANE

"What the hell is going on, Knowledge?" I inquired of my brother as he got into the truck, covered in blood.

He called asking me to pick him up from the police station. I just arrived back in town from New York.

"Someone shot Autumn. I don't know if she's dead or alive!"

He punched the glove compartment.

"I wasn't expecting you to say that. Who the fuck would want to take her out? This shit is crazy."

Autumn didn't appear to be a woman that had enemies out in these streets.

"Bruh, I don't know. Were the bullets meant for me? I'm at a loss right now, but I know one thing for sure. Whoever did this is going to pay for it with their life! And that's on everything."

"Y'all was at the house when this shit went down?"

"Yeah, she walked out the house before me. I was getting ready to drop her off at home. As I was setting the alarm, shots rang out. I looked over at the open door and watched her body fall onto the steps." I've seen my brother shed tears three times in his life. The first time was at our parents' funeral, then when his son was born, and right now. "I ran over to her, called 911, and applied pressure to her wounds until the medics arrived. I never looked around to see if I saw anyone. I just focused on Autumn."

"Well, she's feisty, so let's just hope she pulls through." I rubbed his shoulder, trying to console him.

"It was just so much blood, bruh. I feel like it's my fault because it happened at my house." Knowledge dropped his head in his hands.

"Don't start blaming yourself, and we have to remain positive."

I headed over to the hospital in Long Branch where Autumn and Candy were from. Knowledge said that was where they transported her because of the severity of her injuries.

We pulled up to the hospital and Candy came to mind. I knew she must be going through it. They were so close, more like sisters than cousins. If something happened to Knowledge, I don't know what I would do. As we entered the ER, Candy approached us.

"What are you guys doing here, and why are you covered in

blood Knowledge? Oh, no, she was with you?" Candy started bawling and slamming her fist into Knowledge's chest. "What did you do? What did you do?"

He just stood there and took it until she tired and fell to her feet. I picked her up and held her as she buried her head in my chest, releasing all the pain.

"I got you, Candy, I got you. He didn't do anything. Let him explain." I spoke to her in a hushed tone.

Once Candy calmed down, she went over to the rest of her family. I felt horrible that we had to be introduced to them under these circumstances. They must have thought we weren't shit.

"Guys, this is my friend Kane and his brother Knowledge. Autumn has been dealing with Knowledge and was with him tonight. Hopefully, he can give us some insight on what happened and who did this." She peered up at him with hurt and sadness in her eyes.

Knowledge told them the exact same story he told me. As he was talking, a nurse came out to inform us that we could head up to the ICU.

"Were you at the house when this happened?"

Candy questioned me as we sat in the family waiting room. Her aunts already went in while her mom and brother sat across from us, staring at me.

"Nah, I was just heading home when I got the call. I told you I had to meet the interior decorator at the office in New York. I sent you some pics while I was still in the city, asking for your input, but I guess you were busy."

She seemed a little uneasy and quickly looked away from me, completely ignoring my comment.

"Knowledge, what did the police say? They didn't even talk to us yet."

Candy questioned my brother. Meanwhile, I was still trying to figure out why she didn't respond to me. We would have to address that later.

"They had me come down to the station. I told them exactly what I told y'all. Someone is supposed to come by the house tomorrow to collect a copy of the video footage. We have cameras surrounding the entire property, so hopefully it picked up something or someone."

Knowledge ran his hands down his face. He was so distraught.

"Well, I thank you for being there for my cousin. I'm sure you keeping the pressure on her wounds helped to save her life. I'm forever grateful. I know you wouldn't hurt her, and I apologize for my outburst earlier." Candy smiled at him.

Her aunts came out, and her mom and brother went in.

"You don't owe me no apology, Candy. Shorty not my girl, but I have love for Autumn. We've been rocking hard. I wish whoever did this shit would have shot me instead."

My brother really fucked with Autumn. Besides his crazy ass baby momma, she was the only chick that came to the house. They were like two peas in a pod. Autumn was the female version of Knowledge.

"Ma'am, I'm sorry we had to meet this way. I really care about your daughter and wished I knew who did this. I will pay for all her hospital bills and any other expenses incurred," Knowledge advised Autumn's mom.

"Are you a drug dealer? We don't want no dirty money," her mom shot back.

"Absolutely not. All the money I have is legit. Our parents left us money when they passed away, and my brother invested it. He started his own company, in which I'm a silent partner. We are hardworking young men."

Candy and I walked into the hallway once Knowledge went in. I just wanted a moment alone with her. We haven't seen each other in weeks, and I missed her. I also wanted to know why she didn't know that Autumn was with Knowledge. From the little time I've known them, I could see they told each other everything.

"Is something up with you and Autumn? Usually y'all keep tabs on each other, but you had no idea where she was today. Is she the reason you checked out for the past two weeks?" I inquired.

"She did some foul shit that I don't wanna talk about, and I feel guilty for blocking her calls. Maybe I could have—"

"This is not your fault. Don't do that to yourself. There was nothing you could have done. Obviously, someone had it out for her. We just need to figure out who, and they will be dealt with," I assured Candy.

"I know. I'm the only person she talks to besides Peanut. Oh my fucking God. I was so caught up, I forgot to call her. She's going to lose it. We're all cool, but Peanut has a closer bond to Autumn than she does me."

Candy called Peanut. I could hear her shrilling cry as she received the sorrowful news. Peanut said she was out of town but would make sure to see Autumn when she arrived back in town tomorrow.

Knowledge came out to find us, informing Candy and I it was our turn to go inside.

"Hey, cuz, I love you so much."

Tears trickled down Candy's cheeks as she stood next to her bed. Autumn was hooked up to so many machines. I instantly got a knot in my stomach. Candy rubbed Autumn's hand and shook her head in disbelief. It was eerie because if it wasn't for the difference in their hair, you could have easily thought it was Candy laying there. They look so much alike, which made sense when you saw their moms.

"Cuz, I just need you to get better soon. I will be by your side every step of the way, no matter what. I'm going to find out who did this to you."

I teared up, hearing Candy talk to Autumn. This shit was too much, and I needed to get the fuck up out of here.

We said our goodbyes to the family, and Candy's brother gave me a funny look. It was as if he was trying to figure out why I was with his sister. Candy decided to leave with me and Knowledge, saying she didn't want to be alone.

As we pulled up to the house, you could see the crime scene tape was still up, blocking the entrance to the front door, so we entered from the side of the house, off the kitchen.

I sat the pizza down that we picked up on our way home and grabbed some beverages out of the fridge.

It surprised me that something like this happened in this neighborhood. Autumn had to be targeted. This was one of the most boring areas you could live in.

"Knowledge, did anything crazy happen when y'all was together today? I'm still trying to piece this puzzle together."

Candy was like a dog with a bone. I would be the same way.

"Nothing at all today. She had been here for two weeks. The day I picked her up, she did get into it with Keelie. Autumn hit her in the face with a hot ass drink, burnt the shit outta her. Keelie told her to watch her back, but she's all bark and no bite."

"Please, please tell me you told that to the police before I go bat shit crazy in here."

Candy stared at Knowledge like he better say yes or else.

"No, I didn't because like I said, Keelie doesn't have it in her, but Rah does."

She got real quiet and took a deep breath.

"What the hell is he talking about Candy? I thought he was in jail."

The look she gave me told it all.

"Nah, that nigga home, bruh." Knowledge grinned.

"And I'm the last to know. Explain yourself."

I knew Candy was hiding something when I mentioned she must have been busy at the hospital, and she ignored me. It all made sense now.

"I'm not having that conversation with you right now, Kane," Candy stated as she glared at Knowledge, clenching her teeth.

"Autumn told me he threatened her. So, when you tell the police about Keelie make sure you mention your man. If I find out he had anything to do with it, his ass is dead," Knowledge threatened.

"Rah did not shoot Autumn, so you can stop spewing that narrative."

Candy replied with so much conviction I had to question her.

"How do you know, Candy? Were you with him?"

I really didn't want her to respond, but I needed to know. I'd fallen for Candy, and even though I knew she was involved before we went there, having him physically back in her life changed everything.

"Bruh, you already know the answer to that question. She's not as innocent as she looks."

"Kiss my ass, Knowledge!" Candy took out her phone and opened up the Uber app.

"You already have two different guys doing that. I'm good," Knowledge scoffed.

"Chill, bruh. I know you're feeling a way right now, but don't ever disrespect her or me again!" Knowledge knew I was serious.

Candy stormed out of the house and I went after her.

Chapter Ten

CANDY

"Leave me the fuck alone. Don't follow me! My cousin is laying up in the hospital because someone shot her at this house while she was with your brother, and he wants to talk to me crazy."

Kane picked me up from behind and carried my ass back into the house. He took my phone and canceled my Uber.

"It's too late and dark for you to be running outside by yourself with a shooter on the loose. We don't know if Autumn was the only target. I know you're upset, but you need to think. That shit you just did was reckless as hell. Knowledge didn't mean what he said. Everyone is on edge. You're not leaving my sight, so fix your attitude." Kane stared at me.

"Well, I don't wanna stay here now," I sassed.

"Not a problem. Let me see if one of the hotels around here has rooms available. It's probably not a good idea for any of us to stay here, being that everything is still so fresh."

The DoubleTree in Tinton Falls had availability, so Kane rented out the Presidential suite for us, and Governor's suite for Knowledge. He packed up a bag, and we left.

It was a quiet ride over there. Although Autumn was on my mind, so was Rah. I did text him that she survived but that was it. I knew he was concerned for me and her. I appreciated him being there for Junior and I at that moment.

Once we arrived and checked in, Kane and I went to our room while Knowledge went to his.

"We need to have a conversation about us and what we're doing."

I knew Kane wasn't going to let it go. Finding out Rah was home the way he did was fucked up, and I had no one to blame but myself.

"Can I get in the shower first? If you don't mind."

Kane had been nothing but a gentleman toward me. Since the day we met, he was my Knight in shining armor. He didn't deserve my sarcasm.

As I was in the shower, trying to wash the scent of Rah off me, I couldn't help but wonder where he was, and if he was okay. He had to feel terrible about what he said to Autumn, then she actually got shot. If she told Knowledge he threatened her, who else did she tell?

Autumn wasn't the pillow talk type of person, so I was definitely caught off guard when Knowledge said that. She probably was going through it because I blocked her. It was all my fault. I let the water flow over my face, so it could wash away my tears.

Stepping out of the shower, I dried off with a plush, white towel. I put on one of the robes that was hanging up and wrapped a towel around my head. They even had slippers in there that I slid my feet into.

"The bathroom is all yours, and thank you for the clothes."

Kane was so thoughtful. He had the outfits from our weekend away dry cleaned, and they were in his car. I brought them up with me because I didn't have anything to wear.

While Kane washed up, I used that opportunity to text Rah. I told him I was with my family, and that he should lay low until they found the shooter. Knowledge doesn't know who Rah was, but that didn't mean he couldn't find out. I could tell these property brothers had more reach to the streets than they were letting on.

Kane came out of the shower and stood at the foot of the bed. I had already turned on the double-sided fireplace and ordered room service. We never even got a chance to eat the pizza.

"Listen, I'm feeling you. I want to see where this goes, but I'm a grown ass man and don't eat off the same plate with another man."

He had a towel wrapped around his waist while beads of water still sat on his chest. My eyes made their way down to his six-pack. Just the sight of this man made my juices flow.

"I'm feeling you too Kane, and I'm enjoying the time we are spending with each other, but you also knew I was involved with someone else when we started this."

"He wasn't physically in the picture. Now he is, so you need to end it because I'm not letting you go or sharing."

I planned on ending things with Rah when he came to get the money, but one thing led to another, then the shit with autumn happened.

"Rah and I have history. I couldn't just walk away like he never existed. As far as he's concerned, we are still together and there has never been anyone else. You know about him, but he has no idea about you." I admitted.

"Wait, hold up. You mean to tell me you have never been with anyone else besides him until you met me?"

"Yes, is that a crime?" I cut my eyes.

"No, it makes you that more special. I knew you were cut from a different cloth when I laid eyes on you. Now I understand why he has a hold on you. You have never been with a real man, mentally or physically."

This cocky bastard. He was right, though.

"I don't like having you caught in the middle of my chaos. I don't even recognize myself right now."

"I'm not hiding in the shadows. I want to be with you front and center. Obviously, you want it too. You didn't hide me from your family, and they watched us leave together. Your brother looked at me a lil funny, but he's probably just protective of you."

"He saw me with Rah earlier and probably wondered who

you were. My family doesn't care for Rah at all. They probably were happy I left with you."

I knew what I needed to do, but it was easier said than done.

"I'm not even going to ask you if you fucked him because I already know the answer. I just want to know if he made you feel like this."

Kane released his towel, allowing it to drop to the floor. His shotgun was already locked and loaded, aiming straight at me. He pounced on me like a black panther on its prey in the cover of darkness. We made love for hours, taking small breaks in between. Rah could never.

It was morning, and we were getting ready to head to the hospital. I kept thinking about what Kane said last night. That man wanted me for himself and wasn't taking no for an answer.

He was every woman's dream come true. Kane literally dropped everything to make sure I was straight. When we were together, it was like watching a movie I didn't want to end.

It wasn't about the money or the life he could give me either. I've never asked him for a thing. He just gave from his heart. Kane wasn't trying to buy me. I think that was how he showed his love, through acts of kindness.

Kane checked on me every day and included me in everything that he did. It was so refreshing and gave me butterflies.

Rah, on the other hand, was the total opposite. He gave me stomach cramps instead of butterflies. I was last on his list, and he knew how to play mind games with me to make me feel bad and take him back. I think I felt sorry for Rah, which was why I felt a need to protect him.

"Call Peanut and tell her we are leaving now. I reserved the room for the week, so you can just leave your stuff here."

Kane brought me back into focus with his request. He just handled everything like a boss, making my body tingle.

"Hey, Peanut, we are leaving now so—"

"I'm already here. I wanted to come up early, right when visiting hours started. I'm heading out as we speak. It's too much for my heart to handle. I hate seeing her like that."

She started sobbing so bad. It sounded like Peanut couldn't breathe.

"Awe, I wish I was there to console you. It's rough on all of us, but Autumn is a fighter. We have to stay positive and make sure she knows we are all here for her. You wanna get together later?" I questioned.

"I'm so messed up. I just want to be alone. That's my sister right there, bruh. I'm going to kill whoever did this shit to her! Yo, this shit got me so fucked up right now!"

My heart ached for Peanut. She was feeling exactly how I felt last night.

"Alright, try to calm yourself down before you get on the road. I will check on you tonight. Love you, Peanut, and thank you for always holding us both down." I knew she would take it just as hard as me.

Kane and I made our way down to the lobby. Knowledge was already there waiting for us. We all headed to the hospital together. When we arrived and made it up to the ICU, my Auntie Rose was already in with Autumn, so we went to the waiting area.

Kane immediately jumped on a business call. He was interviewing secretaries for the New York office. Knowledge went to the vending machine to get some snacks. When he walked past me, he tossed peanut M&Ms in my lap, making me smile.

"Thank you, apology accepted." I winked at him.

He gave me a head nod. I hated that awkward feeling between us, and the distance it created with him and his brother. All was well now.

"Hey, Auntie Rose. How are you doing today?" I greeted her when she came out into the waiting area.

She looked like she hadn't slept at all. Bags that looked more like suitcases rested under her bloodshot eyes.

"I'm drained, Candy. I need to go home and get some rest. I never left. They let me stay with her all night. You're here now, so she is in good hands."

Kane needed to finish what he was doing, so Knowledge went in with me after my aunt left.

A police officer was now stationed outside her room. Since it was attempted murder, they needed to make sure no one tried to come back and finish the job.

Autumn was still looking like she did yesterday. I couldn't wait until she was off the ventilator. She needed to breathe on her own, so she could curse me out for blocking her. I just wanted to hear her voice. This was the quietest she had ever been since she was born. My cousin came out of the womb cussing and fussing.

"I'm so sorry, Autumn. Please forgive me, please," Knowledge pleaded as I grabbed his hand, placing it in hers.

Knowledge's heart was heavy with guilt. He thought he put her in harm's way. I told him whoever shot her wanted just her. Otherwise, they would have waited for him to come outside and popped his ass too.

"It's not your fault. If she was awake, Autumn would tell you the same thing." I tried to console Knowledge.

"I know you can hear me, Autumn. Understand I got you. I'm taking care of everything and will make sure you have top notch care. Once your crazy ass is ready to blow this joint, I'll have a blunt ready in the car when I pick you up."

"Y'all belong together because that's some shit she would say." I laughed.

Even though Autumn and Knowledge weren't in a relationship, I felt they were a match made in the hood. Opposites didn't attract in this case. They were the same people. Neither one of them cared about what they said and lived life on their own terms.

"Okay, cuz, we have to go now. I just wanted to see your face. Love you, and I will be up here every day. I'm on this journey with you."

I wished we could stay all day, but she needed to rest and heal. They limited our time anyway, since we weren't considered immediate family. We also had business to handle.

The police needed to come by Knowledge's house to get a

copy of the video surveillance. Hopefully, whoever did this shit was on there because we had no leads.

Rah and Keelie were the only two people who threatened her. I was with Rah, and Knowledge was willing to die on the cross defending Keelie's ass. So, who else would want to cause her harm, and why? Maybe Autumn held the answers to those questions.

Chapter Eleven

AUTUMN

ONE MONTH LATER....

"When am I getting the fuck up outta here?" I questioned the nurse taking care of me.

It was a state of the art rehab facility, but I'd been here long enough and wanted out.

"I have to check your chart, love, to see if the doctor updated it with a discharge date. You have been doing great, so you should be able to continue your physical therapy at home," she answered.

"Great, because I'm ready to go. This place is nice and all, but I'm over it."

I still couldn't believe someone tried to kill me. The shit was crazy, and the police still don't have a clue.

The detectives assigned to my case had no leads, and the video they collected from Knowledge's house was useless. Whoever shot me was unrecognizable, even though I told them it was a man.

They could see him taking off on foot after firing the shots, disappearing through the trees like a thief in the night. Every time I tried to sleep, the vision of him pulling that trigger played over and over in my head.

Knowledge and I were heading out, so he could drop me off at home. The car was parked out front on the circular driveway, so I went to wait outside while he got his keys and set the alarm. As I walked down the steps, a figure appeared from the shadows.

It was a guy dressed in all black from head to toe. The only thing I could see was the white of his eyes. He pointed a gun straight at me. I didn't even have time to react before I felt the bullets pierce my body.

I fell down onto the steps and heard Knowledge scream out my name. As I laid there, bleeding out, he kept telling me to hold on. He called 911. It started getting hard for me to breathe, and felt like I was drowning.

There was a lot of commotion, but I couldn't make anything out. Next thing I knew, my ass was in ICU with a tube coming out my mouth, unable to speak.

"Hey, cuz, did you miss me?"

Candy interrupted my thoughts. She better have what I asked her for. I was happy to see her, even though her ass was always here. My cousin kept her promise to be by my side every step of the way.

"Wassup, if you don't have a blunt for me to smoke, get your happy go lucky ass outta here."

I was in so much pain and discomfort. And these muthafuckas were holding on to the damn pain pills tighter than clenched ass cheeks.

"You have to be nice to me because I might have some edibles for your rude ass," she shot back.

Candy had been sneaking me edibles since I've been here, but I wanted to inhale and exhale that purple haze.

"Are you excited for Family Day? Kane and Knowledge are parking the car. They let me out at the front entrance, since I had the treats. Everyone else should be arriving soon."

This upscale facility Knowledge was paying for did dumb shit like this all the time. Family Day, Taco Tuesday, and Thirsty Thursday, but instead of cocktails we got mocktails. They forgot about Marijuana Monday and Weed Wednesday.

"I'm glad Auntie Bird was able to cancel her trip to come because I get to see everyone all at once, but I want to go home. Y'all can visit me on the outside." I sighed.

"Well, once you leave here, Kane and I will be heading to New York for two weeks. He's finishing up the office. I won't be stopping by every day, like I am now."

"He got your nose wide open. I never thought the day would come that you would finally leave Rah's dirty ass alone. Don't come back with no damn babies." I smiled.

"Kane and I are going for business, not pleasure."

"Stop acting like you're not gonna sit on Kane's face while

y'all are there, bitch! Little Miss Goody Two-Shoes is a hoe now," I snickered.

Everyone started coming into my room just in the nick of time. Candy looked like she wanted to fight me.

Seeing my mom made me smile. This situation has brought us so much closer. She wasn't affectionate toward me at all before this happened, not even as a child. I knew she loved me. My mom just didn't know how to show it.

Now she hugged me all the time and told me how much she loved me. Almost losing me changed something in her emotionally for the better.

The staff set up a table and sitting area for us. I could smell Auntie Lily's fried chicken from down the hall. They each made a dish, except for Junior of course. He did bring me flowers, though.

"I'm glad you guys all came." I never thought the day would come that all three sisters would be together again.

"Anything for you, cuz." Candy smiled.

"Oh, yeah? Break me out of here then."

"You make it sound like you in jail." Knowledge laughed.

I was glad he got to know my family. Knowledge kept his word to my mom and had been taking care of everything. He even made sure she was straight financially and wanted for nothing.

"That's how it feels some days. Anyway, Candy, take a few pics of us with my phone before we start eating. I want to capture this rare moment."

It felt good to get out of that bed and hang out with everyone. Candy took a lot of pics. She even got one of just the sisters. You could tell the smiles were forced.

I was busy cracking jokes and making my way around the room to notice that Candy never gave me my phone back. When I looked over at her, she seemed to be looking through the pictures she just took. I had no idea Candy went through my personal pics until she asked my mom who was the guy in the picture with her.

"Where the hell did you get that picture from Candy?" my mom barked, jumping up out her seat and snatching the phone.

"That's Autumn's phone. I was just asking because I look just like him, and so does she," Candy replied, pointing at me.

"What is she talking about Rose?" my auntie Lily questioned. She stood up on her feet.

"I knew this day would come. Everything done in the dark comes to the light. This is on both of y'all," Auntie Bird chimed in. "You two held on to these secrets long enough. Today is the day you lay it all out on the table."

What the hell was Auntie Bird talking about?

"Excuse my language, but what the fuck is going on. Someone better start explaining!"

Candy was about to lose her shit at any moment.

"Maybe we should excuse ourselves and let y'all handle this amongst family," Kane suggested, wanting no part of this three-ring circus.

"Shit, they the closest people we have to family. Ever since Autumn ass was pumped with lead, we all have been together every damn day. I'm staying. I miss family drama, and I wanna know who's in the pic too," Knowledge voiced. He was ignorant as hell.

"No one is going anywhere! If I can't leave, none of y'all are leaving either," I stressed

My mom started crying uncontrollably. I thought she was going to have a fucking heart attack. I knew she figured out that I was in her diary, but from the way she was acting, that picture held the key to a lot of unanswered questions.

Peanut went over and started rubbing my mom's back, trying to calm her. She apologized for acting crazy on me, and I accepted it. We were both at fault for even crossing that line. It would take something bigger than a little disagreement to end our friendship.

Auntie Lily had the phone now, staring at it as tears fell like raindrops from her eyes. Meanwhile, Auntie Bird was furious, pacing back and forth. I didn't know what was about to go down, but obviously all of them had been holding on to whatever this was for far too long.

"Mommy, I found that pic in your diary. I know I had no business being in your personal stuff, but I felt you were lying about my dad. You were never going to tell me the truth, but today I want it. Is that my dad?"

She looked over at me, lips quivering like she had been sitting in a deep freezer.

"Yes, and I'm sorry for lying to you all these years. It was very selfish of me."

If she wasn't my mom, I would punch her dead in her shit with my good arm.

"What do you mean all these years? All of my life you have been lying to me. You said you didn't know who he was because you had a one-night stand!"

It felt like an elephant was sitting on my chest. The pain was excruciating.

"I was dealing with my own hurt and pain. Telling you that lie was the only way to get you to stop asking about him," she admitted.

"Where is my father? I deserve to know where he is at. Does he even know I exist? Has he ever come looking for me?" I questioned my mom, fighting back the tears.

Auntie Bird's face was suddenly grief stricken. Silence had taken over the room as Candy sat next to me, holding my hand so tight. Kane and Knowledge were both standing with their mouths open while Peanut continued to console my mother. Aunt Lily was off in her own world, still staring at my damn phone. Junior didn't know what to do. Maybe he should have left the room.

"Why do I look like him, though? I thought I was looking in a mirror when I saw that pic. It can't be a coincidence, and it might explain why Autumn and I look more like sisters than cousins. Is he my father too?" Candy inquired, looking toward her mom.

Aunt Lily faints in slow motion, falling to the ground. Junior and Kane picked her up and laid her on my bed. Auntie Bird placed a wet washcloth she got from my bathroom on her face. I was too damn angry and hurt to have any sympathy for either one of these bitches.

"Lily, sit up. You don't get to pass out. Tell your daughter the truth." Auntie Bird pulled her ass right on up.

The way she went down looked fake anyway. I didn't know who was crazier, her or my mom. They were running neck and neck at this point.

"Please, mom, just tell us the truth." Candy cried, letting go of my hand.

"He's your father too. Forgive me for not telling you. It's shameful. I didn't know how to explain such a thing," Aunt Lily sobbed.

"I think I'm going to be sick."

Candy covered her mouth, rushed into the bathroom, and slammed the door.

I just sat there in a state of shock. So many emotions took over my body at once. I didn't know whether to cry, scream, or do both. My cousin was now my sister too, and both our mothers were pregnant at the same time by the same man. They said twins shared everything, but this was too much.

When Candy finally came out of the bathroom, Kane took her into his arms. I knew having Rah locked up was wrong, but they would have never met if I didn't. I'm glad Candy had Kane here to comfort her because we were in the midst of a category five hurricane, and it just made landfall.

Chapter Twelve

CANDY

It felt like I was having an outer body experience. The conversation I listened to as a child made sense now. My mom betrayed Auntie Rose.

"It's all my fault. I did an unthinkable act, ruining my relationship with both my sisters. I also wreaked havoc on you and Autumn's life in the process. You might not ever forgive me, but you deserve the truth."

I started to cut my mom off, but Kane squeezed my hand, so I let her continue.

"One night Rose had a get together at her house. We were all hanging out drinking, playing cards, and enjoying the night. I was too intoxicated to walk home, even though it wasn't far at all. Rose suggested I sleep it off on the couch and go home in the morning."

I could just imagine where this story was heading.

"David, Rose's boyfriend at the time, comes home late. He mistakes me for her, and I just went along with it. I don't know what I was thinking—" Auntie Rose cuts her off.

"You were thinking with your rotten ass pussy, bitch! He told me he realized it wasn't me once he entered your cesspool, but his scum ass finished anyway. You are my sister. My identical twin sister! How could you do this to me, to us?"

I've never heard my auntie talk like that. I was a little taken back.

"Ok, so you got pregnant that night Auntie Lily?" Autumn questioned.

"Yes, and I told everyone it was by this guy I was dealing with. Once Candy was born, there was no denying it. She was the splitting image of David."

Sweet baby Jesus. My mom was crazier than I thought.

"Yeah, and I never knew they slept together until I laid eyes on Candy. By then, I was already pregnant with Autumn, so excited to be a mother. I confronted them both. They had an agreement to never tell me, but David wasn't aware she was carrying his child. She lied about her due date, fucking whore!"

"I might be a whore, but you are a murderer!" my mom roared as she hopped up off the bed.

Next thing I knew, my auntie Rose charged at my mom, knocking her onto the floor, and started wailing on her. Everyone rushed over to break it up, except for Autumn and I. We didn't care if they beat each other senseless at this point.

"Stop it right now. This is just why I don't come around. You would never know you two marinated in the same womb together. Rose, you're the oldest by three damn minutes, act like it. And think about y'all children for once," demanded Auntie Bird.

"Mom, why would she call you a murderer?" Autumn inquired.

Auntie Rose didn't answer. She just adjusted her wig and fixed her clothes.

"Your mother told our brother Pete what happened, knowing he would react the way he did. Pete drowned y'all father in Rose's tub, and we know she had something to do with it, but Pete said it was all him. He was our protector and would never let her spend one day in jail, let alone give birth in one," auntie Bird explained.

"Get out. Everyone, get out. Get the fuck out!" Autumn screamed.

I tried to hug her, but she pushed me away. I glared at her with anger and hurt in my eyes. Grabbing my bag, I stormed out and slammed the door behind me.

I was a victim too. Why would she turn on me?

"Hold up, Candy, slow down. Where are you going? We're in the middle of nowhere," Kane called out.

I stopped and turned around, facing him.

"I didn't do anything to her, or maybe I did. If I was never born then her dad would still be alive, and Uncle Pete wouldn't be in jail. All the sisters would get along, but because I exist my family is in shambles."

I was the eye of the storm. All the chaos centered around me.

"They were the adults, Candy. You and Autumn were innocent children, casualties of the war they created. That was a lot for me to take in just now, so I can't imagine how y'all feel," Kane expressed.

"I wanna get outta here. Can we leave for New York now? A change in scenery might help me digest everything I just inhaled in there. I'm sure Knowledge and Peanut will keep a close eye on Autumn once she processes it all."

I texted my auntie Bird and Junior that I was leaving. They were the only ones who I was speaking to right now.

*　*　*

It had been a little over two weeks since the blow up with my family. Kane and I were still in Manhattan. We decided to stay a little longer since I wasn't in a rush to get back to Jersey.

He didn't care for the people he interviewed and offered me the position. How could I say no? It paid more than my old job, and I got to set my own schedule. The best part was I only had to come into the city when we had appointments. Sleeping with the boss had its perks.

I was sure the fact that I chose Kane influenced his decision to offer me the job. When he told me to choose and stop playing in his face, Kane was right. It wasn't fair to either one of them that I was straddling the fence.

Rah was devastated when I told him about Kane. His devastation turned into rage, and that muthafucka called me all types of tricks and bitches. It was so bad I started to call Kane to come kick his ass, but low and behold, Junior came to my rescue. I could tell he was a little scared, but he got in Rah's face and gave him a piece of his mind.

I didn't even know he was home. Rah probably would have put his hands on me if Junior wasn't there. He had so much hate in his eyes and looked like a damn monster. I've never seen him like this before. Rah eventually left after barking back at Junior. If he would have swung on my brother, we would have jumped his ass.

"Morning, beautiful," Kane whispered in my ear as he kissed my neck.

"Same to you, handsome."

I nestled closer to him. His body was always warm, like a human electric blanket.

We opted for a hotel this time, instead of an Airbnb. Penthouse, of course. Kane enjoyed the finer things in life and spared no expense, but remained so humble. That was one of his greatest qualities. He was so patient, nurturing and generous. Kane was a young man with an old soul.

"What would you like to do for the day? The choice is yours."

It was raining outside, so it was definitely an inside day.

"I would be content with staying in bed with you all day," I confessed.

Lying next to him would be enough for me. I felt safe,

protected and secure with Kane. Plus, this bed was so comfortable.

"We can lay here and talk about how you feel finding out that Autumn is your sister."

Kane was so concerned about my mental well-being. I knew he would bring it up.

"I'm fine with that part. Even though it's a lil weird with us being cousins and sisters. I'm livid that my aunt had my dad killed, robbing me of the opportunity to get to know him. I don't think I can ever forgive her for that. And don't get me started on my mom."

The secrets they kept for so long were damaging, but I couldn't change anything that happened. I just wanted everyone to let Autumn and I handle it our way. Betrayal stung harder when it came from the ones you loved.

"When we get back in town, I think you both need to get together and let them know how y'all feel. Get everything off your chest and leave it there. Don't carry that hurt with you. It will weigh you down. Believe me, I know."

Kane always knew what to say. I wondered what hurt he carried around that weighed on him. I would have to ask him later because right now, I felt ill.

"Oh, god, I think I'm going to be sick again."

I hauled ass from the bed to the bathroom, vomiting as soon as I got to the toilet.

"You didn't even eat anything yet. Do you think it's from what you had last night?" Kane probed, holding my locs and rubbing my back, as I prayed to the porcelain god. I didn't even realize he followed right behind me into the bathroom.

"Probably so, dairy does that to me sometimes."

I rinsed out my mouth then brushed my teeth. That was so unexpected and embarrassing.

"I will have room service send up some ginger ale and saltine crackers. My mom would always give us Pepto Bismol when we had an upset stomach."

He always took great care of me. Kane was going to be an amazing husband and father one day. The father part might be sooner than later. When I became ill during the fiasco at Autumn's rehab, I figured it was my nerves from all the excitement. When my period didn't come on, I didn't panic because it wasn't the first time I was late. But the fact that I would randomly wake up with morning sickness made me nervous.

If I was pregnant, I had no idea who the father was. I could kick my own ass for not getting back on birth control. I got off it once Rah went to jail. The night Autumn was shot, I slept with Rah and Kane unprotected.

Autumn was right. I did turn into a hoe.

I'm usually so careful, I couldn't believe I put myself in such a predicament. Rah caught me off guard, saying all the right things. Kane felt like he had something to prove, and I didn't stop him. At the end of the day it was my fault, and I needed to figure this shit out.

First, I had to take a pregnancy test to confirm my suspicion. Maybe I wasn't even pregnant. It could be food poisoning.

Okay, I was lying to myself. I just didn't want to face the fact that I was out here looking like an episode of the *Maury Povich* show. If Autumn was here, she would help me through this.

"You good? Come lay back down and relax." Kane must have seen the discomfort in my face.

"I'm fine. Just texting Autumn, hoping she will answer me." I crawled back into bed.

"I'll hit Knowledge up. I'm sure he knows what's going on with her." Kane rubbed my back.

A few minutes later there was a knock at the door. Kane got up and came back carrying a tray. They sent up an assortment of crackers and mini cans of ginger ale. I sat up as he placed the tray in front of me and laid back down.

"Were you able to get in contact with your brother?" I asked as I fed him a cracker.

"They're on their way home finally, so I told Knowledge that they might as well come up here. You and Autumn need each other right now. Plus I feel better knowing we are all together."

"Awe, babe, that was so thoughtful of you." I smiled.

After snacking on the crackers and sipping on some soda, I felt a lot better. Kane and I snuggled and listened to the sound of the rain. It was very relaxing. At some point I must have fallen to sleep and when I awoke, I was still in Kane's arms.

"You look so beautiful and peaceful as you sleep," he complimented.

"How long was I out?" I questioned.

"Not long, but your body must have needed the rest."

"That's not all it needs."

I turned to face him and kissed his thick lips. They were so supple. I continued to kiss him, feeling his manhood rise.

Kane threw the covers back, pulled me underneath him, and licked on my neck. I instantly got moist when he pinned my arms down above my head and sucked on my nipples until they were hard, teasing them with his tongue.

This man kissed and licked on my body until he made his way to my pussy and attacked it like a rabid dog. Kane sucked on my clit until I came in his mouth. He sat up and tapped my pussy lips with his dick, then entered me. I dug my nails into his back as he gave me all of him. With each thrust my body seized with pleasure. We switched positions.

I was in control now, grinding on top with my back to him. Kane sat up, and I leaned my head back, rubbing on my titties as he started to play with my clit.

"You make me feel so good, babe."

When I moaned in his ear, he growled and squeezed my pussy. Kane laid back down, and I spun around, never losing my grip on his dick. As we stared into each other's eyes, I rode him like a jockey turning into the home stretch, and he exploded minutes later.

We jumped in the shower and threw some clothes on. Kane had to take a business call, so I decided to call down to the front desk to see if they could send up some food for lunch. We never had breakfast and since Autumn and knowledge was coming, I wanted to make sure we had enough for everyone.

This hotel was so fancy they offered a picnic package for

rainy days like this. Of course I had to have it and told them to bill it to the room. About an hour later, two young ladies turned the dining room area into an outdoor gathering. You would think you were right in the middle of Central Park. Plush blankets covered the floor. There were picnic baskets filled with all types of goodies, and a fresh lemonade stand in the corner. It was amazing the things money could buy you.

"My brother and Autumn are here. I'm going to go get them."

Kane went down to escort Knowledge and Autumn up. My nerves started to get the best of me. I've never been in this awkward space with Autumn before. I thought about how she would react. She pushed me away the last time we were together.

I stood by the door, awaiting their arrival.

"I'm sorry. I miss you so freaking much, forgive me please!" Autumn cried as she entered the room, hugging me so tight.

Tears began to flow like the Nile River down my face. I was so happy to see her.

"Of course I forgive your crazy ass." I felt relieved.

"You two muthafuckas up in here living like kings and queens."

Knowledge looked around as he put their luggage down.

"Whatever, did you guys run into traffic or was it a smooth ride?" I inquired.

"Naw, it was good. We didn't have to drive. Kane had a car at the house waiting to bring us up." Knowledge informed.

I wasn't surprised. This man took care of everyone he cared about.

"Cuz, let me show you y'all room."

I wanted to get her alone, so I could tell her about the romantic entanglement I've gotten myself into.

"You're glowing. Good dick will do that to you. Kane up in here laying that pipe down on yo ass, bitch. That nigga got you up in here being a damn freak. I knew you had it in you," Autumn teased.

"I wish it was the vitamin D that had me glowing. I think I'm pregnant." Autumn acted like she passed out by falling back on the bed. She was so dramatic.

"Ooohhh, I have to be careful. My shoulder is still sore. But back to your hot coochie ass. I thought you were on the pill. And you let Kane deep dive in your ocean without his scuba gear? You a bold bitch, honey." Autumn snickered as she clapped her hands together.

"Once Rah went to jail, I had no need for it. I wasn't fucking anyone else. He's the reason I'm in this predicament—"

"Wait, back the fuck up! Please help me understand how that lil niglet is involved."

"The night you were shot, I was with Rah, which is how I know he didn't do it. Long story short, we ended up sleeping together without protection. I thought about Kane while doing it and let him bust up in me like an idiot. He only lasted like two minutes, so it wasn't even worth it."

"You mean to tell me that Rah might be your baby daddy? I don't have to worry about someone coming back trying to take me out. I'm about to kill my own self." Autumn shook her head.

"It gets worse. Rah dropped me off at the hospital, but I left with Kane. Knowledge punk ass told him Rah was home, which is your fault. Kane knew I slept with him and felt a way about it. So, he wanted to prove he was a better lover, which he is. That man pounced on me and once again, no protection was used." Autumn just sat there with her mouth open.

"You, the perfect one who does no wrong, slept with two guys at the same time. Hours apart. Let's not forget that lil fact. You didn't use protection with either one. Just let them bust up in yo ass like you were a sperm bank. And they say I'm the nasty one." She laughed.

People compared Autumn and I against each other all the time because our personalities were completely different. I was seen as the innocent one, and Autumn the fast in the ass one.

"Now that you got that out of the way. What do I do now? I need your help." I stared at Autumn.

Chapter Thirteen

AUTUMN

"This bougie ass hotel might not have pregnancy tests in their gift shop. We can go check, though. I'm sure a lot of babies were created here."

"Alright, let's go after the picnic, and stop calling me a hoe. I feel terrible enough without your commentary," Candy expressed.

I didn't give a fuck what she was tired of hearing. If Rah was the father, I would choke her ass because he would never go away. One thing I did know, if Rah fucked with Candy, Kane would take his ass out, and I hoped I was there to see it.

Knowledge definitely had some screws loose, but Kane was so reserved it scared me a little. It was the quiet ones you had to be careful of. He was probably a fucking hitta, using that damn real estate as a cover up. They probably both were.

I moved in with Knowledge until I was able to figure things out on my own. He actually suggested it because he still felt guilty about me getting shot, and won't let me out of his sight. If I didn't stay with him, I would have gone to Peanut's house. There was no way I'd go back home.

"What the hell was y'all in there doing, braiding each other's hair?" Knowledge uttered when we finally came out of the room.

"Good thing y'all showed up because the food is almost gone. They even had fried chicken in one of the baskets!" Kane laughed.

He better be joking because if they ate all the food I was going to be pissed. I was so happy to get the hell out of that rehab, my ass was packed and ready at the crack of dawn, so I didn't eat shit. When we got to the house, the car was waiting. All I could do was pack and go. A bitch was starving like Marvin.

"They probably gave us the fried chicken because we're black, muthafuckas." I was happy they did, though.

We sat there tearing that food up, looking more like four bears raiding a picnic, instead of having one.

"I know y'all got a bar up in here." I needed a drink.

"Yeah, I'll grab us some beers. We can save the hard stuff for later," Kane suggested.

He gave us all one, except for Candy. She waved her hand at him.

"Why you not drinking, Candy?" Knowledge questioned.

I swear he was nosey as hell. He had me beat and didn't care.

"I didn't feel good this morning, so I'm just giving my body a rest from the alcohol. I will enjoy this fresh lemonade instead."

"The way you just fucked that food up, you seem fine to me."

Knowledge was an asshole and always had something slick to say. Candy just gave him the finger as she cut her eyes at him.

"We need something sweet to eat. Come on Candy. Let's go to the gift shop downstairs and run up the tab. Kane got it." I was laughing but very serious.

When we made it to the gift shop, the prices on everything were highway robbery. The pregnancy test was forty damn dollars. It better sing the damn results. I got a whole bag of expensive ass snacks for when we smoked later. Candy could sit in their room if she was with child, and sip on some more lemonade.

We headed straight to the bathroom when we got back to the room. I ran the sink water, hoping it would give Candy the urge to pee.

"This is the first time I'm taking a pregnancy test. I just piss on the stick, right?"

"Yes, just piss a lil first, then once you have a flow going, put the stick in midstream."

I took a pregnancy test every month just because. Even though I was safe, shit happened.

When Candy came out with the stick, I was sitting in the

vanity area of the bathroom. She placed it on the counter, sat next to me, and grabbed hold of my hand.

"No matter what the results are, I got you always, sis."

I leaned my head against hers, and we waited until enough time had passed.

"Okay, we are both going to look at it together," Candy instructed as she took a deep breath.

We got up at the same time and walked over to the sink. The test was positive.

"Bitch, you about to be someone's momma," I mumbled, so the guys couldn't hear me.

"Nope, it's a lie! I'm about to take another test, but this time I'm going to piss in the cup."

Candy lost her fucking mind. I knew she was nervous, but the word pregnant was actually visible on the test. This wasn't the one with the lines. I tried not to laugh, but her reaction was hilarious.

"Do you boo, but the shit is still going to say positive. Hurry the fuck up too, though. I'm tired of being in this damn bathroom."

I knew they were probably out there wondering why we were in here together, and what was taking us so long.

Candy crazy ass took the glass cup from the sink and strained the rest of the piss from her bladder into it. I was surprised she still had some left in her, but it wasn't enough to sit the test in the cup. Her slow ass holds the test over the sink and pours the shit over the tip, saturating it. We waited for the results, and once again, it said pregnant.

"I think something is wrong with this box of tests. It has to be. Look, Autumn, it's one test left. You piss on it and let's see what it says," Candy pleaded.

The only thing wrong here was her ass.

"You must be high because I know you're not drunk."

I couldn't stop laughing, my cheeks started burning.

"I'm so serious right now. Stop laughing and take the damn test!"

"Give it here, bitch. I know I'm not pregnant, but yo hoe ass is."

I piss in another cup, sit it on the counter, and put the test in it. It came out negative, just like I said it would. Candy sat on the bench, looking like she was stuck in the Matrix. Next thing I knew, Knowledge swung open the bathroom door. Neither one of us thought to lock it.

"What the hell y'all in here doin'?" Knowledge questioned.

"Get your nosy ass outta here!"

I tried to push him out of the bathroom while Candy swiped all the tests on the sink into the garbage can she was holding. She knocked over the glass of urine by accident. It spilled onto the floor. Candy slipped on the piss when she went to walk away and dropped the garbage can on her way down to the ground.

"Yo, bruh, get in here right now. They on some sneaky shit," Knowledge yelled.

Kane came into the bathroom, and Knowledge dirty ass picked up all the tests that fell out of the garbage can. Meanwhile, I helped Candy pissy ass up off the floor.

"Who pissed on the sticks?" Kane questioned.

"They both did, but one of them is pregnant." Knowledge looked over at me, and I gave him the finger.

"I'm the one who's pregnant. I didn't want to believe it, so I made Autumn piss on one too," Candy answered as she started to cry.

"Let's give them some privacy." I grabbed Knowledge by the hand and walked him out because he would have stayed right there.

We go into our room. I started putting our clothes away, since we were going to be here for the next week. Knowledge was sprawled out across the bed, looking like a whole snack. I'm glad we finally got some alone time because it had been a few months since he laid that pipe on me.

"Yo, I'm really about to be an uncle. I'm just laying here thinking about that shit. My lil man is about to have a cousin to grow up with. It's going to be weird watching Kane be a dad."

"That's if he's the dad. You know she was fucking with both of them," I reminded his ass.

"I'm going to be an auntie no matter what the DNA results are."

I could be petty as hell at times, but no lies were spoken. Knowledge jumped up and sprinted out of the room. I followed right behind him because he better not talk no shit to my sister. Only I could do that.

"Bruh, you straight?" Knowledge questioned.

Kane opened the bathroom door, and they came out. He

looked like someone took all the air out of his lungs. Candy eyes were red as sliced tomatoes.

"You should have got your ass in the shower while y'all was up in there. I know you smell like piss." I was looking Candy up and down.

"Really? You're the reason I fell because you should have locked the door. You already know Knowledge is nosey, just like you," Candy replied.

"When women go into any room together, they up to no good. Y'all went straight to the bathroom from the gift shop, dead giveaway," Knowledge laughed.

Kane was just standing there. I knew he had to be feeling a certain way about everything.

"Well, Candy informed me of her dilemma, and we will get through it, together," Kane explained, taking a deep breath.

"I'm keeping my child regardless, and we will do a paternity test once he or she is born." Candy grabbed Kane's hand and leaned her head on his arm.

"So, are you going to tell Rah's bum ass?" I had to ask, even though I hope she didn't.

"If Kane isn't the father, then yes. I don't want my child to have the same experience as us. The passing down of generational hurt stops right here," Candy expressed.

Kane would make sure they were both good, regardless if he was the father or not. He loved Candy and proved it just now by still wanting to be with her even though the situation they were in was crazy as hell.

"Enough with the baby talk. What are we doing for Candy's

birthday?" I had to change the subject. Thinking about Rah possibly being in our lives forever made me angry.

"Do you want a Halloween party?" Kane asked.

"If y'all do it, make it a masquerade ball? This way it's a lil more upscale. I don't like to look at grown ass people dressing up in silly shit," Knowledge suggested.

"A masked ball does sound better, and you can plan it Knowledge. We all know you can throw a party," Candy responded.

That party he threw was the reason we were all sitting here today, and the first time he whipped that anaconda out on me. I was hooked ever since, which doesn't happen to me. I usually stick and move. I haven't slept with another man since I've been fucking with Knowledge. Peanut ass didn't count.

The sight of him excited me, and when I was in his presence I could be myself without any judgment. The way he cared for me while I was in the hospital and rehab changed the way I felt about him. I had never been in love, so I had no way of knowing if the emotions I felt were the beginning of me loving Knowledge. We would soon find out.

Chapter Fourteen

CANDY

I'm at my GYN appointment, and I was so nervous, my hands were sweating. I couldn't stop tapping my foot. Kane was here as well. There was no way he would miss it. I tried to get him to stay home because Autumn volunteered to come with me, but he wasn't having it.

I prayed this baby was his, so we could be a family without any outside interference. If Rah was the father, he would never let us live in peace. The thought alone made me ill. I just knew I closed that chapter of my life.

The thought of being a mother still weighed heavy on me. I always pictured myself married, living in a beautiful house with my husband, then the kids would come later. The universe had different plans. It was a fast romance with Kane, but I had fallen in love.

I never told Kane I loved him. I'm waiting for him to say it to me. I think as women we always fall first, fast, and hard. We put ourselves out there, and it didn't always play out like we planned. Rah used my love against me.

Once he knew I had fallen for him, he had me right where he wanted me. Rah never loved me the same way in return. He played with my heart and stomped on it. With Kane it was different. I could see the love he had for me in his eyes, in his touch.

That forehead kiss sent chills down my spine. It was so endearing. His actions spoke volumes. He showed me how he felt without saying a word. I knew that eventually Kane would tell me when the moment was right.

He almost slipped a few times when I was making him moan my name. It was on the tip of his tongue. Maybe he thought it was too soon or not the right time. You don't want someone to think it was the sex that made them say it. But the way that man made my body feel, it was enough to make you scream it out loud.

Kane took his time. He showed me a whole different side of foreplay. It started even before we touched each other. From the moment we woke up, and throughout the day, he made me feel so sexy. He would kiss me on the back of the neck, or just hug me and say nothing. If he was out of town on business, he texted me naughty things. He...

"Candy, stop daydreaming. They're calling your name," Kane interrupted my thoughts.

"Oh, wow, I didn't even hear her. Let's go."

Once Kane found out that I was going to the clinic, he had me find a private obstetrician. It wasn't that far from his house. Everyone was really nice and friendly. It sure did beat going to that crowded ass clinic with all of them damn kids running around. They gave you an appointment then made you sit there for two hours before they called you back.

I undressed and waited for the doctor. I'm glad she was a woman because they were gentle. To me, it seemed like the men rushed you and were rough at times. That had been my experience.

"Good morning, I'm Dr. Jones. I will be taking care of you today."

"Morning and thank you for fitting us in on such short notice."

I took a couple deep breaths, trying to hold back the tears. I didn't even know why I was getting emotional.

"Is this your first pregnancy?" she questioned as she put the gel on my belly, so we could see the baby.

"Yes, and we are anxious to see him or her for the first time."

Kane grabbed my hand, and we stared at the monitor.

"Well, the wait is over. Here goes your babies."

"Babies!" Kane and I yelled in unison.

It felt like I was having an outer body experience. I heard what she said, and I could see it on the screen, but it didn't seem real. We were having twins. I was too early to tell the sex, but it was definitely two lil people growing inside me.

I looked over again at Kane, and he still seemed to be in shock. He was smiling but looked perplexed. I didn't know if twins ran in his family, but once he saw my mother was a twin, he knew it ran in mine.

Kane was still holding my hand, so I gave him a little squeeze, letting him know everything would be fine.

Dr. Jones let us hear the heartbeats, and the feeling that came over me was one I never felt before. It was an immense rush of love, and tears flowed like a stream from my eyes. I peered over at Kane, and he must have felt the same way. His tears were proof of that.

"I love you so much, Candy. From our first date I knew you were the one," Kane whispered as he pressed his head against mine.

"I love you too. Thank you for rescuing me." He gently placed a kiss on my forehead.

We were given pics of the sonograms and informed that I was at the end of my first trimester. I couldn't wait to tell Autumn. She was going to lose her shit about the twins. I wish I was on speaking terms with my mother, so I could tell her she was about to be a grandma.

Kane and I left and headed home. He hadn't stopped smiling yet and said he couldn't wait to tell Knowledge. Something in my heart told me that these babies would be Kane's children. I didn't know how he would truly feel if they weren't.

He was being stoic now, but I knew it would hurt him deep down inside if they were Rah's children, Kane was still human. If I could turn back the hands of time, I would have never slept with Rah that night.

I looked up, and we were almost to the house. Autumn

must have seen us pull up on the cameras because she was already outside. Ever since the shooting, Knowledge upgraded the security system. They also hired security for the party, and everyone would be checked upon entering. It was invite only, and we kept it small, close friends and family. They might not have much family, but they did have a lot of acquaintances.

"Get out the car already. I want to know everything that was said, since Kane wouldn't let me go," Autumn demanded, opening my door and cutting her eyes at Kane.

He was used to her now and ignored her antics. I was glad we were all staying together. The house was huge, so we weren't all on top of one another.

"Where's Knowledge? We want to tell y'all at the same time." I went into the kitchen because I was starving, and Knowledge was already in there.

I gained fifteen pounds already, and it was all in my ass and titties, which Kane loved. My ass ate all day and night. I was never full. They were going to have to roll my fat ass up out of this house.

"Good, you are here. All I can say is, Kyle is going to have two cousins to play with."

Autumn ran up and hugged me so tight, jumping up and down. She almost made me drop my damn cookie.

"Bitch, twins? I can't believe this shit." She lifted up my shirt and kissed my belly, twice.

"Congrats, y'all are going to be great parents." Knowledge hugged me then Kane.

"I hope they are boys because we can't take another round

of us," Autumn joked, pointing her finger back and forth between us.

"Shit, me either. It's too many girls in our family," I agreed.

"Is Peanut going to be an auntie or an uncle? You think she will like Auntie Peanut?"

"Autumn, shut ya ass up. You're dumb as hell. Peanut is still a girl, so they will call her auntie. Where do you come up with this shit?" I couldn't believe she asked that.

"She wants to be called daddy by you. Peanut wanna fuck on you, Autumn. I see the way she looks at you," Knowledge sneered.

Everyone laughed except for Autumn. Knowledge must have been wanting to get that off his chest. He was right, though. Ray Charles could see that shit. Autumn knew it too. I'm quite sure Peanut missed her since she had been staying here. I was glad she agreed to come to my party tonight. It would be nice to have the three of us together again.

"Listen, I know how she feels, and we already addressed it. I let her know I don't swing that way, and she understood. So, fuck all y'all questioning eyeballs."

Autumn gave us all the finger while walking out of the kitchen, holding it up behind her head. Kane and I exited out. I wanted to take a nap before we started getting ready for this evening.

It was an all-black affair. Your mask was what would set you apart from everyone else. I had a flamingo mask made. They symbolized beauty, balance and grace. Now that I was going to be a mommy, I represented all of that.

Kane had a black raven mask. It was an omen of death, but it could also be a symbol for change and transformation. Maybe he chose it for both reasons, since he was going to be a daddy. The death of the old him and the birth of a new man who now had a family to be responsible for.

"So, how do you feel about everything? Life is moving fast for us right now." I questioned Kane as we were getting dressed.

I was wearing a dress tonight. It fitted tight up top but flowed the rest of the way. I wasn't even going to wear a bra because when it was zipped up, it gave enough support.

My titties didn't need any more help. They were already getting too big for me. I was starting to show too. I never had a flat stomach to begin with. There were a couple rolls on my sides too, but I loved being thick. I was only trying to cover it up until we are ready to tell the world.

"I'm feeling great. I'm excited for our future, and I think it's time for us to find a home of our own. You being pregnant changes everything. Making sure y'all are straight is all I care about."

"Wow, I wasn't expecting you to say that. I would love for us to have a place of our own together. All of this seems too good to be true." I stood there like a statue, looking down at my feet.

"Like I told you before, the fairytale doesn't have to end. No matter what happens in this life and as long as I have breath in my body, you and my children will never want for anything."

Kane moved in closer, placing his hand on my chin and lifting up my face.

"You better back up because you are saying all the right things, and you look so damn fine in that suit. I'm getting moist in all the right places, and we have to finish getting ready."

Choosing Kane was the best decision I ever made. I didn't think we needed a paternity test at this point. We could just move on with our lives the way it was.

Kane's voice would be the one my kids heard every morning and night, even before they were born. He would be in the delivery room awaiting their arrival, not Rah. Maybe I was more like my mother than I realized. Now, I understood her situation a lot better. There wasn't anything I wouldn't do to protect my babies, no matter who I had to hurt in the process.

"We have plenty of time. The guest of honor is allowed to be late."

Kane showered my neck with kisses, and I could feel his dick getting hard. He wasn't going to let me off the hook.

Chapter Fifteen

KANE

"Kane, put that thing away." Candy giggled while pressing against it with her hand, making it grow stronger and harder. "There are guests downstairs waiting on us. We can continue this later, without any interruptions. I promise you. It will be worth the wait."

She grabbed my face and placed two tender kisses on my lips. When she licked them and kissed them once more, I thought I would erupt instantly.

"See, you're not playing fair. Those melons get me every time." She smiled and turned around.

"Zip me up, please." I grabbed the zipper and pulled it down more. I kissed the nape of her neck and continued downward. Candy allowed the dress to drop to the floor, stepped out of it, then turned to face me.

She looked even more beautiful pregnant, and the extra weight added to her beauty. I loved having something to grab and hold on to. I took two handfuls of her ass and squeezed as my tongue invaded her mouth. Once she stripped me out of my clothes, we made love like time was on our side.

* * *

The house really looked like a haunted mansion with the smoked filled floors and creepy music playing in the background. We descended the staircase, hand in hand, and made our way to the dining area.

"Happy birthday, Ms. Candy. I hope everything is to your liking." Knowledge was wearing a bald eagle mask, which was very befitting of his personality. He did a great job at putting this all together.

"Thank you, and yes this is truly amazing. You and your brother sure know how to go all out for the women in y'all lives. Your father taught you two well. I'm grateful. This is more than I expected." Candy smiled.

"Happy birthday, sis!" shouted Autumn, sporting a phoenix mask.

With all she has been through, she definitely arose from the ashes. Autumn and Candy embraced like they haven't seen each other in years. The bond they shared was beautiful.

"Thank you, sissy. I love you so much!"

The majority of the guests had already arrived and were enjoying themselves. With security around, I felt at ease. We wanted everyone to be able to have a good time without worrying about their safety.

Peanut walked in with a grim reaper mask. I hope she didn't plan on collecting any souls tonight. It was something about her that rubbed me the wrong way lately. I think Autumn being here with Knowledge was affecting her more than they all realized.

Knowledge and I talked about her and Autumn's friendship. I told him I think they fucked around, and Peanut caught feelings. He didn't think Autumn would swing that way. I told him curiosity killed the cat.

"Happy birthday, Candy!" Peanut hugged her.

"Thank you. It seems like I haven't seen you in forever," Candy replied.

The last time they saw each other was the day the ceiling fell in at the rehab. The weight of all those secrets came crashing right through it.

"I just wanted to give y'all some time alone," Peanut explained, looking Candy up and down. "You looked like you put on a lil weight in the face since the last time I saw you."

"Well, I have something to share with you. It's a secret, so you can't tell anyone. You're going to be an auntie," Candy whispered.

"No way! You and Kane are pregnant?" Peanut's voice sounded awkward.

"With twins! Can you believe it?" Candy had a huge ass smile across her face, glowing like fireflies.

Her smile reminded me of my mother. My dad kept her

smiling all the time. They had their regular disagreements like all couples, but he respected her always. That was the difference between a man and a boy.

Peanut stared at Candy with a confused expression on her face.

"No, I can't, honestly. How far along are you?" Peanut inquired.

"A lil over three months. And what about it can't you believe?" Candy fired back.

"That was fast, and why is it a secret?" Peanut questioned.

"Nut, you asking too many damn questions. Just keep your mouth shut about it, shit," Autumn ordered.

"Peanut, I just don't want Rah all up in my business, thinking they're his kids because they're not."

"It's a possibility they could be his, right?"

I didn't like Peanut's line of questioning. It was more of an interrogation.

"What the fuck is your problem, Nut? Who gives a damn about Rah!" Autumn barked.

Knowledge and I just stood there looking on. We weren't about to get involved. Candy and Autumn could handle themselves, especially together. Peanut was family to them. Things shouldn't get out of hand.

"Maybe I should go, since I seem to have ruffled a few feathers," Peanut replied, flapping her arms like she was a bird.

"Oh, you got jokes now? This isn't a laughing matter," Candy pointed her finger in Peanuts face.

I stepped in between them, moving Candy back a few feet. I just wanted her to calm down.

Autumn picked up a bowl of meatballs that look like eyeballs and tossed them at Peanut. She tried to rush her, but Knowledge swiftly grabbed her up from behind. I moved Candy completely out of the way. I couldn't believe what I was witnessing.

"You fucked up, Autumn, trying to put on a show for your nigga and shit." Peanut smirked, wiping the sauce off her face and clothes with some napkins.

"Fuck you, Nut. Yo ass is the one acting funny on us! You just tried to come for Candy, asking all those crazy ass questions. Why are you so concerned about Rah? You've been acting shifty ever since I was shot. Don't think I didn't peep that shit!"

"Fuck me? Fuck me? Let everyone know you already did, and you loved it. I busted yo ass with my fake ass dick, bitch. Tell Knowledge how I had you screaming my name while you came in my mouth."

Peanut made the letter V with her fingers, placed them on her lips and wiggled her tongue in between them. Autumn was squirming, trying her hardest to get out of Knowledge's bear hug.

"Get the fuck out, Peanut, and don't you ever come back here again. I don't know who you are right now! If I wasn't pregnant, I would whip your ass myself." Candy yelled.

I tried to tell Knowledge that Peanut was a woman scorned and now we knew why.

Peanut rushed toward the front entrance, snatching off her cloak and mask. I waited a few seconds and followed behind her. I just wanted to make sure she went quietly. I told Candy to stay put. She had our babies to look after.

Next thing I knew, Autumn charged past me. She chased after Peanut, yelling her name. As soon as Autumn got halfway down the steps, Peanut turned around on the driveway and glared at her. Autumn immediately stopped and sat on the steps. It was like she just saw a ghost.

"Autumn, get up. What's wrong with you?" Candy inquired while shaking her. I didn't even know she was behind me.

Peanut jumped into her car and took off as security made sure we were all straight. I informed them that it was a family squabble, and there was no need to be alarmed. Meanwhile, Autumn was still stuck on the steps.

"Yo, get yo ass up, sitting there looking like a gargoyle," Knowledge jeered, but she just stayed mute.

"Sissy, come on. We're going in the house." Candy grabbed Autumn's hand, forcing her to stand up. They entered the house and went into the bathroom, closing the door.

"Bruh, what the fuck was that bullshit right there?" Knowledge questioned.

"I don't know, but when Peanut turned around, it definitely triggered her."

I went inside and told everyone the party was over, but they could help themselves to all the food and drinks. Security made sure everyone got out safely and secured the house. My main concern was to make sure Candy and Autumn were good.

Knowledge and I headed upstairs to where the ladies were. Candy took Autumn to one of the guest bedrooms to relax in. Hopefully she was up to talking because she had some explaining to do.

Chapter Sixteen

AUTUMN

I was laying across the bed with Candy when the guys walked in. Knowledge probably wanted to talk about everything Peanut dirty ass just said, but I needed to gather my thoughts and put two and two together in regard to her.

"Yo, you into girls? Let me know what's up because I ain't got time to play no damn games. It's to the point that I have to go to Keelie's house to see my son. She don't want him around you, but I fucks with you, so I make the sacrifice."

Knowledge really had put himself out there for me, especially with his son. I needed to apologize to Keelie for throwing the drink in her face.

We have grown closer ever since I went to rehab and got to know each other intimately. When Candy left for the day, he was right there, staying until I fell asleep every night. I saw a sweeter side to him. It made me wonder if we could be more than just fuck buddies. He was nurturing, thoughtful, and had become my friend.

"I know you do, and I appreciate it. No, I'm not into girls. Did I experiment with Peanut, yes? I was curious the first time but didn't like it. The second and last time, I was drunk, high, and in my feelings."

If I hadn't got into it with Candy that day, I would have never slept with Peanut again. I was in a vulnerable state.

"You could have told me, though. We share everything. I wouldn't have judged you," Candy explained.

"I was judging myself! I didn't want anyone to know, and I didn't think she would catch feelings." Peanut caught me off guard, blacking out like that on me at her house.

"Why did you freeze up on the steps is what I want to know?"

Kane looked at me like I had two heads. He probably thought I was bugging, but I was in a state of shock.

"When Peanut turned around, and she didn't have that dumb ass mask and robe on, for a split second she looked like the person that shot me," I admitted.

"You didn't see the person, though. And said it was a man, not a woman."

"I only saw the white of their eyes. She was standing, almost in the exact same spot, and her whole-body frame and stance was just like him. Plus, she looks like a damn dude anyway, so shit."

"Y'all believe she could be so cold and heartless?" Kane asked, putting his hands in his pocket.

"I don't want to believe Nut would do that to me either, then have the balls to come around like nothing happened. She was pissed the day Knowledge came to pick me up, but damn. Maybe I'm losing my mind and being on those steps just fucked with my mental."

"Shit, she had to stick to the script. If she tried to kill you and failed, she couldn't just disappear. Peanut had to play the role of the distraught friend, sister, or whatever the hell y'all call that chick. She's a psychopath. We just saw it today." Knowledge didn't even doubt it from the way he was talking.

It had to be her because no one else knew I was here but her. She knew Candy and I wasn't in a good place. I wasn't speaking to my mom, and I didn't tell anyone else where I was. Everything was adding up to Peanut being the one who pulled the trigger.

"Knowledge, do you have a copy saved of the security video? Maybe we can notice if it's her. I figured it was a dude, but she looks like one, so it's worth a shot."

Why didn't I think to watch the tape sooner? I hope I can stomach it because who wants to watch themselves get shot?

"Kane and I will watch the tape. Y'all don't need to see that shit. It will fuck you up mentally. Candy, you need to be stress free. I don't want my nephews coming into this world too early." Knowledge was acting like a concerned uncle already.

They left to watch the video, and I was consumed with my

thoughts. This the shit you saw on TV but would never think could happen to you.

"What did she say to you exactly when you left? Did it sound like a threat?" Candy interrogated.

"She just told me to get out and said I played on her top, basically. I've never seen her that angry before, but never in a million years thought she was capable of this. We loved each other like sisters."

Tears traveled from my eyes to my cheeks, into the creases around my nose, making their way to my lips.

"She loved you differently, that's the problem. You fucking with her again probably gave her hope for something more than a sisterhood. I'm scared of what I might do to her if she was the one that tried to kill you," Candy stated. Her pregnant ass wasn't doing shit.

"I'm more scared of what Knowledge is going to do to her. He said many times before he was going to kill whoever shot me. I know he meant it." I shook my head.

"He threatened to take Rah ass out too, if he had anything to do with it. Knowledge wasn't joking either and said it with such ease."

The guys came back upstairs, telling us that they sent a copy of the shooting and the video from tonight to some company. They would do a detailed comparison to see if it's the same person in both videos. Some high-tech bullshit. Now it was a waiting game. Sleep wasn't going to be my friend tonight.

* * *

It had been a couple days since Candy's birthday party was a disaster, but a revelation at the same time. The company confirmed it was Peanut that shot me twice, without hesitating once. She not only tried to kill me but actually held my mother's hand while she cried over me.

Peanut knew she was the cause of all the hurt and pain my family was going through, and sat among us, like she was in agony too. It was crazy how you could grow up with someone, spend most of your time with them, and never really know them.

All the sympathy I had for her, the guilt I felt for playing with her feelings, were now gone. I was fueled with rage and hate. If Knowledge killed her ass, I wouldn't lose an ounce of sleep over it. I just wanted to be, so I could witness her demise. The grave she dug for me, will be the one I buried her ass in.

"Morning, sissy, how did you sleep?" Candy was so concerned for me, and I felt horrible. She was the one pregnant. I should be worried about her.

"I slept okay," I answered, taking a seat next to her in the kitchen.

"So, are you going to call the police? They need to arrest Peanut's ass?"

"No one is calling the police. We are going to handle this shit ourselves." Knowledge appeared out of nowhere. "She crossed all lines and violated in a major way. Since Peanut wanna be a man, we about to have a man to man talk," he continued.

"You're making me nervous, Knowledge. I don't want you

to put yourself in harm's way or do something you can't take back."

Candy ass was almost in tears. Her hormones must be all over the damn place.

"Maybe you and Autumn need to go away until everything is handled," Knowledge suggested.

"I'm not going anywhere. That bitch tried to kill me. She's gonna have to look me in my eyes and admit that shit."

Kane came in from a morning run. He ran every damn day, rain, sleet, hail or snow. You would think he was training for a damn marathon. Maybe it was his stress relief or a way to keep fit. Candy needed to be running with him. I knew I would find her ass in the kitchen this morning, stuffing her face.

"Morning, everyone! Hey, beautiful," Kane greeted us as he kissed Candy, rubbing her stomach. They were so freaking cute. Watching him love on her made me so happy. "Y'all huddled up in here like y'all planning something, without me."

"Nah, Bruh. I was just letting your girl know we don't call the police. We handle shit ourselves." Kane nodded his head.

"We need to find out who helped Peanut. She didn't pull this off on her own. The only person I can think of is Rah. He had it out for me too." His ass could be buried in the same grave as her.

"He was with me the night you were shot, so I don't know how that is possible. I also didn't know them to be cool with each other like that, especially to plan a murder," Candy voiced.

"It's possible, depending on the time she was shot. He

could have been in the car waiting for her. Y'all only live less than twenty minutes from here," Kane explained.

"Sis, you were the perfect alibi for him, and no one would suspect Peanut trifling ass at all."

"So, he used me to hurt you? I can't believe he would be this devious. I don't feel so good, please excuse me." Candy got up from the table, Kane followed behind her.

"I'm gonna kill both those muthafuckas, dead ass!" Knowledge promised as he bit into an apple.

"And I'm going to be right there, helping you do it. I want my face to be the last one those muthafuckas see."

"We can't let them know we know. They will just disappear. You threw food on Peanut and tried to swing on her ass, so she unhinged right now. More than likely, she will tell Rah Candy is pregnant. I don't know how things ended with them, but I'm sure he's not happy. First thing first is making sure you two are safe at all times."

It was a week before Thanksgiving, and if I didn't get out this house, I was going to fucking scream. I didn't want to Netflix and chill, play spades, uno, or nothing the fuck else. It was like being back at rehab. Knowledge and Kane wanted to keep us safe, but this shit was ridiculous.

One positive thing that came out of being on lockdown was the fact that we started communicating with our moms. Kane and Knowledge expressed how much they missed their parents and wished they could argue with them. They said we were fortunate to be able to see or call them anytime.

We haven't forgiven them completely because it was a lot, but we were going to spend the holiday together. Our moms were going to come over to the house the night before, so they could start prepping the food. I didn't cook, but Candy did. I would be the bartender. Hopefully we could start the healing process.

Chapter Seventeen

CANDY

Today we find out the gender of our babies. I wasn't only excited to know but eager to get out of this house. We've been working from home. Kane went out to look at different properties, but I only got to look out the windows. We don't know what Peanut had up her sleeve, so the guys were being overly cautious.

My mom and Junior would be here later on today. I didn't want to tell them over the phone that I was pregnant, so I would surprise them all at once.

"Does security have to go with us?" Kane gave me a look that answered my question without him saying a word.

"I'm not taking any chances with my family. Peanut came onto our property and shot Autumn. Someone she loved and wanted to be with. She's not dealing with a full deck and won't get the opportunity to do it again. They have specific orders to use deadly force if they feel any one of us are in danger."

I relaxed back into my seat. This whole situation had become a nightmare, and I wished it would come to an end. I wasn't going to spend the rest of my life looking over my shoulder, being surrounded by security everywhere I went.

We pulled up to the doctor's office. Security rode in a separate car, thank goodness, and would stay outside while we went in. I was worried about how Rah would react once he found out I was pregnant. He didn't handle me choosing Kane over him too well, so this would definitely send him spiraling.

"Y'all can all wipe those ugly ass grins off y'all face!" Autumn, Kane and Knowledge were smiling like they just hit the lottery.

We were back home now and just told them the sex of the babies. I was the only one hoping they were girls, but nope, I'm having two sons.

"Don't be mad, Candy. We only make kings," Knowledge teased while slapping hands with Kane.

"It's okay, babe, you will be the Queen of our castle and have your own personal lil army. They will grow up to love and protect you." Kane always knew how to make me feel so loved.

I gained another ten pounds since my last visit. Dr. Jones wasn't too concerned because I was eating for three, and even though I ate a lot, I did make healthy choices.

"Autumn, we need to make sure the guest rooms are ready

for everyone. They will be here before we know it." She mouthed what I just said, rolling her eyes. She got on my damn nerves.

"Candy, those damn rooms are fine. The cleaning service does them too, every week."

"We can put candles on the nightstand and leave some chocolate on the pillows. I can have fresh flowers delivered to put in there too."

I just wanted our moms to feel welcomed. They were struggling too with what they did. Having them together again was a lot.

Junior would stay in the finished basement. It was basically a hangout area, but it had a bedroom down there with its own master bath. There was a kitchen, sitting area, pool table, and gaming systems. He would love it. I was also glad Juinoe would get to spend some time with Kane and Knowledge.

"Do you want me to take towels and make them look like dolphins and place them on the sink? This ain't no damn hotel. You're doing the most," Autumn said with a fake ass smile.

"Knowledge and I will go pick them up later. Let me know if you need me to grab anything while we're out," Kane stated.

"We have everything. Our moms gave us their list, and I ordered all the food online and had it delivered yesterday. You guys have done enough, thank you."

I knew family was everything to Kane and Knowledge, so I had a surprise for them. Tomorrow wasn't just Thanksgiving, but the anniversary of their parents' death. I ordered memorial lanterns for all of us to light and release into the night sky in their honor. I wanted Kane to know that even though he was consumed with taking care of me, I got him too.

These babies I was growing inside of me will intertwine our families forever. I'm going to stand firm in my decision not to get a paternity test. I just had to inform Kane.

Him and Knowledge left to go pick up our mothers and Junior, so I went to get the rooms ready without the help of Autumn's lazy ass. It didn't take me long, and I knew they would appreciate the extra effort I put into making them comfortable.

I had just finished with the guest rooms when Kane and Knowledge arrived with my family. I didn't realize how much I really missed them until they were standing in my face. The tears just kept coming, nonstop. I wore leggings and a tank top, so you could see my bulging belly.

"Oh, wow, Candy! You're pregnant, my lord!" my mother exclaimed, hugging me so tight. She was crying harder than me now. I took both my hands and wiped her eyes.

"I'm sorry." She held her hands on my stomach. I kissed her on the cheek.

"Thank you, I needed that." This was a time for healing, no more pointing the finger.

"Candy, you're making me a great auntie." My auntie Rose stated as she rubbed my belly with tears still lingering in her eyes. It was great seeing her and Autumn embrace when she walked in.

"Twice. I'm having twin boys. They will be here in the springtime."

My mother covered her mouth in excitement while Junior just stood there with eyes as big as dinner plates.

"I'm going to be an uncle? That shit is so cool!" My mother popped him on the back of his head for cursing.

We showed them to their rooms, so they could put their stuff away. Junior freaked out over the basement and wanted to move in permanently. He stayed down there with the guys, so they could hang out and get to know each other better. I was so glad my brother finally had male figures in his life to guide him.

Kane said he could work with him during the summer and school breaks. He was going to teach him the realty business and how to invest in the stock market. This way he could make his own money and stop hanging with the wrong crowd. I might not say it all the time, but I loved Junior and wanted the best for him.

All the ladies met up in the kitchen. It was time to start prepping for tomorrow. My mom and Aunt Rose quickly made the kitchen their own. My auntie Lily started washing collard greens in the sink while my mom peeled sweet potatoes. This was the first time we all cooked together. It made my heart smile.

I put on some classic R&B and listened to them sing along to the songs as I leaned against the wall, taking it all in. This was what family was all about.

"Whew, that was delicious, I'm stuffed. I can't tell you the last time I had a Thanksgiving dinner like this, thank you ladies." Kane sat back from the table, rubbing his belly.

"Shit me either, everything was rocking," Autumn commented.

She did make the biscuits. They were canned though. Me, my mother, and Auntie Rose made everything else. We threw down. Fried chicken, Cornish hens, turkey ham, potato salad, collard greens, baked beans, Mac and cheese and sweet potato pies for dessert.

We were up at the crack of dawn getting everything done. After the surprise memorial for the guys, I was heading off to bed.

Their parents were cremated together. They had their ashes in the great room sitting on a table, along with their wedding picture. The sunlight shone in on them every day. I placed two large candles on the table next to them this morning. I told Kane and Knowledge to each light one, and they would burn all day in their parents' honor. They both teared up.

"Junior, help me clear off the table, so we can set up for pie and eggnog."

I didn't know where Autumn snuck off to, but she needed to help.

"Candy, we got this. Go sit down with your mom and aunt and relax. Y'all did enough." Knowledge could be such a gentleman when he wasn't being a smart ass.

Autumn finally joined us again, dressed in all black. She looked like a damn cat burglar. I knew we were about to do a memorial, but it was a celebration of life, not a damn funeral. Autumn gave me a sly grin, which meant she was up to something. I pulled her off to the side.

"Why are you dressed like you're about to go fight?" She also had on black Air Force ones with her hair slicked back into a ponytail.

"I need you to cover for me. Please don't ask me any questions, Candy. Once we let the lanterns go, I'm going to dip out. Just keep Knowledge distracted long enough for me to leave." A lump instantly grew in my throat.

"You know the cameras will alert their phones of any movement on the property. They will be on your ass like white on rice, especially since they gave security the night off to be with their families."

I wanted to convince Autumn to stay, but I could tell by the look in her eyes she wouldn't.

"Have everyone leave their phones in the house. Make up something. I'm meeting my Uber on the street. It will be here in twenty minutes. I need you to do the memorial now. I will already be on the parkway by the time they realize I'm gone."

All I could do was nod my head yes. There was no stopping Autumn when she already had her mind made up.

Chapter Eighteen

KNOWLEDGE

Today was a rough one, emotionally. Losing not one, but both your parents at the same time changed you internally. You didn't know whether you were coming or going. Then to be ripped from the only home you've known made the pain even deeper.

My mother's family wasn't shit. Those muthafuckas were dead to me. They could have taken us, but instead they let us go into the system. The only good part about it was them keeping Kane and I together. We bounced around from foster homes to group homes because nobody wanted two teenage, black boys.

We had each other, and that was what got us through it. Kane was the quiet one that kept his head down and did as he was told. Me on the other hand, I got into trouble all the time. I always had something to say and would fight at the drop of a dime. I didn't know how to control the hurt and pain I was feeling and took it out on everyone.

Kane always had my back, though, and saved me more times than I could count. He would only fight if pushed to the limit and wreaked havoc when he did. I would warn everyone that Kane was the one they needed to be scared of, not me.

He was calculated with his shit. Kane wouldn't cause a scene or feed into the bs like me. His ass sat back in the cut, analyzing and strategizing his revenge. You never saw him coming, and by the time you did, it was too late. I had to stop my bullshit, once I realized I was doing more harm to Kane than myself.

My brother was forced to become someone he wasn't in order to save my ass. I was putting him in situations he had nothing to do with. Kane wanted to read and educate himself. He kept all our dad's books and writings on the stock market and financial literacy. He was a lover not a fighter, but he loved me more than himself it seemed.

Kane always felt he had to protect me, even now, because he wasn't just my older brother, but the only family I had left. When I had my son Kyle, I was excited for my legacy to live on, but I still didn't feel like I was part of a family. Kane and I were still two lone wolves. Once we met Autumn and Candy, all that changed. I wasn't a guy that was ready to settle down, but Autumn makes me want to sit still.

She was supposed to be a smash and dash, but something

about her kept drawing me back. Autumn was a guy's girl. Her energy matched mine every time. I've never been in love, or even had a stable relationship, so all this was foreign to me. Keelie only got pregnant because I was drunk and high as hell. I let her fuck on me without a condom, changing the course of my life.

Even though I had it rough for a few years, my foundation was solid. My parents were love and showed love. I knew what it felt like to grow up with unconditional love from both parents, and that was what I wanted for my children. I wanted to be a husband one day, even though I came off like I didn't.

I just hoped that Autumn felt the same way that I did. She was starting to soften up some and became more affectionate toward me, giving me facial rubs and kisses out of the blue. I could definitely say she was one of the closest people to me besides Kane. Kyle liked her too. He took to her instantly and asked about her all the time.

"Why you dressed like you about to rob a bank?" Autumn looked like she was about to go on a secret mission.

"I wanted to dress warm since we were going to be outside. You can't go wrong with all black."

Autumn's thick ass was distracting me. She looked good no matter what she had on. I felt her up before we headed out back.

We all stood outside and gathered around. Candy was kind enough to put a memorial together in honor of my parents. Usually, Kane and I spent this day alone, drinking, smoking, and reminiscing on our childhood. It felt good to be surrounded by people that cared for us and wanted to help celebrate their lives.

We each had a paper lantern to hold. They were bigger than I thought they would be. We lit the fire pit to provide some heat, so we formed a circle around it. It was cold as hell out this bitch, so hopefully we wouldn't be out here too long.

"I just wanted to do something special for you guys. You both have been so kind and generous not to just me, but my family as well. I'm sure it's hard living without your parents. Even though they are not here in the physical, they live on through you and their energy is out in the universe. We can't make the pain go away or the hurt any less, but we will be here to support you. You don't have to mourn alone anymore." Candy's words were solid and emotionally affected everyone.

Kane lit all of the lanterns, and it was a beautiful sight. I've never done no shit like this before. It was different. We counted to three and let the lanterns go at the same time. Oddly, there was no wind tonight. They floated into the sky effortlessly. Candy said they will float back down once the fire burns out, and they were hundred percent biodegradable.

I was concerned that we might set some shit on fire. Autumn said she had to use the bathroom and would be right back. Candy wanted to conclude the night with a champagne toast. Her and Junior had apple juice. I went over and talked to Autumn's mom and auntie. I couldn't tell who was who. They look like bookends.

Autumn was taking a minute to come back. Her ass must be on her phone. Candy made us leave our phones in the house, so there wouldn't be any distractions. She seemed to have thought of it all.

"Are we doing this toast without Autumn? We need to get everyone back inside," Kane questioned, looking directly at Candy.

"Ummm, yes, let's toast and head back in. To family, love, and legacy!" Candy raised her glass, and we all did the same. I cut off the fire pit and escorted the ladies back inside.

I looked around for Autumn. She wasn't here and her phone was gone from off the table. I picked mine up and saw there were alerts from the security system. Something definitely was up.

"Candy, you know where Autumn dipped off to?" She turned around, looking at me like a kid caught sneaking a cookie.

"No, I don't. She just said it was something she had to do and not to ask her any questions."

"You let her go out there alone, knowing Peanut crazy ass has it out for her?" Kane joined in on the conversation.

Candy started crying. You couldn't say anything to her lately without the waterworks. Now I felt like shit when she wasn't the one in the wrong.

"Please stop crying, please. I'm about to track her ass."

Kane and I linked both their phones to ours, just in case we needed to locate them. I knew Autumn thought like me and would stop sharing her location, so I put a tracking chip in her phone as a backup.

"Why would Autumn be at a damn cemetery this time of night and go by herself?"

Candy covered her mouth and took a seat on the couch. The way she was reacting to my question, she must have known exactly why Autumn was there.

"Peanut visits her deceased great aunt every holiday. She raised Peanut after her parents' lost custody. Autumn and I usually went with her. I was so consumed with everything going on here, it didn't dawn on me until now. Oh my god, she must be going to confront Peanut. We have to go get her!" Candy cried out.

"I'm going by myself! Kane will look after y'all here."

"What's going on? Is everything ok with Autumn? Where is she?" Autumn's mom questioned. I headed out. Candy could deal with her people. I had to get to Autumn before shit went left.

When I pulled up to the cemetery that my gps led me to, I drove around with my headlights off, trying not to draw too much attention to myself. I could see on the map I was getting closer to where her phone location was signaling. This shit looked creepy as hell. It felt like I was in a horror film.

The moon was full and hung in the sky like an oversized flashlight. The night was still. Besides the sounds of my tires riding over the dirt path, it was dead silence. There were a lot of trees scattered throughout the cemetery, most of them bearing no leaves, looking like they were reaching out to each other.

I saw two people to the right of me and assumed it was Autumn and Peanut. Parking over by the side of a tree, I got out. It was better to be on foot, so I didn't startle them. Getting closer, I could see Autumn pointing a gun at Peanut. My gun.

When I went upstairs looking for Autumn at the house, I noticed my drawer where I kept my gun was open. It was gone, along with the silencer I had for it. I purchased it after Autumn was shot. Kane would go the fuck off if he knew I had a gun, especially in the house.

"Knowledge get the fuck outta here! This has nothing to do with you. It's between me and this bitch!" Autumn barked once she noticed me.

I could see she was serious as hell, and I was going to have to work hard at getting her to put the gun down.

"You don't wanna do this, Autumn. Once you pull that trigger, you will never be the same person again. Trust me, I know first-hand. This ain't what you want."

She didn't even flinch. Autumn kept her eyes on Peanut, and her hand on the trigger.

"This muthafucka tried to kill me! She left me for dead, all over some ass. Nut didn't care if my mom had to bury her only child. This crazy bitch actually held her hand, watching her cry over me. Then had the audacity to shed a few tears herself, like she was really hurt. Now I know those tears were just for show." Autumn wasn't trying to hear me.

I stood on the side of her, so I could have a clear view of

Peanut's bipolar ass. She might have a damn gun on her too. I knew if she made any sudden moves, that was her ass. Peanut was standing there with a smirk on her face, basically not giving two fucks that her life could end at any moment. I needed to figure out how to get the gun out of Autumn's hand before she made Peanut take a permanent dirt nap next to her aunt.

Chapter Nineteen

PEANUT

I was trying to pay respect to my auntie, and Autumn snuck up behind me, pointing a gun in my face. I guess she finally figured out it was me that put two in her. When she froze on the steps at Candy's birthday party, I knew then it was only a matter of time before she put it all together. That was why I got up out of there with the quickness.

Autumn thought I was some fucking toy she could play with. That bitch knew exactly how I felt about her ever since we were kids. I first met her and Candy when I moved in with my great aunt, when I was six. Both my parents were drug addicts, and CPS removed me from my home. We lived in Virginia, and they couldn't find anyone to take me. My auntie got word and drove down to get me.

She didn't have any kids, so when I met Candy and

Autumn, they became my sisters. We played every day together. Whenever you saw one of us, you saw all of us. We were inseparable. Autumn and I connected more. Our personalities were similar and so was our attitude. Candy was a girly girl while Autumn and I were climbing trees, racing cars, and getting into fights. As we got older, we got even closer.

Autumn was my first kiss. We were fourteen. I always knew I liked girls, but I started liking Autumn more than I should have. One night I slept over at her house, like I always did, and we were joking around. When she went to hit me back with the pillow, I grabbed it out of her hands and kissed her. Autumn was definitely caught off guard.

She just stood there, so I kissed her again. This time she kissed me back. It never went any further than that, and we acted like it never happened. I could tell she didn't enjoy it like I did, but ever since that day, I was in love with her. I knew she wasn't into girls, but that didn't stop me from wanting her.

Autumn knew back then my feelings for her were strong, so when we finally slept together for the first time, I thought she was coming around. She would always flirt with me, knowing it lit a fire inside me that burned only for her. Then she crushed me and had me promise to never tell anyone about that night, including Candy.

I agreed because I loved her. Even though I fucked with other girls, my ass would never commit to a relationship. I always held out hope that one day Autumn would have a change of heart. Silly me.

Then I thought that day had arrived when I picked her up

from the courts. She knew when she climbed into my bed that night what would happen. Autumn could have slept out on the couch. She wanted me to make love to her and enjoyed every minute of it, throwing it back at me. Her pussy was dripping wet. When I said I love you while I was deep inside her, she said it back.

The next morning when Autumn informed me she had called Knowledge to come get her, I saw red. I've never been so furious in my entire life. It felt like someone took my heart out my chest and stomped all over it. That heartless whore had hurt me for the last time. I knew I would get her ass back, just didn't know how or when. Then along came Rah and a plan was formed.

"Why did you do it, Nut? What did I do that was so bad you thought taking my life was the only solution?" Now she wanted to play dumb.

"You know exactly what you did! Don't act stupid now. You're a selfish bitch, only thinking about yourself. Don't ask me no fucking questions you already know the answers to."

"You're the selfish bitch, trying to make someone want you in a way they don't! Just because I slept with you doesn't mean we were going to ride off into the fucking sunset together! I was honest with you, but you keep forgetting that part."

"You used me! I would have done anything for you. All that flirting you did, saying you loved me, you only love yourself."

"What I want to know is who helped you? We know you didn't do the shit alone."

Now this muthafucka wanted to join in on the conversation. I should have shot his ass too. All I did was push them closer together. They got to be a couple because I was an inch off. He was enjoying what should have been mine.

"Who else wanted revenge on Autumn just as much as I did? She knows the answer to that. Once again, she was selfish and had to have things her way. Put that man underneath the jail because he mistreated Candy. That wasn't none of your fucking business."

I didn't have shit to lose at this point but my life, but in reality, I was already dead. Once my auntie left this earth, I felt like I died with her. She passed away right after I graduated high school. Autumn's mom let me stay with them until I got on my feet. My auntie had left me a lil life insurance policy. I used that to get my own place, started working, and sold some weed on the side. I've been taking care of myself ever since. My parents never checked for me.

They saw me two times after my auntie took me in, once in court and at her funeral. They just hugged me and said they were sorry for *my* loss. This was my mother's aunt that took me in, and she never once told her thank you. I lost the only person in this world that loved me unconditionally, no strings attached.

"So, this wasn't no spur of the moment, I'm drunk and high, bullshit. You two muthafuckas put a plan together to take my ass out. Well, dumb and dumber couldn't pull it off. Now here I stand with your life in my hands." This bitch was getting on my nerves.

"Pull the trigger like I did, or take yo weak ass back home. I'm sick of listening and looking at your ass."

Chapter Twenty

CANDY

I listened to my auntie Rose ask all these questions, but I couldn't stop thinking about Autumn. Maybe I should have told Knowledge Autumn was up to something. At least this way he could have gone with her from the start because he wasn't going to stop her either.

Hopefully nothing happened before Knowledge got there. Peanut always made sure she was at her auntie's gravesite at the exact time she passed away. That was how Autumn knew she would be there. She knew Peanut wouldn't miss it no matter what.

"Candy, why are you just sitting there? You hear your auntie talking to you? Answer her now!" my mother ordered with so much bass in her voice. It startled me.

"We figured out it was Peanut that shot Autumn. Knowledge went to go after Autumn because she went to confront Peanut." My aunt was instantly filled with rage.

"Peanut tried to kill my child? Why would she wanna do such a thing? Come on, take me to where they are. I'm gonna kill Peanut's ass myself. Get up, Candy, let's go." My auntie pushed me on my shoulder, trying to get me to stand up.

"No one is going anywhere, especially Candy. Ms. Rose, I know this is a lot to take in right now, but you have to calm yourself down. My brother is handling it. He won't let anything happen to your daughter, and I'm not going to let anything happen to any of you. Just trust me when I say we got this." Kane sat next to me on the couch.

My mom took my aunt into the kitchen to get her something to drink. She didn't go quietly. Auntie Rose talked shit about how she let Peanut into her home, and how she loved her like her own child. She had every right to feel the way she was feeling. Peanut had us all fooled. Her ass belonged on the psychiatric ward. You have to be a sick muthafucka to do the shit she did.

Peanut was on some *Lifetime Movie Network* performance. She probably was laughing at us the whole time, like look at these fools. I still couldn't get over the fact that Rah might be in on it. Just the thought of it made the hair on the back of my neck stand up. He deserved whatever fate Peanut got.

I hoped Knowledge called soon to say that everything was okay. I just needed to know that Autumn wasn't in harm's way. Junior came over and sat in the chair across from us.

"You good, Candy? Do you want me to get you anything?"

Junior had been a totally different person ever since the shooting happened.

It scared the shit out of him that he might lose one of us. Now that he knew I was pregnant, he would really worry about me.

"No, I'm okay. I can't eat or drink anything right now. I just need Autumn and Knowledge to come walking through that door."

I was trying not to stress because it wasn't good for the babies, and I could feel them fluttering around in there.

"You're gonna be a good uncle Junior. You're already looking out for your sister." Kane complimented him.

"I'm glad she's having kids with you and not Rah. I hate him. Especially after how he treated Candy when she broke up with him." I shot Junior a look that made him hang his head.

Kane scooted forward, resting his arms on his knees and folding his hands. I could feel him burning a hole in the side of my head with his eyes. Junior didn't mean any harm. He was just expressing how he felt, not knowing I never told Kane about Rah's reaction.

"What did he do to you, Candy? Tell me now!" The sound of his voice made me jump a lil.

Kane had never talked to me in such a manner. It wasn't loud, but it was piercing. I could see the vein in the side of his neck pulsating.

"This is why I didn't wanna tell you. I knew it would make you go insane. I'm alright, It was just words. Junior stepped in and made him leave."

I could tell by the look on his face he didn't give two fucks about what I just said.

"So, if Junior wasn't there, he was gonna put his hands on you? Don't lie to me either because if your brother had to step in, then the conversation escalated to more than just words." What started out as a beautiful day, has now turned into a shit show.

"I don't know if he ever put his hands on her before, but he definitely would have that night. They never argued, so I was surprised by it. He was in her face, spit flying and everything, calling her all types of vile names. There was fear in her eyes. I was nervous too, but he was going to have to fight me before I let him do anything to her. I've never seen him like that before, Junior confessed.

Kane was up on his feet, pacing back and forth. I had to say something.

"He has never put his hands on me, ever! I wouldn't tolerate that from any man. What Junior said is correct. He was definitely a different person. I told him that I was leaving him for you, and it enraged him. I shouldn't have told him about you and ended our relationship all at the same time."

Kane lifted me up and stared deeply into my eyes. I tried fighting back the tears, but it was no use. They win every time.

"Stop blaming yourself and don't make excuses for him ever again. He helped Peanut shoot Autumn, and you know it, whether you wanna believe it or not. I was gonna let Knowledge handle him, but now, he's my problem." This was exactly what I was trying to avoid.

"He can still be Knowledge's problem. Let him handle it. He said he would if he found out he had anything to do with it, remember?" I was pleading with Kane at this point.

"That muthafucka disrespected you, not aware you were carrying our children. He violated you and has to answer to me for it. You won't ever have to worry about him again, I promise."

There was no reasoning with Kane. I prayed that him and Rah never had to cross paths. By the look in his eyes, that prayer wasn't getting answered.

Chapter Twenty-One

RAH

These muthafuckas thought they got one over on me, but Peanut already informed me on what was what. Candy never planned on telling me she was pregnant, knowing there was a possibility that they were my kids. Twins ran in my family too, so that made me feel more confident that I was the father. Peanut looked out for me, even though I was two seconds off her ass.

I was pissed at Peanut for not getting the kill shot off on Autumn's trifling ass. Her telling me about the pregnancy made up for it. Autumn was a tough cookie. Her ass pulled through. It would take more than two bullets to put that trick down. I would have aimed for her head, but Peanut let her feminine side pull the trigger.

She felt Autumn put a hole in her heart, so she wanted to

do the same to her. I don't even know what Peanut saw in Autumn. Her ho ass was for the streets. I've been plotting on her ever since I found out she put me in jail. I wanted her dead but didn't know how to get it done.

When I was at the liquor store picking up a few items, Peanut happened to be there picking up more shit than me. I got weed from her here and there, so we were cordial. She seemed aggravated, and I just asked her what was good. This nigga unleashed on me like a broken fire hydrant.

We decided to head back to her place, hangout, and shoot the breeze. She let me know what transpired between her and Autumn. I never knew Autumn's door swung both ways, but whatever she did had Peanut's nose wide open. Once I saw how distraught she was, I knew I could convince Peanut to help me kill Autumn's ass. The crazy part was it didn't take much convincing.

Peanut said Autumn was at some dude named Knowledge house. Even though it was two weeks ago when she was last with her, Peanut was sure Autumn was still there by her social media post. Autumn just so happened to make a status that said she enjoyed her time away from the hood but it was time to head home.

The timing was perfect. What were the odds of everything falling into place like that? We decided to take her out at that very moment. I felt Peanut should be the shooter because if she got caught on the property, her ass could play it off like she was coming to visit Autumn to apologize or some shit.

Peanut already had the heat because she lived alone and sold weed, so she stayed strapped. She said the gun couldn't be traced back to her. We had to move fast because Autumn could have left by the time we arrived there.

I parked on the side street, where I couldn't be seen. The entire property was surrounded by dense trees but no fence. Peanut said that they didn't leave yet because Knowledge's car was still parked in the driveway in front of the house. She was able to squeeze through the trees and squatted on the side of the car.

We waited for like forty minutes before Autumn came out. Once I heard the shots, I started the car. Peanut came busting through the trees like a jackrabbit, hopped back in the car, and we were out. I needed to finish covering my ass.

Before we left Peanut's house, I texted Candy that I wanted to come by and get my money. I needed to make sure she was my alibi, since I had threatened Autumn in front of her. Peanut told me Candy and Autumn weren't speaking because of what she did to me, so I knew Candy would be vulnerable. I dropped Peanut off at home and went straight to her house.

I told Candy everything she needed to hear, so I could get her out of her clothes. I had to be with her long enough for her to defend me if my name came up. Autumn had told Peanut I threatened her, so she could have told others.

It happened to work out that Junior told Candy Autumn had been shot while I was there. He was another witness for me. After I dropped them off at the hospital, I met back up with Peanut. I let her know that Autumn wasn't dead from what I heard, but it didn't look good for her either.

She knew then Candy was seeing someone else but never said anything. Peanut had no reason to tell me, so I understood. It was my karma. I just didn't think Candy had it in her. My ass thought I had her wrapped around my finger, but obviously she had enough of my bullshit. I drove Candy into the arms of another man.

Into the bed of another man I should say because she was definitely pregnant and claimed they were his. That shit sounded so crazy, and I still couldn't wrap my head around it. I thought this was someone she just met, but from what Peanut told me this little romantic entanglement they were involved in started when I was still locked up.

Candy tried to play dumb when I mentioned something felt different. She knew exactly what I was talking about. Now I was out here looking like a creep. I had been watching them ever since Peanut told me she was knocked up. It blew me away to find out Kane was Knowledge's brother. They kept this shit all in the family. It was a sibling love affair. Yeah, Peanut also told me that Candy and Autumn were sisters.

I didn't know exactly what went down at Candy's party, but it had Peanut singing like a canary. She was pissed all over again, like the day I saw her in the liquor store. I'm glad she sang because Candy was going to give me a paternity test when she dropped that load. If she thought they were about to play house with my kids, she was sadly mistaken.

They had a pretty nice house too. These brothers must be sitting on some bank to afford property like this. The guys seemed to move about freely, but they had their women under lock and key. I only saw Candy leave that house once to go to the doctors. They had security with them, so I kept my distance when I followed them. I couldn't afford to draw attention to myself.

They must have sent their security home for the holiday because none of them were on my radar, and Autumn never left the house when they were around, until today. She was on some sneaky shit too because she jumped into a car out on the street, dressed like she was about to pull off a hit herself. Her dude left out about twenty minutes later, probably looking for her ass.

I couldn't worry about them, though. The two I was looking for were still in the house. I've been sitting out here all day, waiting on the perfect opportunity to knock on the door. I'm just glad this was the last house on the block. Otherwise the police would have been on my ass. This was the type of neighborhood where you couldn't loiter.

With security not around, and Autumn and Knowledge gone, now was the perfect time. Once I approached them, I exposed Peanut. They would know she told me about the pregnancy, but I didn't give a fuck. Making sure I didn't have kids out here being raised by someone else was more important than her fucking feelings. I had to let my presence be known.

I started the car and headed toward the house. I'm sure they could see me approaching. These muthafuckas probably had a state-of-the-art security system. I parked behind a Bentley truck. They must be some high-ranking drug dealers or some shit. I didn't think that was Candy's type. She was definitely living the life, but I was about to disrupt that shit.

Chapter Twenty-Two

CANDY

I didn't know what was taking Knowledge and Autumn so damn long. Kane could see from his phone that they were both still at the cemetery, so at least we knew he made it to her. He won't let me call her. Kane kept saying Knowledge got it. I believed him, but I wouldn't be able to relax until they were back home and safe.

Meanwhile, I was trying to keep my auntie and mom calm as well. They couldn't believe Peanut would do such a thing. It was also crazy that Peanut shooting Autumn brought them together. They were back to being sisters and looking out for each other. I laughed when they promised to jump Peanut the next time they saw her.

"Who the hell is this driving up to the house?" Kane asked out loud, looking at the security cameras from his phone.

He got up and headed toward the foyer. I followed him. We weren't expecting anymore company. I knew it wasn't Knowledge and Autumn, so I was baffled. Who the fuck randomly showed up to someone else's house, especially on Thanksgiving?

Kane had to be regretting letting security be off today. I was probably the reason he did it and now wished they were here.

What if Peanut sent someone here after us? What if something did happen to Autumn or Knowledge, and this person was coming to tell us. Just because their phones were pinging to that location didn't mean that they were alright. Peanut could have known Autumn would show up for revenge and set a trap for her. All these crazy thoughts and questions were racing through my mind.

Knock! Knock! Knock!

Kane started walking toward the door, and my heart started racing.

"Don't open that door. We don't even know who it is."

I couldn't see who it was or what the car looked like. Kane had his phone down at his side.

"Back up, Candy. Go into the great room with your family. I got this." Pregnant and all, I wasn't going anywhere. "Whoever this is came alone and must be lost. I'm just going to send him on his way."

Kane knew I wasn't leaving his side. He swung open the door, and I almost passed out. My eyes have to be deceiving me. Peanut betrayed us once again.

"What the fuck are you doing here?" I could feel my blood pressure rising.

"Wait, you know him, Candy?" Kane glanced over at me.

"Of course she knows me. She's carrying my kids."

This smug bastard had the nerve to crack a smile when he spoke those lies.

"So, you're Rah. The one I heard so much about." Kane's voice was so calm. "The one who disrespected my queen when she's carrying *my* sons. You're that Rah?"

"Those are—" Before Rah could even finish his response, Kane moved me out the way while snatching him by the throat with one hand, lifting him off the ground. He threw him onto the floor inside the house and slammed the door shut.

Chapter Twenty-Three

KNOWLEDGE

"**D**on't listen to her Autumn! She wants you to pull that trigger and take her out of her misery. She knows that it's all over now and has nothing to lose. Let her stew in her own shit. Don't give her the easy way out." Autumn loosened her grip off the gun, eventually lowering it to her side.

I couldn't help but think back to that very moment when seeking revenge altered who I was. Even though I pushed what occurred that day to the back of my memory, I would never forget what happened.

Timothy Conner was nineteen years old when he drove drunk, ran a red light, and crashed into my parents' car. He's the son of a judge, so he not only had white privilege on his side but the law too. Timothy pleaded guilty to reckless driving and underage drinking, vehicular manslaughter was no longer on the table because of that. He received probation. That was it, Fuck the fact that he killed my mom and dad.

I figured justice would never be served. We were teenagers at this time. What could we do? I had no idea Kane had been plotting our revenge ever since that day. He saved every newspaper clipping of the story, even the police report that had Timothy's address listed.

Kane had just closed on his first piece of property. An abandoned building that used to be a factory. He had me meet him there. I figured he wanted us to toast to his accomplishment. Plus, it was the anniversary of our parents' death.

Timothy was on his knees pleading for his life when I entered the building. Kane had a 9mm pointing at him. I never even bothered to ask Kane the details on how he got him there. I didn't care. This muthafucka needed to be dead, just like my parents were. I wanted his family to feel the pain, sadness, and hurt we felt every damn day.

Kane was patient for five years and really thought this shit through. He had plastic laid out on the floor, duct tape, and a silencer on the gun he was holding. I looked up at Kane and could see a little doubt creep up on his face. I guess planning it was the easy part. The execution wasn't.

"Yo, bruh, you good? I'm here now. You can lay his ass down. He deserves it for what he did. This muthafucka took mom and dad from us. Fuck him!"

Sweat was now forming across Kane's brow. He wasn't built for this shit.

"He does, and I want him dead. It's just for some reason I can't bring myself to pull the trigger."

I walked over to Kane and took the gun out of his hand.

"And you don't have to. You protected me our entire life. You came to my rescue more times than I could count. Now, it's my turn to do the same for you."

I faced Timothy, stared him dead in his eyes, and unloaded on his ass until there weren't any bullets left.

We rolled him up nice and tight in the plastic and taped his ass up like a rug. There was an area in the back of the building that was fenced in. It must have been the hangout area for the staff. It was full of picnic tables, and a few scattered trees were planted out there.

We dug a 6-foot grave and tossed Timothy into it, poured lime over his ass, and filled it back up with the dirt. Kane scattered grass seeds all over his grave. Eventually it would look like this area was never disturbed.

Seeking revenge could make you feel better, temporarily. It would never make you whole again. That void in your heart remained. I didn't even care that I murdered that man, and it scared me to feel that way. I had tapped into a part of me that I didn't even know existed. I was a cold hearted killer when it came to the ones that I loved. That same feeling reared its ugly head again when Autumn was shot. I was out for revenge and didn't care who I had to take out to get it.

Standing here at this very moment I realized I loved

Autumn, and I didn't want her to do something she couldn't take back. Autumn wasn't a killer, and if she ended Peanut's life tonight, she would end hers too. The person she was now would no longer exist mentally.

"Give it here. I love you Autumn, and I got you."

Keeping my eye on Peanut's no-good ass, I removed the gun from Autumn's hand. I wasn't finished with her yet.

"Awe, isn't this sweet? Look at the beautiful couple. He loves her!" Peanut spoke sarcastically as she stood there clapping her hands. Next thing I knew, Peanut quickly reached behind her back and pulled out a gun.

Instead of pointing it at us, she held it up to her own head. I was now pointing my gun at Peanut because I didn't trust this shifty muthafucka. Tears spilled out of her eyes and ran down her face. Maybe this tin man did have a heart.

"I loved you, Autumn. More than you will ever know. All my cards are laid out on the table now for everyone to see. I can't come back from this. It's over for me. I'm not rotting in a jail cell while you two sail off into the sunset. And I'm sure Knowledge and Kane won't even let me make it to the jail, so fuck both of y'all!"

BOOM!

Peanut's lifeless body fell to the ground, landing right on top of her aunt's grave. The blood leaking from her head stained it. Autumn tried to run over to Peanut, but I grabbed her and pulled her into me. She was shaking and crying uncontrollably.

I knew she was emotional and conflicted. This was a person

she called her sister and loved all the way to the very end. Peanut was a wolf in sheep's clothing and was only out for self. I wished things could have ended differently, but it didn't. There was nothing we could do now.

"Get in the car and don't look back. This is all on her. We have to go." I helped Autumn into the car and drove out faster than I drove in.

Peanut committed suicide. It was an open and shut case. We had the video evidence that she shot Autumn. All we had to do was give it to the police. I know I didn't fuck with them, but for a future with Autumnm I was willing to change my ways.

"Did you really mean what you said back there, that you love me?" Autumn questioned me as I turned onto the street, leaving Peanut in our past once and for all.

"Yes, I love you. I'm not afraid to let you know how I feel. I've never felt this way before, and I know I will probably fuck up, but I'm willing to give this thing a shot if you are."

"I love you too, and we can fuck up together because I ain't going nowhere."

She stared out of the window as tears continued to cascade down her cheeks. We didn't say a word to each other the rest of the ride back to the house. I think we were both overwhelmed with emotions and needed to process everything.

"What the fuck is he doing here?"

Autumn sat forward in her seat with a scowl on her face. We just pulled up to the house, and there was a car I didn't recognize parked behind Kane's truck, but obviously she did.

"Whose piece of shit is that?" Now I was on alert and needed answers because of the way Autumn reacted.

"Rah's dirty ass!"

We both rushed out of the car and headed for the house. I could feel that feeling trying to take over me again.

Chapter Twenty-Four

CANDY

"Kane, please stop!"
"You're gonna kill him!"
"Oh my god, noooo!"
"He's not worth it. Think about our kids!"

I was screaming at the top of my lungs at Kane, but he wasn't listening. He kept beating the hell out of Rah.

With each blow that connected to Rah's body, it sounded like bones were cracking. Kane must have slammed him on this hard ass floor about four times. One of Rah's eyes was completely shut, and his mouth was busted open. Blood leaked out every orifice on his body.

Junior, my mom, and auntie came rushing out after hearing my shrilling pleas for Kane to stop. He had completely blacked out and disconnected from reality. They watched in horror with me as Kane lifted Rah's body up once more, slamming him onto the floor.

The door opened up, and I looked over to see Autumn and Knowledge walking in. I was so relieved that they were fine, but even more grateful that Knowledge was here to end the vicious thrashing that Kane placed upon Rah.

Knowledge rushed over and grabbed Kane from behind, finally stopping him from pummeling Rah to death. Autumn had a grin on her face that showed her enjoyment. She had been waiting for this moment for years.

I went over to Autumn and hugged her. She had my nerves so bad, I thought something awful happened to her. Now that I could see that she was in one piece, I put my focus back on the situation at hand.

Rah was stretched out on the floor, looking like a deer that had just been struck by a car, straight roadkill.

"Bruh, relax! You can't kill this man in front of everybody like this. Think of what it would do to Candy. She can't unsee it."

Knowledge tried to calm Kane down while still holding on to him.

"Good for his ass! I wish he was dead, then he could join Peanut's ass." Autumn spewed.

She stared down at Rah with pure disgust as he laid there helpless.

"Wait! What? Peanut is dead? Did you do it, Autumn?" I held my breath.

"No, I went there to off her ass, but that crazy bitch still had to have the last word. She shot herself in the head. As much as I wanted her gone, that shit hurts my heart." Autumn's eyes fattened with tears, but she didn't let them fall.

"Y'all trying to send me into labor early. It's just one thing after the other. I need to wake up from this fucking nightmare."

I rubbed my belly. My poor babies didn't deserve this stressful shit.

Auntie Rose came over and took Autumn by the hand, walking away with her into the next room. Meanwhile, my mom was trying to help Rah's ass. Why, I didn't know. Junior told her to leave him alone. He placed his hand on her back and motioned her to join her sister and niece.

After she walked away, Junior turned around and kicked Rah in the side, causing him to roll over, then stomped him in the face. He deserved it, and as much as it saddened me that Peanut was dead, she got off easy. Rah would meet his fate too, whatever it was.

"I'm calling the police, so they can lock his ass up. If he stays here a minute longer, Kane is gonna finish him," I announced.

"Don't call the police, Candy. I will handle it." Kane saw me pull out my phone. "I know the chief of police personally. I got it from here. Go relax and check on your family."

He finally calmed down and was back in control.

*** * * ***

"Well, I can't say that I'm not happy to see this day come to an end."

I was exhausted, mentally and physically as I climbed into the bed and snuggled up next to Kane. He took the ice pack off his hand and placed it on the nightstand. The swelling went down a lot.

"Let me apologize for losing my temper tonight. That's a side of me I hope you never have to see again. I just couldn't believe his arrogant ass was bold enough to knock on our door. I lost it. All I saw was red. If Knowledge hadn't walked in when he did, I don't know what would have happened."

Kane placed a gentle kiss on my forehead and rubbed my shoulder.

"I don't even want to think about it. The thought of losing you scares me more than anything. I just knew they were gonna take you to jail tonight after seeing what you did to Rah. The paramedics thought he was in a car crash."

"The chief wasn't gonna let that happen. He was best friends with my dad and actually wanted to take us when our parents were killed, but he was going through a divorce at the time. The state said no because he was already involved in a custody battle for his kids."

They didn't lock up Kane, but Rah wasn't so fortunate. They arrested him for being Peanut's accomplice, handcuffed him right to the stretcher. We explained everything that happened, but left Peanut's suicide out. They could find her on their own. The police were aware she was the shooter and took the video evidence that confirmed it.

"You've been through so much, and now you're dealing with all my family drama."

"It's ok, y'all are my family too now. I go hard for mine and will deal with the consequences. Whatever they may be. Don't worry about all that now. Let's just focus on our future together." Kane kissed my belly then kissed me.

I could feel myself getting wet. Kane slid his hand over my pussy and played with it before inserting two fingers. He made me cum instantly. I was super sensitive now and the slightest touch sent a vibration throughout my whole body.

Turning my back to him, so that we were in the spooning position, I rubbed my ass up against him. His hard dick poked me from behind as I reached back and gently massaged his nutsack. Kane lifted my leg up and entered me.

"Shit, Candy, it's always so tight. It drives me insane."

Kane whispered in my ear while thrusting in and out as I did a slow grind, squeezing his dick at the same time.

"Stop that before you make me cum before I'm ready."

I did it on purpose because I knew that was his weakness. He needed to recognize who was really in control.

Kane had me get on my hands and knees, with my legs spread wide. His hands were on my hips as he thrusted in and out of me with such precision and skill. I was soaking wet. He took his left hand and played in my pussy.

"Damn, babe, you taste like sweet nectar."

I looked back to see Kane licking his fingers. It aroused me even more. I started fucking him back, throwing my ass in a circle. He tried to fight the urge to erupt like a volcano but couldn't.

"Aaahhhhh!" Kane moaned out as he released into me.

He pulled out, and my pussy throbbed with pleasure. Kane laid me on my back and ferociously feasted on me, sucking on my clit until it swelled up.

"Yes, yes, Kane. Mmmmm, mmmmm. Right there. Uugghhhh, yes, right there!"

Kane was hitting my spot, causing my body to respond with spasms as I arched my back. A tingling sensation rippled throughout my body as it heated up. I came so hard it curled my toes.

Kane looked up at me, grinning. His beard was drenched in my wetness. He laid next to me and wrapped me in his arms.

"Candy, will you marry me?"

"You wanna run that by me again." I sat all the way up, so I could hear him better.

"You heard exactly what I said. Will you do me the honor of becoming Mrs. Kane Alexander? I will buy you a ring later. That's not important right now. I don't want my sons born into this world without us officially being a family." Tears clouded my vision.

"I want us all to have the same name. Our sons need to know that they were created in love. They will never have to question who they belong to. You are the one Candy, my beginning and my end. Please say yes." Kane wiped the tears from my eyes.

"Yes! Yes, I will marry you. I don't care about no ring as long as I get to go to sleep and wake up to you every day for the rest of my life. That's all I need."

He grabbed my face and kissed my lips, tasting the salt from my tears.

"You have made me the happiest man alive. Let me show you how grateful I am."

Kane started nibbling on my neck. It was going to be another sleepless night.

Chapter Twenty-Five

RAH

I couldn't believe Peanut put her own self down. That shit was crazy but was beneficial to my case. Since she was no longer among the living, she couldn't testify against me. All the evidence they eventually collected showed I was involved but didn't prove I was the mastermind behind it all. I pleaded guilty to conspiracy to commit murder in order to avoid a trial.

They sentenced me to ten years. I've been in the county for a few months now, but they were transferring me to New Jersey State Prison today to finish out the rest of my time. I was ready to get this bid over with, so I could seek my revenge on those muthafuckas.

I ended up losing the sight in my left eye after Kane snuck me and continued to assault my body like I wasn't human. How he wasn't charged remained a mystery to me. He may have cracked a few ribs and knocked some teeth loose, but he didn't damage everything. My trigger finger still worked, and I was going to kill all of them, including Junior's punk ass for kicking me while I was down.

"Johnson! Let's go. You're shipping out!"

It wasn't long before I arrived at my temporary home in Trenton. A maximum-security prison. They had me locked up with real killers. These muthafuckas took all damn day processing me too. As soon as I finished eating, it was lights out already. At least I didn't have a roommate, or so I thought.

Right after they locked us in for the night, the CO came to my cell, opening it. In walked this older dude, looking like he had been in jail half his life.

"What's going on? Who the fuck is this?" I questioned.

Why would y'all wait till now to put someone else in with me.

"Shut the fuck up, inmate! You don't get to question shit around here. Now, you two gentlemen play nice." The CO walked off.

"I'm Raheem, but you can call me Rah. The top bunk is all yours."

This weirdo just stood there, looking at me like I was speaking a foreign language. Maybe he was hard of hearing or just slow as fuck.

He reached into his pants and pulled out some rags, then went over to the toilet and shoved them into the bowl. This muthafucka kept flushing it until it filled up with water. The rags he stuffed in there created a plug. I guess he wanted to go swimming because it looked like a little pool.

"Yo, you aight man? Are you about to soak your feet? It's too late for the bullshit."

I turned around to go lay down, and this crazy muthafucka put me in a full nelson.

"This ain't the WWE. Unhand me you son of a bitch!"

I tried to get out of his grip, but this old bastard was strong as hell. Even though I screamed for help, no one came to my aid.

"My name is Pete, and the only bitch is yo punk ass! You think you can try to kill my niece and live? Family is everything to me, and I'm about to show you just how much. You ready to be baptized, so we can wash your sins away, Raheem?"

"I'm sorry. I didn't mean it," I lied.

He walked me over to the bowl and before he placed my face in it, Pete spoke to me for the last time.

"Tell the devil I said hi, nigga."

Chapter Twenty-Six

KANE

"Push, Candy, push! You're doing a great job, babe."

I wiped her brow with a cool washcloth. The time had finally come for us to meet our sons. She was thirty-eight weeks, but they said that was considered full term for twins. I just wanted them to be healthy and strong.

"Alright, Mrs. Alexander, give me another big push. He's almost out."

Candy pushed again, and the doctor pulled our son out. He let out a little cry, and my heart fluttered with joy. She laid him on Candy's chest, and I cut the umbilical cord. They took him right away to get him cleaned up and to make sure he was okay. I held Candy's hand and kept my eye on my first born. He was a feisty one already.

"You're doing so good, Candy. I can't believe I'm a grandma."

Candy's mother was here too, right on the other side, giving her all the support she needed.

"Alright, are you ready to push again? On the count of three. One, two, three, push!"

Candy followed the doctor's orders, and in two more pushes, out came our other son. He was handsome like his brother and just as feisty. They both came out kicking and screaming.

"They are perfect, just perfect. I can stare at them all day and never grow tired. I can't believe they are ours." She looked up at me and smiled.

There was nothing I wouldn't do to protect them. They were my world. The day before Candy went into labor, I took a drive to see her uncle Pete. I made a few calls for Rah to be transferred out of the county jail to the state prison where he was. I let her uncle know what went down with Rah and his family.

Before I left the visit, everything was set in place for Rah's first day there to be his last. Once I received the call that all the loose ends were tied up, I could enjoy my family in peace.

"I'm gonna go get the rest of the crew, so they can say hi real quick before I send everyone on their way," I informed Candy as I gently kissed her forehead.

She performed a miracle today and needed to get all the rest she could.

Chapter Twenty-Seven

CANDY

I couldn't stop staring at my two bundles of joy. They looked exactly like their father. Kane had a birthmark on his back that looked like a brown kidney bean. It was the first thing I noticed on each one of our sons when they laid them on me. That was all the confirmation I needed.

I prayed long and hard that they didn't come out looking like Rah's ass. When the police called to inform Autumn that he was found dead in his cell, I knew Kane had something to do with it. I didn't ask and never would. Some things were better left unsaid.

My husband did whatever he had to do to protect us. I liked how that sounded, *my husband*. Kane and I got married on New Year's Eve. It was a small, intimate ceremony held right in the house. As a child I always dreamed of a huge fairytale wedding, but this was just as grand. Kane made sure of it. The entire first floor was transformed into a wedding venue, and he spared no expense.

Everyone I loved was there. Kane had Knowledge as his best man, and Junior escorted me down the aisle. Autumn was my maid of honor of course, and Kyle was the ring bearer. Keelie finally let him come back to the house after Autumn apologized to her. They would never be best friends, but they all agreed to be cordial for Kyle's sake.

My mother and aunties cried the entire time. We ain't nothing but a bunch of cry babies. They even cried at the reception that was held afterwards during our first dance. We did a mother daughter dance as well.

A photographer and videographer captured the entire affair. I wanted to be able to show my sons our union and reminisce on this day with them in the future.

People might have thought Kane and I were moving too fast, babies and a marriage all in a short amount of time. But when you know, you know. Falling in love didn't come with any instructions or a timeline. There was no handbook or manual to follow. You step out on fate, hoping that the person you chose to be vulnerable with and love wholeheartedly had the same intentions for you as you had for them.

Speaking of a timeline, Kane purchased us our first home. He had been looking ever since he found out I was pregnant. We want to be out of Autumn and Knowledge's way within the next month. It was located thirty minutes west of them in Freehold.

It had six bedrooms, seven baths and sat on three acres of land. My sons would grow up with plenty of space to run around in and be surrounded by nature. Deer and wild rabbits would be in their backyard. I wanted them to have everything I didn't. But no matter how privileged their lives were, I'd teach them to remain humble.

My mom and Junior were moving in with us as well. Kane had to get back to business, and I didn't want to be home alone. Plus, there was no way I could live such a lavish lifestyle and have my family still in the projects.

Having my mom with me would strengthen our relationship, and she'd be a huge help with the boys. It took a village, and I needed all the guidance and wisdom she had to offer me.

"Oh my goodness, look at my nephews!" Autumn came in being loud as usual.

My mom was holding Kairo, and Kane was holding Kanen. I let Kane choose their names, and I loved them. Their names were strong just like his.

"Don't be scaring my babies, being all loud and what not."

"Candy, hush, they are used to my voice. They know their auntie is extra. All that yelling I did into your belly, telling them to hurry up. Whew, child, Kane they have your whole entire face. All Candy did was push them out."

"They still have to grow into their looks, so they might start changing a little and resemble me too. I'm hoping they have my eyes."

"Much respect, Candy. Thank you for bringing my

nephews into the world." Knowledge was smiling from ear to ear.

I'm glad he and Autumn were officially together. One day it would be us visiting them in this capacity.

"Candy, you don't even look like you just gave birth. You're so beautiful, and so are they." My auntie Rose and I have gotten so much closer.

We were finally building the relationship I always wanted. The wounds her and my mother caused were still there, but it was finally starting to heal.

Junior hadn't said a word. He just stood next to Kane, rubbing Kanen's little hand. No family was perfect, and we all had issues we needed to work through. They said love conquered all, and as you could see that was true for us.

It was our love for each other that had us all here today, welcoming a new generation. They were my peace, my heart in human form. I guess my Cinderella ass finally got a happily ever after!

This next story starts the spin-off series about Autumn and Knowledge.

S ome information may seem like it's being repeated, but this was done on purpose for the readers who might not have read the original standalone. This way they wouldn't be completely lost. Thank you for reading, enjoy!

Chapter Twenty-Eight

AUTUMN

TWO YEARS LATER...

"Get up off your knee like that. I keep telling you I'm not ready to get married yet, but your annoying ass just won't take no for an answer."

Knowledge had asked me to marry him more times than I could count over these last two years. He refused to take no for an answer.

This nigga just came into the bathroom while I was brushing my teeth, got down on one knee, and pulled out a goddamn ring pop. I started to kick him in his dick, but I was about to sit on it tonight, so I needed it to be in supreme condition.

"I'm gonna keep asking until yo crazy ass say yes. I love you, and you're going to be Mrs. Alexander one day."

Knowledge smacked me on the ass as he stood up. I twerked for a few seconds because I knew he liked it when I made it bounce.

"And I would never accept a marriage proposal from a man with an edible ring."

I laughed, rinsed out my mouth, and turned around to face him.

Knowledge was as fine as they come. He blew my mind the very first day we met.

"Stop playing with me. You already know what it is. I told you once you say yes, I will have our jeweler design your ring exactly how you want it. Don't nobody wanna hear your fucking mouth if I pick it out and your ass don't like it."

He gazed into my eyes and invaded my space. I licked his lips then stuck my tongue in his mouth. We kissed like it was the first time.

"The ring pop isn't the only edible thing around here."

Knowledge scooped me up, carried me out of the master bathroom, and into our bedroom.

He dropped me on the bed like I was a piece of luggage. I giggled and played hard to get as he undressed me. His ass only had on some boxers and was out of those muthafuckas in a blink of an eye.

"I just put those pajamas on when I got out of the shower, and now you have me in here naked as a plucked chicken."

He climbed onto the bed and pinned me down by my wrist

as he stretched out over me. I wrapped my legs around his waist. It caused a smile to creep across his face.

"Why did you come to bed dressed like that anyway? Stop actin' like you don't know how we do."

Knowledge gave me a kiss on the lips, then softly bit my chin. I relaxed my legs, and he applied gentle kisses all over my body until his face was positioned in between my thighs.

"I know, but I thought we were going into the theater room to watch a movie tonight."

Knowledge glanced up at me with a sly grin twisting up his lips.

"Why watch a movie when we can make one?"

Before I could even answer him, Knowledge tried to take my whole pussy in his mouth. His long, wide tongue moistened my pussy lips as he licked and sucked on them. I could feel the juices starting to seep out and trickle down my ass cheeks. He placed a hand on each knee and pushed my legs open wider.

Knowledge tickled my clit with the tip of his tongue and teased it by slowly licking all around it. He was driving me insane. I was soaking wet at this point and started whining my hips. My pussy massaged his face as his tongue darted in and out of it.

"Yes, babe. Mmmmm, hmmmm. Right there. Sssssss, uggghhhhh. Yes, right there!"

I could feel the tension building up as I fucked his face. He viciously sucked and slurped on my pussy. A wave of heat came over me, and my legs shook while muscle spasms invaded my pelvic floor.

I groped my own breast as I came in his mouth. Knowledge palmed my ass with both hands, pushed my pussy further into his face, and sucked up all of the sweetness.

"Damn! Your pussy tastes like candied yams." Knowledge complimented me.

He looked like a basted turkey on Thanksgiving. His face glistened from all of my wetness covering it.

Knowledge climbed onto the bed and laid down next to me. His dick looked like a missile ready to be launched. I straddled him backwards. He loved it when I rode him this way.

I grabbed his dick and guided it to my opening. The head found its way in, and I slowly but surely engulfed the rest with my pussy. He let out a long moan when we became flushed against each other.

My hands rested on his knees while I rotated my hips in a circular motion. I squeezed my pussy muscles, so they would clamp down on his dick. This always sent him to another realm. I looked back and watched his reaction. His mouth was slightly opened, and his eyes rolled in the back of his head.

"How does that feel, babe? You like the grip this tight ass pussy has on you?"

Knowledge couldn't even respond. He just licked his lips and held onto my hips.

I picked up the pace and started bouncing my ass up and down. He sat up, took his hands off my hips, and placed them on my titties. I removed my hands from his knees and played in my pussy. My clit swelled up even more.

My head rested in the crook of his neck as I grinded on him.

Moans and groans escaped both our lips. Our bodies were attuned, and a natural rhythm developed between us.

"Autumn, you about to make me cum. Shit... it feels so damn good. You got that virgin pussy, always tight."

Knowledge laid back down, and I spun around, so I could finish him off. While looking him in his eyes with one hand on his thigh and the other on his stomach, I rode him until we both climaxed. I heard his toes crack as his body tensed up, and his eyes dilated.

"Whew! That was everything."

I was out of breath trying to talk. My body collapsed on top of his, and he wrapped his strong arms around me.

"Love you, Autumn." Knowledge whispered and kissed the top of my forehead.

"Do you know that your eyes get really big when you cum?" I giggled.

"No, I don't. I'm too busy busting a nut. Who gives a fuck about my eyes? You always tryna clown a nigga."

Knowledge started tickling me. I laughed so hard I snorted.

"Damn, Petunia!" Now he was laughing harder than me.

"Oh, I'm a pig?" I looked up at him with a twisted grin.

"No, you're my queen and future mother of our lil princess one day."

Knowledge rubbed my back, and I rested my head back on his chest.

If he only knew. I had more reservations about being a mother than I did about being his wife. With everything I've been through and my family history, I didn't think I was fit to be either one.

* * *

"What am I doing here, and why the hell are you here with me?" I questioned Peanut.

We were standing at her aunt's grave in the same cemetery where she ended her life. I was dressed in the all black outfit I wore that day, but I don't have any shoes on. Peanut also wore the same clothing, and you could see the bullet hole on the right side of her head.

"You know exactly why we are both here, Autumn. Did you really think I would just go away? Was I supposed to die and all would be forgotten? I know you are smarter than that. My blood is on your hands!"

She nodded her head toward my hands. I peered down at them, and they were now covered with her blood. I tried to wipe it off on my pants, but it was useless. They were stained.

"You took your own life. That shit ain't on me!"

I turned to walk away but was pulled back as if someone had snatched me from behind. Peanut was now standing in front of me, and I was being held in place by some invisible force.

She had a mischievous smirk across her face as she started tapping the sorcerer staff she was holding on the ground. I could feel a burning sensation on the bottom of my feet. It felt like I was standing on a bed of hot coals.

"You knew from our first kiss how I felt about you, bitch!"

I could see the rage in her eyes.

"We kissed once as teenagers. I didn't realize you were fucking crazy and would become obsessed with me. If I knew, believe me, I would have never kissed you back, or fucked with you in my adult years. It was the worst mistake of my life."

"Fucking with me once may have been a mistake, but you let me play in your pussy twice. So, that leads me to believe you wanted me just as much as I wanted you." Peanut licked her lips.

"I see you are still delusional. The first time was me being curious, and the second time I was drunk and in my feelings. And your lips do look dry as fuck, so I hope that's the only reason you just licked them."

She laughed and pointed at me.

"Your humor is what attracted me to you. We were best friends, and you always made me laugh. Watching you smile was the highlight of my day whenever we were together. I can't believe you switched up on me for a nigga."

Peanut had to be out her rabbit ass mind.

"Oh, please, Nut. Everything was fine, and you didn't have a problem with who I dealt with until I started fucking around with Knowledge. Your miserable ass tried to kill me because you were jealous of the time I spent with him. You shot me, you stupid muthafucka! And—"

"No, I shot you because you played on my top and had me wrapped up in your web of deceit. All the fucking you did finally caught up to your hoe ass when I pulled that trigger," Peanut replied.

My body was an inferno at this point. It felt like I was inside of a wood burning stove.

"Well, thank you for shooting my ass. It's the reason why Knowledge and I are even together. We fell in love during my recovery. All you did was push us closer together you dumb duck."

I started laughing, and I could see it made Peanut even madder. Her face tightened, and her eyes widened.

"You are going to burn in hell for everything you have done. All your demons have come to collect your soul. You're laughing now, but I will have the last laugh!"

Peanut snapped her fingers, and I was engulfed in flames. All I could do was scream and...

"Autumn! Autumn! Open your eyes. It's just a dream," Knowledge yelled.

The sound of his voice woke me up and ended my nightmare. I was sweating profusely. My pillow and sheets were soaked. I had tears in my eyes, and my heart rate was elevated.

"Yo, you have to talk to someone about these crazy ass dreams you're having. They're increasing, and I'm starting to worry. You won't tell me about them, and you refuse to go to therapy, so maybe it's time for you to discuss it with Candy. She's your sister and will never judge you."

Knowledge climbed out of bed and headed toward the bathroom. I knew he was concerned for me. I used to only dream about Peanut here and there. Now, it was like once a week. I'm afraid to tell anyone who my dreams are about or what goes on in them. I don't want them to think I'm crazy or try to psychoanalyze me.

Knowledge was the only person who knew I was even having nightmares. I felt bad for him too and tried to sleep in the guestroom, but he wasn't having that shit. He was a glutton for punishment I guess because one time I punched him in his face when he tried to wake me up. I was in the middle of fighting Peanut's ass.

I got up and joined Knowledge in the bathroom. He was already in the shower and had the glass doors steamed up. I opened them and stepped inside. His arms were extended out, welcoming me into a warm embrace.

No words were spoken. Knowledge just held me tight as tears ran down my face. He let me have my moment while the water beat down on both of us. I was mentally exhausted, and the tears I cried were proof of that. I couldn't keep on holding everything inside. Today was the day I finally released it all.

Chapter Twenty-Nine

KNOWLEDGE

Autumn cried and all I could do was hold her close to my heart. I wished I could take away all her pain. Besides my mother, I've never felt this way about another woman in all my life. There was nothing I wouldn't do for Autumn, and I loved her with everything in me.

Never in a million years did I think I would settle down, let alone want to commit to just one woman. I was content with sowing my wild oats until Autumn came along and found a way to capture my soul. If my mom was still alive she definitely would have been happy I found someone to match my energy.

She always said I was the wildcard out of Kane and I. My mom and dad used to joke that I would be alone forever because I was so set in my ways.

I wished they were both here to see us now. We were doing

great in this life and had found women who reflected the same qualities as our mother, with just a lil extra spice.

"Let it out, Autumn. You can't keep on carrying whatever this is. The load is too heavy."

I rubbed her back.

"I know. I'm going to talk to Candy today. She's the only other person I trust with my secrets besides you."

Hopefully Autumn wasn't giving me lip service and would actually confide in Candy. My gut was telling me it had something to do with Peanut since Autumn's nightmares started after her suicide. If I knew Autumn like I thought I did, she probably didn't want me to try to fix it or her, which was why she wouldn't tell me.

Autumn thought I overreacted sometimes, and maybe I did. When it came to the people I loved, there were no boundaries I wouldn't cross. I wanted them to be the best and have the best.

We washed up and got out of the shower. I grabbed towels from the warmer for us and wrapped one around Autumn's body as she held her arms up, then one around my waist. The hydronic chrome heated towel warmer was the best feature I installed in the bathroom, and it reminded me of my childhood.

My mom would always put our towels in the dryer while we were in the tub as kids. When we stepped out, she would wrap us up like mummies, and the warmth felt so good against our skin. I do the same thing with my son Kyle whenever he visits, and I couldn't wait to do it for the kids Autumn and I would have together.

"I have some business to handle with Kane this morning, so we can drive over to their house together." I informed Autumn.

"Yeah, we could actually walk over. They live right across the damn street."

A few months after Kane and Candy closed on their property in Freehold NJ, I purchased the home across from theirs. Being that Kane and I were in the realty business together I had access to information and connections the average homebuyer didn't.

I was able to convince the previous owners to sell to us. Most people had a price, you just needed to find out what it was. For those that didn't, there were other means to make them see things your way.

Even though we used to live only thirty minutes away, having Candy and Autumn within arms reach of each other was important. After how everything played out with Autumn and Peanut, I wanted her to have her family as close to her as possible.

We moved in right away and made the needed renovations and additions. Autumn's mom stayed on the property too. She had her own two-bedroom guesthouse right out the backdoor. There was no way we were leaving her in their hometown of Long Branch by herself. Plus, when we finally started a family of our own, having grandma right here would be a blessing.

"You're right. I need to stop being lazy."

I kissed Autumn on her forehead, grabbed my phone, and headed downstairs.

As I walked into my office my cell phone went off. Once I saw who was calling I didn't even bother to answer it.

It's too early in the morning to deal with Keelie's bullshit.

I hit decline and sent her ass to voicemail. My son had his own cell phone I gave him and knew to call whenever he needed me.

Having a child with Keelie was the only regret I had in this life. I love my son and wouldn't trade him for nothing in this world, but his mother. If I could trade her ass in I would have done that shit seven years ago. She was annoying, irresponsible, and vindictive. I found this out after our son was born.

Keelie was cool as hell when we were just fucking around. Once she became the mother of my child, the snake finally shed her skin, and the true Keelie appeared. I was disappointed in myself for having a child with a woman I really didn't know.

One of my friends from the neighborhood I grew up with threw a party. I decided to go and see what was good. After being there for about an hour, I ran until this redbone with a big ass and loud mouth.

I was young, dumb, and reckless. One drunk night turned into a lifetime connection with a woman I couldn't stand. We were never in a relationship. It was smash and dash everytime.

Even if Keelie stayed at my house, her ass was out of there once she opened her eyes. When she had Kyle everything changed. Keelie knew there was nothing I wouldn't do for him or her. I made sure they both were straight. There was no way I would have the mother of my son wanting for anything because if she wasn't good, then he wasn't either.

The problem arose when she wanted us to be a family and I didn't. Once she realized she couldn't tie me down, she used my son as a pawn. If I fucked Keelie, then I could see Kyle. He was her way into my house and my bed.

I went along with her bullshit for as long as I could. One day I got off the merry-go-round she had me on and suffered the consequences of not being able to see my son.

Then along came Autumn. She was supposed to be a hit and no commit too, but we vibed and I loved her energy. Autumn started showing up consistently and staying over for days at a time.

Once Keelie caught wind of this, all of a sudden she wanted to start coming back around and let me see Kyle. I was messy and fucked with both of them. Autumn didn't mind because she was just like me and didn't want a relationship, but Keelie did.

She was so used to controlling the narrative and didn't have any competition when it came to other women until Autumn. Keelie tried to fight her on multiple occasions not realizing Autumn was with the shits.

I would always intervene, but the situation got out of hand one day and Keelie was on the losing end. She took Kyle away from me once again, and we were back at square one. Soon after Autumn's best friend shot her.

It was crazy because this horrible incident made us realize our feelings for each other had reached another level. Autumn had to go to rehab, and I was by her side every day. We decided to make it official. Things were great. I just didn't have my son in my life.

Eventually Autumn sincerely apologized to Keelie, and they were able to resolve their differences for Kyle's sake. I explained to Keelie that Autumn wasn't going anywhere. She was officially my lady, and whatever we had going on was finished. I explained to her that our son deserved for the adults in his life to act accordingly. She agreed, and all was well until I purchased this house for Autumn.

When Keelie found out I was moving further away and gave Autumn the house she thought she deserved, she started to tick. Once Kyle told her I proposed to Autumn, even though she didn't accept it, Keelie went boom. She took her monkey ass down to the courthouse and filed for full custody of Kyle. She even requested child support.

Keelie lied and said my line of business didn't allow for me to be a full-time parent. Once my lawyer submitted proof that I owned my own company and worked from home eighty percent of the time, the judge granted us joint custody of Kyle. He was homeschooled, so splitting the time evenly wasn't an issue.

I was ordered to pay Keelie a set amount each week for Kyle since I made more money than her. She didn't work at all. It was funny because I actually gave her more without the courts being involved, so she screwed herself in the end. I used to pay her rent, all her bills, and purchased everything Kyle needed.

On top of that, I made sure she had money in her pockets

and purchased her a new car. It was my job to make sure Kyle knew as a man you take care of your responsibilities. I couldn't have her drive him around in some piece of shit while I rode around in luxury every day.

And even though Keelie couldn't get shit from me now, besides what I was ordered to pay, Kyle would never want for anything in this life while I was breathing or in my death. I already set him up to live like a king when he turned twenty-one.

"Why won't you answer your phone for Keelie's ass? You know she always calls me when you don't." Autumn questioned, interrupting my thoughts as she entered my office.

"Because she doesn't want shit. We just dropped Kyle back off to her yesterday. What could she possibly need from me, especially this early in the morning?"

Keelie was probably mad because I didn't say shit to her ass unless it was regarding our son. Once he walked into their house I peeled off. I didn't even give her the opportunity to say boo to my ass.

She had no choice but to find an ally in Autumn since I wasn't fucking with her. Keelie crossed the line when she allowed them white folks to get involved in our business and put a price on Kyle's head.

"Well, Keelie said Kyle has been acting up ever since we dropped him off. He's been disrespectful, and this morning he called her a bitch." Autumn laughed.

"That shit is funny, but I'm going to get his ass. He knows better than to call any woman out their name, especially his mother. We have our differences, but I will never let him disrespect her or you."

"Shit, it's her fault because we don't curse around him, and no one is being called a bitch over here. We monitor everything he watches and listens to. Keelie has no filter when it comes to her mouth, and you know she calls me a bitch all the time because Kyle tells me when she does."

She was right. Kyle snitched on his mom like he was being paid. He loved Autumn and got upset every time his mom talked about her. Autumn treated Kyle like he was her own child. She was hands on with him.

"I wanna tell her about herself, but I'm afraid she will take it out on Kyle. She's dead ass wrong for talking about you to him or around him. He's a child and doesn't need to be involved in our bullshit or forced to choose sides. We are all on his side, and he can never have too much love."

"Welp, you stuck your dick in her and busted all over her weak ass walls, so deal with it."

Autumn walked out of my office and gave me a nice view of her thick ass in those leggings she wore.

It looked like they were painted on. If I didn't have to meet up with Kane, and now stop by Keelie's house, I would have bent her over my desk. Autumn's pussy was so damn good I could sleep in it and have.

I got up and followed behind Autumn. She was already waiting for me at the front door with my keys in her hand. We got into the truck and drove off.

"I'm not coming with you, so you can drop me off first. I

already spoke with Candy and Auntie Lily and my mom are both over there making breakfast for all of us. You know how they throw down in the kitchen, and I want my food hot."

Autumn didn't play when it came to food, especially when her aunt and mom had their hands in the mix.

"You rather take your greedy ass over there instead of riding with me real quick to handle Kyle. I would do it on Facetime, but I want him to look me in my eyes, so he understands how serious I am."

"Well, you go look him in his eyes, and I will put your plate in the microwave until you get back. I'm not waiting over an hour to eat. It's like a forty minute drive each way to Keelie's house. Nope, fuck that."

I pulled up to Kane and Candy's front door. They were both standing in the doorway. Autumn kissed me goodbye and got out. I rolled down the window and told Kane I had to handle something real quick and would be right back.

As I drove off I called Keelie to let her know I was on my way. She asked if Autumn was with me because Kyle was asking for her once he heard them talking this morning. This the shit I was talking about, not letting kids be kids. Kyle had no business being all up in their conversation. I know she probably hung up and called Autumn a bitch right in front of him.

I let her know I was coming alone and wasn't staying no longer than ten minutes.

Chapter Thirty

KEELIE

I was livid when Kyle asked for Autumn when I was talking with her. When he reached for the phone I wanted to pop the shit out of him. I was his mother, not that bitch. He loved him some Autumn, and it really got under my skin.

We were able to put our differences to the side, but it didn't make us best buddies. Autumn was just my go to whenever Knowledge's ignorant ass didn't answer my calls. I would never truly fuck with Autumn after what that bitch did to me.

Everytime we saw each other words were exchanged, but one day the shit hit the fan. She threw a hot ass drink in my face when I ran up on her while she sat in Knowledge's truck outside his house one day. This was before they became a couple, and he had his cake and ate it too.

My face immediately blistered up and even though it wasn't severe enough for me to go to the ER, I still wore a mark on my face from that day. There was a discolored spot underneath my eye from one of the blisters, and it won't clear up no matter what. I tried everything.

Every time I looked in the mirror I was reminded of what that trick ass bitch did to me. Autumn was a hoodrat, and I figured eventually he would let her go and be on to the next. Once she was shot their relationship blossomed out of nowhere.

They really became a couple, and Autumn apologized. It took her a minute but she finally saw the error of her ways. I only accepted her apology in order to get back in communication with Knowledge, figuring the opportunity to have him back in my bed where he belonged would present itself.

The fact that Autumn wasn't coming with him today was the universe letting me know my opportunity had arrived. Knowledge and I haven't had a moment alone in forever. I needed to remind him of how it used to be. We had our own little family and were doing just fine until the wind blew Autumn our way. Eventually I would have been Mrs. Alexander not that ho.

I took a shower, lotioned up, and slipped on a pair of short shorts and a lace bra. With my ass cheeks hanging out and my titties pushed toward the heavens, there would be no way Knowledge could resist all of this goodness. I put on my silk robe to cover up what I wore and sprayed perfume all over me.

Knowledge would be here in the next ten minutes, which gave me enough time to do what I needed to do. I went into the living room to wait for him to arrive. Everything was set in motion and sooner than later he would be back in my arms.

Knock! Knock! Knock!

Yes! My future husband was at the door, and I sashayed over to let him in. I peeked through the peephole, just to make sure it was him and not my annoying ass neighbor I fucked here and there. If he didn't have a nice size dick and money, I would cut his ass off.

"Hey, babe, glad you could make it," I greeted Knowledge's fine ass.

He stood there looking like a chocolate warrior. Tall, dark, and handsome was an understatement. Knowledge's waves stayed on swim with his caesar haircut. His mustache was nicely trimmed above his thick ass lips. I stared into those hypnotizing eyes of his and regretted everything I ever did to him, to us.

"I'm not your fucking babe! Don't start no shit, Keelie. Where's Kyle? He's the *only* reason I'm here."

Knowledge shoulder checked me as he entered my home.

Well, that was rude.

I closed the door and started walking toward the hallway then looked back over my shoulder before I spoke to Knowledge.

"Follow me, he's in his bedroom playing the game."

Licking my lips, I strutted off to Kyle's room. I could hear Knowledge let out a deep sigh.

"Kyle, daddy is here. He's about to get your ass for calling me a bitch!" I announced and opened his door.

Knowledge ran his hands down his face.

"See, that's the problem now. Watch your mouth, and he might just watch his. He's only repeating what he is hearing. I'm going to set him straight, but you have to do your part too."

Knowledge pushed past me and shut the door in my face. He just left me standing out in the hallway by myself. I guess my presence was no longer needed, so I went to my bedroom to find my photo album.

I laid across my bed, flipped through the pages, and reminisced over better times. All the pictures I had were the ones I took of Knowledge and Kyle by themselves. They looked so happy. If everything went the way I hoped it would, my whole house could eventually be filled with photos of us three together.

"Alright, I'm out," Knowledge yelled, interrupting my trip down memory lane.

His ass was barely here for ten minutes. I couldn't believe he was leaving already. I jumped up off of my bed, grabbed my perfume, and rushed out into the hallway. He was standing in Kyle's doorway, and I didn't want him to leave.

"Kyle, stay in your room and continue to play with your game while I talk to daddy real quick. Make sure you have your headset on and turn it up," I ordered him as I peeked my head in his room.

I closed Kyle's bedroom door and followed behind Knowledge as he swiftly walked toward the living room. This nigga was almost floating. His feet were moving like they were on fire.

"Damn, Knowledge, slow down. I want to talk to you for a minute."

I untied my robe, so he could get a good look at all my curves.

He stopped and spun on his heels. Knowledge stared at me like I disgusted him. If looks could kill my ass would be dead. I really didn't understand why this man was so hostile toward the mother of his only child. My body birthed a son who would continue to carry on his legacy, not Autumn.

"We don't have shit to talk about, Keelie. You asked me to come speak to our son and I did. I have no idea why your ass is dressed like a low budget stripper, but if you thought for once second it would make my dick hard—"

"Wait, you can curse but I can't?" I cut Knowledge off and placed my hands on my hips.

"I said don't curse at or in front of Kyle. He's in his room with the sound of his game blasting in his ears and can't hear us. You made sure of that. And I don't know why because the days of putting our son in his room in order for us to fuck are over. It's been over," he spewed.

"You have that funky ass bitch in your life, so you don't need me to get on my knees and suck your dick anymore, huh? I was your woman before that trick showed up, and now, you just tossed me on the side of the road like a dead deer." I glared at him.

"Are you serious right now? We were never together! I don't know what fantasy you created in your mind, but it's false, and you know it. It's been over two years since my dick made you gag. And watch your mouth when it comes to Autumn."

Knowledge pointed his finger at me.

I wanted to punch Knowledge right in his face. His words cut like a knife and were hard to hear, especially the part where he defended her. Tears filled the brim of my eyes.

"You're making it seem like we were a couple and decided to start a family. You got pregnant on some drunk shit. I love my son with everything in me, and I'm glad he is here, but the truth is the truth. Your eyes are tearing up, so I know you're about to twist up my words and be dramatic for no reason."

"He wasn't planned, but we didn't take any precautions to avoid our situation either. And once he was born that made us family, nigga!"

I was seething at this point. Everything I felt for him before he arrived quickly exited out of my system. Now, I was on some fuck him type shit.

"You ain't no kin to me. The only person in this house that's my family is our son. Kyle is part of my bloodline and carries my last name, not you. I only went over and beyond for your ass because you are his mother. That gravy train stopped the day you brought the state of New Jersey into our personal business."

I knew it wouldn't be long before he threw the court bs in my face. Yes, I was on some get back shit when I took him to court, and it backfired on me. That was the reason I started fucking my neighbor. He fulfilled my needs sexually and financially since Knowledge cut me off. The money I received for Kyle covered my rent and all my bills, but I needed money for myself.

Sean worked on wall street and didn't mind paying me for

my services. He was like a Knowledge replica when it came to sex and money, but nothing compared to the original. Plus, Sean had these weird sexual requests that creeped me out sometimes. I had expensive taste, so I did what I needed to do. Working a nine to five was not my forte.

"No, it stopped once Summer, Winter, Spring, or whatever her name is came into our lives. It seems like everything revolves around her now. I wish the bitch who shot her had better aim when she pulled the trigger. Autumn should have d—"

Before I could finish my sentence, Knowledge's hands were around my throat. He lifted me up by my neck and slammed me onto the couch.

"She should have what? She should have what?" He pressed his hands harder into my neck.

As I struggled to breathe, Knowledge must have snapped back to reality because he suddenly let me go. He has never put his hands on me before, and his reaction revealed everything I needed to know. She was his Achilles heel. Knowledge risked it all when it came to Autumn. How do I compete with that?

"I can't believe you just choked me out, you stupid muthafucka," I murmured as I sat up on the couch.

Knowledge stood there and looked down at me.

"Get the fuck out my house!" I pointed toward the door, and Knowledge quickly exited.

You could see the look of fear written all over his face. He probably thought I was about to call the cops, but I wasn't. There was no need to bring the law into our lives again. I had Knowledge right where I wanted him.

I walked over to the mirror that hung on the wall by the door. His fingerprints were clearly visible on my neck. I'm light skinned, so it looked really bad. That was what probably had him rattled.

Knowledge was truly a good guy, and I knew if I spoke on Autumn in the manner in which I did, I would awaken the beast lying dormant inside of him. He reacted exactly as I hoped he would. I was now the puppetmaster and planned on pulling the strings whenever I felt like it.

Smiling, I stood in the window as he drove off to be with whore who didn't even want to marry him. She had his nose wide open, though. I would definitely give her that. Her pussy must be laced with crack cocaine because Knowledge was definitely hooked on it.

He wanted no parts of me, and I looked damn good. When he wrapped his hands around my neck, my kitty cat definitely started to purr. Just feeling his hands on me moist. I couldn't let all this wetness go to waste, so I called Sean to see if he would pick up where Knowledge left off. He never said no.

Chapter Thirty-One

AUTUMN

"What's on your mind, sissy? I know something is weighing heavy on your heart. It's showing in your eyes."

Candy always knew when things weren't right with me. She was one of the closest people in my life and knew me like the back of her hand. I adored her and the time we spent together.

We sat on one of the plush couches in her sunroom, full from the amazing breakfast our mommas cheffed up. They kept Candy's boys entertained in their playroom while we relaxed and talked. Kane went into his office to wait on Knowledge to return.

"A lot, sis, a lot. Whew!"

I took a deep breath and leaned my head back in order to

keep the tears that threatened to fall at bay. Candy moved closer to me and took my hand in hers.

"Talk to me. You know you can tell me anything. Did you kill someone because I will help you hide the damn body?"

Candy was serious as hell as she rubbed my back with her free hand. We were as close as sisters could be. There was nothing we wouldn't do for each other. We've been this way our entire lives, and the older we got, the stronger our bond grew.

"I've been wanting to tell you this for some time now, but didn't know how and was afraid—"

"Afraid? If Knowledge did something to you his ass is good as gone. I have love for him, but I will take him out when it comes to you!" Candy barked.

She caught me off guard because she was usually the calm one and Knowledge's cheerleader.

"Relax, killa. Knowledge is the one who suggested I talk to you, and you know he's not crazy enough to do anything to hurt me. He loves me more than life itself."

"Then why won't you marry him?" Candy questioned, and it caused me to think back to the first time Knowledge proposed to me.

"Babe, where are we going and why do I have to have this hooded covering over my head? I feel like I'm being led into a death trap."

It was breathable and very light, but that wasn't the point. I've been riding in this car like a hostage for almost thirty damn minutes. If all the windows didn't have the celebrity tint, people that drove by would think I was taken against my will.

"I had a blindfold for you, but your ass is nosy as hell, so I had to use the hood instead. We're almost to our destination so just chill. I got you."

He grabbed my left hand and kissed the top of it. Knowledge had been acting weird all day, so I knew he was definitely up to something, and I wanted to know what it was.

"Well, I hope you are driving us to the airport, and there's a private jet waiting to whisk us away to the islands. You've been working a lot lately and could use the break. And you know my ass wants unlimited food and drinks."

"What I have planned is even better than that. We're here, so sit tight while I come around to your side and let you out."

After Knowledge parked the car, he came around to my door and opened it. He held on to my hand as I stepped out. My heels hit the pavement, he closed the door, and we started walking.

"Just hold onto my hand and let me lead the way. Trust in the fact that I will never guide you in the wrong direction."

"I trust you with my life, sir. Now take this damn hood off my head before I lose my fucking mind." *Knowledge and I both laughed.*

We finally stopped walking. Knowledge removed the hooded covering from off of my head, and I gasped. My knees trembled, and I felt faint.

"You bought this for me, for us? You never cease to amaze me."

I grabbed Knowledge by his face and kissed him on the lips.

Tears ran down my cheeks, and my heart was filled with so much joy.

My mom, Auntie Lily, Kane, Candy and my nephews stood in front of a house with signs that read, "Welcome To Your New Home, Autumn".

Well, Kairo and Kanen sat in a little gold wagon with their toys.

This was the day I found out Knowledge purchased the house across the street from Kane and Candy. I knew he had his eye on it but people were still living in it. There was no way they would give up such a beautiful piece of property willingly.

It took up half a block and was surrounded by so many beautiful trees. I was in awe of it and now it belonged to us.

As I cried and hugged everyone, Candy whispered for me to turn around. Knowledge was on bended knee and held a ring in his hand that had to be around six carats. I instantly started to sweat and thought I would vomit. My nerves got the best of me.

"I know neither one of us thought we would get to this point when we first met, and our relationship hasn't been without its fair share of drama. But if you will do me the honor of being my wife, I promise you a lifetime of happiness, love, and peace."

My heart dropped into my feet. All types of crazy thoughts swirled around in my head.

"I'm so sorry, but I'm not ready to get married. Please forgive me."

I ran back to the car, and Knowledge chased after me. I felt horrible turning him down, but I also didn't want to accept a proposal I wasn't ready for.

"Autumn! Autumn! Stop daydreaming and answer my question." Candy demanded, snapping me back into reality.

The proposal I just reminisced on wasn't the one Kyle told his mother about. Knowledge asked me again one day in front of him, thinking Kyle's presence would help convince me, and I still said no, and no again to all the other times he asked after that.

"I love Knowledge and want to spend the rest of my life with him, but I'm scared. What if it doesn't work out? What if we decide in five years we don't like each other and want out of the relationship? I can't just walk away. We are still young. Time is on our side. I feel like we don't need to rush into something we might regret."

Candy gave me her *whatever* face. She sat back and folded her arms.

"Why are you focusing on the negative? You're basically doing everything a wife does, so I don't see the issue with making it official. Once he puts a baby in your ass you will change your mind."

I rolled my eyes at Candy. It was easy for her to say that because she and Kane were over here smelling like gumdrops and lollipops. Meanwhile Knowledge and I smelled like a forty ounce of Olde English, a pack of Black & Milds, and regret.

Our lives were completely different. Kane and Candy have their own little family that they created themselves. Rah, Candy's ex, who gave them hell and tried to destroy their situation was deader than a doornail. Mine was alive and well. I created a life with a man who already had a child and an evil, miserable ass baby momma who was hell bent on revenge.

If Keelie thought for one minute I trusted her just because she gave me a fake ass smile and waved whenever we picked up or dropped off Kyle, she could kiss my ass. I was a woman first, and we knew when other women were counterfeit and jealous.

I saw the permanent stain left on her face from when I threw my drink on her. If Keelie was anything like me, she wouldn't be satisfied until she got payback. On top of that, the life I was now living with Knowledge was what she wanted for herself. There was no way in hell she would wave her little white flag and surrender peacefully.

"Well, Candy, I'm not ready, and I don't want to marry him because everyone else thinks I should. When the time is right I will, but until then, let's talk about the real reason I needed to speak to you."

I cleared my throat and sat back on the couch with my legs intertwined like a pretzel.

"Ever since Peanut killed herself I have been having these awful nightmares. In the beginning I would only dream about her every once in a while. Over the last few months, they have been increasing and are very vivid, down right scary."

I could tell by her body language that Candy was taken back by my confession.

"If I didn't sneak into Nut's funeral and see the casket for myself, I would think the bitch was still alive. That's how realistic these dreams are."

Candy covered her mouth with her hand, and her eyes, which now were the size of dinner plates, had tears in them.

"It's to the point that I wake up crying, sweating, yelling, or fighting. The shit is out of control. Knowledge is aware of the nightmares, but he has no idea they are about Peanut. I don't want to tell him because he will try to make me go to therapy or start hovering over me."

The tears Candy tried to keep from falling finally made an appearance. This was why I didn't want to tell her either. Candy was too emotional, and ever since she became a mother, it had gotten worse.

"I knew you would react this way, and I should have just kept my mouth shut. What the fuck are you crying for?"

I tried to contain my laughter but couldn't. Candy was crying like I told her I was dying or going to prison. She was worse than Knowledge when it came to overreacting on shit. Any other time she wanted to fix my life. Now, she was the one falling apart.

"You're suffering, and it's not funny, Autumn. Obviously there are some unresolved issues, which are causing you to dream about her. Maybe you should see a therapist like Knowledge suggested."

"Bitch, you are my therapist! Now stop crying and do your sisterly duty. I've been holding all of this in, and it's taking a toll on me. I figured if I finally talked about it, maybe I can get some relief. Get your fake, Iyanla Vanzant ass together, so you can help me."

Candy wiped her tears, sat back on the couch, and placed a

decorative pillow on her lap. She motioned for me to lay down. I spilled my guts out to her while she played in my hair.

It wasn't easy being vulnerable, even with my sister. I've always held shit in and worked through my problems alone. Everyone had their issues they dealt with. They didn't need me to add on more.

I told Candy about every dream I had and how each one made me feel. It was weird because most of the time you only remembered bits and pieces of your dreams, but I knew every detail about mine.

"I'm still stuck on the part where you had no shoes on in your last dream. What did you do with the clothes and the sneakers you wore that day?"

"Knowledge told me to throw everything out, but I kept my all black forces. I just got those muthafuckas and wasn't tossing them out in the trash. The outfit was actually yours, so I didn't care. I figured you wouldn't miss it."

I laughed so hard my cheeks started to hurt.

"You know what. I thought the clothes you wore that night looked familiar."

"Girl, bye. You wouldn't even have known if I didn't tell you. I had that outfit for months. I'm sure you have some of my things as well."

"Yeah, right. Anyway, I think you should burn the sneakers. They are a reminder of that day, and you only wear those forces when you are about to fight. The days of you brawling in the streets are over."

I stuck my middle finger up. Most of the fights I had were

because of Candy. If you fucked with her, you fucked with me. She could fight, but you had to hit her first, then she would hook off. Not my ass. If you approached me on some rah rah shit, it was lights out. I wouldn't even let you finish what you were saying to me.

"I'll think about it. I might need them for Keelie's ass one day."

"Seriously, though. Sometimes our dreams have a message in them. Maybe Peanut is trying to tell you something."

"What, you're a Medium now? Bitch, pick a career."

Candy stared down at her phone. She had an alert on it, which went off whenever someone entered their driveway. They have sensors and cameras hidden all around their property. Even though Rah was no longer a threat, they still remained cautious.

"Your man is back. He just parked and entered the house. It looks like he's going straight to Kane's office," Candy informed me as she stared at the video on her phone.

"His ass took longer than he should have."

I turned up my face when I noticed he had been gone for over two hours. If he wasn't in a car accident, he better have a good excuse ready. I started to get up but sat back down once Candy moved her lips.

"Where are you going? I can tell by your body language you about to start some shit."

"No, I'm not, sistercousin. He didn't eat, so I know he's hungry. I'm about to heat up his food and give it to him."

When Candy aggravated me, I called her by that name. It

still creeped out a little when I thought about how our mothers, who were identical twin sisters, slept with the same man.

"You're lying. He'll find you when he's ready to eat."

I jumped up fast as hell before Candy could stop me again. There was a feeling in my gut that something wasn't right, and Knowledge's eyes were about to reveal it. I could always look into them and tell if he had something weighing heavy on his heart.

"Autumn, come here."

Candy's peaceful ass was right on my heels as I entered the kitchen. I went over to the microwave and started it.

"You have three minutes to say what you need to say."

I crossed my arms and leaned back against the counter.

"Take a deep breath and relax. Knowledge could have got stuck in traffic. He could have stopped somewhere and picked you up something nice. You just don't know, so stop thinking the worst."

"You don't know what I'm thinking, and you are down to two minutes." I kissed my teeth.

"Ummm, yeah I do. I may not be as experienced as you are when it comes to men, but I'm not naive either."

Candy must have left her mind back in the sunroom, and she needed to go find it before she got her feelings hurt.

"I don't know if you are lowkey calling me a hoe, but I'm going to need you to stop talking."

We both looked over at the microwave.

"I have a minute left and didn't mean to insult you. Maybe what I'm trying to say isn't coming out right. All I know is

Knowledge wouldn't risk what you guys have, especially with Keelie's trifling ass."

The microwave beeped, letting me know the food was ready and that Candy ran out of time. I grabbed Knowledge's plate, a fork, and a napkin. Candy's aggravating ass followed me over to Kane's office. Knowledge sat in one of the chairs in front of Kane's desk.

"Hey, babe, why didn't you come find me and say you were back?"

I placed his plate, along with the napkin, down in front of him. I held on to the fork.

Chapter Thirty-Two

KNOWLEDGE

"I figured you were chillin' with your family. I'm already late for the meeting Kane and I had scheduled this morning, so I came straight to his office. What's the big deal?"

Autumn looked as if she wanted to gouge out one of my eyeballs with the fork she held in her hand.

"Nigga, are you stupid, or do you think I'm dumb? I smelled her perfume the minute I walked in here."

I smelled it on me too, but figured it would wear off by the time I saw Autumn.

"She sprayed the shit on herself, right next to me, when I was standing in Kyle's doorway about to leave. It's not what you think," I explained.

When Keelie answered the door, the scent of her perfume

hit me right in my face. She probably sprayed it again just to be smart. Her ass knew the shit would get on my clothes.

"The fragrance is rather loud, but I thought it came from Autumn, damn."

I looked at Kane with a scowl on my face.

"Yo, bruh, you're not helping. She's ready to attack me, and that's all you could come up with?" I quizzed.

"That funny smelling shit didn't come from me. I wear oils," Autumn clapped back. "Kane, you know better to think I would walk around smelling like toilet water and kangaroo piss mixed together."

"Let's not do this here, please. Can we finish this conversation at home? I just need to handle some business with Kane, and then you will have my undivided attention."

Autumn leaned over and got in my face. Candy reached over and grabbed Autumn by her shoulder and took the fork out of her hand then sat it on my plate. My appetite was null and void. They left the office, and I ran my hands over my face.

"Fuck!"

I rested my elbows on my knees and hung my head. When I looked up, Kane stared at me like I was the dumbest muthafucka in the world.

"Why would you come in here smelling like another woman? What the fuck is wrong you, bruh? Are you trying to die today? Autumn is not Candy. I ended up with the calm before the storm, your ass got the storm. A goddamn tornado."

Autumn definitely was a firecracker, but I liked that about her. She kept me on my toes, and there was never a dull moment. Each day with her was an adventure. Autumn gave my life the spark it needed.

"Candy wouldn't have stood for this shit either. She's quiet, but no woman wants to feel how Autumn just felt. I'm surprised she was so calm."

Kane raised his eyebrow and turned his head to the side.

"You call that calm? Did you see how she held the fork in her hand when she got in your face? She almost poked your ass, bruh. I need to know what happened at Keelie's house."

I explained everything to Kane, and he seemed disappointed once I finished. When we were growing up, he was always the level headed one and guided me through this life. After the death of our parents, Kane became my father figure and mentor. The way he glared at me didn't sit well in my spirit.

"Once Keelie answered the door in her robe, you should have stayed your black ass outside. I'm surprised she wore clothes under it, well, pieces of clothing. You could have talked to Kyle in your car. She set a trap, and you walked right into it."

My head hung low again while Kane spoke the truth to me. I fucked up and got entangled in a web spun by Keelie, which more than likely was created to destroy Autumn and I. How did I not see this coming?

"Do you think she will get the police involved?"

"I don't know, bruh, Keelie is unpredictable. I'm more worried about her telling Kyle than anything. I don't want him thinking I'm some sorta monster when I'm not. Keelie wished death upon Autumn, and I flashed back to the day Peanut shot her on my steps and lost it."

When Autumn was shot, I didn't think she would make it. I had already lost the most important woman in my life and didn't want it to happen again. We have developed a solid friendship in a short amount of time.

"Listen, you need to tell Autumn everything you just told me."

I lifted up my head and looked Kane dead in his eyes. He must have forgotten that Autumn was the same person who took my gun and went looking for Peanut's ass like a bounty hunter.

"Naw, she will go over there and beat the last breath out of Keelie, then both our asses will be in jail. You and Candy would have to take Kyle because I'd be damned if he went to stay with his trifling ass grandma."

Keelie's mom had to be in her late sixties, early seventies and acted like she was our age. I heard the way she talked to Keelie, and I actually felt bad for her. She even cursed me out a few times because Keelie would tell her everything. Mostly lies, though.

"You know we have too much pull and money for either one of y'all to stay one night in jail, but I get what you're saying."

Autumn and I were solid, and this situation threatened the very foundation on which we stood upon. If I could turn back the hands of time I would, but I can't. I just have to toughen up and take it on the chin like a man. All of this was my fault and like Kane said, I should have never stepped foot in Keelie's house.

"Listen, you are your own man. Handle the situation how you see fit. Just be ready to suffer the consequences. I will always have your back no matter what, but I'm also going to let you know when you're wrong."

"And I respect you, always. I'll figure it out, big bruh. Now, back to business. Did we close on the land out in Cali, and where is Junior? Why isn't he in on this meeting?"

Junior was Candy's younger brother. He was a young bull we took under our wings to keep him out of trouble and off the streets.

"I sent him on his first international assignment. He's over in Dubai scouting out some land, getting to know the people."

Kane and I elevated to the next level in this realty game. We have one of the top real estate companies on the East Coast. Kane was a beast when it came to researching areas and determining where hospitals, outlets, stores, etc. should be built.

Everyone knew it all came down to the right location, but Kane took it a step further. He made sure we physically visited every city in which we wanted to purchase land. He wanted to know about the people who lived and worked there, to see it with his own eyes.

The raw data we collected, along with the other information he used, determined if we purchased the land or not. Kane never bought land in an area that would take away homes and businesses of local residents. He understood the value of Mom & Pop stores and only wanted structures to go up in neighborhoods like that if they took nothing from it but added to it.

"That's what's up. Junior is a fast learner and a smooth

talker. I was very impressed with him when he shadowed me. He wasn't nervous traveling alone?"

Kane leaned back in his chair with a slight grin on his face.

"You know the assistant we hired to help Candy?"

"Shorty with the purple hair? I think her name is Jade"

"Yeah, her. She went with him. Candy doesn't like the fact that I sent them together. She feels like they might start fucking around, and if they don't work out, Jade might quit. I think Junior already closed that deal. He lives here. She works here. They're both single. If it hasn't happened already, it will."

"It's like a soap opera in this muthafucka today. Let's finish up with everything, so I can get Autumn and go home. I have to get myself out of the doghouse."

"Are you going to ignore me all night?"

Autumn gave me the cold shoulder ever since we got home, and that was four hours ago.

"Knowledge, I'm pissed. I don't want to talk to you because I'm afraid of what will happen if I do. A million questions are racing through my mind. If I ask and you answer incorrectly, I might punch you in the face. And this time it will be on purpose."

I heard the frustration in Autumn's voice. If she came around me and smelled like another man, I would have lost my fucking mind. All my thoughts would have gone exactly where hers did. She sat on the edge of the bed and flipped through the channels on the tv.

"Autumn, I did not fuck with Keelie, and that's on everything I love. I went there to talk to Kyle, and that's exactly what I did. When I entered the house, I went straight to his room and stayed there until I left."

I took the remote out of Autumn's hand and knelt down in front of her.

"Don't get nervous, I'm not proposing to you. You said no too many times, and I've finally decided to never ask you again. We're good the way we are."

She cracked a smile, and I felt a little bit of relief.

"I need you to understand you are the only woman in my life, and there is no one in this world who could take your place. My heart belongs to you and only you. I apologize for making you upset and for my actions that caused you to think, for one second, I would betray you in any way."

Tears streamed down Autumn's cheeks, and a lump formed in my throat. It was devastating to my soul to know I was the reason she cried. I wiped her face and kissed her full, soft lips. Autumn's beautiful eyes peered down at me.

She had her hair pulled back into a ponytail. I reached up and took it out. Her hair fell down onto her shoulders and rested against her dark brown skin, which glistened from the coconut oil Autumn put on when she got out of the shower.

Autumn held onto my face as she kissed my forehead and leaned her head onto mine. I removed her clothes and buried my face in between her legs. She arched her back when I pushed her legs open and licked her inner thighs. I slowly grazed my tongue up and down the length of her pussy, then kissed all over it before sucking on her swollen pearl.

Her juices saturated my face as I devoured my first meal of the day. Autumn squirmed and lifted her ass up, pushing her pussy further into my mouth. After a few minutes of Autumn fucking my face, I held her pussy lips open while I inserted two fingers into her tight opening.

As my fingers moved in and out, I massaged her clit with the tip of my tongue. Autumn moaned like a wounded animal as she creamed all over my hand. I removed my fingers and replaced them with my mouth, so I could slop up all of her juices.

Autumn climbed onto the bed and got down on all fours. She looked back at me and bit down on her bottom lip. My dick jumped from excitement, and I proceeded to take off all my clothes. I stood behind her and slid into her warmth as I held her waist. Autumn gripped the sheets, and I delivered stroke after stroke while I watched my dick glide in and out of her pussy.

"Uh, uh, uh, Knowledge. Oooohh, babe, yes, it feels so good. Fuck me harder. Fuck me until I cum all over you."

I started pounding in and out of Autumn's pussy, and she tried to crawl away.

"Where you think you're going? This is what you wanted, right?"

Autumn thought she was slick. She talked big shit then tried to escape the assault.

I climbed onto the bed without sliding out, so I could make sure Autumn's ass stayed put. She was ass up, face down, like she was about to do a push-up. With one hand pressed down on the small of her back while the other one massaged her clit, I gave Autumn every inch of my dick.

"Aaaaahh, damn babe, sssssss."

"Yeah, talk that shit now. I'm about to make your ass feel your words."

A few minutes later Autumn's body began to tremble and jerk beneath me. I exploded right after she came. When I pulled my dick out, it was coated with her nectar. Autumn rolled over onto her back, and I leaned down and kissed on her plump, naked pussy.

I got up, walked into our bathroom, and started a bubble bath. After the tub was filled up halfway, I went back into the bedroom and scooped Autumn up. She wrapped her hands around my neck and kissed the side of my face.

"I love you, Knowledge, I really do."

Autumn was my peace and even if she never accepted my proposal, I would still make sure she lived a life fit for a black queen.

I put her down, and we both stepped into the jacuzzi style tub. Once I sat down, Autumn straddled me and took my dick into her hands.

It never took me long to power back up. Autumn guided my dick into her opening and began a slow grind. All I could do was hold on and enjoy the ride.

Chapter Thirty-Three

AUTUMN

It had been a couple weeks since I shared the details of my nightmares with Candy. I did what she said and burned the sneakers in a fire that night, along with the clothes Knowledge wore to Keelie's house. I haven't dreamed about Peanut's ass since.

I don't know if it was a coincidence, or the fact that I got it off my chest, but I was grateful. So was Knowledge, who was downstairs in his office while I headed to my GYN appointment.

Candy said she would come with me. I was having my IUD removed and wasn't ready to have a conversation with Knowledge about children yet, so I made him stay home. He didn't understand what a woman's body went through mentally and physically during a pregnancy.

I watched my sister change into a completely different person. She bounced back with her body, but as a woman, Candy became someone else. A mother. Her life now revolved around her children. Kairo and Kanen were her beginning and her end. The old Candy no longer existed.

Knowledge wanted exactly what they had, what his parents had, and he wanted it sooner than later. I haven't adjusted to the life I was currently living. All of this still seemed new to me even though it had been over two years. I missed the projects, not enough to move back but definitely needed to visit my old stomping grounds.

After I got ready, I went downstairs and kissed Knowledge goodbye. He tried to question me already, and I told him we could talk when I returned home. I grabbed my keys and headed out to pick up my sister.

"Hey, sis, I'm outside." Candy came out and climbed into the car.

"What's good, sissy? Did you decide what you're going to do?"

Candy barely buckled her seatbelt before she interrogated me.

"Damn, can I pull out the driveway before you turn into Olivia Benson?"

"Oh, hush, you get on my nerves."

Candy pushed me on my shoulder. I loved fucking with her. It was my job as the little sister.

"I only had this IUD in for seven months, but I want it out. One month I get a period, one month I don't. Sometimes they're heavy, sometimes they're light. I'm over this bullshit. I've been on some form of birth control since I started fucking. My body needs a break, but I don't want to be someone's momma."

The universe knew I loved being a woman, but life wasn't always easy as one. We worried about so many things, and whether to continue with this birth control shit or not annoyed the hell out of me.

"You think Knowledge will mind if you have him use condoms? That's always an option for you guys. Then you can let your body take a breather while you figure it out."

"Fuck Knowledge, I mind. The way that man is hell bent on putting a baby up in me, his ass might poke holes in the condoms or act like it busted when he really took it off. And I don't trust his ass to pull out in time."

"Shit, we're the ones who can't be trusted to get off in time." Candy laughed.

"You right. When you on top, about to rock that nigga to sleep, the shit feels so good, and you get caught up trying to get yours and forget to jump off."

Candy put her arms up in front of her and started doing a rocking motion in her seat. She looked like she was skiing. We both busted out laughing. This was the Candy I missed. I'm glad she came with me.

"On a serious note, what's going on with you for real? You don't want to get married, and now you don't want kids. You're so good with your nephews and Kyle. You would be an amazing mother." I cut my eyes at Candy.

"You're just saying that because I'm your sister. We both know I'm not mother material. I like to smoke, drink, sleep in, talk shit—"

"Stop it. I'm not going to sit here and let you degrade yourself. You are intelligent, beautiful, tough, thoughtful, nurturing. I can go on and on. I wish you could see what we all see, what Knowledge sees."

Tears clouded my vision as I pulled into the parking lot of the doctor's office. I knew Candy loved me, but I had no idea she thought so highly of me. It made me very emotional. I found a spot, parked the car, and killed the engine.

"Our mothers really did a number on us, Candy. All the secrets, the lies, and honestly, they didn't even raise us. They were physically there, but we raised ourselves. I'm afraid I will do to my child what my mom did to me."

Candy unbuckled her seatbelt and turned to face me.

"Awe, sissy. We are not our mothers. We are not their mistakes. Our children are not going to have to figure out life by themselves. They will have healthy relationships with their fathers and will get to experience life in a way we didn't get to. Our goal was to break the cycle, and we did."

She tucked my hair behind my ear and smiled before continuing.

"Our mothers weren't perfect and made their mistakes. They were dealing with their own demons and did the best they could with us. We accepted their apologies and have forgiven them. Now, our moms have the opportunity to get it right with our kids. Being a grandma is a second chance at motherhood for them. You have to give your mom some grandkids first, though."

I unbuckled myself and hugged Candy to the point I didn't want to let her go, but we were about to be late for my appointment. Dr. Jones would give you the side-eye if you weren't on time. She was the same doctor that delivered Candy's boys.

Candy started seeing Dr. Jones when she became pregnant and loved her. Since I was still going to the clinic, I switched over to her upon Candy's recommendation. Dr. Jones was an OB/GYN, so I didn't have to be pregnant in order to be one of her patients.

"I think I will stop taking birth control completely and let nature take its course," I informed Candy as we exited the car and headed toward the office. She smiled so hard it looked painful.

"So, does this mean you will finally accept Knowledge's proposal?"

"Slow your roll, mother hen. I didn't say all that."

I held the door open for Candy and we went inside.

"What do you mean you don't feel the strings! Oh, lawd, I'm about to die."

I was laid back with my feet up in the stirrups while Dr. Jones tried to retrieve the IUD.

"Calm down and stop talking crazy, Autumn."

I reached over and plucked Candy, who sat next to me, on her lips.

"Owwww, what the hell was that for?"

"Because you need to be quiet. There's a device floating around in my vagina and unless you plan on helping her find it, let me talk crazy."

Dr. Jones tried to hold in her laughter but couldn't.

"It's fine ladies. I will just use the ultrasound to see where it floated off to. Even though it's rare, sometimes they can move or even fall out of your vagina."

I covered my forehead with both of my hands and took a deep breath.

"If it fell out into Knowledge's mouth, and he didn't say anything, I'm going to kill him."

They both laughed, but I was serious as hell. I wanted to stick my hand up there and search for it myself. Dr. Jones was moving too slow to me.

"If it did fall out, more than likely it happened during your period."

"That's why I want this muthafucka out because my periods have a mind of their own now. Please excuse my language. I'm just a little agitated."

I closed my eyes, relaxed, and Dr. Jones did what she needed to do in order to locate the IUD. Candy hummed like an old ass lady in church while she rubbed my arm. She was the best sister I could ever ask for, but I wanted to elbow the shit out of her.

"Well, the ultrasound showed it's in your cervix. It also revealed a baby in your uterus. You're pregnant, Autumn."

I wanted to kick Dr. Jones right in her mouth when she uttered those words.

"How did this happen?" I was in a complete state of shock.

The whole point of me getting that stupid ass, T-shaped, piece of shit inserted in me was to prevent this from happening.

"At some point your IUD shifted positions. It's no longer effective when this happens, and you are able to get pregnant. Most pregnancies conceived with one present results in ectopic pregnancy, but your miracle baby is growing in your uterus where it belongs."

"This has to be a mistake, and I didn't have any signs or symptoms of a pregnancy. Candy, you go look. Maybe it's a gas bubble she's looking at and not a baby."

Candy got up and stood behind Dr. Jones.

"It's definitely a baby, sissy. I can see him or her."

"You're around seven weeks, and your baby has a very strong heartbeat. Now, I have to remove the IUD because it poses health risks to you and the baby. I know you didn't plan on getting pregnant, so I have to ask if you are going to continue on with the pregnancy?"

"Yes!" Candy answered before I could.

"I need your sister to answer me."

Dr. Jones looked back at Candy, who was still standing behind her, looking like she just won the lottery.

"I'm not ready to be a mom, but he or she is here for a reason. Yes, I will keep my baby."

Dr. Jones removed the IUD and gave me pics of the ultrasound. It was crazy to see this tiny little human Knowledge and I created.

"I'm going to leave you guys alone, but I want you to wait ten minutes before you leave. You can change back into your clothes. If you feel good after the time expires you're free to go, but I want to see you every two weeks for the next two months. We need to monitor you closely just to be sure there are no complications with your pregnancy."

"Thank you so much, and I will schedule my next appointment on my way out."

"I'm going to be an auntie!"

Candy covered her mouth and screamed into her hands. She was so excited.

Chapter Thirty-Four

KNOWLEDGE

"What are you doing here, Keelie?"

I couldn't believe she just showed up out of nowhere. If Autumn pulled up and she was still here, all hell would break loose.

"Ummm, I called you multiple times. You didn't answer, so I figured I would just stop by."

"You on some bullshit. What do you want? It can't be about Kyle because he's here. That's why I didn't answer the phone for you."

I stepped outside and closed the door because I didn't want Kyle to know this jackass was here but not to see him.

"My car is getting old, and I want to trade it in for the newest model."

Keelie had a Lexus LS, and every two years I would have the latest model sent over to her but that stopped.

"I don't know why you came all the way over here to tell me that."

She laughed, but I didn't find shit funny. Neither would Autumn if Keelie didn't get her ass out of here.

"You're so entertaining. I came over here because I want you to call up your guy, and let him know I'm on my way over to upgrade what I have. If not, I can wait here until Autumn gets home, and we can all have a little talk."

She rubbed on her neck. I knew it was only a matter of time before Keelie started her bullshit.

"How did you know Autumn wasn't here?"

"I saw her in my neck of the woods earlier and figured it would be best if I came over when she wasn't here. I'm pushing it, though. I made a stop on my way, so we need to hurry this up before she pulls up."

Dr. Jones' office wasn't far from where we used to live in Red Bank. Keelie still lived in the same area.

"She saw you?"

"No, I saw her and her sister going into the same office I just came out of. I was already sitting in my car, two rows back, about to leave when they arrived. Dr. Jones has been my gynecologist for the last four years."

"I don't need to know all that. And you can take your car over there tomorrow. I will give him a call later. Now, please leave."

As I went to walk back into the house, Autumn pulled up.

When it rained, it poured. She exited her car and walked up toward the house.

All hell is about to break loose.

If I could have snapped my fingers and disappeared, my ass would have been gone.

"Oh, yeah, I'm also going to need one of those Birkin bags Autumn has. It looks so good on her arm. It even matches the interior of her car. Must be nice to be the wife, I mean girlfriend, of Knowledge Alexander," Keelie whispered.

Autumn had a custom made, charcoal gray Maserati with a dark purple interior. Before I could respond to Keelie's messy ass, Autumn closed in on us. She kissed me on the lips then turned around to face Keelie.

"Hey, girl. Are you here to get Kyle? I hope not. I had a fun evening planned for us."

I was completely thrown off by Autumn's undisturbed demeanor. So was Keelie.

"Umm, no... I just stopped by to get some information for my car. I'm getting an upgrade, and since Knowledge purchased it, he had what I needed."

"Well, I'm glad he was able to help you out."

Something was definitely going on with Autumn. She couldn't stand Keelie's ass, and now she talked to her as if they were cool as hell.

"Knowledge always takes care of the women in his life."

Keelie batted her eyes at me, and Autumn's entire demeanor changed. I knew she couldn't keep up her nice girl act for long.

"Are those false eyelashes you're wearing sticking together when you blink, or is something wrong with your eyes all of a sudden?"

Keelie sucked her teeth and blew her breath. Autumn threw her keys in her bag then shoved it into my chest.

"I'm just being friendly, Autumn. There is no need to get all worked up." Keelie smiled, pissing Autumn off even more.

"Yes it is because you're being disrespectful when I was the one being friendly. I walk up, and you're standing at my door, looking like the bird that just swallowed the canary. I don't know if you just got here or been here, but I kept my cool and—"

"I'm standing at your door? Bitch, please. This is not your house. You couldn't even afford Barbie's Dreamhouse." Keelie laughed.

I quickly stepped in front of Autumn to prevent her from hooking off on Keelie.

"Move, Knowledge! I'm not about to fight her, especially with Kyle in the house. I have more respect for her son than she does."

Autumn pushed me in my back, and I stepped to the side.

"Yes, my son! The son Knowledge and I made, hoe. You need to have one of your own, so you can stop playing house with mine. Your pussy has more miles on it than a Rent-A-Center truck. You probably can't have none, insides all fucked up from diseases and shit."

"Get your disrespectful muthafucking ass off *our* property before I let her dog walk your ass," I spewed.

Keelie crossed the line. She only felt comfortable doing it because she knew she had me by the balls. If she ran her mouth now, I would just have to deal with the repercussions.

"Yeah, right. Ain't nobody scared of Autumn, even though I heard about how she rocks out with her ghetto, street rat ass. Just know, I throw hands too," Keelie responded as she slowly walked backwards to her car.

"Then your sour patch pussy having ass knows I'm undefeated, bitch. You're just mad because you think I took your son's father from you. The truth is you never had him, you fake ass Lisa Raye, or should I call you Diamond? Yeah, I know you used to be a back alley stripper for the niggas on the block. I hope Kyle never finds out his mother slid her crusty ass cheeks down a dirty utility pole for a few dollars."

Keelie cleared her throat and spat at Autumn, but she was too far away for it to land. I walked toward Keelie, so she would move faster.

"You out here hock spitting green phlegm like an animal and have the nerve to call me ghetto? Bye, Keelie the Llama. You might want to go get checked out instead of worrying about my insides. It looks like you have an infection in your throat from sucking on dirty dicks, bitch."

She finally got in her car and drove away. I was glad our house sat in the back, away from the street. The trees outlining the property blocked it completely. If Candy would have seen them going at it, she would have ran over and hit Keelie herself. I was still shocked that Autumn didn't.

"Sylvester, do you want to tell me why Tweety was really

here? You dislike her more than I do, and now y'all out here grinning and shit." Autumn questioned me as we entered the house.

"I didn't even know she was coming over here. She only showed up because I ignored her calls. You think I wanted this to happen?"

I followed Autumn into the kitchen and sat her bag down on the island. She washed her hands and grabbed a bottle of spring water out the fridge.

"Well, you better put a leash on your dog. I'm not going to get her now, but she will have to see me in a little over seven months."

Autumn piqued my interest with her response.

"I really don't want y'all fighting at all. She's still Kyle's mother, and I don't want him to be mad at you for hurting his mom. I worry about how all of this affects him. And what's with the timeline? I thought I was going to have to pull you off of her today."

Autumn took a sip of her water then reached into her bag.

"Well, worrywart, now you can be concerned with how it affects both of your kids. I'm pregnant!"

She handed me the pictures from the ultrasound. This explained why Autumn tried to stay calm and didn't turn Keelie into fertilizer.

"I planned on putting together a scavenger hunt for you and Kyle later tonight. The treasure box would have had the pics inside. Candy was going to help me set it up because you know, I don't do shit like that. But you and the yellow power ranger ruined everything, so here we are."

She sighed and walked away. I could hear the sadness in her voice. Autumn didn't want this right now, maybe never, but obviously the universe had other plans for us, once again.

It must have been an emotional experience for her today, but she still wanted to make it special for us. I really felt like shit. Even if I wanted to, now that she's pregnant, I couldn't tell her the truth on why Keelie was here. She doesn't need me to add any more stress to her life than I already have.

I went to look for Autumn, and she was in the arcade/playroom with Kyle. He assembled a lego kit while she sat across the room on one of the bean bag chairs and watched him. I grabbed one of the chairs and sat behind her. She leaned back into my chest. I placed my hands on her stomach.

"I'm scared. I planned on stopping my birth control, so eventually this would have happened, but I thought I had more time," Autumn confessed.

"Please don't be scared. I got you and will be by your side every step of the way. Neither one of us expected this. I wanted it to happen of course, but knew you took precautions to prevent it. Obviously, my little men are strong swimmers and break down barriers to get the job done."

We both laughed. I tried to bring some joy back into the moment.

"Yeah, the cannon they were shot out of is probably the reason my IUD shifted. I still can't believe this shit. It seems so unreal. When Dr. Jones told me I didn't believe her and wanted it all to be a dream."

Autumn laid her hands on top of mine.

"It's not a , and this child is already lucky to have you as their mother. I apologize for you having to deal with Keelie today. You don't deserve to be disrespected at all, especially at your own home."

"She's bitter. Her words don't affect me at all because they're all lies, and she isn't someone I care about. I'm going to whip her ass because it's the only way to get her to stop fucking with me, though. Keelie doesn't have to like me, but she will learn to respect me."

"I don't deserve you."

"That's the smartest thing you said today." Autumn grinned.

"Who else knows besides Candy?"

"No one. Candy promised not to tell anyone, not even Kane. I want all of us to be together when we announce it, but I don't want to say anything until I'm safely through my first trimester. My mom is going to be so happy. Ever since the twins were born, she wanted her own grandchildren to spoil."

Momma Rose, that was what I called Autumn's mom, was definitely going to be ecstatic. She always said it wasn't fair her sister Lily got to have two grandkids and she had none.

"Look at Kyle. He is so engrossed in what he's doing. I can't wait for us to tell him," Autumn smiled.

We spoke low the entire time, so he couldn't hear us, and Kyle paid us no mind anyway. The legos had all of his attention.

"Our lives are about to change drastically. You have to stop smoking too. If I can't indulge, neither can you," Autumn demanded.

"We will have to compromise on that. I won't smoke around you, the same way I don't around Kyle."

"Yeah, ok. You know I always get my way. Now pull me up. You are taking Kyle and I out to dinner tonight, and I'm ordering everything on the menu. I want to shower again and take a nap before we go, though."

Autumn was right. She always got her way in the end. I pulled her up, and she left to go handle her hygiene and relax. My phone vibrated, and I removed it from my pocket. The devil herself sent me a text message.

Keelie: I want my birkin by the end of the week

This muthafucka wasn't going to stop until she made my life a living hell.

Chapter Thirty-Five

AUTUMN

It had been a little over one month since I found out I was going to be someone's mommy, and I've seen Dr. Jones twice so far. Everything looked great during each visit, and Knowledge and I heard the heartbeat together for the first time.

I'm just happy it was one child and not two. We told Kyle already, and he was excited. I knew he would tell his mom because that was what kids did, so I had Knowledge tell her before he could. Even though I despised Keelie, she shouldn't have to hear the news from her child.

Not that it was any of her business, but our situation now affected their son. Therefore, Keelie should have known in case Kyle became sad or had questions. He would have to get used to not being the only child, and it might be hard for him.

"Everything is set for tonight. The caterer will be here around four to start prepping, and the cleaning service just left. They will come back in the morning."

Knowledge basically put the announcement dinner we were having tonight together by himself. He just came into the family room and updated me on the progress.

"They don't need to come back tomorrow. I can clean up everything myself. I'm pregnant, not disabled. I'm almost finished with the gift boxes."

Knowledge had to have something made that marked the occasion. He had the ultrasound pic printed on the front of t-shirts for everyone. On the back of them it said "Baby Alexander's" and whatever relation you were. So, my shirt had "Baby Alexander's Mommy" on it.

"You are not cleaning up anything. Dr. Jones said you are still considered a high risk pregnancy because of the IUD being present when you conceived. Even though everything is going as planned, you still need to take it easy."

"If I need to take it easy then we should stop having sex. The way we around here fucking, I'm sure it's considered a strenuous workout."

I puckered up my lips, and Knowledge kissed them before he sat across from me.

"You talking crazy. There's no way in hell I'm not sliding up in that pussy. I swear it seems like it's wetter and tighter, if that's even possible. And your ass was already nasty before. Now you're a straight freak."

I held my mouth open in disbelief. He really tried to play me out.

"You got a nerve calling me a freak when your ass is up in here trying to turn our bedroom into UniverSoul Circus. You got me flipping around on your dick like I'm an acrobat, talking about 'call me the ringmaster' and shit."

"I'm just trying to control the performance. You are the star of our show, you know."

"That's because my hormones are out of whack. I'm horny all the time. I could be brushing my teeth and thoughts come to my head about how I'm going to sit on your face and ride it until I bust all up in your mouth."

Knowledge stood up, walked over to me, and took me by the hand.

"Where are we going?"

"Upstairs, so you can show me your thoughts instead of telling me about them."

This man was something else, and I loved it.

"Come in, come in. So glad you guys could make it," I greeted everyone.

Candy, my nephews, and auntie Lily entered the house with Kane right behind them. My auntie Bird, the youngest of the sisters, traveled to Turks and Caicos a few days ago for work. She won't be able to attend. I Facetimed her, so she could see my little belly.

Junior and his girlfriend Jade were already here. They were the first to arrive. I'm pissed he was fucking Candy's assistant, and so was she. It was something about her I didn't like, but she worked for them and not us.

I led everyone into the dining area. The chef had the entire house smelling like a five star restaurant. Knowledge and I decorated everything. It looked damn good too. He chose the colors black and gold.

"Once you guys get settled, you can wash your hands in the bathroom off to the left."

"Autumn, you guys did an amazing job. I'm still trying to figure out why we all are here tonight."

My mom questioned me all week after she found out about the dinner. She had no idea I was pregnant, and I've been avoiding her like the plague. I always wore a robe or one of Knowledge's shirts when I was around her.

"Thank you, mom, and you will find out soon enough. Meanwhile, let's go get some food. I'm hungry like always."

The chef set the food up, buffet style, along the back wall of the dining room. She made soul food and Caribbean style food. My eyes were about to be bigger than my stomach. I put a scoop of everything on my plate.

"Sissy, I see Knowledge's party planning skills are rubbing off on you."

Candy made two small plates of food for the boys.

"Not really, I helped with the decorations, but he did everything else. Wait until you see what's in the gift boxes sitting under our chairs. I know you saw the two gold highchairs he purchased for Kairo and Kanen. Knowledge doesn't play when it comes to the kids."

"I know, and as soon as I saw them, I told Kane we were taking them home with us."

We walked over to the table and sat down. Once everyone had their plates and were seated, Knowledge took control of the room.

"Autumn and I would like to thank all of you for taking time out of your day to enjoy this special evening with us. Everyone we love is here tonight, except for our lil man Kyle who's with his mother."

Once Knowledge told Keelie we were expecting, she didn't receive the news with a loving heart. He asked her if he could get Kyle for the night, and she said no. Usually she would let him come, even if it wasn't our time to have him, but those days were over now. Hell would freeze over before she accommodated us anymore.

We were going to wait until it was our turn to have him, but Knowledge and Kane's work schedule was crazy. They had a slew of upcoming business deals that required them to travel a lot starting next week, so we had to get it done now.

"If you look under your chair, you will find a gift box. The answer to the question of why we are gathered here tonight is in that box," Knowledge continued.

We did not get Jade a shirt. What would it have said? Baby Alexander's uncle's piece of ass? Nope! Junior better share his shirt with her.

Everyone opened their box, and the sound of joy erupted in

the room. They all jumped up out of their chairs and started clapping. They yelled congratulations as they put on their shirts. Knowledge and I put ours on as well.

"I'm so glad the cat is out of the bag. I almost slipped up a few times and told Kane," Candy admitted as she rubbed on my belly.

"Why did Candy know before me?"

My mom's eyes were filled with tears. I went over and hugged her.

"Awe mom, Candy happened to be with me when I found out. The same way I knew she was pregnant before auntie Lily did. We're sisters, we know everything about each other before anyone else does. You know how that is."

"Okay, and these are happy tears. I'm finally going to be a grandma. I love you guys." Knowledge joined in on the hug.

"And we love you." I kissed my mom on the cheek.

"Yo, bruh, congrats! Now you're about to have two like me. I'm so excited for you both. And Autumn, he couldn't have found a better woman to continue to build our family with. Thank you." Kane embraced us both.

After everyone got all their excitement out, we sat back down, finished dinner, and awaited dessert. The chef prepared peach cobbler and a blueberry cheesecake. My greedy ass requested both. If I continued to eat like this, I was going to get as big as Candy did when she carried the twins.

I looked around the room and saw nothing but happiness. Kane loved on Candy, my mom and auntie Lily loved on the twins, Junior loved on Jade, and Knowledge felt me up under the table. Love was definitely in the air.

Candy knew what she was talking about when she said my feelings would change when Knowledge put a baby up in me, and they did.

"Ask me again." I looked at Knowledge.

"Ask you what?" He stared back at me like I had six heads.

"Ask me to marry you." Silence took over the room.

"Why, so you can break my heart again in front of everyone? Nah, I'm good."

"I promise, I will never hurt you again." I reached over and placed my hands in his.

Knowledge got up then down on one knee. I could see the hesitation in his eyes. It was only right that I finally accepted his proposal in front of the same people who witnessed his disappointment.

"Autumn Johnson, will you finally marry me?"

"No... I'm only playing! Yes! Yes, I will marry you. I love you."

I leaned over and kissed Knowledge like we were the only two people in the room.

"Aight, that's why you're pregnant now." Candy always had something slick to say.

Dessert was served and after we indulged in the goodness, our guest got ready to leave. The chef and her crew packed up as well. It was time for everyone to go so I could be alone with my fiance.

"You and Candy have a wedding to plan," Knowledge informed me as we walked our guest to the door.

"Yes, we do, Knowledge, and I can't wait to annoy her like she did me."

"Good night, Candy. Kane, take your wife home."

I kissed my nephews goodbye, and Kane put them in the stroller that was outside the door. Everyone else followed right behind them, except for my mom. She went out the back door.

"Why can't we just go to city hall and call it a day?" I asked Knowledge after I closed and locked the door.

"I will do whatever you want, but in all honesty, you don't want that. You're just feeling the pressure of everything. Give it a week, and if you still want it just to be me, you ,and a witness, that's fine with me."

Knowledge took me by the hand and led me upstairs. I truly lived a life I thought only existed in fairytales. It was now time for me to write my own happily ever after story.

Chapter Thirty-Six

MISS DANIELLE

TWO MONTHS LATER...

I couldn't believe this stanking ass bitch lived a life of luxury, and my child was buried in the ground next to my aunt. Autumn didn't even show up to the funeral. It was the least she could have done since she was the reason Peanut was dead.

When the police contacted me after her suicide, I was shocked they were able to get in touch with me. My aunt who raised Peanut died years ago and at her funeral, I gave Peanut my phone number, but I didn't think she saved it. We didn't have the best relationship.

They found it folded up in her wallet. It was funny because she never called me once, and I don't blame her. Our situation was complicated. But the people who Peanut considered family, Autumn and her raggedy ass sister Candy, abandoned her.

I found Peanut's journal when I went through her things. She had an unhealthy obsession for Autumn and according to what she wrote, the feelings were mutual. Candy's name was mentioned a few times but in a sisterly way. Even though I hated her too, her sister became my target.

From what I read, Autumn strung Peanut along and used her. Peanut was very detailed in her writing, especially when it came to their sexual escapades. She definitely loved Autumn more than she should have. My daughter did everything for her, only to be tossed to the side once she met Knowledge.

You don't do that to someone you claimed to have loved. Autumn drove Peanut to kill herself. Since she was having a child of her own, she needed to know what it felt like to lose one. I always believed in an eye for an eye, and now the time had arrived for me to balance out the scales.

A little birdie told me Knowledge and his brother Kane were going out of town today for business. I devised a way to get myself into the house since Autumn would be alone. They would be gone for a couple days, but I only needed a couple hours.

It had been two months since I found out she was pregnant. Even though I wanted to get her ass right then, I had to wait for the perfect opportunity. Autumn and I needed to spend some quality time together.

I drove up and parked down the street from Autumn's house. Thirty minutes had passed by when the car service finally arrived to pick up the brothers. They exited from Candy's house. These bitches actually lived across the street from each other.

They must have some magical ass pussies to have pulled this shit off. What were the odds of both of them hooking up with wealthy men who waited on their low budget, hoe asses hand and foot? It had to be one in a billion.

As soon as they pulled off, I waited ten minutes before I got out. The van shouldn't draw any attention since I had the local utility logo put on it. Dressed in full uniform, with a clipboard in my hand, I walked up to Autumn's house and rang the bell.

I had a hard hat on and kept my head down in case she viewed me from a camera inside. Even though I only met her once at my aunt's funeral, I was sure she remembered my face. Peanut looked just like me.

"Good morning. How can I help you?"

Autumn greeted me when she opened the door. She sounded so sweet and bubbly.

"Hey, Autumn. It's a pleasure to see you again."

I lifted up my head and smiled at her. Autumn looked like she just saw a ghost.

"Miss Danielle? Why the fuck are you at my house dressed like *Bob the Builder*?"

WHAP!

I struck Autumn across the face with my clipboard hard as hell. She stumbled backwards and dropped the cell phone she held in her hand. Her nose started to bleed. After what Peanut wrote about Autumn being the undefeated neighborhood bully, I knew I had to catch her young ass off guard. I quickly entered the house, closed the door, and locked it.

When I turned around from locking the door, she sucker punched me in the face. It dazed me for a moment and knocked my hat off, but I recovered and grabbed my stun gun from the utility belt I wore. I zapped Autumn on the arm when she swung again. The zap was quick, like a half of a second, but just enough to stop her.

If Autumn landed that second punch, my ass might have gone down. I dragged her into the kitchen by her hair. Autumn's thick ass was heavier than she looked. She punched at my hands and kicked the air until I let go of her in front of the sink.

"Stop moving before I zap your ass in the stomach!"

Once I said that she calmed down. She probably wondered how or if I knew she was pregnant. Autumn answered the door in a short, terry cloth robe. You couldn't tell just by looking at her.

"Sit up and don't turn around. Stay facing away from me."

I opened up the cabinet doors in front of the sink and took out my handcuffs. When I first came up with my plan I wanted to tie her up to a chair, but the circumstances have changed. Autumn was stronger than an ox, so she needed to be secured better.

"Slide over closer to the sink, and put your right hand out to the side. Don't try no funny shit either. My hand is on the button. I will fry the back of your neck."

Once she obeyed my request, I cuffed Autumn's hand to

the pipe. Their kitchen was huge, some shit you only saw in magazines. I walked from behind Autumn and stood in front of her.

"You're a weak ass bitch just like your daughter. She definitely had your blood running through her veins. Her auntie was strong, beautiful, loving, nothing like you two raccoons. I never understood how Nut turned out to be such a fucking failure, even though she was raised by greatness. Now I know why. DNA doesn't lie."

I reached down and smacked Autumn across the face, and she swung at me with her left hand. This bitch punched me hard as hell in my ear. I fell to the side and had to quickly roll away because she started kicking at me.

Once I got back up on my feet, I picked up my stun gun and walked back over to Autumn.

"Swing at me again, and I will break your fucking arm. You're a tough one. I will give you that. Your dumb ass is still talking shit and fighting with one hand."

I stomped on Autumn's left foot with the steel toe boots I wore, and she yelled out in pain. The sound of her voice made my heart rejoice. She needed to feel how I felt. How Peanut felt when she broke her heart.

"I'm still trying to figure out why your trifling ass is even here? Are you trying to avenge Peanut's death? Where were you when she still had breath in her body?"

Autumn tried to shake loose from the pipe. She even grabbed it with her free hand and tugged at it. This girl was crazy as hell.

"Don't question me you Jezebel. My relationship with my daughter is none of your goddamn business."

"Yes it is because I was there for her when you weren't. You can't even blame it on your drug addiction either. Your ass still never showed up once you got clean. You or her father. Both of y'all ain't shit, bitch."

I pulled out my rope and tied Autumn's free hand to the faucet, then I tied her legs together at the ankles. There was a wooden spoon set that sat on the counter in a cute, little container. I grabbed the longest one and slapped Autumn in the face with it.

"I want you to admit you are the reason my child is dead. She killed herself over your nasty, pussy licking, dick sucking, confused ass. All she wanted to do was love you, and once you found a nigga to take care of your broke ass, you no longer needed Peanut."

"What the fuck is wrong with you? You're just as delusional as she was. I never loved her like that, and you don't know a damn thing about my relationship with her or Knowledge. You must have read her journals and believed what she made up. They say the apple doesn't fall far from the tree."

Autumn had a lot of heart and talked too much shit.

"I believe my child, and you had something to do with her death. She wrote about all of y'all, but mainly you. You don't know what it feels like to lose a child, but today you're going to find out when I murder yours."

Autumn's eyes widened, and she appeared shocked for a moment, but quickly went back to being stoic.

"Nut tried to kill me! Did her *Moesha* ass write that down? And I don't know what you are talking about, but I don't have any children."

"Little girl, I know more than you think. Now admit you killed my daughter. I don't have time to play around with your rancid ass."

I stomped on Autumn's other foot and popped her in the lips with the wooden spoon. She didn't scream out loud this time. Instead, she clenched her teeth and a tear ran down her cheek.

"Fuck you and your daughter! Don't worry, you will be seeing her soon, so you can tell her what I said. You signed your death certificate the minute you crossed my doorstep."

I laughed in Autumn's face. Peanut said she was funny, and she didn't lie about that.

"Who do you think will kill me? Knowledge? He should be at the airport by now. I watched him and Kane as they left this morning from your sister's house. That's some messy ass shit too. You and Candy being sisters and cousins. Your momma was the original hoe."

"Don't you ever speak on my mother, or my sister, you human cesspool. Let me go so I can beat the shit out of you."

Autumn looked like a fish out of water the way she flopped around. She tried her hardest to get free, but couldn't. I laughed, grabbed a can of disinfectant spray that sat on the counter, and sprayed her in the face. She started coughing and shaking her head.

"Maybe that might cool you off some."

I took a deep breath and sat my stun gun on the counter. Autumn wasn't going to admit she caused Peanut's death no matter what I did. There was no need to prolong the situation.

"Your family will have a closed casket funeral for your ass too."

How the fuck did she know it was a closed casket if she wasn't there.

"I will be long gone before anyone comes to your rescue. I'm going to slowly zap every part of your body until you pass out. By the time Candy comes to check on you, your baby will be dead."

Autumn wore pajamas under her robe. I untied it and pulled up her shirt. It looked like she swallowed a basketball. Autumn was all baby.

"Awe look, I can see your pregnancy line. You are definitely far enough along where they will make you deliver the baby, so you can bury it."

Autumn started screaming so loud I thought she ruptured my eardrum. She wasted her time doing all of that. No one could hear her ass from inside this mini mansion. Shit, the walls might be soundproof. I leaned over toward her face.

"Shut the fuck up!"

Whack!

Chapter Thirty-Seven

AUTUMN

My mom struck Miss Danielle in the head with a bat and knocked her ass out. If she didn't come over when she did, my baby would have died. For all I knew, my child could be in distress right now. When she zapped me in my arm with that fucking stun gun, I felt an electrical shock throughout my body. I broke down and cried.

"Mommy, I prayed you would show up."

My mom untied my feet and my hand. She was visibly shaken.

"I came over to check on you, and when I opened the door I heard you screaming. You always keep a bat by the backdoor, so I grabbed it and raced toward your voice. When I saw what was going on, I lost it. I think she might be dead, Autumn."

My mom's voice cracked when she spoke. She grabbed a

hand towel and ran it under some water. She gently wiped the blood off of my face. My eyes still stung some from when Miss Danielle sprayed me in my face.

"If she's not dead, she will be. Can you get my phone by the front door? I need to call Knowledge. Hopefully he hasn't boarded the plane yet."

While my mom got my phone, I went through Miss Danielle's pockets with my free hand. I thought she might have the keys to the handcuffs on her person, but she didn't.

"I have your phone. It was next to this hard hat, which I'm guessing belongs to her. Who is this woman, Autumn?"

My mom handed me my phone and tossed the hat on the counter.

"She's the human portal in which Peanut entered into this world." I answered my mom as I called Knowledge.

They were still at the airport waiting to board the plane. Once I explained to him what happened, Knowledge had Kane call their car service to bring them back. He also said he would call the police and paramedics.

"What are we going to do with her body?" my mom questioned after I disconnected my call with Knowledge.

She thought she killed Peanut's mom, but she didn't. I felt her pulse before I checked her pockets, and that crazy bitch still had breath in her body, for now. Before I could answer my mom, my phone vibrated.

Candy: I'm at the door and it's locked. I don't have my key.

"Mom, can you please let Candy in. Kane must have called her."

When my mom left the room, I kicked Miss Danielle in the side of her head. She started to move a little bit, and I kicked her again.

"Oh, hell no!" Candy yelled when she saw me.

She immediately started stomping Peanut's mom in her face.

"Aaaaghhh," Miss Danielle hollered out in pain.

"Thank goodness she's not dead. I thought I killed her."

My mom placed her hands over her heart. She already had one body under her belt. I'm sure she didn't want another one.

After Candy finished getting her kicks in, she came over and sat next to me. She placed her hand on my belly, and we both cried. I haven't felt my baby move since Miss Danielle knocked on my door.

About ten minutes later the police were the first to arrive and uncuffed me. They placed Miss Danielle under arrest. Her face was leaking blood all over the floor.

"Cover her head with a trash bag. I don't want that bitch dripping her tainted blood inside or outside my house."

The police laughed at me and left with Miss Danielle. The way she looked, I was surprised they didn't call an ambulance for her. Usually they waited for the ambulance to arrive.

"Sis, throw those sneakers in the garbage and run and grab the pair I keep at the back door." Candy had Miss Danielle's blood all over her kicks.

I could hear the sirens from the paramedics, like they were

in my house. I was glad they were close by because I needed to get to the hospital right away. My nerves worsened with each second that passed by.

A few minutes later, the paramedics pulled up. My mom stayed behind to secure the house while Candy rode with me to the hospital. She held my hand the entire ride and prayed over me.

When we arrived at our local hospital, they sent me straight to the maternity floor. Once they got me into a room, Candy helped me change into a hospital gown. When I took off my panties, I noticed some blood drops.

"Candy, look! I'm bleeding!" I started to panic.

"Relax sissy, it's going to be alright. It's not a lot, just some spotting and sometimes that can happen. Especially after what you just experienced."

Candy had me take a few deep breaths and helped me onto the bed. One of the techs hooked me up to all the monitors. The doctor came right in and performed an ultrasound. I cried once I heard my baby's heartbeat.

It was crazy because I never wanted to be a mom. Now, there was nothing I desired more in this life than being this child's mother. This little person grew inside of me everyday. I looked forward to the flutters I felt when he or she moved around. If anything happened to my baby, I would lose my mind.

"Your baby is doing fine, and the heartbeat is strong. Would you like to know the gender?"

"No, we want it to be a surprise. I have a question, though. Is it normal to be spotting this far along in my pregnancy?"

"From the report they gave me, you just went through a traumatic experience. I'm sure it's the cause, but I will do an internal exam just to make sure nothing else is going on. I also contacted Dr. Jones, and she will be in to see you. You need to stay overnight, so we can monitor both of you. If there are no issues, you can go home in the morning."

The doctor performed the exam and everything appeared to be fine. My vitals were good, but my body was a little sore, especially my feet and nose.

"Thank you for being here, sis. I appreciate you more than you know." Candy just smiled.

"You know I always got your front and your back."

"Hello, I'm looking for my fiance. She was brought here by the paramedics. Her name is Autumn Johnson."

We heard Knowledge's voice out in the hall. Candy got up to go get them. As soon as they came into the room, Knowledge rushed over to my side and kissed me on my forehead.

"How are you? How is the baby?"

He started rubbing my stomach, and I became so overwhelmed with emotion. I couldn't even answer him. I'm worse than Candy with the crying shit.

"Autumn and the baby are fine. She just has to stay overnight, so they can keep an eye on her."

Candy filled them in on everything that occurred since we arrived.

"I hope this isn't the room they think we're staying in?"

"Oh, lawd! Babe, stop it. We don't need five star treatment everywhere we go."

Knowledge stared directly in my eyes.

"When it comes to you and our kids, it will always be the best or nothing at all. You both have been through a lot today. I can't take away the pain physically or mentally, but I can make sure you are comfortable as you heal. I'm about to go and see if the V.I.P. room is available. All floors have one. They just don't want you to know about them." Knowledge exited the room.

"Well, we are going to head home since you guys are good. I left the boys with my mom and Jade."

I rolled my eyes everytime Candy mentioned that girl's name.

"Why don't you like her, Autumn? She's been with us for almost two years now." Kane inquired. I guess Candy rubbed off on his ass.

"And I disliked her the entire time. Something about her aura disturbs my energy."

"Jade is very sweet and a great help." Candy added in her two cents.

"Is she sweet when she's riding Junior's dick in your house and cumming on your Egyptian 800 thread count sheets?"

Candy always wanted to find the good in people. The only way another woman could be around Knowledge and our kids everyday was if she had eight teeth, one good eye, four strands of hair, webbed feet, and skin that felt like fish scales.

I wasn't jealous or insecure, but I was a woman, and I know how we operate. Jade witnessed everyday how Kane catered to

Candy and their boys. She probably wanted to take her place, but set her sights on the next best thing, Junior.

Junior was Kane and Knowledge in the making. I'm sure Jade wanted the same treatment we received. When he brought her to the family dinner, I knew then she had his ass under her spell. He followed her around like a puppy. I just hoped Jade's intentions with Junior were genuine because if they weren't, she would regret the day she entered our lives.

"Everything is set. We're moving to the V.I.P. room."

Knowledge returned, and the sight of him made me smile.

"Autumn, we will pick up this conversation at a later date. Get some rest, sissy, we love y'all."

Kane and Candy said their goodbyes and went on their way. Knowledge sat down next to me, and all the emotions he tried to hide surfaced.

"When you told me the baby hadn't moved after she shocked you, I thought the worst."

Knowledge softly laid his head on my chest and rubbed the side of my belly. I massaged his head while he cried. I've never seen him like this, and it broke my heart. It took alot of restraint for him to hold all of this in until we were alone.

"We're good, babe."

"I'm never leaving y'all again. Junior will have to take on a bigger role and go with Kane when certain business deals require our presence. You need to rest tonight, but I want to know exactly what Peanut's mother said, word for word. I have to get to the bottom of this whole situation."

I knew the Alexander brothers already put things in motion

on their ride from the airport to the hospital. You couldn't threaten the lives of the people they loved and continue breathing. Knowledge wanted to know who helped her, and so did I.

* * *

"You did not need to take the wheelchair from the hospital. I can walk from the car to the house, Knowledge."

This crazy muthafucka stole the wheelchair from the hospital. Well, sort of. He paid the tech that wheeled me out a thousand dollars to put it in the back of his truck. I called the hospital on our way home to see how we could donate a new one to the maternity unit.

"You heard Dr. Jones. She wants you to take it easy and stay off your feet as much as possible. I already talked with your mom, and she's going to move into one of the guest rooms until the baby is born."

"My mom doesn't need to do all of that. You're doing too damn much."

"Either it's your mom or a full time nurse. Take your pick."

"My mom. You get on my nerves." I laughed.

Knowledge always went to the extreme with shit. Keelie's mutt face ass was right when she said Knowledge always took care of the women in his life. She almost lost an eyeball, but she was correct. Her ass probably had something to do with what happened to me.

"Do not bring this dirty ass wheelchair into the house. Put it in the storage shed in the back," I informed him.

Knowledge helped me up, and we entered our home. I cringed as I walked past the kitchen and thought about yesterday. It smelled like Pine-Sol and bleach. My mom must have done one of her old school, Saturday morning cleanings after the detectives left.

"I hired the chef we used at the dinner to work for us. She will be here every Sunday to meal prep lunch for the week and cook dinner. Two nights a week Latrice, that's her name, will cook whatever you want. I know your mom will do what she does, but I also want her to relax and be catered to as well."

Knowledge picked me up, like I was a baby, and carried me upstairs to our bedroom. Fresh flowers filled the room, and he used one of my favorite candies, Almond Joy, to make the shape of a heart in the middle of the bed.

"Awe, babe, you are too good to me."

I grabbed Knowledge's face and kissed his supple lips.

"Aight now, don't get me started. You know Dr. Jones said no sex for a week because of the spotting."

"She didn't say I couldn't please you."

He had a big ass grin on his face.

After Knowledge put me down, I smelled some of the flowers, grabbed a candy bar, and opened the balcony doors. It was a beautiful day to sit outside with my feet up. He took a seat in front of me, placed my feet in his lap, and started to massage them.

"I'm hungry, and my nose is still a little sore."

I still couldn't believe Miss Danielle held on to that clipboard with her man hands and smacked the shit out of me. As much as I fought in the past, I knew how to take a hit. If that was the first time, my ass would have been disoriented.

"Every time I think about how she violated you... Man, it doesn't even matter. She's already been handled. I—"

"What does that mean?" I cut Knowledge off.

"You know exactly what it means. Don't ask questions you already know the answer to."

"When the detective took my statement yesterday, they said she was being transported to the county later that—"

"I know exactly what she said. I told her to say it. She wasn't even a detective. I had to make it look real or your sleuthing ass would have figured something was up. If you knew about it last night, you would have never gone to sleep. You needed to rest."

My mouth hung open in disbelief. That explained why Knowledge had to leave in the middle of the night. He said he had some business to handle with Kane, but wouldn't leave until I fell asleep. When I woke up this morning he was lying right next to me, with his hand on my stomach.

"Were the officers who showed up and the paramedics real?"

Knowledge stopped massaging my feet and looked at me like I just asked a dumb question.

"Of course! Listen, the less you know the better."

As much as I wanted to continue to interrogate him, he was right. I just ate my almond joy and kept my thoughts to myself.

"The only thing left to do is to figure out who helped her. What exactly did she say to you?"

I told Knowledge everything Miss Danielle said, word for

word. He looked as if he was about to explode. My eyes filled with tears. It hurted my soul to have to repeat the shit, but he needed to know exactly what she said.

"Everything she knew about us was personal. It has to be someone we know that fed her the information. There is no way in hell she could have known Kane and I was going out of town all on her own."

"And she knew I was pregnant. We only told our immediate family and our circle is small as hell. Yes, two months have passed since we announced it, so other people could have found out by now, but no one around here knows her."

Knowledge shook his head and blew out his breath.

"She knows someone around here, and I'm going to find out who the fuck it is. And when I do, they won't be able to tell no one else a damn thing."

"Honestly, Keelie was the first person that came to my mind. I'm sure her ass isn't happy about us having a baby, and that bitch not only upgraded her car, but she has a brand new Birkin bag. You cut her off, so where did her broke ass get the money from to do all of that? Miss Danielle could have paid her." Knowledge's face looked blank. "I know she's Kyle's mother, but if she participated in this, I want her dead."

"It is what it is. If Keelie aided the monster that harmed you and tried to kill our child, she would meet the same fate as her."

"I'm glad we are on the same wavelength."

I leaned back in my chair and stared up at the beautiful view.

"Did Peanut have any siblings?" I frowned my face up at Knowledge.

"Not that I'm aware of. Why would you ask such a question?"

"Nothing, forget I even asked. I need to go pay Keelie a visit. Let's get some food in our system first. You think your mom feels like cooking? I'm going to have to do something really nice for her. I'm forever indebted to Momma Rose for coming to y'all rescue. I know she did some fucked up shit in the past, but she went into momma bear mode for you yesterday."

"Yeah, she did. I'm sure she won't mind feeding us. Facetime her and see what she says."

My mom had been great since the truth was revealed. Our relationship improved tremendously, and I'm sure she would be an awesome grandma. She was already off to a great start.

Chapter Thirty-Eight

KEELIE

"Hurry up, Kyle. We ain't got all day."

He walked slower than a tortoise on purpose.

"I hate going to grandma's house, it stinks just like her."

"Stop being rude and disrespectful before I pop you in your damn lips."

I didn't like visiting my mother any more than Kyle did, but I had no choice. As her only child, I needed to make sure she was alive and well. I visited her twice a week, and I called every Sunday to hear her voice. I unlocked the doors, and we got in the car.

"Buckle your seatbelt and keep your hands off the door."

I pulled off and headed to my mom's house. She only lived

ten minutes away in the senior housing projects, but the drive there felt much longer.

"Kyle, how do you feel about being a big brother?"

"I'm happy and mommy Autumn said I can help her when the baby comes."

I almost crashed my damn car when he uttered those words.

"Who the fuck told you to call her mommy Autumn?"

My face was beet red.

"Nobody. If the baby and I have the same dad, doesn't it make her my mommy too?"

"I'm your mommy, and Autumn will be that baby's mommy. Do you call her that when you're at your dad's house?"

I glanced at him through the rearview mirror, and he looked confused.

"No."

"Good, and don't ever let me hear you say it again. Now, if Autumn married your dad, then she would be your stepmom, but it will never happen."

We rode in silence the rest of the way. I pulled into the parking space assigned to my mom and killed the engine. She didn't have a car, so it was always available to me.

"When we get in there, you better speak and give her a hug. Don't touch shit and don't ask for a goddamn thing. Do you understand me?"

Kyle nodded his head yes. I grabbed him by the hand when we exited the car and started walking fast as hell. I basically dragged him. He pulled away from me.

"Owww, you're hurting my arm," Kyle yelled.

Everyone who was outside looked over at us. I swung him around to face me and leaned in close, so only he could hear me.

"Shut your ass the fuck up before I break your arm. If you scream out like that again, I'm going to whip your ass when we get home," I threatened Kyle.

His eyes swelled up with tears. He stood there looking just like Knowledge. It made me even madder.

"I want to go with my dad and Autumn," Kyle barked as he folded his arms and pouted his lips.

"The only place you're going is to bed when we get back to the house."

I took him by the hand, again, and walked up to my mom's door. I rang the bell and waited for her to answer. She opened the door and gave me a dirty look.

"Well, it's about time you showed the fuck up. I've been waiting for your monkey ass all morning."

"Hello to you too, mom."

I pushed Kyle into the house and closed the door behind us.

"Hey, grandma."

He greeted her like it pained him. We followed my mom into the living room. She sat back down in her recliner. Kyle walked over and hugged her. When he let her go, he placed his hand over his nose.

"Hey, boy. What's wrong with you?"

"Something smells bad."

I pinched Kyle on the side of his neck when he sat next to me on the loveseat.

"Ouch!" he yelled.

The apartment did have a funny smell to it because you really couldn't clean it well. My mom was a hoarder and had been her entire life. Her apartment was in the same condition as the one she raised me in. I never let any of my friends come over to my house because I used to be embarrassed.

My mom only threw stuff out when housing threatened to call code enforcement on her. She would get rid of enough items to where it was no longer a fire or safety issue. As soon as they deemed it liveable again, she started right back piling shit up.

It was crazy because almost everything she collected came from her neighbors. She dumpster dived everyday, and the community room attached to her building had a table of donated items. If you were a resident you could take the stuff for free. Her ass went there multiple times a day.

We had to throw stuff out the last time I was here. It was the only reason we were able to sit on the couch today.

"Take your ugly ass outside if you wanna yell," ordered my mom.

Kyle put his head in his lap.

"So, mom, how you been? Did you take a walk this morning?"

She cut her eyes at me.

"Don't nobody have time for no small talk. I need you to get your ass up and start on my head, so you can take that lil niglet of yours home. Leave him in the car the next time you come."

I wished I did leave Kyle in the car. He acted like a fool today. We both were sick of him. It was okay because as soon as I'm done here, he was going right to his dad like he requested. I needed a break.

Whenever I came to my mom's house, I always rolled up her hair for her. She washed it during her morning shower and blew it dry after she got out. I got up, gathered everything I needed, and started on her hair.

"You still didn't get back with his father?"

She said she didn't have time for small talk.

"No, but I'm trying. He just got me a new truck and an expensive pocketbook."

I parted her hair, greased the scalp, and used old school pink, sponge rollers in her head. Sometimes I forgot my mom was much older than she looked or acted. She had me late in life. I was twenty six to her seventy.

"Well, try harder. That bitch he's with now don't got shit on you. Plus you have his only child. Kyle's annoying as hell, but he's your golden ticket."

"Don't call Autumn bad names."

Kyle butted into our conversation.

"Boy, shut your trap. He hates when anyone talks bad about *his Autumn.*"

"He better learn to mind his business and stay outta adult conversations. I will call her anything I damn well please. I'm grown as hell, and this is my house."

"I won't have his only child anymore. She's pregnant."

My mom turned her head around to me so fast she

scared me.

"You stupid muthafucka! It's over now. Autumn won. That trick has the man, the house, and now the baby? Her pussy must be made out of kryptonite. He slid up in there, and she took all his power. She runs things, not him."

It was fucked up, but I became immuned to the horrible names my mom called me. She talked to me like this my entire life. Once I turned sixteen, I stopped reacting to her words.

"I'm not worried. I have a little kryptonite of my own. When I say jump, he says how high."

"You're crazier than I thought. Finish up my head, so you can be on your way."

My mom knew nothing about how to get or keep a man. My father was for the streets, and eventually it caught up to him. One of the many ladies he dealt with shot his ass dead one day, in broad daylight.

I was fifteen when this happened, and I could count on one hand how many times I saw him. At least Kyle's dad loved him, and he made sure to be a part of his life. Shit, Knowledge would keep him full-time if I allowed it.

"Alright, you are done. Kyle, let's go."

He didn't even say bye to my mom. He hauled ass out the front door. I followed right behind him.

Kyle took off running once we got outside, and I didn't know why until I saw Knowledge's car. He got out and Kyle jumped into his arms.

What the fuck did he want.

"How did you know I was here?" I questioned Knowledge.

"I tracked Kyle's phone. We need to talk and not in front of him."

"Daddy, my grandma was talking about you and Autumn."

I wanted to slap the shit out of Kyle.

"It's okay. Sometimes adults say things they shouldn't in front of kids. Your grandma is older, so she gets a pass."

Knowledge puts Kyle down.

"Mommy isn't old. She said stuff too. And she pulled my arm and pinched me."

I was going to fuck him up.

"Kyle, go get in my car. It's already unlocked. Put a movie on and relax."

Knowledge glared at me with nothing but pure hate in his eyes.

"I was about to drop him off to you anyway," I sassed.

"No, you weren't. You mean you were going to call me, and I would have met you somewhere in public to pick him up. Your ass tried to spit on Autumn and disrespected the fuck out of her. You will never step foot on our property again."

I've seen Knowledge angry before, but never like this. His eyes didn't even appear this wicked when he choked me out.

"I have a serious question to ask you and don't play no fucking games with me. Autumn was attacked in our home, and I want to know if you had anything to do with it." He peered at me.

"What? I know I wished death on her, but that was before the pregnancy. I'm a bitch, but I would never physically attack Autumn while she's pregnant."

Knowledge closed his eyes and leaned his head back. He took a deep breath and ran his hands down his face.

"My ear is to the streets, and I have feelers out. I'm going to find the person, or people, who helped the muthafucka who did this. If your name is in the mix, Kyle will be minus one parent."

Did this nigga just threaten my life?

I heard stuff here and there about how powerful Knowledge and Kane were, but figured it was just rumors. I've been around them for almost eight years and never seen anything of the sort to make me a believer until today.

"And that extortion bullshit stops right now. I rather tell Autumn what I did, and why I did it before I give you shit else. Don't text me unless it involves my son. Don't fucking call my phone unless he requires medical attention."

All I could do was stand there as Knowledge tore into me.

"If you see Autumn on the same block as you after she has our child, your ass better turn around and drive in the opposite direction. I kept her off you for the last two years, but that's over too."

Knowledge got in his car and pulled off. He never said when he was bringing Kyle back.

Chapter Thirty-Nine

KNOWLEDGE

I never wanted to question Kyle about his mother. It had always been my goal to never put my feelings about her on him. He already had to deal with being transported back and forth between two homes that operated on different sides of the spectrum.

After he told me his mother hurt him twice today. I have no choice but to find out if there was a pattern of abuse. Sometimes kids exaggerated situations or made them up. Keelie never confirmed or denied Kyle's accusations, so her silence about it was an admission of guilt to me.

She was his mother and had a right to discipline him. I didn't have a problem with that. I do have an issue, though, if she bullied him or reacted out of frustration. He said she pinched and pulled his arm. I wondered if this was a pattern of abuse.

Kyle didn't need to have his arm pulled out of socket or bruises from the pinch in order to prove to me she did it. Most abusers knew just how hard to hit you without leaving a mark.

Keelie could have verbally abused him as well. Her mouth was just like her mother's, toxic as hell. I'm sure she was only doing what was done to her.

"So, Kyle, I want you to know you are not in trouble. I'm glad you told me what happened today at your grandma's house. Now, I want you to be honest with me when I ask this question. Even if your mom said don't tell me, you can. Does your mom hit you all the time, or only when you are doing something you shouldn't?"

"Both. She said she doesn't like my face because I look like you and smacks me in it sometimes. Mommy was nicer to me when you lived in the other house."

My throat felt like it was on fire as I swallowed my tears. I continued to question Kyle the entire ride home. He responded in such a mature manner to only be seven, and it was a lot to digest. We pulled up to the house. I parked the car and killed the engine.

"Do you want to go back home with your mom tonight?"

I never planned on taking him back to Keelie's house after all the stuff he told me. I just wanted to hear his response.

"Noooooo! She's going to lock me in the bathroom and cut off the lights for telling on her and my grandma."

"Go ahead and start heading to the house. I'm right behind you."

Kyle exited the car, and I repeatedly punched my steering wheel. I was so hurt, I actually felt the pain in my heart. As far as I was concerned, Kyle never had to go home ever again.

I got out of the car and caught up to my son. He looked up at me. I picked him up and swung him around in the air. He laughed so hard it caused me to laugh. His smile and happiness meant the world to me.

When we entered the house, Kyle kicked his sneakers off and started hollering for Autumn. They had a special bond no one could ever come in between, not even me. She was downstairs in the reading room. It was her favorite space in the house.

I had a large, circle reading nook built into the wall that had a view into the backyard. She laid in there with her feet elevated. Kyle went over and laid next to her. She kissed him on the top of his head and rubbed his back.

"What is my favorite person in the world doing here?"

"My dad picked me up."

Kyle smiled and rubbed on Autumn's stomach. She wore a tank top and shorts, so her belly was visible.

"Well, I'm glad he did. I missed you. Tonight we can make salted caramel popcorn balls and watch a movie outside, but you have to make sure your room is clean before we do. It looks like a little crazy person sleeps in there."

"Yay! I'm about to go clean it now."

Kyle kissed Autumn on the cheek and ran off to his room.

"You make him so happy, thank you."

"No need to thank me. He makes me happy. Now, tell me what's going on. It's written all over your face"

It was my turn to lay next to Autumn.

"Keelie has been physically, verbally, and emotionally abusing Kyle. I'm trying to remain calm, but I feel like I'm about to explode. I blame myself. It's my job to protect him, and I didn't."

I watched as Autumn's entire expression changed. She put her hand over her heart and tears ran down her cheeks.

"You are not about to blame yourself for something you had no idea was going on. If that's the case, put the blame on me too because he's with me more than you when he's here, and I didn't see it. Keelie isn't a stranger from down the street. That's his mother. She's the last person you would think you needed to protect him from. This shit is crazy."

Autumn always knew how to reel me in. Even though everything she said was right, it didn't make me feel any better. I wouldn't be good until Kyle lived with us permanently.

"Do you know his grandma called him a niglet today? A fucking niglet."

I sat up and rested my elbows on my knees.

"I don't think he needs to be around any of them by himself," Autumn expressed.

"He's not going back. They would have to kill me before I let them destroy my son. On another note, I don't think Keelie had anything to do with what happened to you. Her ass is still on my radar, but it has to be someone who not only knows us intimately, but Miss Danielle as well."

As I talked to Autumn I thought back to when I hung up with her at the airport.

"Kane, call Candy and tell her what's going on. I'm about to hit up our contact at the police headquarters. I can't have just anyone show up to the house. She would legally be in their custody before I could get my hands on her."

I spoke to my man, and everything was set in motion. He would send out the paramedics and the officers that were under his control. They would drive Peanut's mom to the dropoff location that was previously established and wait with her until we got there.

Kane and I sent for our personal driver, and once he arrived, we headed straight to the hospital. Later on that night when Autumn finally fell into a deep sleep, Kane came back and picked me up. Once I was in the car, we left to handle the person that was crazy enough to fuck with our family.

Thirty minutes later we arrived at the warehouse. Kane pulled in around the back. We jumped out and walked up to the officers. I gave them an envelope of cash for their troubles, and they removed Miss Danielle from the back of their car.

"You can leave the handcuffs on her," I instructed the officers.

They pushed her toward us, got in their car, and left.

"I don't know what went through your raggedy ass mind when you were plotting and scheming, but you didn't think it through all the way. And I know you had help, and when I find out who, they're going to die too."

Miss Danielle laughed in my face. She knew she wasn't making it out alive, so I didn't expect anything less from her. We *threw her ass in the back of Kane's trunk, got into the car, and headed to her final resting place.*

The warehouse we just left was for pick-up and drop-off only, nothing else. Kane and I were the only ones who knew where the bodies rested. We drove Miss Danielle to the same abandoned building where we buried the bastard that murdered our parents.

This was Kane's first property he ever purchased, and it would forever remain in the family. We made a few improvements to it over the years, but it still required a lot more work.

Kane drove around the side of the building to the loading dock. Once he stopped, I jumped out. I unlocked and opened one of the bay doors, then he drove all the way inside. I closed it and walked up to the parked car.

He popped the trunk, and I snatched Miss Danielle out by her hair. We laid out some plastic on the floor, and I threw her ass on it. Kane loaded up the cordless nail gun and passed it to me.

"Now, I'm going to ask you nicely. Who helped you?"

"Ya daddy!" she fired back.

"Wrong answer."

I shot a nail into her thigh. She screamed out in pain, but no one could hear her.

"I'm going to ask you again. Who fed you information about me and my family?"

Miss Danielle looked me in the eyes.

"I don't give a fuck how many times you ask me, my answer will not change. As a mother, I did what I had to do for my kids, the same way you are doing what you have to do for yours. My

only regret is I didn't get to kill one of yours, like Autumn killed one of mine."

As soon as the last word she spoke left her lips, I unloaded the nail gun into her entire face. I tossed it onto the plastic, and Kane and I wrapped her body up. He grabbed a few rolls of duct tape, and we had her ass looking like a mummy within ten minutes.

We dug another six foot grave in the picnic area in the back. After we dropped her body in, Kane and I poured lime over it and filled the hole back up with the dirt. It was nice and leveled. I tossed the grass seeds all over it, and we were done.

Soon enough this patch would blend in with the rest of the area, just like Timothy's grave did. I hoped they both continued to rest in pain.

"Babe, do you hear me talking to you?"

Autumn nudged my arm and snapped me out of my thoughts.

"I apologize. What did you say?"

"I said Peanut had no family up here at all besides her dead auntie, and she never had any kids of her own. Nut's parents lived in Virginia, and she never spoke of any other family."

"There's always a trail of breadcrumbs left to follow. I won't rest until I have all the answers. I did have the van she parked down the street picked up by this guy who owns a chop shop. He said there wasn't shit in there. Hopefully we get a hit off the plates."

"She had to be staying somewhere around here. I know she didn't drive up from Virginia the same day. And where is her phone? I checked her pockets and didn't find one. Whoever helped Miss Danielle had to keep in contact with her."

Autumn got up on her knees and rested her chin on my shoulder. Whenever she did that, she wanted something.

"Not to change the subject, but I think we should get married sooner than later. I know I decided to go with a big wedding, and Candy and I have been planning everything for the last two months, but I changed my mind, again."

"Are you serious right now?"

"With everything that happened to me, and now Kyle, we could use some cheer around here. Plus, I don't want a big wedding anymore because I don't know who to trust. We need a mental break from all this right now."

Autumn made a valid point with the trust thing. I looked at everyone differently now.

"Whatever you want to do, I'm down with it. I just have to make sure the rings you picked out can be done ahead of time. I'm sure for a few extra bands he will get the job done."

"Great, so we can get married in two weeks in the backyard. There's plenty of space back there. I will handle everything. All you have to do is show up. I'm about to go tell Kyle and call Candy."

Autumn talked so fast it made me dizzy. Damn, two weeks. I thought she meant like in a month or two.

She grabbed her phone, got up, kissed me, and left out. It felt good to see that bright smile across her face again; even if it was temporary. I pulled out my phone to call Kane.

"Hey, bruh, you know the surprise you are working on for Autumn? I'm going to need you to make that happen ASAP! We're getting married in two weeks."

Chapter Forty

KEELIE

Knowledge took Kyle to his house a week ago and refused to bring him back. This black bastard called me up and said Kyle was staying with him permanently. He actually told me that the only way I could see my son was during supervised visits.

When I asked him why the visits had to be supervised, he said Kyle would never be alone with me, or my mom, until he could physically defend himself against us. He made it seem like we were animals and attacked Kyle like a pack of wild hyenas.

Knowledge told me if I called the police, or involved the courts, he would put me back into the pussy I slid out of, bury us both in his backyard, and build a playground on top of our graves for the kids to play on.

In all honesty, I'm glad to be child free. I could go about my life as I pleased and didn't have to worry about Kyle's cry baby ass always complaining. He was where he wanted to be anyway.

Like my mom said, Autumn won. When I told her what was going on, she suggested I let it go and see my son on Knowledge's terms. I was fine with everything until I stopped by Knowledge's jeweler's store a few days ago and overheard his conversation with him.

Since Kyle ran his mouth and told our business to his dad, I decided to trade his jewelry in and get something nice for myself. Knowledge purchased our son so much jewelry over the years, but on his birthdays, Kyle got big items. He gave him a diamond necklace for his fifth birthday, and a diamond encrusted Rolex when he turned seven.

It just so happened that while I was in the store picking out my diamond tennis bracelet, he called Knowledge. I couldn't hear Knowledge, but the jeweler mentioned his name and told him Autumn's rings were ready. He said that an armed guard would drop them off that night.

I almost passed out at the counter. Autumn must have finally accepted his proposal. I was hurt all over again. My heart had been crushed into a thousand pieces once more.

When they hung up, I asked him if he was going to the wedding too. My ass tried to play it off like I was invited. He said no, he had a prior engagement next weekend.

After I left the jewelers that day, I drove over to my mom's house to give her the earrings I got her. She treated me like shit, but she was still my mom, and I loved her. No matter what, my mom always had my back.

"Why do you look like you've been crying? Goddamn, you're worse than Kyle's eggheaded ass."

I handed her the box with the earrings in it and wiped my eyes.

"What the fuck is this? You don't ever bring me shit."

She opened up the box and twisted her face up at me.

"Why did you get me these? I hope you didn't steal them."

"I don't steal. It's just a little something to say thank you. You never turned your back on me."

My mom had always been hood and was never going to change. Even though her words were abrasive, she had always been by my side through it all. I'd never forget the time these girls followed me home and tried to jump me.

My mom came outside with a spray bottle of bleach and a sock full of nickels. She told me and the girl I had the problem with to fight one on one. If any of her friends tried to jump in it, she would spray the bottle and swing the sock at them.

"And I never will. I might talk my shit, but I will always ride for mine."

She gave me a hug, and I leaned up against the side of the couch. It was back to being cluttered, so I couldn't sit down. My mom plopped down into her recliner.

"Knowledge and Autumn are getting married next weekend."

I broke down and cried like a newborn baby. Snot escaped my nose and dripped down the top of my lip. As much as I tried to act like I didn't care, I did.

"Shut the fuck up and pull yourself together. If you don't, I will take this fly swatter and slap you so hard, you will leave here with little squares all over your face," my mom threatened. "Crying over a man that's not yours is foolish. You had your chance and blew it. You and your rotten ass pussy."

The shit that came out of her mouth was wild.

"What you need to do is learn to recognize when a great opportunity presents itself. I'm sure that boy of yours will be in the wedding. The last person Autumn wants to see when she walks down the aisle is you. Tell Knowledge you want to see your son participate in the wedding and let it count as a supervised visit. It will ruin her whole day."

"He told me I was banned from their property. That's not going to work."

My mother scratched her forehead then snatched off her wig and threw it at me. I caught it and sat it with the rest of the junk on the couch. She looked like Patrick Star from Spongebob without her hat hair.

"You the type of muthafucka that would fuck up a wet dream. Ask him anyway. All he can say is no. You said you had some kryptonite of your own. Well, now is the time to use it. I swear, I think they gave me the wrong baby at the hospital."

Beep! Beep!

The people behind me beeped, and it snapped me out of my thoughts. I was in the fast food drive-thru line and held everyone up as I reflected on the conversation I had with my mom. After I got my food, I parked in one of the spaces to eat.

Knowledge said he would rather tell Autumn. He didn't say he would tell her, so maybe I did have a way in. I took pictures of my neck after he left the day he choked me. The marks were superficial, and I knew a few hours later they would lighten up, so I put makeup on them. The way they showed up on camera was scary. You would have thought I was lying dead in a morgue.

I decided to text Knowledge and take back some control.

Me: I know about the wedding and I would like to come see Kyle in it

Knowledge: You funny as hell... get off my line

Me: I just sent you some pics and they have the date and time stamp on them

Knowledge: WTF

Me: I guess you saw them. I'm going to send them to Autumn next unless you let me come

Knowledge: I will send you the info the night before... oh yeah, fuck you

Chapter Forty-One

CANDY

"Sissy, you look so beautiful. I really can't believe you are getting married today."

"I can't believe it either. I tried to avoid getting married and being pregnant like the plague. Now, they're both happening at the same time."

Autumn looked absolutely stunning. She was the most beautiful bride I had ever seen. Her dress was from a local black-owned boutique. It was coral colored, strapless, and fitted her body like a glove. It stopped right above the knee. The perfect dress for Autumn and her baby bump.

She didn't want to go the traditional route with the white dress and veil. Autumn was very chill and carefree. Even though she always wanted to look good, today she desired simplicity. They even chose to get married barefoot.

This was a union no one thought would ever happen, especially Knowledge, and they wanted to enter into it grounded. They needed to feel the earth and the energy of the sun beneath their feet before they walked down the aisle, and that day had arrived.

I didn't know how we pulled this off in two weeks, but we did. Knowledge gave me his American Express black card and told me to spare no expense. Autumn told me what she wanted, and I did my best to make it happen.

The event planner I hired transformed their backyard into a wedding venue that took your breath away. They built an entire hardwood dance floor and enclosed it inside of a tent that looked more like a real structure. When you entered it, you didn't even know you were outside.

Since this was going to be a small, intimate ceremony. We didn't have a wedding party. Therefore, we didn't have a flower girl. I had them make a runner out of fresh flowers for Autumn to walk down the aisle on instead. It was made out of Calla Lily Bulbs. I knew my aunt and Autumn would like that.

Chairs were set up on each side of the aisle. They were covered in white chair covers with a champagne colored satin bow tied on them. After the ceremony they would be removed to set up for the reception. The entire ceiling of the tent was adorned with strings of lights that contained soft, coral colored bulbs.

I had a fresh flower wall built out of cream roses to serve as the background for where Autumn and Knowledge would stand for their nuptials. Kane knew someone who performed non-denominational weddings, and he agreed to marry them after we obtained the marriage license.

Autumn and I only invited three of our closest friends from our old hood to the wedding. We knew they had nothing to do with Miss Danielle demonized ass. Knowledge and Kane didn't invite anyone. But a few of the guys from the security detail Knowledge put on Autumn after the incident were in attendance.

All the other guests were everyone who attended the announcement dinner, but this time Kyle and my auntie Bird would be here. Autumn promised to be nice to Jade, and I made sure she had a seat next to Junior.

After my conversation with Autumn at the hospital about them, I did tell Junior he couldn't fuck in our house. He made enough money, and so did Jade, for them to go to a hotel if they wanted to get their freak on.

We did have an uninvited guest coming who weaseled her way in. She would be seated in the back by herself. Security has already been warned about her ass. If Keelie moved up out of her seat or opened her fly trap of a mouth during the ceremony, they were to physically restrain her after we got Kyle out of there. She was made aware of what measures were in place for her and agreed.

"Are you sure you're good with Keelie being here? You are a better woman than me," I asked Autumn.

"I only allowed it because of Kyle. Even though he doesn't want to live with her ever again, he still loves her. He said he likes it when he gets to see his mom."

You couldn't pick your parents and had to play with the hand you were dealt. Autumn's mom, my auntie Lily, had our dad killed. If we could forgive that, then eventually Keelie, Autumn, and Knowledge could make things work for them. Kyle was still a child right now and needed to be protected.

"When Knowledge asked me I couldn't say no. I'm going to be a mother soon, and I know I don't want to miss out on anything my child does, and she shouldn't either. Some memories you can't recreate. According to Knowledge and Kyle, Keelie's mother is horrible. Maybe that's why she's the way she is. Unfortunately, Keelie is part of this package deal right now."

"And you said you weren't mother material. You're already thinking and acting like a mom. You put your personal feelings to the side in order to make sure Kyle's happiness came first. You've always been a mom in your own right. You're just making it official with your own baby."

The ceremony started in less than an hour, and Autumn was ready. I just needed to make sure the guys were good, and that the event planner had everything under control. I headed into the guestroom Knowledge used to get ready.

Knock! Knock!

"Can I come in? Is everyone decent?" I asked as I cracked open the door.

"Yeah, come in, my soon to be sis-in-law," Knowledge answered. I pushed the door all the way open and entered the lion's lair.

"You look so handsome!"

Knowledge had on a cream linen suit with a coral colored

shirt underneath. He had a fresh line up and smelled like a million bucks.

"I'm not going to get emotional, but I want to thank you for loving my sister the way you do. That's it. No long, drawn out speech or tears. Just a simple thank you, and I love you."

"You're welcome, and there's no need to thank me. It's easy to love your sister. We are two of the same. She's my everything. And thank you for giving my brother a family of his own. Y'all boys are the best thing to ever happen to him besides you."

Knowledge and I embraced, then I left, so he could finish writing his vows. I was headed downstairs when I saw Kane standing in the doorway of the upstairs lounge area. He was clearly talking to someone but abruptly closed the door when he noticed me.

"Who were you talking to?"

"I can't tell you. It's a surprise and don't ask me any more questions with your fine self."

Kane grabbed me and started kissing on my neck. He tried to distract me, but it didn't work.

"We can save all of that for tonight. I want to know who is in the room."

"Candy, go be the wedding planner, and let me handle the surprise."

He was right. I had shit to do and headed downstairs. Once I made my way outside, I saw that all the guests had arrived. They were already seated and everyone looked beautiful. The event planner had everything under control.

It had been so long since I got to hang out with my friends

and looked forward to chilling with them today. Once I had the boys I rarely went on social media, and I never posted. My only communication with them was via text, here and there. I was only around my immediate family after everything that happened with Rah and Peanut.

Like funerals, weddings brought everyone together, so here we were. After I hugged and kissed everyone, I left to make sure Autumn had finished writing her vows. Time was flying by, and we had to start soon.

"Candy, let me talk to you for a minute."

One of my friends, Kisha, stopped me before I got to the house.

"Hey, is something wrong?"

I was confused as to why she chased me down. Whatever she had to say could have waited until later.

"I'm just shocked you guys would accept Peanut's sister Jade into your family after everything that happened, and I don't want to sit by her because I'm ready to fight. I know y'all moved out the hood and shit, but bitch, did you leave your mind there when you left?"

My mouth wouldn't even form the words to answer her back. I tried to take a deep breath to gain my composure, but it wasn't working.

"Oh, shit, you didn't even know. We're whipping her ass for real now."

Kisha could tell by my reaction, I had no idea I brought the enemy into my home, around my husband and kids. I not only brought her into my home but into all of our lives. Autumn kept saying she didn't like her, and I didn't listen. She had me playing the role of a fool for two years.

"How do you know she's her sister?"

I was finally able to speak. My hands felt warm and clammy, and I still felt weak.

"I'm originally from Virgina. I have family who still live out there. When Peanut offed herself, her mom placed the obituary in the local newspaper in Virginia instead of the paper up here. I guess she did that because they have no family in Jersey."

I stared at Kisha like she spoke a foreign language.

"One of my uncles sent me a screenshot, and asked me if I knew her because it mentioned Long Branch. When I read it, it said she was survived by her sister Jade Dotson of Virginia. I never said anything to y'all because Peanut's ass was dead, and I told my uncle fuck her and her family."

"I'm still confused. How did you know it was her today?"

"We sat down and said hello. You know how we are, we keep it short and cute. I guess Junior wanted to show off his lil boo thang to us and gave her whole government when he introduced her. A light bulb went off in my head because her name is ugly ass fuck when you say it altogether, just like her, so it was hard to forget."

Kisha took so long to spit it out, making me get upset. I could see she was higher than five kites on a windy day.

"Bitch, you been smoking?

"Of course... anyway! I searched her ass on instagram and facebook just now, and her pic came up. It's her, so what are we going to do? I see y'all have the SWAT team out here. Let them take her out, and say she tried to kill Autumn. The other two tried and failed, maybe she thought the third time was the charm."

"I have to go. Don't say anything to anyone, and please don't touch her. I have to get Autumn down the aisle before we take out the trash."

Chapter Forty-Two

AUTUMN

I didn't know why it took Candy so long to come back, but I was about to head downstairs. The wedding was set to start in five minutes. As soon as I grabbed my phone and headed toward the door, Candy came busting in.

"Why the fuck do you look like a vampire drained all the blood out of your body?"

"I'm not feeling well. I think it's something I ate."

"Damn, I hope it wasn't from the catered food. If so, throw that shit out."

Candy looked like she fell head first into a used porta potty. Something was definitely up with her, but I didn't have time to figure it out right now.

"Sissy, let's go." Candy grabbed my hand.

We walked out of the room and ran straight into Kane.

"Whatever surprise you have for Autumn, don't do it. We have bigger fish to fry, and I can't explain it right now. Just trust me and keep whoever is in that room there until after the wedding."

We made our way downstairs, and she looked more nervous than me.

"Kane, please make sure Autumn gets down the aisle. Don't wait for me. I need to use the bathroom. I'm not feeling well, and I don't want to hold everyone up. My mom has the boys."

Candy rushed back into the house.

"Something is going on with Candy. I don't care what she said. As soon as I get you down that aisle, I'm going to check on her." Kane looked concerned.

"It damn sure is. She better not be pregnant because I'm going to kick her ass if she is. I need her to help me with my baby."

The music started, and I walked down the aisle to the man who waited patiently for me. He looked so fine standing there like the king he was. It felt like it took me forever to get to him.

Once I did, Knowledge took my hands into his, and we faced each other. The officiant began to speak, and a calmness came over the room. When we got to the part where we had to exchange vowels, Knowledge went first.

"You are the most beautiful woman in the world, and I'm honored to stand before you, our friends, and family to profess my love. You complete me in each and every way. The road we traveled to get here wasn't an easy one. There were many twists and turns we had to take. Detours and roadblocks designed to alter our course tried to stop us but couldn't."

My eyes began to burn, and I rubbed his hands while I listened to him speak.

"We made it, and there is no other woman I desire more than you. There is no other woman I love more than you. Thank you for loving me, protecting me, honoring me, and giving me the greatest gift in the world, another child."

Knowledge's words made my heart skip a beat, and I fell in love with him all over again at that very moment. Now it was my turn to say my vows.

"Well, let me first start by saying, you couldn't have chosen a better person to stand beside you than your son Kyle. He is very much a big part of this union as we are, and I love him with all of my heart. Now on to you, the head of our home, and the master of my heart. You make me want to do and be better. The chemistry we share is beyond measure."

I started to get a little choked up and took a slight pause, so I could hold back the tears.

"You saved me from myself. You showed me what unconditional love looks and feels like. You are not just my lover and friend, you are my peace. With you I know I am safe and cared for. We are bringing forth a new life, and there is no other person I would rather do it with than you. Thank you for putting us before yourself. Thank you for being you."

After the vows we exchanged rings and before the officiant could pronounce us husband and wife, everyone's phones started going off, then my friends started cussing up a storm.

I looked around and everyone had shocked expressions on their faces. When I looked over at my mom, she shook her head. I walked over and took my phone she was holding from her. A video had been air dropped to everyone. When I opened it up, I saw Keelie and Knowledge at her house. She walked over and answered the front door with nothing on but an opened silk robe.

The video had no sound, so you had to read her lips. Keelie clearly said hey babe when she greeted him. Knowledge entered her home. She walked ahead of him then turned around and told him to follow her to the bedroom. His dumb ass followed right behind her, and they disappeared.

I glared at him, and Knowledge couldn't even look at me. If that wasn't enough, this trick ass bitch stood up and said she was pregnant by Knowledge. Security was ready to take her down, but I stopped them.

"That's right. You're not the only flower bed he planted seeds in."

She lifted up her shirt and actually had a little belly.

"We've been fucking around for a minute. That video was just one of many."

Before I could react to Keelie, the paramedics pulled up. Kane came running out of the house with Candy passed out in his arms and Uncle Pete hot on his trail.

So many things were happening at the same time, it made my head spin. All I wanted to do was disappear.

"Where the fuck did uncle Pete come from, and how did he

get out of jail?" my mother spewed. She was already out of her seat and looked pissed.

"Don't nobody give a damn about him right now, mom. My only concern is my sister. Can you get Kyle and take him in the house? Thank you."

My mom always worried about the wrong shit sometimes. Her niece was being put in an ambulance. That trumped everything going on right now.

"Oh no, Candy!" screamed my auntie Lily as she held onto the twins. They started to cry.

"Auntie, go with my mom. The boys don't need to see all of this. I will call y'all from the hospital when I know what's going on."

Before they could take Candy away, I rushed over to the ambulance. She was on the stretcher, and I could see a little knot on the side of her head.

"Kane, what the hell? One minute she doesn't feel good, the next minute she's laid the fuck out. It doesn't make sense."

"I know. Something is definitely going on, and I will explain what I think it is later. Uncle Pete, you can ride with us."

"Alright, I'm right behind y'all," I told Kane.

They climbed into the ambulance, closed the doors, and drove off. My nerves were shot to hell. I rubbed my belly because my baby was kicking like crazy.

"Are you alright, Autumn? Is something going on with the baby?" Knowledge questioned me with a concerned look on his face. I didn't even realize he followed behind me.

"Muthafucka, if you don't get away from me. Go check on

your stank ass baby mother and her new child that's on the way. You don't need to concern yourself with me and mine."

Knowledge's eyes filled with tears, which was something that didn't happen too often. I could see the hurt and pain written all over his face. Now he knew exactly how I felt a few minutes ago when Keelie's vengeful ass ruined my day; and my life.

"You know her fucking baby is not mine. I meant what I said when I told you I didn't fuck with her. She's lying and wants to destroy us."

All I could do was laugh to keep from crying.

"The video isn't a lie. Something happened. I gave you the opportunity to come clean, and you didn't. So, if anyone wants to destroy us, it's you. My sister is on her way to the hospital, and I need to be there when she wakes up. If she wakes up. I'm not doing this with you right now."

I went to walk away from Knowledge and heard a bunch of commotion coming from the backyard. When I made my way back there, Kisha had Keelie's ass hemmed up. Junior and Jade were making their way toward me.

"We're going to head over to the hospital. Do you want to ride with us?" Junior asked as Jade smiled at me. This bitch knew I didn't mess with her.

"Fuck no! You know I don't like this trick."

I wasn't in the mood today to bite my tongue. Junior's expression showed he wanted to cuss me out, but he knew better. Even though Knowledge was on my shit list, he would protect me against anyone, including him.

"Y'all better get this hood booger away from me before I have her ghetto ass arrested!" Keelie barked.

I hurried over to them because I could tell things were about to go left. Kisha was with the shits, just like me. She would fight at the drop of a dime.

"Bitch, I've been to jail before, and I don't mind going back over my friends who I consider family. You brought your trifling ass to this wedding just to fuck shit up, and now, I'm about to kick that baby out yo ass."

Kisha cocked her hand back, and I grabbed her by the arm before she could swing on Keelie. If anyone was going to whip her ass it would be me.

"She's not worth it. I'm going to get her ass in due time." I pulled Kisha back.

"There's no need to wait. She's here right now. Look at her grinning and shit. She thinks it's funny." Kisha was thirty-eight hot.

"Look at the angry birds. Y'all big mad. Well, my job here is done. Fuck all—"

POW! POW!

Before Keelie could finish her sentence, I hit her with an overhand right punch then followed it up with a left hook. She fell backwards, onto the cake that sat on the table she stood in front of.

"Autumn! You can't be out here fighting while you're pregnant."

Knowledge grabbed me from behind, which prevented me

from jumping on top of her. I wasn't even going to hit her, but she kept on with the disrespect.

"Yeah, friend! That's what I'm talking about, two-hitter quitter."

Kisha laughed and clapped her hands as she celebrated me putting Keelie on her ass.

Keelie pushed herself up, and blood trickled down the side of her mouth from her busted lip. She pulled some of the cake out of her hair and threw it on the ground.

"I didn't even get your ass like I wanted to. That's just a preview of what's to come. Talking about you throw hands too, but your scared ass threatened to call the fucking police when Kisha was about to put you down. We don't do that where we come from."

"You got that off, Autumn. You're still not married, though."

I tried to break free from Knowledge, but he wasn't having that.

"Keylolo, you're just jealous of my friend because she put that good wap on your son's father, and he didn't want your stale, day-old bread ass pussy anymore. That shit is past its sell-by date, hoe." Kisha kept talking shit to Keelie.

"Who the fuck is Keylolo?" Keelie questioned.

"You, bitch! Don't act like you don't watch *Martin*. Now, get to stepping."

"Escort her off our property. She's no longer welcomed here. If she steps back on it, shoot her ass," Knowledge instructed security. Keelie's eyes got big as hell when he said that.

"Oh, you want them to kill me and our child? I'm telling everything now! Autumn, how does my pussy and ass taste? He licks me from top to bottom every single time, then comes home and kisses you in the mouth. I know you smelled my perfume on him from our last love session." Keelie laughed.

Security snatched her up, but it didn't stop her from running off at the mouth.

"Thank you for my new car, the Birkin bag, and the cash you put in it, babe. I guess I'm lying about that too. Autumn can call the dealership and your personal shopper if she thinks I am. I'll be at the house waiting for you to come over."

Knowledge released me from his grasp, and as soon as he did, I turned around and slapped fire out of his ass. Spit flew out his mouth and everything. He rubbed his jaw and took a deep breath.

"I deserve that and more. Even though she made most of that shit up just now, I should have never put you in this position. I'm sorry, just let me explain everything to—"

"It's a little too late for that right now, Knowledge," my auntie Bird cut him off. She stepped in between us and looked me in my eyes. "You have to calm down before you send yourself into early labor. Go check on Candy. I will stay out here until the event planner, and everyone else, packs up and leaves. Then I will help my sisters with the boys."

My lips began to tremble as tears glossed over my eyes. I

refused to let them fall. I wanted to scream from the top of my lungs, but I knew I had to hold it together for now.

"You're right, auntie. I'm just embarrassed you had to witness all of this craziness."

She wrapped her arms around me and kissed the side of my face.

"Please, let me drive you to the hospital."

I stuck my middle finger up at Knowledge while holding on to my auntie. He knew damn well I wasn't riding with his ass.

"Kisha, I'm going to ride with you guys as soon as I put something on my feet."

I had Candy put a pair of flip flops for myself, and some comfortable loafers for Knowledge, in a basket under our table for when the wedding was over. Knowledge went over and got the basket when he heard me mention I needed something for my feet.

After I put the flip flops on, we all walked to the front of the house where the cars were parked. Kisha unlocked her doors and opened her mouth.

"Don't be talking shit about my car, Autumn. It's not as fancy as yours, but it takes me where I need to go."

Kisha knew me better than that. I didn't even have a car until Knowledge bought me one, so I would never judge anyone. With that being said, I didn't think it was safe for me to ride with them.

"Bitch, how do you have four donuts on your car? Usually people have one, but you managed to defy all odds. What happened to all your tires? This muthafucka looks like a clown car. I don't even think you should be driving it, for real, for real."

Kisha put her hands on her hips and blew her breath at me.

"Fuck you, Autumn. Jerome and I got into a fight, and his bitch ass stabbed all my tires. I'm in between jobs and couldn't afford to buy new ones. I had one donut already, then I took the one from my momma's car, her boyfriend's car, and my cousin's car. A bitch had to get creative."

"Ladies, I will drive everyone. Autumn, get in the truck and don't argue with me about it."

Knowledge caught me off guard with his aggressiveness. As much as I didn't want to, I got my ass in the truck. My pussy had to be reminded we were on bad terms with him right now. She loved when he took charge and tried to respond to his tenacity. Not this time, though. There was no way I would give in as easily as I did when he came home smelling like Keelie.

Once everyone was inside, Knowledge started the truck and pulled off. I glanced over at him from the corner of my eye. In my heart I knew he didn't sleep with Keelie, but something definitely went down. He didn't give her everything she named for nothing.

Knowledge was buying her silence. For what I didn't know, but I was going to find out. Keelie thought she got the last laugh with her little performance today. Little did she know, the only thing she did was confirm what I already knew. This world wasn't big enough for the both of us to coexist. One of us had to go, and it wasn't going to be me.

Chapter Forty-Three

KNOWLEDGE

I felt like shit. Hindsight was twenty twenty, and allowing Keelie to come to the wedding ended up being the wrong move. She had my back against the wall, but if I would have just listened to Kane when he told me to tell Autumn everything from the beginning, my stupid ass wouldn't be in this predicament right now.

Autumn never treated me like the opp, and honestly, it had me fucked up right now. She had been pissed at me before. That was just normal relationship shit, but this right here was different. It felt different. I could see Autumn looking at me out of the corner of her eye. If only she could hear my thoughts and read my heart, she would know I was truly remorseful for the part I played in hurting her.

We finally pulled up to the emergency room, and I valet

parked the truck. I went around to help Autumn out of her seat, but she ignored my extended hand. Autumn proceeded into the hospital, with her friends right behind her, once they all got out. I gave the attendant some cash for his troubles and went in after them.

Kane, Uncle Pete, Junior and Jade were all sitting in the waiting area. My brother looked like he had been run over by a Mack truck. From his expression I could tell something was not right. He got up and came over to us.

"How's Candy? Why are you sitting out here and not in the room with her?" Autumn immediately questioned Kane before he could even say one word.

Kisha went and sat next to Junior, and the other two ladies sat down by uncle Pete.

"Your sister is going to be fine. She gained consciousness in the ambulance before we even got to the end of the block. They're running every test to make sure there are no underlying issues and examining the bump on her head. When I came to check on Uncle Pete, Junior and Jade were out here. Then you guys just walked in, so now I can go back in there with Candy."

"Why does she have a speed knot on her head, like someone popped her ass?"

Autumn continued to interrogate Kane.

He placed his hand on her back and ushered her toward the corner of the room, away from everyone else. I followed right behind both of them.

"She hit her head when she fainted. There was an empty glass and an open bottle of Ciroc on the counter. Obviously something heavy was weighing on her mind. Candy would never take shots straight up like that, especially in the middle of your wedding. Uncle Pete said—"

Autumn didn't even let Kane finish his sentence before she cut him off.

"Uncle Pete said what? I don't even know what type of voodoo you did to get his ass out, but I know it was your doing. If that crazy muthafucka did something to my sister, his ass is grass."

"Relax, Uncle Pete has nothing to do with why she passed out. He came downstairs to watch the wedding from the window, since he couldn't walk you down the aisle. That was my surprise for you." Autumn was clearly taken back by what Kane just said.

"Why would I want the person who killed my father to take his place in walking me down the aisle? Are you smoking on something else besides that loud, my nigga?"

"He did not kill your father, which is why I was able to get him out. When you two decided to rush the wedding, it fucked up my original plans. I wanted him home a month before y'all got married, so you guys could get to know each other and hear his side of the story."

Autumn took a deep breath and rested her back against the wall we were standing by. She bent over, placed her hands on her knees, then looked up at Kane. I tried to rub her back because she appeared to be in distress, but she swatted my hand away.

"Who killed my father?"

"I don't know. That's a question for your mother at a later time. Right now, we need to figure out who the fuck Jade is."

"What the hell are you talking about?" I finally let my voice be heard.

Kane made absolutely no sense right now. Autumn started shaking her head. She was already on one from the wedding. I hope this didn't push her over the edge.

"Uncle Pete said Candy didn't even see him standing in the window when she came into the house. She walked straight into the kitchen and was talking to herself. He said he heard her say she can't believe she let the enemy into her home and around her family. Whose else could she be talking about? Jade is the only person who wasn't family and around us everyday."

"I fucking knew it! I tried to tell you muthafuckas, but y'all made it seem like I was crazy and being mean for no reason. I'm whipping her ass."

Before we could even react, Autumn kicked off her flip flops and ran over to Jade. She hiked up her dress and kicked her straight in the face. Junior jumped up and stood directly in front of Autumn.

"Yo, what the fuck are you doing?" Junior barked.

Jade's nose was leaking.

"Listen, I know y'all family, but you better take the base out your voice talking to her and back the fuck up."

I moved Autumn behind me and stepped to Junior. He must have lost his fucking mind.

"Alright, take a pause for a minute. Emotions are running

high, and everyone is upset. We can't be out here cutting up in the waiting area like this." Kane looked at me.

I backed up and took a hold of Autumn's hand. Kane just saved Junior's ass because no man will ever approach Autumn and not feel my wrath. Everyone needed to understand I would die protecting her and my kids.

When Junior sat back down next to Jade to make sure she was alright, Kisha immediately reached over him and punched her in the eye. Once that happened, the other two girls hopped up like they were trained to go. They grabbed Jade by her feet and snatched her out of the chair onto the floor. All three of them tried to pull her out of the hospital entrance like a pack of wolves, but Junior intervened.

He hocked his arms underneath Jade's and pulled on her. They were all in a tug of war until security came over and broke it up. They threatened to kick everyone out, but Kane smoothed it over as usual.

Kisha had Autumn's back without a doubt. They all did.

"I don't understand what the fuck is going on. Why are y'all attacking my girl like this?" Junior asked, looking crazy as hell at everyone.

Jade stood next to him trying to pull her dress down with blood still dripping from her nose. The shit might be broken. Autumn kicked her in it, hard as hell, with the heel of her bare foot. Jade's eye appeared to be swelling up too.

"She knows what the fuck is going. That bitch is the reason why our sister is in this fucking hospital. If Jade doesn't start explaining herself, she's going to be the next patient they wheel into the back. And if your dumb ass defends her one more time, you will join her."

Autumn pointed her finger in Junior's face as she walked up on him. I still held on to her other hand just in case I needed to pull her away. She might swing on his ass next, and I had enough of her trying to beat on everyone with our child nestled in her womb.

"I don't know what you are talking about. How could I have done something to Candy when I was with Junior the entire time. None of this makes any sense. I'm not staying here any longer listening to this nonsense and being y'all human punching bag. I need to have my nose and eye looked at."

"Oh, bitch, you will stand here. You are two seconds from being toe tagged and sent to the morgue. Matter fact, I think we should walk her ass down there right now, and put her in the fridge until she's ready to tell us who the fuck she really is," Autumn voiced.

"Candy will just have to be mad at me because she told me not to say nothing to nobody, but fuck this shit. This fool is Peanut's sister."

We all turned and looked at Kisha. I couldn't believe she knew this the entire time and never said a thing.

"Bitch, why didn't you tell us this shit on the way over here! What the fuck is wrong with you? When did y'all figure that shit out?" Autumn was fuming.

"I figured it out right before you walked down the aisle, when Junior said her entire name to us. Candy swore me to secrecy, and said she would handle it after the wedding. I didn't know she would pass the fuck out. Shit, I punched this bitch in her face. I'm trying to do my part as a friend, so stop yelling at me. Let's just take her to the morgue like you suggested." Kisha placed her hands on her hips.

Jade sat back down in her seat. The look of guilt was written all over her face.

"Is this true Jade? You weasled your way into our lives, just so you and your mother could hurt Autumn and try to kill her unborn child? Candy treated you like family, and this is what you do to her." Junior started choking Jade's ass. He shocked me with his reaction.

"Stop before they throw your black ass in jail. We will definitely handle her," Kane yelled.

He removed Junior's hands from around her neck. She started coughing and tears ran down her cheeks. Uncle Pete sat there completely unbothered.

"Peanut never mentioned having a sister. This shit is unreal, but it all makes sense now. Here I was thinking Keelie had something to do with it, and all along Jade was hiding in plain sight. Whew... this has turned out to be the worst day of my fucking life." Autumn rubbed her temples.

"Excuse me, Mr. Alexander? Your wife is done with all her tests and is asking for you."

A nurse came out to the waiting room and spoke to Kane.

"Autumn, you and Junior go with Kane to check on Candy. I'm going to stay out here and make a few phone calls." I handed her the flip flops she kicked off to put back on.

They all went to the back, and I went into the bathroom to

get some wet paper towels. Jade couldn't continue to sit out here with dried up blood on her face, drawing attention. I walked back out and tossed them on her lap.

"Here, clean your face up." Her left eye was almost closed shut at this point.

"I have to step outside for a minute. If she moves from her seat, close up her other eye."

Kisha's crazy ass gave me the thumbs up, and I continued out the front entrance.

When I looked back, I noticed uncle Pete had followed behind me.

"You know I handled Rah for your brother when he fucked with Candy, and I don't mind handling Jade for you. Just say the word, and her ass is out of here. She got the game fucked up."

Uncle Pete approached me on some gangsta type shit. I could only imagine all the shit he had seen and been through during his time inside.

"That she does. This one is personal for me, though, so I need to handle it a certain way. I appreciate your offer, and just know we got you for life." I dabbed him up, and uncle Pete went back inside.

After making the necessary phone calls, I breathed a sigh of relief knowing the muthafuckas who fucked with me and mine were about to wish they never crossed paths with us. When I went back into the hospital, Autumn and Junior were in the waiting area.

"Candy is okay physically, emotionally she's a wreck. They

wanted her to stay overnight as a precaution, but she refused. She wants to get home to the boys. My aunt will be there to help, so she'll be fine. Now, what are we going to do with this trick?" Autumn stared at Jade like she wanted to kick her again.

"There is no we. You had enough action for the day. I already called my car service to take your friends home and a tow truck to get that hazardous piece of metal out our driveway."

"Wait a minute now, Knowledge. Why are you having my car towed? You can just have the car service drop us off at y'all house, and I can get it myself. You, and your almost wife are going to stop disrespecting my shit."

"You didn't let me finish, Kisha. Since you provided us with some much needed information, I'm having a new car delivered to your house tomorrow. All you have to do is text Autumn a screenshot of your license, so I can have the title put in your name. I will take care of the insurance and registration every year." Kisha jumped up and hugged me, then Autumn.

"Friend, I know he did some bullshit. But this is a good man right here, girl. Don't let Keylolo get her claws on him again. It's exactly what might happen if you let him go. Y'all about to have a baby, and he took your ass out the hood. Don't end up back there by letting your pride get in the way."

"Sit your annoying ass down somewhere."

Kisha smacked her lips and cut her eyes at Autumn before turning around to face me.

"Now, am I getting a Maserati like my friend? It's just a question you know. This way we can match and shit. If not, I would be good with a KIA. My grateful ass will appreciate whatever you give me, and thank you. I should have said that first." I looked down at my phone to read the alerts going off.

"It will be a Lexus, and y'all ride is outside."

Kisha bit down on her fist as she screamed into it. The two ladies with her hugged Autumn then headed toward the door.

"Bye everyone except Jade. I hope your ugly ass dies tonight. Autumn, I will call you tomorrow."

I thought Autumn was wild. Her and Kisha were running neck and neck.

"Junior, take them with you and meet me at the house. Let uncle Pete ride in the back with Jade, and put the child proof locks on the doors after they get in." Once they left it was just Autumn and I.

"Then there were two. It's been a long day, and it's about to get even longer. I need to get you home, so you can shower, get some food, and relax."

"I'll relax after Jade becomes worm food, and you come clean about Keelie. What the fuck happened?"

Chapter Forty-Four

KEELIE

I couldn't believe that bastard told his rent-a-cops to shoot me if I stepped foot on their property again. It was okay, though. Seeing the look on everyone's faces when that video popped up on their phones made it all worthwhile. And knowing Autumn didn't get the opportunity to become Mrs. Alexander today made me want to celebrate.

She just knew her little day would go off without a hitch; not on my watch. Yeah, Kyle had to see his mother act a fool out there, but he was used to it. And since his little punk ass wanted to be over there with them, fuck his feelings too. I was going to do whatever I could to make all of their lives a living hell. Why should they get to live happily ever after? This ain't no goddamn fairytale.

As I walked into the bathroom to undress, pieces of cake were still falling off the back of my shirt. I couldn't take it off in the car without exposing myself, so I just brushed off what I could and drove home. I was still in shock from Autumn hitting me.

Everything in me wanted to rush her ass, but I knew her goons would jump me. I looked at my face in the mirror. My lip was swollen. It also split open when it hit my teeth on impact. I definitely underestimated her strength.

Autumn was the type of chick you had to fight dirty. And as soon as she had that baby, I was on her ass with salt in one hand and a bat in the other. She snuck me today, so it was only right I blind the bitch before I beat her down.

Now I understood why Miss Danielle was unable to complete her mission. I would never know what actually took place inside that house, but obviously Autumn was able to overpower her, or someone came to her rescue. Either way, Autumn was still pregnant, and I was pissed.

When Knowledge approached me about it, I wanted to crawl in my skin and die. I played the part of the fool in order to save myself. There was no way he would ever connect Miss Danielle to me. We only crossed paths out of pure coincidence.

The day I left from arguing with Autumn outside "her house", I pulled out of the driveway mad as hell. My mind was so preoccupied with the fact that Knowledge defended and protected her once again, I didn't even realize a woman in a utility van had followed me home.

When I exited out of my car, she hopped out of the van and approached me. At first I thought she was trying to kidnap my ass. She had on a black sweatsuit, some steel toe boots, and gloves. I walked backwards toward my house in order to put some distance in between us. It also allowed me to keep my eyes on her at the same time.

"Excuse me, I don't mean to alarm you. I just need your help. My name is Miss Danielle, and I noticed we have a common enemy."

"I don't give a fuck who you are. I'm about to call the police on your crazy ass in two seconds." *I took my phone out of my bag and unlocked it.*

"Please, don't do that. If you do, I can't help you get your revenge on Autumn."

Once she said that, I let down my guard and tossed my phone back into my bag. I have no idea how this lady knew Autumn, but any enemy of hers was a friend of mine.

"I'm listening."

"Do you mind if I come inside? I don't want anyone to see us out here talking."

I was hesitant to let her in at first, but my hate for Autumn outweighed my apprehension. Once we were inside, I offered her a seat on the couch. I remained standing, just in case I needed to make a mad dash out the front door. My guard may have been down, but I still didn't trust Miss Danielle.

"First off, let me start off by telling you who I am. I'm not sure if you know the young lady who shot Autumn over two years ago, but she was my daughter. They called her Peanut. She committed suicide because Autumn left her for Knowledge. It's my understanding you have a child with him."

"Yeah, we have a son. I heard about the shooting and prayed she wouldn't pull through. But as you can see, the universe doesn't answer my prayers." She smiled.

"Well, maybe I can be the answer to those prayers. If you are willing, you and I can team up to make her pay for all the pain and suffering she has caused us. My child is dead, and she's over there playing house with yours."

"How do you know so much about what's going on at their house?"

This lady was like the fly on the wall. She knew everything about their household like she lived in it.

"I had my other daughter, Jade, infiltrate Autumn's sister's family. When I read Peanut's journal, she mentioned how naive and gullible Candy was. I figured if she got in close with them, they wouldn't suspect Jade was a mole. Well, her stupid ass had the nerve to fall in love with Candy's brother. She stopped providing me information months ago, talking about how they were good people, and she didn't want to hurt them."

The more Miss Daniell spoke, the angrier she became. She definitely was out for blood, and I was more than happy to help her get it.

"So, what's your plan now?"

"I'm patiently waiting for her to get pregnant with a baby of her own. Autumn needs to know what it feels like to lose a child. I just can't afford to keep coming back and forth up here, I live in

Virginia. After Jade flaked on me, I had no choice. When I'm done with Autumn, her ass is next."

"Your wait might be over. I saw her go into the OB/GYN office today. She could have been there for a regular appointment, but she had her sister with her. If she is pregnant, my son will spill it. I always make him tell me everything that goes on over there." Miss Danielle's eyes got so bright, they almost glowed.

"I hope she is. I've been up here for the last week, scoping everything out, and was about to pack it up and head home until I heard y'all yelling insults at each other. I was parked in front of the house next door. Every month, for the last three months, I rented out a AirBnb for a week. Usually I leave here emptied handed and hopeless, but not this time."

"Okay, so let's figure out how we are going to go about this if she is. You have to wait until she is alone to get her ass. Knowledge goes away with Kane for business sometimes and lets me know when he does, just in case there's an emergency with Kyle."

I didn't lie to Knowledge when I told him I would never attack Autumn while she was pregnant, because I didn't. Miss Danielle did, and she was probably floating in a river somewhere right now. That was what she got for deviating from the plan.

She was supposed to zap Autumn in the neck as soon as she opened the door with the stun gun, this way she couldn't fight back. Then tie her ass up to a chair, tape her mouth shut, so she couldn't scream, and beat her in the stomach with a hammer. Obviously she didn't do that because Autumn's baby was still healthy and growing, and Miss Danielle was MIA.

If Knowledge didn't figure out the role I played by now, he never would. I just provided her with some information. She didn't follow the blueprint anyway, so my hands were clean in my eyes.

As I removed my clothing, I took off the fake baby bump suit I was wearing and sat it on the closed toilet seat. My neighbor Sean had his sister create this work of art for me. She was a professional makeup artist who worked on movie sets in New York and LA.

Even though we gave her a short turnaround time, she killed it. The bump matched my skin tone perfectly and felt realistic to the touch. It wore like a bodysuit with a belly. I probably could have fooled Dr. Jones, until she put me on the monitor.

Sean also edited the videos I took and made them into a magical little bomb to airdrop on their asses. He knew everything about computers and all types of crazy shit you could do with them. Making my video was light work to him.

I started the shower and stepped in, so I could wash the day off of me. Sean would be here soon. He wanted to come by to collect his payment for helping me out. I rather he waited until my lip healed, but he wasn't having any of that. His ass always had to stick to the schedule.

After I finished up with my shower, I threw the clothes I wore to the wedding in the trash, and put the bump in the hall closet. As I was lotioning up in my bedroom, there was a knock at my door. I put on my robe and walked over to the window to see who it was.

"Hi, can I help you?" I asked the cable guy who stood

outside my door when I opened it. He wore a lanyard around his neck with a badge clipped to it that identified him as a worker for the cable company that serviced our area.

"Yes, ma'am. There seems to be a neighborhood outage, and I was just stopping by each house to make sure the cable is up and running."

My ass never turned on the TV when I came home, and this was the first time I heard about some outage. Therefore, I didn't know if he was lying or not.

"Wait right here and let me check."

I left him standing on the outside while I grabbed the remote to turn on the TV in the living room. When it came on, it said "no signal" across the screen.

"Oh shit, it really is out."

"I can troubleshoot all your boxes for you real quick if you don't mind. It will only take a few minutes."

"Umm, yeah, come on. You can start with the one out here while I throw something on." I closed the door once he entered the house.

He started working on the cable box, and I went to my room to get dressed. Sean texted me saying he would be over in ten minutes. This muthafucka cable guy better hurry his ass up. I threw on a cute little romper and walked back out into the living room.

"I'm finished with this one. If you could show me to the next room, I can be out of your way shortly."

"Yes, you can go to my room all the way in the back. My son isn't here, so there's no need to bother with his box."

While the cable guy did what he needed to do, I went to the kitchen to put some champagne on ice. Sean and I were going to toast our accomplishments. I managed to get back at Autumn and Knowledge at the same damn time. My momma said if you want something done right, you have to do it yourself.

"Alright, I'm all done. I just have to check the wires outside and once the boxes reboot, you should be good to go."

"Thank you and have a good night."

"The same to you ma'am."

As I let the cable guy out, Sean was coming up to the door.

"Hey, beautiful," greeted Sean.

"Don't you look handsome."

Sean knew his weird ass was fine as hell. He walked into the house. I followed right behind him and closed the door.

"I hope you are prepared to pay off your debt." He started rubbing on his dick.

"Yes, I have everything we wore from the last time."

Sean wanted me to dress up as Lil Bo Peep, and he would dress up as Old McDonald. This nigga really cut a hole in the overalls for his dick to poke out through. When we were fucking, he wanted me to make the sounds the animals made on the farm. Instead of a moan, it was a moo. I couldn't say ahh, it had to be baa baa; like a goddamn sheep.

We did crazy shit like this all the time. I'm just glad I didn't have to spread cheez whiz all over my pussy today, and let him lick it off while dressed like a big ass rat. The last time we did that, I caught a yeast infection.

Sean had fetishes and fantasies he felt safe acting out with me. And as long as he kept on helping me to make Autumn and Knowledge lives miserable, I would do anything he wanted. They say revenge was a dish best served cold, and today I left them shivering.

Chapter Forty-Five

AUTMN

"You know what really hurts? The fact that you lied to my face. We're supposed to be better than that."

"I didn't lie... I just didn't tell you what happened because I thought you would view me differently if you knew what I did to her."

Knowledge and I were on our way back to the house from the hospital. This muthafucka finally told me what really occurred between him and Keelie, and now he wanted to insult my intelligence.

"That absolutely makes no fucking sense! If I flat out ask you a question and you don't tell me everything, it's a lie by omission. You were only worried about yourself, and that's fucked up." Knowledge glanced over at me.

"I just didn't want you to think less of me."

All I could do was take a deep breath to try and calm my nerves. I really wanted to reach over and punch him in his mouth for talking stupid.

"If you were defending me, why would I think less of you? We both know Keelie said that shit on purpose. Her demonic ass wanted you to act a fool because she knows you better than you think. The problem right now is you don't know me like I thought you did."

"I do know you. I was just thinking you—"

"You don't get to think for me! Your black ass should have said what happened and allowed me to decide how I wanted to handle it."

I cut Knowledge because I had enough of his sorry ass excuses.

"And your handling it would have involved you going over there to whip her ass. I was just trying to protect you."

"Protect me? Were you protecting me when you gave her the upper hand? You provided the person who wants to destroy my life with ammunition to use against me. You loaded the gun, and she pulled the trigger."

Tears flowed like a waterfall down my face. Knowledge had no idea how deep he cut me.

"Autumn, please stop crying. It pains me to know I'm the source of your hurt. I never wanted any of this to happen."

All the feelings I've been suppressing finally surfaced. I let out a cry that came from the pit of my soul. Knowledge pulled over to the side of the road and put the hazard lights on.

"I'M TIRED! I'm tired of being strong. I'm tired of

protecting everyone else's feelings. I'm tired of you, and I'm really tired of Keelie." He tried to hold my hand, but I snatched it away. "This is supposed to be a joyous time for us. We should have gotten married today, but instead we got embarrassed. The people I love and care about had to watch my fiance and his baby momma look like they were about to fuck. Why didn't you just leave when she came to the door half naked?"

Knowledge blew his breath and looked straight ahead. I grabbed some tissue from the glove compartment to clean my face.

"Don't look stupid now. You know that bitch has it out for me and wants you back. She would do anything to have me out of the way. Your ass should have been straight up from the jump, then we wouldn't be sitting here right now looking like the black people who are about to be killed first in a movie. Please get me away from these damn woods."

Knowledge took the car out of park, turned off the hazard lights, and pulled off.

"You're right. I fucked up, and now I have to suffer the consequences of my decison to keep everything from you. And I don't know who she's pregnant by, but it damn sure ain't me. I choked her, but it wasn't in a sexual manner. If I could rewind time I would do everything differently, but I can't."

I could see the tears falling from his eyes now. Any other time I would try to console him, but not today. He needed to cry and feel just an ounce of what I felt.

"We can't start our new life off like this. There can be no secrets or lies between us. I need to know the man I'm willing to spend the rest of my days with will never let someone else control our narrative. I'm the only woman, unless we have a daughter, that should have you out here buying bags and cars."

"Autumn, I promise you, I'm never going to do no dumb shit like this ever again. You, our baby, and Kyle are my life. Together we make our own little family, and I won't ever let anyone, or anything, come between us again. My only fear is losing you."

"When we drove off from the cemetery after Peanut killed herself, do you remember what you said?" I questioned Knowledge.

"I said I loved you, and I wasn't afraid to let you know how I felt. I also remember saying I would fuck up, which I just did."

"Then I said, we can fuck up together because I'm not going anywhere. I meant that, Knowledge. I'm here for the duration, ten toes down always... just don't fuck up again."

We finally made it back home. Knowledge helped me out of the car and when we entered the house, I could hear my mother, auntie Lily and uncle Pete going at it. They didn't even notice us until I spoke.

"Mom, if y'all want to argue, take them to your house in the back and have at it. It's been a long day, and I can't deal with this right now. Did y'all forget the kids are here? Where are they anyway?" Everyone stopped talking and stood there with a dumb ass look on their faces.

"Junior is in the playroom with them," my mom answered.

"Uncle Pete, where the hell is Jade?" Knowledge asked.

"I locked her ass in the hall closet. We didn't want to leave her out in the car alone."

Knowledge walked over to the closet and opened it up. Uncle Pete had Jade's hands tied behind her back with a shoe string and a plastic bag over her head. I looked down at his sneakers and sure enough, one of them had no laces.

"She can stay in there just like that until everyone leaves. I'm about to go check on the kids." Knowledge closed the closet door back.

"What happened to auntie Bird? I didn't see her car outside." I asked.

"Your mother chased her away." My auntie Lily laughed like it was funny.

"Bird was talking about how happy she was that both her nieces were giving her more babies to love and spoil, and all I did was tell her she needed to settle down and start a family of her own."

"No you didn't. You said her eggs were going to be scrambled by the time she decided to start a family."

"Lily, it's the same thing." They both laughed.

"No it's not, mom. That was mean and hurtful, but y'all laughing. It's not funny and mind your business. Auntie Bird will have kids when she's ready, and she might not want any after seeing how you two did y'all kids. Now laugh at that." I cut my eyes at both of them.

"Is Candy alright? You never called us." Auntie Lily changed the subject real quick.

"Yes, they were about to discharge her when we were leaving. I didn't call because all hell broke loose in there... just like here. I'm sure by now you know Jade is Peanut's sister."

"Yeah, Junior told us. I still can't believe it, she had us all fooled. I'm around her almost everyday and never would have guessed that."

"Candy is definitely going to need your help and support, Aunt Lily. She blames herself for bringing Jade into the family, but later for that. Why were y'all acting like wild animals up in our house?"

"Lily never got the chance to tell me how she really felt about the whole situation to my face, so I understood her frustration. But your mother got a lot of fucking nerve when I went to jail to save her ass. She came at me sideways, and I don't appreciate that shit. Her ass got me fired up." Uncle Pete joined in on the conversation.

He was steaming mad. His lips were tight as hell as he spoke. My mom glared at my uncle like a mountain lion ready to pounce on their prey. He must have said something she didn't appreciate, probably the truth.

"Uncle Pete, did you kill my father? Kane said you didn't. We just need to know what really happened, so we can put all of this behind us." He looked at my mom before he answered.

"When I got to the house he was already dead. Your mother had been putting antifreeze in his juice all day without him knowing. It's odorless and sweet tasting, so David had no idea he was being poisoned. I put him in the tub and filled it up with water to make it look like I drowned him. There was no way in hell I could let my baby sister go to jail, especially pregnant."

My mom started crying. Auntie Lily shot daggers at her even though I think she knew my mom did it, but hearing how, made her feel a way. She had all this anger for her brother and sister when all of this was really her fault.

"I knew if I confessed they wouldn't do an autopsy or question your mom. All they cared about was locking my black ass up. The truth didn't matter to the police. That's how Kane got me out. He hired some high powered attorney who reopened my case. They never read me my rights, so my confession was thrown out. Your father was cremated. The DA office didn't have enough physical evidence to retry me. They had no choice but to release me."

Kane knew he was a smooth muthafucka. He stayed in the background, but was always ten steps ahead of everyone. One of the greatest qualities of these brothers was their love for family. There wasn't anything they wouldn't do for the people they loved.

"Mom, you need to put all that hostility you have for uncle Pete to rest. If it wasn't for him you would have given birth to me in a damn jail, and your ass would still be there right now."

She looked up at me with sad, puppy dog eyes. My mom knew how to play the victim very well. Her ass had been doing this my entire life.

"I was just mad because he never even told us he was coming home. Then he shows up and says he was going to tell y'all the truth about him not killing David. He should have given me the opportunity to tell y'all myself."

My mom always had to make everything about her.

"Did you even stop and think about how uncle Pete felt? He has been rotting away in a cell all these years for a murder he didn't commit. Candy and I hated his ass because of what we thought he did. You could have cleared his name with us when it all came to light a couple years ago. Everyone knew it was more to the story, but we forgave you anyway and moved on. You need to show your brother the same grace we showed you."

Junior and Knowledge came into the living room right on time with the kids. I needed a mental break from the craziness and seeing them always made me smile.

"Kane and Candy are at the house, so I'm about to take the boys home."

"Kyle is going to go with them. We can pick him up in the morning." I nodded my head at Knowledge.

"Uncle Pete, you might as well come with us too." Junior rounded everyone up, including my auntie Lily, and left.

"I'm going upstairs to bed. I love you guys and will see y'all in the morning."

"We love you too mom, and you need to apologize to auntie Bird and uncle Pete tomorrow." She waved me off as he headed toward the steps.

"Once Kane gets Candy settled, he's coming over, so we can deal with Jade. You need to go shower and relax. I'm sure all the food is still here. I will warm you something up and bring it to you."

"I'm not going anywhere until she explains herself. We also need to make sure she's the only one left. Muthafuckas keep coming out of the woodwork."

"That's true. I'm about to let her ass out of the closet. Once she tells us everything, you are done. Kane and I got it from here."

Knowledge let Jade out of the closet and walked her into the dining room. He sat her down in one of the chairs and took the bag off of her head. I punched her hard as hell on the side of neck. Jade's head swung to the other side like it was about to fall off.

Chapter Forty-Six

KNOWLEDGE

"Damn, Autumn. If you close up her throat she can't tell us shit."

Autumn hit Jade with the force of a bat. I knew firsthand how hard she hits. My face still was sore from that slap she laid on me earlier. I'm just glad it wasn't a closed fist.

"I owed her that. Her mother tried to kill my child with her help. She's lucky she's still breathing. If I didn't want her blood all over my house, I would stab her in each ear with a paring knife and let her bleed out."

"Please, don't kill me. I will tell you everything. Just hear me out." Jade pleaded for her life.

"Before you start lying, why didn't Peanut ever say she had a sister?"

"Peanut didn't know I existed. I'm a year older than her. We share the same mother, but not the same father. Our mother was on drugs when she had me too, and my father's family took me in. I didn't get back acquainted with my mom until I turned eighteen."

Jade shifted her legs as she spoke. Her hands were still tied behind her back. You could tell she was very uncomfortable. She held her head down as she continued to talk.

"She was clean by then and wanted nothing to do with me at first. I always loved her even though I didn't know her. Eventually my mom accepted me into her life and told me I had a little sister. It was her idea to keep me a secret from Peanut. Why? I don't know."

"Because your mother was a sick bitch, just like your sister." Jade peered up at Autumn.

"What do you mean *was*?"

"Did you think I would allow the blood in her body to keep flowing through her veins after what the fuck she did to Autumn?" I sat down in one of the chairs and leaned back.

"Don't worry, you will be joining her soon enough. Hopefully you are the last fruit from the poisonous tree." Jade started to cry when Autumn said that. "Please stop crying. You look like a wet otter. It's not a good look."

"Who else helped your mom besides you? Are you and Peanut her only children?" Jade looked over at me.

"As far as I know, yes. And I keep trying to tell you guys I didn't help my mother attack Autumn, and I didn't do anything to Candy." Tears still trickled down Jade's face.

"Candy passed out once she learned who you were, muthafucka! It was too much for her heart and soul to take. It is your fault. All of this is your fault. You purposely sought after her just so you could feed your heartless mother information about me. I told them you were no good, but they trusted you. They spoke highly of you because you were so convincing. You held my nephews, bitch!"

Autumn slapped Jade so hard I thought her handprint would be burned into her face. I knew she needed to get this off her chest, so I didn't say anything. These animals tried to kill our child. This was just the beginning of Jade's real life nightmare.

"And I'm sorry. I didn't want to do it, but my mother said we had to honor Peanut and get revenge for her. She said you killed my sister. My mother had me get close to Candy. She knew she was my way into your family. The story I told everyone was that I relocated up here for a new start, and was a college student. We had to make it look real, so I signed up at the local college. If anyone ran a background check on me it would show up."

"Finally we are hearing the truth. Keep going." Autumn finally took a seat.

"Somehow my mother found out that Candy went to Dr. Jones' office. I started volunteering there a few days a week. Whenever Candy had an appointment scheduled I made sure to be working. I went over and beyond for her when she was there. We became very friendly, especially during her last trimester. She would come like twice a week because she was considered high risk with the twins. One day, after Candy already had the boys, she asked me if I wanted to work for them." I looked over at Autumn and shook her head in disbelief.

"What I don't understand is why Miss Danielle waited so long." She was on some stalker type shit.

"My mother wanted to wait until Autumn had a kid so she—"

"Your Rumpelstiltskin ass mother purposely waited around for my first born child?" Autumn cut Jade off.

"Yes. I know it's horrible, and that's why I wouldn't help her anymore. I stopped feeding her information before you were pregnant. Being around your sister and her family every day did something to me. I really started to care for them and wanted no parts in hurting you or them. My plan was to leave one day and never come back, but then I fell in love with Junior."

"If you didn't tell her about my baby, who did?"

Autumn slammed her fist down on the table. I saw the rage in her eyes and thought she would beat on Jade again, but she remained seated.

" I honestly don't know. If I did, I swear to God I would tell you."

"Don't swear to him now. You should have thought about God when you were plotting and scheming to kill my child. I'm not going to kill you, though. You said you didn't have anything to do with it, and I believe you."

"Autumn, thank you so much, and I'm sorry for everything.

Whew... I just knew I wasn't going to make it out of here alive." Jade breathed a sigh of relief.

"You're not. I said I wouldn't kill you. Knowledge isn't so forgiving, so he's definitely going to stand over you until the last breath leaves your body. Just because you grew a heart along the way doesn't excuse what you did, or give you a pass. Bitch, you're dying today."

The doorbell rang, so I headed over to answer it. I knew it was Kane. Junior wanted to be a part of this tonight, but I told the young bull he wasn't quite ready yet. Taking someone's life wasn't something to take lightly. You had to have the right mindset to block that shit out after it was over.

I knew he wanted to punish Jade for what she did to his family, but the fact that he understood family came first over everyone else made me see him in a different light. Junior was ready to put Jade down like an animal at the vet because she violated the people he loved.

He had me worried at the hospital when he jumped up at Autumn. I thought I would have to bury two bodies tonight. Junior quickly gained his senses when he found out what was going on, so we were good. I opened the door for Kane, and he had a bag in his hand.

"You come bearing gifts, bruh? What's good with you?" He entered the house, and I closed the door.

"I made a stop on the way home from the hospital. It's for tonight. Are you ready to get this over with?"

"Absolutely, but we have a problem. Someone else helped Miss Danielle. Jade claims she stopped feeding her information months ago, and I believe her, so does Autumn. I didn't want to say anything in front of her, but the only other person who knew we were going away that day was Keelie." Kane dropped his head.

"After what Keelie pulled at the wedding, she's capable of anything."

"It's all good, though. I got my people on her ass. If she did have anything to do with it, they will find out."

Autumn met us in the hallway on our way to the dining room. She looked completely drained.

"Hey, Kane. How's my sister doing?"

"She's having a hard time with the whole situation. Once she saw the boys she perked up some. I told her Jade had us all fooled. Well, except for you. We even did a background check on her, and everything looked good. No one else will ever step foot in our house again. I'm hiring an outside agency to do what Candy was doing. This way she can just focus on being an amazing mother and wife. I also want her to take some time for herself."

"Shit, Jade had me fooled too in a way. I knew her ass wasn't right, but I thought she would try to seduce you. Her being Peanut's sister never even crossed my mind. Well, I'm going to shower and get in bed."

"Don't forget to eat something. You have to feed my daughter. She's hungry as hell."

"You better be careful what you wish for. If it is a girl, she's going to act just like me."

"That's true. It's okay, though. If she's anything like you, one day she will make someone's son as happy as I am." Autumn smiled.

"Awe, babe. You're still sleeping alone tonight."

Autumn walked off and left us standing there. I thought shit was sweet between us, obviously she was still in her feelings.

"Damn, she fucked you up with that one. I have a full house, but you know you can always stay with us."

"Fuck you, bruh."

"That's what you won't be doing anytime soon."

Kane laughed like that shit was funny. I'm sleeping in my own damn house, in my own damn bed. I don't care what Autumn just said.

"You ready, Jade? It's time for us to go." She sat in the chair scared as hell.

"Where are we going?"

"We have a dirt hotel we started, and a space just opened up for you. It's nothing too fancy and you can only check in, not out. You can rest in peace knowing your mother will be in the room next to you." Kane wasn't shit. His ass was full of jokes tonight.

We took Jade to my car and tossed her ass in the trunk. It didn't take us long to get there. Once we were inside, I popped the trunk. Kane grabbed the bag he had and exited the car. I got out and went to get the plastic to put down on the ground.

Kane and I had our little routine down pact. It was like we could read each other's minds. We barely said a word. He already had pulled Jade out and untied her hands.

"Please, you don't have to do this. Just let me go, and you will never see me again."

"You had your chance to leave when you decided you made the wrong decision by helping out your mother. Instead, you stuck around and tried to become part of our family. What was your plan? To get pregnant and hoped having a child would save you if we found out? We would have still killed you, and Junior would have been a single dad."

Jade could save her crocodile tears. I didn't give a fuck about them or her. Kane opened the bag and pulled out four tasers.

"Since your mother decided she wanted to shock my niece or nephew to death, I felt it was only right we did it to her child."

Kane handed me two of the tasers. I told Jade to stand in the middle of the plastic and as soon as she did, she pissed herself. We aimed the stun guns at her.

"On the count of three," Kane instructed me. "One, two, three."

At the same time we pulled the triggers. We aimed for her chest and face, she was immediately paralyzed on contact. Jade was almost lifted into the air from the voltage. She fell to the ground hard as hell, busting her face open.

Kane and I dropped the stun guns and started rolling her ass up in the plastic. She was ready to be placed in her plot, but we had to dig it first. This was the part I hated the most, but with both of us working together it went by fast. We lucked up with the soil being optimal for digging, it only took us a few hours.

"How many more bodies do you think we have to bury after this one?" Kane was just as exhausted as my ass.

"To be honest I don't know. It seems like everytime we think it's over and done, shit hits the fan again. I have some things in motion and pretty soon all the snakes will be revealed. Everything seems to be pointing towards Keelie, but she's not smart enough to have come up with this shit by herself."

The hours seemed to race by and before we knew it, grass seeds were being tossed on the dirt. We cleaned everything up and headed home. All I could think about during the ride was Autumn. I had to make it right with her. She needed to see and not just hear that I was sorry.

Chapter Forty-Seven

KEELIE

"Come the fuck over here right now! They are trying to kick me out, and I know you had something to do with it, you funky bitch!"

My mom hung up on me before I could even get a word in. I had no idea what she was talking about, but I needed to get over there and figure it out. When I looked at the time on my phone, I realized it was only a little after eight in the morning.

I really wasn't in the mood to deal with my mom's bullshit. There were other pressing matters which required my attention. It had been a week since I showed my ass at Autumn and Knowledge's wedding, and that fucker cut me off financially.

His lawyer served me with paperwork yesterday and basically forced me to sign it. He had two big ass goons with him and said if I didn't comply, they had orders to snatch my ass up and bring me to Knowledge. I didn't know what would happen if they did bring me to him, but I wasn't going to find out. After Knowledge told them to shoot me, I knew he killed Miss Danielle.

If he was capable of doing some shit like that, I needed to keep my distance. I believed the only reason I was still breathing had everything to do with the fact that I was Kyle's mother. He loved his son more than anything and wouldn't want to see him hurt.

The paperwork said I gave Knowledge full custody of Kyle, and as of that day I would no longer receive child support payments. Now, I needed to find a way to get money to pay my bills. Last night I listed my Birkin bag on one of those online consignment shops. The money I would get from the sale should hold me over for six months.

Sean was a source of income as well, but that required me to put my body through unnatural sexual scenarios. He would be my last resort. I still had a few pieces of jewelry left that Knowledge purchased for Kyle. If I had to, I would sell those as well.

I jumped in the shower, got dressed, and headed over to my mom's house. Starbucks was on the way, so I stopped there to get a cup of coffee to wake me up. As I sat at a red light, I grabbed my cup out of the holder to take a sip, and it slipped out of my hand.

The shit spilled all in my lap and burnt the fuck out of me. When I jumped as a reaction, I took my foot off the brake and rear ended the car in front of me. The person started waving their hand out the window for me to pull over. They pulled off to the side of the road, and I parked right behind them.

When the lady got out of the car and started walking to the back of it to assess the damages, I realized it was Autumn's friend from the wedding who tried to fight me. I'm telling you, when it rained, it poured. I was not in the mood to deal with her ghetto ass shenanigans today. There was barely a scratch on her bumper.

After she looked over her car, she walked over to the passenger side window. She tapped on the glass, and I rolled it down.

"Bitch, I know muthafucking lying! Your trifling ass probably hit me on purpose, hoe. Get out of the car. I'm about to whip your ass for real this time. Autumn isn't here to hold me back." she threatened.

"First of all, I took my foot off the brake by accident when I spilled my coffee. Second of all, I didn't even know you drove a Lexus. I was sure the piece of shit car with the micro tires belonged to you, or one of the other girls you were with. And last, but not least, you ain't whipping nobody's ass." I laughed.

"You got jokes? Ok, bitch. I hope you still think shit is comical when I leave you out here looking like one of those groundhogs who wasn't quick enough to make it across the road."

Next thing I knew, Autumn's friend leaped into my car, head first, through the open window. She was like a rabid raccoon and immediately started attacking me. I tried to defend myself, but she wouldn't stop swinging. When she raised her arm to hit me again, I leaned in and bit her in the tittie.

"Aaaahhh!"

When she screamed and grabbed her chest, I was able to open my door. I was halfway out of the car when she grabbed me by the back of my shirt. She pulled on it so hard, the only thing I could do to get away was slide up out of it.

There I was, on the ground with cars flying by, honking at me. I stood up, and this maniac was coming around to my side of the car.

"Hey, Kangaroo. It looks like your pouch is missing its joey. Where did the baby bump go, ho? Wait until I tell Autumn this shit."

I didn't put the suit on because I didn't plan on being attacked and snatched out of my clothes. And out of all the people in the world, it had to be her car I hit.

"My name is Keelie, you fucking hoodrat. I'm sick of your ass calling me everything else that starts with a K. Fuck you and Autumn. Tell her whatever you want. Get back in your rental and go somewhere."

I was already defeated. They took my son and stopped my funds. There wasn't anything else they could do to me.

"Rental? If you only knew. Girl, go get in your car and cry. You're out here in a bra and leggings. If that ain't hoodrat behavior, I don't know what is. All you're missing is a bonnet and some Uggs. Bye, Keylolo the kangaroo."

After Autumn's friend got in her car and started to pull off, I didn't notice she had my shirt until she stuck her hand out her window waving it. I got back in my car and cried. As I'm buckling my seatbelt, getting ready to drive off, my mom sends me a text message.

Mommy Dearest: Where the fuck are you? These people are on my ass.

Me: I'm on my way now. I got into a little accident. I'm down the street.

Mommy Dearest: You can't do shit right. I bet you it was your fault too. Hurry your dumb ass up.

I reached in my backseat to see if I had a shirt thrown back there. The only thing I could find was one of Kyle's tank tops. It would have to do because if I turned around to go get a shirt, I would have to fight my mom.

When I pulled up to her complex, she was standing outside with a suitcase. I parked in her space and killed the engine. Her standing out here like this could not be good.

"Don't just sit there like a dummy, pop the trunk so I can put my suitcase in it."

My mom was literally yelling at my window like a crazy person. I did as she requested, and she placed her luggage into the trunk then slammed it hard as hell. It closed automatically on its own, but she probably broke it now.

"What's going on? I'm so confused right now."

My mom shifted her body and looked at me like I said something wrong. She pointed her finger in my face and proceeded to cuss me out.

"Your conniving, no good ass wants to sit here and play stupid. I know you had something to do with them putting me out. You always hated me, even as a child. When you come over, I see the way you look at me and my house. It's like we disgust you. You probably called the people on me or know who did. I should have aborted your ass when I had the chance. You ain't worth two dead flies."

"Why would I want you to be homeless? I need to talk to someone to find out exactly what the hell is going on. All of this isn't making any sense right now, and you're mad at me for no reason. I didn't do this."

"This morning the city came over and put a sticker on my door, saying my home was uninhabitable, and they were condemning it. They said I had too many complaints by the Board of Health for hoarding. I was allowed to pack up some of my things, but that's it." I couldn't believe my ears.

"Did they at least put you up in a hotel until we get the place emptied out?

"Yes, they are putting me up at Buckingham Palace. Stop being as dumb as you look. Why the fuck would they put me up somewhere. I have no choice but to stay with you. Kyle isn't there no way, so I can just stay in his room."

I instantly became ill. All I could think about was how she would have his room looking like the set of *Sanford and Son* in three days. With Knowledge cutting off my money, I couldn't afford to put her up in a hotel, not even a damn motel.

It would take them weeks to clear her house out. I'm sure they couldn't just throw her stuff in the garbage. She would have to have some say about what stayed and went. Knowing my mom, she would act just like the people on the show

Hoarders. I could see her now with the keep pile bigger than the throw away pile.

"I'm going to call the city tomorrow and see what I need to do. Honestly, I don't want you staying with me longer than a week."

"I wish I didn't have to stay with your monkey ass for no longer than an hour. This is your doing, like I said. Everything was fine until you went over there fucking with them people's wedding. Now all of a sudden the city gets involved."

"It was your idea for me to go. Don't forget that while you're blaming me for this."

I told my mom everything that happened at the wedding. She thought it was funny as hell, but now she's trying to turn against me.

"Bitch, I told you to go to the wedding, not start your own reality show when you got there. Then you had the nerve to get popped in the mouth by the bride. It's a damn shame you still getting beat the fuck up as an adult. You look like you were just in another fight and lost. And I know that's Kyle's tank top because it's wearing on you like a belly shirt."

All I could do was start the car, turn up the music, and pull off. My mom had never been to my house, and I secretly never wanted her there. I always feared she would catch bed bugs from all her dumpster diving. Those little hitchhikers catch a ride on any damn thing.

"We need to pick up some food on the way home. Your ass can't cook, and I don't need to add food poisoning to my list of troubles."

The more she talked, the more annoying she became. She reminded me of the mother on *Throw Momma From The Train*. We stopped and picked up some breakfast sandwiches and made our way to the house. When we pulled, she started talking shit again.

"I finally get to see how the other side lives. It must be nice to have a beautiful house and manicured lawn. Your pussy might not be rotten after all if Knowledge paid for you to stay in a place like this."

"It's a small, ranch style house mom, nothing to write home about."

"Shit, your ass lived in a hole in the wall before you became the goose that laid the golden egg. This is definitely a come up."

She never had nothing nice to say to me. I was going to have to pray real hard for the patience and strength to endure her disrespect, now that she needed to stay with me.

"I'm not sure if the cable is working in Kyle's room. There was an outage, and I didn't have them check his box because he wasn't there," I informed my mom as we headed into the house.

"If it's not working, I'm going to stay in your room, and you can sleep in there."

"No you're not. I will make you comfortable out in the living room if need be, but you are not going to bully me in my own home. You keep talking to me like I don't have feelings. I'm a grown ass woman, and you need to give me the same respect I give you."

I swallowed the lump that formed in my throat. It felt good

to finally stand up to her, but I also braced myself in case she hauled off and slapped me.

"You finally grew a pair. Good for you. Just know if you ever speak to me like that again, I will punch you in the face in your own house. Now show me to my room."

The day was just beginning, and I wanted it to end already.

Chapter Forty-Eight

KNOWLEDGE

Kisha called Autumn and told her about her run in with Keelie. I already knew she lied about the baby being mine, but to find out there never was a baby blew my mind. That was some sick shit to do. I'm glad my son no longer had to deal with her bullshit. He asked about Keelie having another kid when he saw her stomach at the wedding. I had to tell him it was a prank she played on everyone.

A couple weeks had passed since we found out, and Autumn was still down in the dumps emotionally. Her hormones were all over the place, and she still had me sleeping on the chaise lounge chair in our room. I refused to go into one of the guestrooms. As long as I was near her and my baby, I didn't care where I slept.

The people I had collecting information for me came

through with everything I needed. It was just a few more loose ends that needed to be tied up, then I could wreak havoc in the streets. Before I did, home needed to be taken care of first.

"Are you ready to go?"

Autumn was putting on her sneakers when I walked into her massive closet. It had to be the size of a one bedroom apartment.

"Yeah, and I wish you would tell me where we're going."

"It's a surprise, you will see when you get there."

Even though I knew she hated surprises, she would definitely enjoy this one. All I wanted to do was put a smile back on her face. This hasn't been an easy pregnancy for her, and the last few weeks have been hectic. What I have planned will definitely put her in a great mood.

"I'm going to go see your little surprise, just know I'm not happy about it. I rather lay in the bed and watch ratchet ass shows while I eat hot wings and celery sticks."

Once she finished complaining, we exited the house. The chauffeur was already standing outside the truck. He opened the door and Autumn climbed in. I walked around to the other side and got in. There were an assortment of beverages on ice for us to choose from and a platter of hot wings. A big ass smile appeared on her face.

"I swear you can read my mind. You make it hard for me to be upset with you."

Autumn grabbed a wing, dipped it in the blue cheese, and devoured it. She definitely could put some food away. And I loved the fact that she didn't care about counting calories or watching her weight. If Autumn was hungry she ate.

"How much longer do you plan on treating me like this? I miss sleeping next to you and rubbing on your stomach in the middle of the night. We're not roommates, and you have to stop treating us like we are."

"Believe me, I don't enjoy sleeping alone and miss you next to me just as much. It's just that whenever we have issues, you have a way of saying the right things to have me naked in seconds. We make love, and it's like nothing happened. The issues are still there, but we just ignore it. We can't keep doing that."

Autumn was right. I figured if I made her feel good physically, then whatever weighed heavy on her mind would just go away.

"I will do better with communicating with you and won't use sex as a weapon to silence you. Now that I am aware of how my actions make you feel, I will do my best to consider your feelings first and stop being selfish."

"And I will do better expressing my feelings to you. I bottle everything up, which is not good. I should have kept pressing you that day for answers instead of falling under your spell. It's my fault too. I love you and don't like it when we aren't centered."

"I love you too. You are my life. There's no me without you."

We ate on the wings, washed it down with some mineral water, and relaxed until we reached our destination. The partition was up, so Autumn couldn't see in front of her, and I had the shades pulled down on the windows.

"Why does it sound like planes are flying over our heads?"

The chauffeur opened Autumn's door and helped her out. I grabbed the small carry-on bag I had packed and exited the truck.

"The last time I tried to surprise you, you were hoping I was taking you to the airport with a private jet waiting to take you to the islands. Well, your wish is my command. I already checked with Dr. Jones, and she said you are cleared to travel."

I grabbed Autumn's hand and led her to the red carpet. The flight attendant and captain greeted us as we boarded the jet.

"Babe, I didn't even pack anything. What am I going to wear? Do they have Dove soap and all my smell goods wherever we're going?"

"Everything is already taken care of. I have a bag of your personal items right here. All you have to do is relax and enjoy the next seven days."

I knew it wouldn't be long before her tears made their way on the trip. Autumn tried to wipe them away, but they kept falling. We sat across from each other and buckled our seatbelts to prepare for take off.

"Thank you so much. I really needed this. Here I was still in my feelings, giving you attitude, and you were planning this amazing trip for us. I'm sorry, babe."

"It's all good. I know you didn't mean it."

A few minutes later we were in the air and on our way to

our own private island in the Caribbean. If this didn't get us centered, nothing would.

Once we were able to unbuckle and move around, Autumn and I went to the private bedroom on the jet to relax. There was a king size bed, bathroom, sitting area and flatscreen tv on the wall. We kicked off our shoes and climbed onto the bed. I put a movie on, and Autumn laid down beside me.

She kissed me on the cheek and slid her hand under my shirt. Her fingers massaged my chest, and my dick immediately jumped up trying to figure out what the hell was going on. Autumn hasn't touched me like this in weeks, and it felt good.

Everything in me wanted to turn her over on her side and slide up in her, but I kept my cool and let Autumn control the situation. She straddled me, then leaned in close and placed kisses all over my face. Our lips connected, and I slid my tongue into her mouth. We kissed as I ran my hands up and down her back.

Autumn sat up and took off my shirt, then climbed off me to remove my sweats and boxers. I laid there with nothing but my socks on. She stood at the end of the bed and gave me a strip tease. Her titties looked like two big ass, brown coconuts with nipples. I just wanted to put them in my mouth.

I had to rub on my dick to calm him down. He was ready to put in that work. Autumn turned around, threw that thing in a circle, and I thought I would bust in my hands. Her ass had a mind of its own. Each cheek bounced independently, then in unison. I called it the twerk jerk. She twerked, and I jerked.

After the show was over, Autumn climbed back onto the

bed and in between my legs. She guided my dick into her mouth with no hands. It tried to bob and weave, but she captured his head and softly sucked on it.

Her tongue slid up and down its length before she engulfed it. Autumn's head moved up and down as I watched, wanting to please her as well.

"Move over closer to me, and do it from the side."

Autumn did as I instructed. Without taking me out her mouth, she moved from between my legs and positioned her body where one elbow was on my thigh and the other on my stomach. Her ass was in the air as she arched her back. I massaged each cheek with my hand while she continued to try to suck the skin off my dick.

My fingers found their way to the center of her wet pussy. I massaged her clit, then slid two fingers into her opening. Autumn started to bounce her ass up and down. I finger fucked her faster, and she slobbed all over my dick. When she looked over at me, licked her lips, and twerked faster, I removed my fingers and slapped her ass.

"Sit on my face. I want you cum in my mouth."

I removed the pillows from behind my head and laid flat on the bed. Autumn squatted over my face and rested her belly on my forehead. I kissed on her thick pussy lips and ran my tongue up and down the inside of her pussy. She started slowly rocking back and forth on my face. Soft moans escaped her lips as I tickled her clit with the tip of my tongue.

"Oh, babe, I missed this so much. You make me feel so good. I can't wait to bust all over your face."

I licked and sucked on Autumn's pussy, and her juices dripped from her sweet peach into my mouth. She continued to grind on my face. I gripped her ass and pushed her pussy further into my mouth.

"Ahhh, yes, babe, yes. Just like that, just like that. I'm almost there."

Listening to Autumn talk sexy had a nigga going insane. The sound of her voice excited me, and I couldn't wait to make her feel every inch of me.

She fucked my face, nd her legs started to shake. Autumn exploded in my mouth. I kissed her pussy as she relaxed and got her breathing under control.

"Whew, my body needed that."

"We're just getting started. Lay on your back."

I cleaned off my face with my shirt as Autumn got comfortable on the bed. She was so beautiful. Seeing her naked body, which housed our child, lying there waiting to receive me, sent a warm sensation throughout my body.

She rubbed on her titties and started playing with her nipples. My mouth replaced her fingers as I hovered over her and gave each one the same attention. I used my tongue to trace the outline of her areola, then applied gentle kisses all over them.

Autumn squirmed underneath me and massaged my dick. She ran her hand up and down its length while squeezing it.

"Whose pussy is this?" I asked Autumn while spreading her legs open. She reached up, grabbed my face, and brought it close to hers.

"It's yours. What are you going to do to her?" she whispered.

"I'm about to teach her a lesson. She ignored me these last few weeks, and I didn't appreciate it. I think she deserves a beating."

Autumn placed her legs on my shoulders, and I guided my manhood into her opening. I stared into her eyes as the head of my dick tested the waters. It was nice and warm, just how I liked it. She gazed back into my eyes and bit down on her lip. When I pushed him in a little further, I could see her body react to my girth.

"Oohh, shit," she murmured. I wasn't even halfway in.

I removed her legs from my shoulders and placed my hands on the bend of her knees. With her pussy in full view, I watched as my dick slid in and out. Her juices were flowing, and now she was ready to take all of me.

When I plunged all the way in, I could feel her walls tighten around my dick. I delivered long, deep strokes as my balls slapped against the base of her ass. Autumn licked her fingers and started rubbing on her clit. That shit drove me wild. I started going faster and harder.

"Aaahh, sssssss, damn, Knowledge."

I slammed into her over and over again, making her moan louder each time. She grabbed a pillow and placed it over her face to muffle the sounds.

"Go ahead, cum for me. I want to see your face when you do."

Autumn tossed the pillow onto the floor, and I dug in

deeper, making sure to hit her spot. Before long, her body started convulsing as we locked eyes. Whenever I watched her have an orgasm from us fucking, it felt good to know I was able to make her experience something a lot of women didn't.

One thing she could never complain about was not being sexually satisfied. Even though I wanted to cum when she did, I held back. I needed to feel her next to me when I did.

"Get on your side."

Autumn turned over with her back to me as I laid down next to her. She lifted up her leg, and I entered her once more. It always felt wetter after she released. Our bodies were meshed together, and I placed my hand on her stomach. It wouldn't take long for me to unleash my seeds into her warmth. The way her pussy seized my dick upon entry, she wasn't playing fair.

Chapter Forty-Nine

AUTUMN

As soon as Knowledge entered me from behind, I latched onto his dick and put him in a headlock. He rubbed on my stomach, then worked his way up to my titties. His fingers grazed my nipples, making them stand at attention. I grinded my ass on him in a rocking motion. Each time I rocked forward, I clenched down on his dick.

"You keep doing that shit on purpose. Your ass knows it makes me cum each and every time." I laughed.

Knowledge became attuned with my rhythm as he placed his fingers in between my legs. He stimulated my clit and sucked on my neck. I was so aroused from the sensation I couldn't contain myself.

"Stop playing around and finish me!"

The next I knew, he had me get on all fours, and I regretted everything I just said. This muthafucka pushed my ass cheeks apart and drilled my pussy until he creamed inside me. When he was finished, I rolled over onto my back. My pussy was throbbing.

Knowledge got up and went into the bathroom. He came back out with a cool, wet rag for me. I placed it on my pussy lips. It provided me with some relief.

"Yeah, talk your shit now."

"Whatever, punk." I stuck my middle finger at Knowledge and got up to take a shower.

"Can you pass me the bag, so I can go wash my ass."

He handed me the bag, and I disappeared into the bathroom. I started the shower and climbed in. As soon as the water hit my face, I cried like someone just died. These were happy tears, though. I was thrilled to get away from everything and everyone, and Knowledge and I were back on solid ground.

Being home in that house was a constant reminder of everything horrible that happened there. I didn't have time to heal and get past it. I still didn't know who helped Miss Danielle if Jade didn't. Knowledge probably knew and didn't want to stress me.

"Would you like some company?"

Knowledge came into the bathroom and joined me in the shower. We washed each other up, got out, and dried off.

"This is exactly what my soul needed, thank you!" I kissed him on the lips.

The captain called over the intercom and said we would be landing soon. I couldn't believe we were in this room for that long. We put our clothes back on and went to sit back in our seats.

"Wow, it's beautiful!"

I could see the island as the plane was making its descent. The sea was a beautiful shade of turquoise, and lush, tropical trees and vegetation covered the island. We braced for the landing.

As we exited the plane, the warmth of the island greeted me, and all I could do was smile. There was a young man waiting for us at the end of the red carpet. He stood in front of an all black Rolls-Royce Cullian SUV.

I felt like royalty. It was very overwhelming, but I think I could get used to this. We were such home bodies, and I never really wanted to go anywhere. Knowledge traveled for business, but as a family we didn't. After this trip right here, all of that was about to change.

He opened the door for us to climb in. After we buckled up, the driver pulled off. I looked around in awe of the ride. The interior was the color of a baseball mitt, and it smelled like money. When I met Knowledge I knew he had bank, but all of this was on another level. They were treating us like celebrities.

We never discussed finances, and he always made sure I wanted for nothing. Over the past two years their company expanded and grew, so I knew he had millions, but this right here had to be on some billionaire shit.

"Babe, you really outdid yourself. I feel like a beautiful, black queen for real."

"That's exactly who you are. You deserve this and so much

more, and I'm going to give it to you. All I want is for you to be healthy and happy in this life. I want the same for myself and our kids."

"We appreciate you. Well, the baby might not because you made this little person do the wobble in my uterus on the plane." We both laughed.

"After all the fighting you did, I'm sure a few backshots felt like a little ripple to our baby."

"I'm done fighting. No I'm not. I definitely will retire my boxing gloves and black forces after I whip Keelie's ass. I'm definitely putting hands and feet on her." Knowledge just shook his head.

"You're right, but we are not mentioning her name again. We only want good vibes and energy. This trip is all about you and my little princess you are carrying. I'm going to spoil you to no end the entire time we are here."

Before long, we pulled up to our destination. The driver helped me out of the car, and Knowledge took me by the hand after he got out.

"Why are we at the beach? Are we going on an excursion already?"

"We are taking a speedboat to a private island. That's where we are staying. It should take us about twenty-five minutes to get there."

I just stood there with my mouth hanging open. My ass was excited to stay on the main island, now we get one all to ourselves. We put on our life jackets and boarded the boat. With the wind blowing in my hair and the sun shining on my face, I enjoyed the ride over.

As we stepped out of the boat onto the dock, I saw two huge homes on the island. They were both gated and looked exactly the same. They appeared closer than they really were from the boat. At the end of the dock were a line of electric scooters. We got on one and rode it up to the house.

Knowledge parked the scooter after we got off. He entered a code on the gate, it unlocked, and he pushed the door open. It automatically closed and locked back behind us. There was a pebble walkway leading up to the front door.

The door wasn't locked, and we walked right in. A young lady greeted us with two bottles of mineral water and warm, damp rags on a tray. We cleaned our hands with the rags then took the water.

"Dinner will be ready in an hour. In the meantime, relax and get acquainted with the house. I will show you to your room. When the food is ready to be served, I will alert you." She took two Apple style watches out of her pocket and gave them to us to put on.

"These are for the staff to communicate to you."

We put them on, and she led us to our room. The bedroom was very similar to the one at our house back in the states.

"How do you like everything so far, beautiful?" Knowledge took me into his arms. He always gave the best hugs.

"I love it all. This room reminds me of home. I wish it was my home."

"It is." I raised my head from off of his chest and looked him in the eyes.

"You want to run that by me again, sir."

"I purchased this island for us. Well, Kane and I bought it together for our families. The house next door is for his family, and this one is ours."

"You have to be shitting me. This must be a joke."

I could tell Knowledge was serious as hell.

"We will split our time between the two homes. For the six months of hurricane season we will stay in New Jersey. The other six months will be spent here."

To say I was speechless was an understatement. This right here literally blew my mind. Growing up the way I did, I never thought I would ever live this type of life. And to know my children would never have to struggle brought tears to my eyes.

"Go open the closet."

I walked over and slowly opened the door. My knees got weak from excitement. It was the exact replica of my closet at home, and it was fully stock. I mean clothes, shoes, jewelry, everything.

"When did you find time to do this?"

"We started this over a year ago. The locals on the main island are excellent skilled workers and were more than happy to take our money to build these homes. We sent videos and floor plans of our houses to an interior decorator. As you can see, her company is amazing."

I was ugly crying now. I'm already emotional, so it doesn't take much to make me cry. We changed our clothes and took a tour of the rest of the house. It had seven bedrooms and ten bathrooms. An additional small home that housed the staff sat in the back, off to the side. They would live there full time, but would only have access to the main house when we were there.

He even had them build a classroom where the kids would be homeschooled. The kitchen was state of the art. My mom would definitely have to give me cooking lessons. I wanted to be able to prepare meals for my family as well. There were so many other rooms, but my favorite was my reading room.

Knowledge had it built on top of the house. You could only enter it from a hidden spiral staircase located in our bedroom. The room had a full 360 view of our island. All of the walls, including the ceiling, were made of impact resistance glass.

Different shapes and sizes of bookshelves, full of books, filled the space. There were several areas for me to lounge at and even a children's reading corner. I'm sure most of my time would be spent up here.

An alert came across the watch that dinner was ready. We made our way to the dining room, and I almost passed out when I saw everyone who attended the wedding sitting down ready to eat, including Kisha. I saw on the gram that my other two friends caught Covid, so I'm assuming it was the only reason they were not here.

"When? How? What are all you guys doing here?"

"I needed a do over. You deserve to be the most beautiful bride and to have a wedding that people only dream about. Two days from now you will have it. For now, I just want you to enjoy your friends and family." Knowledge kissed me on my forehead.

"Girl, your man flewed us out on a private jet yesterday. We've been at Kane and Candy house across the way. I need a man who can buy me a private island too, so I can get rid of Jerome's ass." Kisha was funny as hell.

"We surprised you, Autumn." Kyle ran up and gave me a hug.

He had a big ole smile across his face. Seeing him happy, and knowing he would be with us forever made my heart full.

"I promise not to pass out this time." Candy and I embraced.

We held on to each other for what felt like an eternity.

"Yeah, because if you do, I'm going to kick your ass."

Hopefully no one would get sick or require medical attention. If they did, the brothers thought of that too. There was a helicopter landing pad in between our homes. If we needed immediate assistance, medics would be here in minutes.

I made my way around the room and greeted everyone. When I got to the officiant, I felt the need to apologize.

"Listen, there will be no foolery like the last time. Please accept my apology, and I'm glad you could make it."

"It's perfectly fine. Everything happens for a reason. Look at your new wedding venue, it's literally in paradise. The universe makes no mistakes." We hugged, and I sat down to eat.

The chef, the same one Knowledge hired for us, was here as well. She prepared a three course meal consisting of appetizers, dinner, and dessert. The kids were satisfied with their grilled cheese sandwiches and chicken fingers.

Afterwards, the guys went off to Knowledge's island man cave room he had built. My mom and her sisters took the kids off our hands. It was almost their bedtime anyway. Us ladies sat in the family room and talked the night away. Kisha kept us entertained with stories about her and Jerome. Their relationship was a complete comedy show.

It was great to see all of us laughing together and enjoying each other's company. Knowledge outdid himself once again. There was one surprise after the next. I couldn't wait to marry the man who captured my heart and changed my life forever.

Chapter Fifty

KNOWLEDGE

Today was the day I finally made Autumn Mrs. Alexander. I laid next to her watching her sleep. She looked radiant and peaceful. I didn't know what I did right in this world to deserve her, but I'm glad she was the one I got to grow old with.

The sounds of birds chirping could be heard through the opened terrace doors. We kept them open all night to enjoy the wonderful island breeze. There was no need for air conditioning at night. The ceiling fan circulated the cool air, making it very comfortable.

"I can feel you staring at me." Autumn spoke with her eyes still closed.

"I'm just admiring your beauty."

She stretched and yawned before looking at me through her enchanting eyes.

"How long have you been awake?"

"Not too long. I'm excited for today and can't wait for you to see everything that has been prepared for you."

Autumn had no idea what she would even be wearing. Candy knew her sister like the back of her hand and handled everything. She would be over later to get the ball rolling.

"We all will be meeting up for breakfast. The ceremony doesn't start until three, but I have a full day already planned out for you."

"I'm still waiting for someone to wake me up from the dream I am in. This all seems so unreal."

"It's no dream. This is your reality. And before we get up and prepare to go downstairs, I'm going to eat a lil something right now."

I threw back the covers and revealed her naked body. She smiled and got on all fours. This woman was something else. I grabbed her by her ankles and pulled her down to the edge of bed. After I got on my knees on the floor, Autumn looked back at me and started twerking.

She immediately made my dick hard. I grabbed the front of her legs and pulled her closer to my face. Autumn opened her legs even more and her pussy was right in front of my mouth. I kissed it, then licked her inner thighs.

My tongue explored the outside of her plump pussy before tickling her clit. I sucked and slurped on her succulent pussy as her juices began to flow. She was so wet, and I made sure to catch every drop that dripped into my mouth. Her low, soft moans excited me even more, and I couldn't contain my desire to be inside her.

I got up off the floor and back on the bed. "Get on top."

Without hesitating, Autumn mounted me. She took my dick in her hand, guided him to her opening, and sat on his head. I palmed her ass with both hands and pushed him all the way in.

"Sssssss, oooohhhh. Babe, you have to ease him in."

"Don't act like you can't handle this dick. You know what to do."

Autumn started rocking back and forth. Her pace was slow at first then she picked it up. I loved watching her titties bounce up and down. They were perfectly round and full. She placed her hands on my chest and began to ride me like a cowgirl.

"This is what I'm talking about. Oh, yeah, just like that."

"Whose dick is this?" She rode me harder and faster. I didn't answer on purpose.

"Don't make me have to ask you again."

This time she leaned toward me and slammed her pussy up and down on my dick. I was ready to explode.

"It's yours, and always will be. Now drain him."

Autumn hopped off my dick and took him into her mouth. She licked and sucked my man down. In less than a minute, I filled up her cheeks with my seeds.

"Now, we both had some protein before breakfast." All I could do was laugh.

After handling our hygiene, we got dressed and headed over

to Kyle's room to get him ready. He was already up and had taken a shower. He had his own bathroom in his room and everything in it could be turned on by pushing a button. The temperature of the water had been permanently set to warm, this way he couldn't burn himself.

The staff showed him how to work everything last night. He was a mature kid and a fast learner. My son never gave us any trouble and was my pride and joy.

"We're about to head to breakfast. Put something on your feet."

Kyle did as he was told and we headed downstairs.

You could smell the goodness throughout the entire house. Everyone was already seated, except for Kane's household. They were on their way over.

"How is everyone doing this morning?" They all looked like they slept well.

"We're straight. I see you and Autumn are all smiles. Y'all must have been up there being grown." Kisha was on go from the time she woke up, until she went to bed.

"Girl, bye. Your ass always has to be the one." Autumn responded to Kisha.

"This place is amazing, Knowledge. I have to include it in one of my blogs."

"Aunt Bird, you can come here anytime you like, even if we are not here. Just let me know ahead of time, and I will make sure you are accommodated, I informed her.

She was chill and never involved herself in the drama. Hopefully Momma Rose apologized to her and Uncle Pete, and all was good. Autumn had told me what she had said.

Kane and his crew finally arrived. The chef and her staff served everyone and we dug in.

"After we are done here, all the ladies will go over to the salon located next to the gaming room to get it all done up. There's a person assigned to each of you to make it go by faster. The fellas will keep an eye on the kids. We don't require as much as y'all."

I had a salon built because no one had time to keep going back and forth to the main island to have stuff done, especially with the kids. We needed to have everything on the premises. I'd rather have someone take a boat to us.

After everyone ate, we all went our separate ways. The officiant had an online wedding to do today as well, so I let him use my office. He would get back with us when it was time to get dressed. I needed to fill my brother in on everything I had going on and the information I received from my peoples.

Once Junior and uncle Pete were settled with the boys, Kane and I took a walk out in the garden. It was a place for us to have picnics in and a space for Autumn to relax with the kids whenever she wanted a change in scenery.

"What's going on, bruh?" Kane got right to it.

"Yo, Keelie was the one who helped out Miss Danielle. I had someone go in as the cable guy and bug her house. He installed microphones in the cable box in the living room and her room. She's fucking with some nigga named Sean, and he helped her with the video. You know he had her ass in there sounding like a whole farm while they were fucking. I don't know what type of zoophilia or bestiality type shit they got going on, but I'm glad my son no longer has to be subjected to that shit." Kane blew his breath.

"That nasty bitch gotta go. I understand she's my nephew's mother, but should have been buried when we found out her and her mom were mistreating him. Keelie is a waste of space and needs to be eliminated. She will do more harm to Kyle alive than dead. He won't miss her."

"I agree with you 100 percent. It was hard to pull the trigger back then because I thought he needed her. Kyle has Autumn, so he's good. I'm killing her funky ass mother too. My guy just sent me recordings last night of her and Keelie talking in the house. She's the one who told her to come to the wedding in the first place."

Keelie's mom should have minded her own fucking business. She knew how trifling her daughter was because she was the same person as her. Now they could die together.

"Damn, you're not sparing the mom?"

"Hell no, not now. She deserved to get got for fucking with Kyle. I thought having her evicted from her apartment was punishment enough. But since she sent her daughter to ruin our day, fuck her life too." Kane laughed.

"Why you put that old ass lady out on the streets like that? You foul as hell." I laughed.

"I knew she would have to move in with her daughter, and they deserved each other. Her mom is a hoarder, and I figured eventually she would drive Keelie into an early grave. Now we're going to dig a grave for both of them."

"What about the Sean dude?"

"Don't worry about him. I'll handle it."

We made our way back inside the house. After the ladies were done, it was our turn to get tightened up. Kane flew in our personal barber to get us right.

I had a masseuse set up in the great room to give the ladies each a massage and unlimited mimosas. They would serve Autumn orange juice with sparkling water. I wanted every guest here to feel special too. It was Autumn's day, but I knew they all needed to create these memories together.

All the fellas gave me their sizes, and I had my tailor make sure everyone had a nice linen suit to wear. Mine was a champagne color, and theirs were all white. We all wore coral color shirts underneath. I had slides for everyone to wear, this way they could easily take them off.

Candy picked out white flowing, strapless dresses for all the ladies, she wouldn't let me see Autumn's dress. Her and Kane flew everything over with them. This way Autumn couldn't find out about it until I told her. If it wasn't for Candy helping, once again, today wouldn't be possible. I couldn't thank her enough for her help.

The ceremony and reception would take place by the sea. At the very edge of our backyard, there was a road that led to the beach on the other side. The island was small, which was perfect for us, so it wouldn't take long for everyone to be driven there.

We had three, eight passenger, stretch limo golf carts delivered to the island for occasions like this. Autumn would be the last to arrive with Uncle Pete, who would finally get to walk her down the aisle.

"Daddy, do I get to be in the wedding again today?" Kyle came running up to me.

"Yes, son. You need to get your haircut first."

"Is mommy coming? I don't want her to. She's mean to me and Autumn." I squatted down in front of him.

"You won't ever have to worry about your mommy being mean to anyone ever again. Okay?" He gave me the tightest hug ever and kissed me on the cheek.

"Thank you, daddy."

He ran off again to be with his little cousins. Even though he was older than them, Kyle loved to be around the twins. He got a kick out of telling them what to do. I followed behind him, so I could get everyone into the salon and get this show on the road.

Chapter Fifty-One

AUTUMN

This woman had magical hands. She started at the top of my head and worked her way down to the bottom of my feet. I don't know what type of concoction she whipped up and applied on my skin, but it smelled amazing and had my body feeling brand new.

Sometimes you don't realize how much stress your body holds onto, and my body was tight. I could literally feel the tension being released from it. I'm going to have to start having this type of treatment twice a week. She finished my left side and started working on the right.

"How do you feel about all of this, Autumn? This truly is a dream wedding," questioned my mom.

She was across from me getting rubbed down by a sexy island man. Hopefully she could find her a boo if we visited the main island the next time we came back. My mom deserved to love again, and we all want someone to grow old with at the end of the day.

"From the moment I left my house yesterday, I have been on a high. It really is amazing, and the fact that I get to experience it with you guys is icing on the cake. I don't like to make a big deal out of myself, but Knowledge does."

"You guys are perfect for each other, and I'm proud to have him as my son-in-law."

"We definitely compliment each other. I thought this day would never happen, but here we are. My stomach has been doing flips all morning. I'm sure it will calm down after the ceremony."

"Candy was pregnant when she got married, now you. Y'all do everything the same, down to marrying brothers," Auntie Bird added.

She didn't lie. Candy and I really have been doing everything the same our entire lives. If she wasn't in my life, I would be lost. Our relationship means more to me than she realizes. I'm always acting like I'm the oldest and felt a need to protect her, but Candy really was my safe place.

"Do you guys think Jerome will marry me one day?" Kisha asked.

"He needs to grow a pair first and stop running around like a little girl, cutting up your tires."

Kisha mouthed "fuck you" to me.

"You say something, Kisha? I couldn't hear you." I cupped my hand around my ear and leaned my head toward her.

"Remind me later to cuss your ass out when I'm not in front of your mom and aunties."

We finished up with the massages and headed upstairs to start getting ready. Candy and Kisha were getting dressed in my room, and my mom and aunties were getting dressed in hers.

When Candy showed me what I would be wearing, I was in awe. It was a champagne colored, strapless dress. The part that covered my breast was made out of sequence and the rest out of tulle. When I put it on, I felt like a queen.

"Autumn, you look radiant. Like a star in the sky shining down on us. Oh, sissy."

Candy teared up, then I started. Kisha was too evil to cry, and just stared at us shaking her head.

"If y'all keep crying, you won't have any tears left for the ceremony." We ignored her.

"This is really happening. It's starting to feel real now. I pray there is no tsunami or tropical storm. It seems like something bad always happens to me. All I want to do is get through today."

"And you will. Nothing bad is going to happen. We get to have the same last name again, and nothing is going to stop that. Positive vibes only, sissy." Candy gave me a hug. "We have to go. They are about to start taking us over to the beach. You stay up here until I come back. I just want to make sure Knowledge leaves first and doesn't see you yet."

They left me alone with my thoughts. Sometimes it was a scary place to be. You started to overthink everything and prayed you made the right decisions. Your thoughts were powerful and could fuck you up if you give the negative ones too much energy.

"Alright, the coast is clear. I put the guys on the first cart, and sent them on their way. Uncle Pete is waiting for you downstairs. I'm going over with the ladies now and ten minutes after we leave, you will come. We just need time to get everyone in their seats."

I took a deep breath and followed Candy. When we got to the steps, she held my hand as we headed downstairs.

"You are a beautiful bride. It is my honor to escort you to your new beginning."

"Thank you, Uncle Pete. I'm glad you are here."

They left and soon after, we were on our way. When we arrived, there was a woven basket for our slides. We placed them in there, and uncle Pete and I locked arms. Knowledge and Kyle stood on the gazebo with the officiant. All the chairs were in a semi-circle facing the water. They left an opening big enough for us to get through. The aisle for me to walk down was made of fresh flowers. There was a photographer and videographer. Everyone stood when they saw us.

Suddenly I heard music. It was "Spend My Life With You" by Eric Benet featuring Tamia. It sounded like they were standing right next to me. I looked over to my left, and there they were. My heart always jumped out my chest. We walked down the aisle as they sang to us. My eyes were filled with so many tears, I almost couldn't see out of them.

With each step I took, I was closer to my other half. To the man who kept on making my life happier with each passing moment. I finally made it to him, and the tears wouldn't stop flowing. Uncle Pete kissed my hand and gave me over to Knowledge.

He took my hands into his and the ceremony started. This time there were no interruptions, and we finally became Mr. and Mrs. Alexander. It felt amazing to kiss my husband on our own island, in front of the Caribbean sea with the sun shining down on us. It was the best day of my life.

"We did it! You are mine forever. I'm the happiest man alive right now. Once our baby arrives, our family will be complete."

We hugged each other, then I leaned down to give Kyle a kiss on the cheek.

"Can I call you mommy Autumn now?" Kyle whispered in my ear.

"If you want to, and if it's ok with your dad. I didn't give birth to you Kyle, but I promise to love and raise you like my own son. You are safe with me."

"I already asked my dad before you got here, and he said yes." I just smiled at him.

"I'm sick y'all. It's goddamn celebrities singing at the wedding. Who's showing up to the reception? Rihanna? All jokes aside, congrats, friend. I'm so happy for you guys. This was beautiful." Kisha came up, talking shit as usual.

We did a photoshoot on the beach with everyone while they set up for the reception. Our special guests were out of here faster than they sang.

"Babe, how did you manage to get them to come sing, especially on such a short notice?"

"I keep telling you everyone has a price, but you don't believe me, though. Money talks and bullshit walks. This is what they do. They get paid to sing at private events all the time."

"Whatever. Thank you again for this mind-blowing experience. I love you with my whole heart." He leaned into my face, and we started kissing.

"Save all of that for tonight." There goes Candy with her slick ass mouth.

"I would say someone is about to get pregnant tonight, but y'all already jumped the gun on that one." Kisha had to chime in as well.

"Candy you'll mess around and be knocked up again while you all up in mine. With your twin producing ass."

"I've been trying to get her pregnant again every night." Kane came up behind Candy and wrapped his arms around her.

"This is the perfect place to do it, bruh. I'm about to put another baby on top of the one Autumn is carrying tonight."

Knowledge rubbed his dick up on my ass. I told him to stop being fresh, and we all headed over to the reception area.

They put three long tables together covered with white linen and lined both sides with chairs. Knowledge, Kyle and I had our own round table at the end. Tiki torches were lit all around. There was a bar set up next to us, along with a buffet of every kind of food you could think of. The seafood looked so damn good, it had to come right out the sea.

After everyone ate until they were about to bust, and

enjoyed a few beverages, we all headed back to the house. They had me open the door and when I did, there were rose petals on the floor leading to the great room.

When I entered, it was set up like a casino. How they were able to set this up in a couple hours was beyond me. They had to have everything hiding in the house somewhere. Knowledge knew I loved to gamble. I played online casinos all the time on my phone.

There were tables set up to play blackjack, roulette and the money wheel. They had slot machines lined up in a row with chairs in front of them to sit down. Knowledge gave everyone a stack of cash to play. He even had a sitter for the boys. Kyle was with them, so if she pinched one of them, he would tell us.

Waiters came around taking drink orders and offered cupcakes as dessert. It was like we were at a real casino. We laughed and played until it got late. Kane and his crew went home, then all of us headed to our rooms.

I plopped down backwards onto the bed. My magical day was coming to an end. Knowledge came over and lifted my dress up.

"If I knew you didn't have any panties on all this time, I would have slid my hand up your dress when we were on the beach."

"You're so nasty."

"And you love it, Mrs. Alexander."

Knowledge buried his face in between my legs. I put my knees up and rubbed on his head while he devoured my pussy. It was about to be a long night.

Chapter Fifty-Two

KNOWLEDGE

Even though we had a great time on the island, I was glad to be back in Jersey. There were a lot of people who needed to be handled. These muthafuckas thought they had one up on me. They probably were sitting around laughing and shit, thinking they pulled it off.

I thought about what they did to my wife and my son everyday. Them fucking with me didn't mean shit. I knew I was just the causality of the war Keelie started with Autumn. She set out to destroy her but fucked herself in the end.

Keelie was warned about what would happen if I found out she had anything to do with attacking Autumn and our child. Her life had been spared too many times, but not anymore. I'm coming for her and the bitch that had her.

From being in those group homes when our parents were

killed, I learned to never show my hand early. If a nigga knew what you were planning, they had time to come up with a defense or straight disappear. They always saw me coming because I was a hot head.

Once I learned the power of patience, they couldn't stop me. Kane showed me the way, and I never slipped up again. It was the same thing right now. I been had the drop on Keelie and the hoarder, but they had no idea.

I needed her to think I was so focused on my family, I didn't have time to worry about her. She wouldn't try to run because she was comfortable. The more time that passed by, the more confident Keelie became with thinking I had no idea it was her. Little do she know, I was coming to end her life but first, I needed to handle Sean the neighbor.

There were some things he said on the recordings I didn't appreciate. He needed to face me man to man, or should I say man to boy. One thing I would never tolerate was another man speaking on my son. This was why I told Kane don't worry about him, his punk ass belonged to me.

Sean wasn't going to the pet cemetery we created. I wanted them to find him rotting away in his house. Usually I didn't leave a body to be found, but in this case I had to. If I just made him disappear, Keelie would figure out it was me, then she might try to run.

I had someone following his every move. Sean lived a very predictable life and never broke his routine. Even if you weren't a criminal, you should always switch up. A predator always found its prey based on their activity. They learned all your patterns, then used it as an opportunity to get your ass.

Every Friday night, he ordered the same meal from the Chinese restaurant around the corner of his house. The order was always delivered at seven like clockwork. When my guy followed the delivery driver out the store one day, he noticed some writing on the menu stapled to the bag. It said "no peanut sauce/allergies".

If Sean had a severe allergy to peanuts, then more than likely he had an EpiPen, or two, in the house. It was the first thing I looked for when I broke in. I had to make sure it wasn't anywhere near his immediate reach. He needed to go into anaphylactic shock while I watched.

Getting in his house during the day wasn't easy, especially with Keelie's ass right next door. I had to come up with a disguise no one would recognize me in. I got dropped off blocks away and walked to his house. Entering from the backyard was the safest bet because it faced an empty field.

He didn't have any cameras outside his house, and Sean also felt safe enough on this block not to alarm it. I even had a copy of his house key made. My guy followed him to the gym, took it out of his jacket pocket, and placed it in the key molding kit.

I used the key to get in the house. Since he only had one house key, I knew it had to unlock the front and back door. He would be home in a few minutes, so I hid in the hall closet. I needed to stay there until he got his food. My plan would only work if his routine stayed the same.

Sean entered his home and was none the wiser to me being

there. He did his regular shit and waited on his food. Once it arrived, I exited the closet when it got quiet. This muthafucka was lame as hell. He sat in a recliner eating his food. I walked up behind him.

"If you scream or move, you're dead."

I took the small bottle of peanut sauce out of my pocket and poured it all over his food while standing behind him.

"Who are you and what are you doing?" I could hear the fear in his voice.

"I'm the Devil and here to collect your soul."

"What did I ever do to you, Mr. Devil?"

This nigga was so scared he didn't know what to say.

"Nothing directly. When you talked about my son to his mother, you indirectly disrespected me and violated the code of ethics."

"W-w-who is your son?" I laughed

"Don't start stuttering and getting amnesia now, muthafucka. You know who he is. Your fucking his mother and making her bark like a goddamn dark, you sick bastard."

"Oh, Kyle. I like him. He's a sweet little boy."

The tone in his voice changed when he said that. It was a clear indication he was lying.

"No you don't. You said you were glad he wasn't there anymore because he was a punk ass little bitch who always wanted his mommy. You and his whore ass mother sat around and laughed when you referred to him as Kylena. Don't worry, though. I'm going to kill her too."

"I'm sorry. Really, I am. We were just joking around."

"Well, the joke is on you now. Eat up." He sighed and dropped his shoulders.

"You poured that sauce on my food. I can smell the peanuts in it, and I'm allergic."

"I'm aware, and I will shove it down your fucking throat if you don't eat it."

I walked around his chair, so I could have a front row view. He looked up at me with tears in his eyes.

"You like editing videos too, huh? I know everything."

His hand was trembling so bad, I thought he would drop the fork. He managed to get it in his mouth.

"Hurry the fuck, bitch. I have shit to do."

Sean ate some more and within minutes his lips were swelling up.

"My throat is starting to tighten. Please don't do this." He struggled to talk.

"You did it to yourself. We all make mistakes, some are just deadlier than others. When you fuck with people's kids, they might kill you. Let this be a lesson." He grabbed at his throat.

"Please, help me."

"Since you said please, you can go get your EpiPen."

He sat the bowl down, jumped up, and headed toward the bathroom. I followed behind him. When Sean opened the medicine cabinet, he knocked everything into the sink trying to find it. With shaky hands, he tried to get the EpiPen out the box while gasping for air.

I kicked him in the back of his knee, and he fell to the ground. There was no way he had enough energy to get back up. A few minutes later he was dead. I had to let him die in the bathroom, this way the police would think he was trying to save himself. One down and two to go.

After making sure no one was in the backyard, I exited his house and traveled the same path which led me here. My ride pulled up. I got in, and he drove me back home.

As soon as I entered the house, Autumn was standing in the foyer rubbing her stomach.

"I'm glad you are back. I think there's more than one baby in my stomach."

"You play too much."

"I'm serious. I called Dr. Jones, and she said she can fit us in. You can't go looking like that, so shower and put something decent on. I told Kyle he could come with us."

It seemed like I haven't stopped since we've been back. When I finished handling my hygiene, I made my way back downstairs. They were standing at the door waiting for me.

"Finally." I ignored Autumn's comment, she was just anxious.

We got into the car and headed to see Dr. Jones. Traffic was a bitch, but we arrived right on time. Instead of trying to find a space to park with them still in the car, I let Autumn and Kyle out at the door.

"Go check in while I look for parking."

If she really was pregnant with twins, I wouldn't mind. Filling up our house with kids was my goal. I parked the car and went inside. They had already called her to the back that fast.

"Look, daddy, we're about to see the baby on the TV."

Kyle was excited, and Autumn looked nervous.

"Whether it's one or four, I got you."

She smiled and reached for my hand. Dr. Jones put the gel on her stomach and moved the wand around.

"I knew I felt someone else kicking me." I was happy as hell, two in one shot.

"It happens, sometimes. They play hide-n-seek. Your babies look good and their heartbeats are strong. This pregnancy has been fascinating from the very beginning."

"This is wild. There's nothing I can do now but prepare to be a mother of three kids at the same time."

After Dr. Jones cleaned off Autumn's stomach, Kyle touched it. She placed her hand over his, and I put mine over both of theirs. This moment right here meant everything in the world to me. It was all about family, and mine was growing in leaps and bounds.

Chapter Fifty-Three

AUTUMN

A FEW MONTHS LATER...

Every day for the last week, Knowledge and Kane have been digging up my backyard. When I asked him what the hell they were doing, he said building a playground for the kids. I didn't want to come straight out and call him a liar, but I think he told me a half truth. Those muthafuckas look like they were digging a grave.

I was due to have these babies any day now, and I didn't need them burying people back there while I was in the hospital. My bags were packed and waiting by the door. I originally wanted to do a home birth, but since I'm having twins I couldn't. They said it was too risky and complications could arise.

We set up our room to accommodate both babies. Our kids are sleeping with us. I don't like the idea of putting babies in their own rooms down the hall and using a monitor to listen or watch them. The only monitor I needed were my eyeballs.

I've been experiencing pressure in my pelvic area and back all morning. I couldn't sleep at all last night and thought I might be in labor. When I got in the shower, the heat on my back felt good and provided some relief, but once I got out the pain was still there. If I go downstairs and tell Knowledge he would panic and make me nervous. Telling my mom would be a better choice.

"Mom, I need your help." I didn't even knock. I just walked in her room.

She has been great with me over these last few months. Having her here was a blessing, and it allowed Knowledge to work without worrying about me.

"You're in labor. I can see it in your face. Let's get you downstairs."

I didn't even have to say a thing. She already knew. The contractions were like ten minutes apart. Each time they came it got a little worse.

"You sit down over here and let me get Knowledge."

My mom had me sit in the dining room chair. I did the breathing exercises Candy taught me in order to calm my nerves. I sent her a text when I was upstairs, so I'm sure she would be over at any moment. In walked Knowledge and Kyle. They must have been out back throwing the ball.

"You okay? Do we need to call an ambulance?"

"No, babe. Calm down. We can drive over there. Please call Dr. Jones and let her know we are heading over to the hospital." I could see the excitement in his eyes.

I was excited and scared at the same time. All these wild thoughts came in my head, like what if something was wrong with them? What if I died giving birth? Will my pussy still work the same? It sounded crazy, but these were real questions I had.

Knowledge helped me up, and we all headed out to the car.

"Mom, call Candy and tell her they can meet us at the hospital. Thank you."

"Oh shit, your bag." Knowledge ran back inside to get it.

I totally forgot about it after these contractions started kicking my ass. He got back in the car and we left.

It didn't take us long to get there. The pain was getting worse. When we pulled up to the valet at the ER, Knowledge jumped out and ran inside. Seconds later, he came back out with a wheelchair.

"Thank you, babe." He kissed my lips, then helped me out of the car and into the wheelchair.

They took us straight to the maternity floor. My mom and Kyle waited in the waiting area inside my room until they got me changed and hooked up to all the monitors. Even though everyone had their own private room, once again, Knowledge had to have the best.

He made sure we had the VIP suite which was enormous and had everything we needed. It looked like I was about to give birth in a five star hotel. I'm sure his donation to the hospital had something to do with it.

Candy and her entire household arrived ten minutes later. My circle was small, but it was strong. Knowledge sat right next to me rubbing on my belly. The contractions were getting closer and stronger. It felt like they were minutes apart.

"You good?" asked Knowledge.

"Not really. I'm in a lot of pain. I just want to get this over with and never do it again."

"You don't mean that. It's the pain talking."

"It's my pussy talking, and she said we're not doing this shit anymore," I murmured.

"How's my favorite patient doing?" Dr. Jones came in to see how far along I was.

"Hey, I heard that." Candy laughed.

"Whoever is giving birth is always my favorite patient. I've been watching your monitor out there, and you keep having contractions."

"Yes, they are horrible, and I want them to stop." Dr. Jones smiled and checked me.

"You have a high tolerance for pain. You're fully dilated and ready to push."

Knowledge started clapping. He stood up and kissed my forehead.

"Let me know the two people staying with you. Everyone else needs to go to the waiting room."

"My husband and my mom." Dr. Jones left out then came back in with her team.

"You're going to do great, sissy." I squeezed Candy's hand and didn't want to let it go.

Knowledge and my mom stood on each side of me.

"When I tell you, I want you to give me a big push. Okay?" Dr. Jones was positioned in front of me.

"You got this Autumn. Push with your ass, but don't shit yourself." Everyone laughed at my mom.

It felt like forever, but eight minutes later both my babies were out and being cleaned up. I gave birth to two, healthy, handsome little boys. My biggest worry was them being underweight, but they each weighed six pounds.

When they placed them in my arms, I broke down crying. It was an overwhelming feeling of love. They looked like the perfect mix of both of us. The rest of the family was able to come out and see them. Everyone was so happy and couldn't believe it was two more boys added in the mix.

"Two more kings. You did it, bruh." Kane and Knowledge hugged.

"Candy, you're going to have to get pregnant again, and try to get us a girl. I'm done."

"Well, hopefully this one is a girl." Candy rubbed her belly.

"Are you serious? You really let him knock you up in the islands."

"Yup, it was those mimosas." We laughed.

Candy and her crew left. They took my mom with them, but we kept Kyle. We wanted him to be part of this moment. Knowledge, Kyle, Kason, Kiaan and I together completed our circle. We were now a family of five, and I looked forward to making a beautiful life with my guys.

Six weeks later...

I had my six week check up today and everything went well. Kason and Kiaan already had their one month pediatric appointment and were doing great. Life with three boys wasn't as hard as I thought it would be. My mom and Knowledge were a great help and made it easier on me.

He even took a two month leave from work to give us all of his time. In a couple weeks he'd be back at it with Kane and Junior. In the meantime, we had a situation to handle. Knowledge told me Keelie and her mother were the last to go.

How Miss Danielle and Keelie hooked up was irrelevant at this point. No more questions were being asked. I was straight fucking her up. The fresh pair of black forces I ordered came in and were on my feet right now. Knowledge and Kane finished the grave in the backyard and put two fifty-five gallon steel drums in there.

The house was completely empty besides Knowledge and I. We were just waiting for our guests to arrive. His personal driver went to pick up Keelie and her mother. They thought they were coming over to visit Kyle.

Knowledge went over there and told her I wanted to call a truce. Since having my boys I understood how she felt as a mother and her presence was important in Kyle's life. Her stupid ass fell for the bait, especially when Knowledge said he would give her the money for all the weeks he didn't pay.

As I pulled my hair back in a ponytail, the doorbell rang. In my mind, I heard the boxing bell go off for the twelve and final round.

"You ready?" Knowledge went to answer the door.

"Born ready." They came walking in smiling and shit.

"This is nice. I've never been inside. Congrats on the babies and the wedding. You guys finally did it. Woo-Hoo." This bitch was still slick with the mouth.

"Don't worry, this is your first and last time here." She looked at me with a crazed face.

"Where's Kyle?"

"With his family. Something you know nothing about." Knowledge walked over and stood next to me.

"What the fuck is going on?" Keelie looked over at her mother. She shrugged her shoulders.

"I'm about to beat your ass, then you both are going to die. Like they say on *American Idol*, it's the end of the road for you today."

"What the fuck I do? Just kill her." Keelie's mom was trifling down to the very end.

When I approached Keelie, she blew her breath then tried to swing on me. I stayed ready and saw it coming. After I slipped it, I proceeded to beat the skin off her ass. She never had the opportunity to swing again. Blow, after blow, I delivered to her face.

Her body dropped to the ground, and I stomped her in the face, neck and chest. I snatched her up by her hair and flung her into the wall. After sitting on top of her, I pummeled her body until Knowledge pulled me up. My knuckles were burning and bloody, but I could have kept going.

"This is some sick shit." I tapped Keelie's mother's jaw, and she went down like a bowling pin.

Knowledge called Kane, and he came right over. After they put on hazmat suits, gloves and goggles, they threw each of them in a drum and poured sulfuric acid over their bodies. Once the lids were on, they filled the grave back up with dirt.

These muthafuckas really are crazy.

I went into the kitchen to rinse my hands off and put them in a bowl of ice. Knowledge walked in and started talking.

"Now Kyle is minus one parent and a grandma. The people will be here tomorrow to start working on the playground. Don't panic when you see them putting cement down. It's just the bottom layer. I'm going to have them put that sponge-like material as the topper. This way when the kids fall, they won't get hurt."

"I'm glad to see both of them go. They deserve everything they got and more. It's fucked up, but that's life sometimes."

"Yeah, and that bitch Keelie made an anonymous call to the police on me when they found her neighbor Sean dead in his house. They transferred her to the detective who's in my pocket. Her house is still bugged, so I knew when she did it."

"Well, let's go shower, then pick up the kids."

Life was unpredictable. At any moment it could make a turn for the better or for the worse. We were able to survive situations that should have destroyed us. Knowledge and I vowed to always stand Alexander strong through any storm.

Chapter Fifty-Four

FAMILY UPDATE...

CANDY

TEN YEARS LATER...

"Can you believe Junior is about to be a father? I still can't wrap my head around it."

Autumn sighed and put her money in the vending machine, ignoring me. We were currently on the maternity floor inside the waiting area at the same hospital we had our kids.

"I'm still trying to get used to the fact that Kisha is going to be his baby momma. How those two got together is beyond me. She is going to drive his ass crazy."

She pushed the button for the Twix candy bar and grabbed it when it dropped down.

"At least it's with someone we already love and consider family. With everything we've been through, it's hard to trust outsiders."

"Whatever, you want one?" Autumn handed me the candy bar.

We had no idea Kisha and Junior were even seeing each other. Jerome had been out of the picture, and we knew she had a new man in her life but never met him. Little did we know we already had. They hid their relationship from us because they said Autumn and I would have been against it, and they were right.

I didn't want one of my closest friends fucking my little brother. Yes, Junior was a grown man, but he would always be my little brother. It was my job to protect him.

Once they told us, after Kisha was already knocked up, I accepted it. She loved him, and he loved her. At the end of the day, that was all that mattered.

"I just want it to be a girl. If we add one more boy to this family, I'm going to scream."

Autumn nodded her head in agreement.

"Yes, because you and I aren't producing shit, so our only hope is Junior."

Kane and Knowledge both got snipped. Knowledge was the first one on the chopping block after Autumn found out she was pregnant again at her six week checkup from having the twins. That pull out method didn't work for them.

She was so mad and cried for a month straight. And it was another boy, which made Knowledge happy as hell.

I also gave birth to another boy before Autumn did. Kane and I tried for a girl two years later and ended up with one more rock head, so we raised the white flag.

"Kane just texted me and said our moms cooked enough food to feed a small army. They always have to go overboard."

Since Kisha had her mother and Junior in with her, our moms decided to stay home and cook a huge dinner to celebrate. They started last night when Kisha went into labor. Kane and Knowledge stayed behind to keep an eye on the kids.

They finally took a backseat from the business and put Junior in charge. This allowed them more time to be with us and the kids. Kyle was learning the ropes as well. He would be eighteen soon, but Knowledge and Kane started grooming him when he turned sixteen. It was their dream for all our boys to run the Alexander empire together one day.

"It's a girl. She had a girl!" Junior came running into the waiting area.

The excitement in his eyes made me emotional. He was so happy. Autumn and I started jumping up and down with him. We finally had a niece. A little girl we could spoil to no end. She was going to be the true queen of the castle with all these brothers and cousins to look after her.

"I'm so happy for you. You're going to be an amazing father."

My brother came a long way. To witness him mature until the young man before me was a beautiful thing. He was a homeowner now and lived ten minutes down the road from us. Today he added daddy to the list, and one day would be a husband.

"She weighed eight pounds even and is nineteen inches long. We named her Kali with a K, but her middle name is Candy, after you, sis."

"Here come the tears," Autumn teased.

"Awe, I'm honored," I responded as the tears fell.

"Thank you for everything." We hugged.

Today was a good day and tomorrow would be even better. Even though the family we created for ourselves started from romantic entanglements that almost destroyed us, we survived it and came out stronger. I wouldn't change anything because all the choices we made led us here. Life was definitely what you made it.

The End!

Author Charisse C. Carr Catalog:

Novellas

Valentine's Day With My Landlord
https://amzn.to/3OJxcbo
BCE: Beast Coast Entertainment: Diary Of A Secretary
https://amzn.to/3uLGFrt
Summer Luvin' With A Neighbor's Son
https://amzn.to/3zUw9A5
The Lake House: A Murder Mystery
https://amzn.to/41CfNcw
The Housewives of the Drug Game: Kalee & Bronx
https://bit.ly/410ETjA
A Billionaire's Christmas Wish
https://a.co/d/iZ6NuqB
Mutual Obsession
https://a.co/d/aI3hkdw
A Bully's Promise

https://a.co/d/gHfFe6M

Series
A Countdown To His Love
https://amzn.to/3CbVXJL
Harper & Stone: A Family Affair
https://bit.ly/442pD8f
Mali & Chaquille: A Dangerous Hood Love
https://amzn.to/3hQUf9i
Mali & Chaquille: A Dangerous Hood Love 2
https://amzn.to/3DlGBTD
Toxic Traits: A Collection of Domestic Violence Short Stories
https://a.co/d/f9CgFQh
The Asaad Brothers
https://a.co/d/7UxFfq8
The Asaad Brother: A Hitta's Revenge
https://a.co/d/2ufRR7O
Breathless
https://a.co/d/40FbH4i
Breathless 2
https://a.co/d/dayCOoR

Social Media:

Click on the link below to follow me on Facebook!
https://www.facebook.com/profile.php?id=100077944875169&mibextid=eHce3h

Click on the link below to follow me on Instagram!
https://www.instagram.com/authorcharisseccarr?igsh=Z3FtcWtwdjl6ZWt6&utm_source=qr

Click on the link below to follow me on TikTok!
https://www.tiktok.com/@authorcharisseccarr?_t=8ibAddJaArz&_r=1

Made in the USA
Middletown, DE
01 December 2024

65500113R00245